NO ORDINARY GENTLEMAN

DONNA ALAM

The moral right of this author has been asserted.

All rights reserved. No parts of this publication may be reproduced, stored in a retrieval system, or transmitted in any form or by any means, without the express permission of the author

This book is a work of fiction. Any reference to historical events, real people or real places are used fictitiously. All characters and events in this publication, other than those clearly in the public domain, are fictitious and any resemblance to real persons, living or dead, is purely coincidental.

© Donna Alam 2021

Cover Design: LJ Designs
Image: Rafa Catala
Editing: Editing 4 Indies

ALSO BY DONNA ALAM

The following are standalone titles, often set in relating worlds

MY KIND OF HERE

No Romeo

No Saint

THE WHITTINGTONS

The Interview

The Gamble

NO ORDINARY MEN

Love + Other Lies

Before Him

ONE NIGHT FOREVER

Liar Liar

Never Say Forever

LONDON LOVERS

To Have and Hate

(Not) the One

The Stand Out

PHILLIPS BROTHERS

In Like Flynn

Down Under

Rafferty's Rules

GREAT SCOTS

Hard

Easy

Hardly Easy

HOT SCOTS

One Hot Scot

One Wicked Scot

One Dirty Scot

Single Daddy Scot

Hot Scots Boxed Set

Surprise Package

AND MORE!

Soldier Boy

Playing His Games

Gentleman Player

*I'd like to dedicate this book to the women who stand with me.
Those who take this sows ear and help fashion it into a silky
purse. The women who soothe my needy soul with words of
encouragement and realness.
Elizabeth, Lisa, Michelle
Michelle & Annette
The Mo-Fos
And also to Codral Cold & Flu medicine. 'Nuff said about that the
better.*

*I refer to this book as my big boy.
It's my version of an old-time historical romance and the words
are many.
I hope you'll love it x*

Love is an irresistible desire to be irresistibly desired.
~Robert Frost

1

HOLLY

I LOVE OLD PEOPLE.

I enjoy their company. I like hearing about the things they've seen and done, and the stories they have to tell. You can learn a lot from hanging out with older folks. And while I can't explain my affinity, it's fair to say I've always preferred their company.

I even like the crotchety ones.

It's not just seniors, either. Take the couple I'm currently sharing a table with—thanks to happy hour and the local thirsty office crowd—they aren't old exactly. Just older. But such cool company. How I come to be in the hotel bar at all is thanks to my rumbling stomach, a hankering for company, and an aversion to paying the ridiculous room service surcharge for a coffee and a sandwich.

So here I am, basking in the remains of the day's sunshine as it streams in through a huge window overlooking one of London's quieter streets. The bonus of my extended lunch is Lukas and Annika, the older (but not old) couple I've spent the last hour with. It seems they've travelled the world several times over and have already visited a bunch of places on my bucket list. I am *absolutely* drinking up their stories while swapping a few of my own.

Interesting, see?

"So you just arrived in London?" Lukas smiles encouragingly. He's tall and angular and reminds me a little of Tom Brady. Or what Tom might look like in ten years or so.

I nod in agreement and take a quick sip of my drink, having moved on from a cappuccino to a glass of wine at their invitation.

"I flew in from Florida yesterday, but I'm originally from Oregon." Buttphuck Oregon. Otherwise known as Mookatill, home of the cheese by the same name.

"I don't think we've ever been to Oregon," Annika says, glancing at the hubs. He shakes his head.

"Home of tall trees and even taller mountain ranges." Sheesh, I sound like I work for the tourism board. Mookatill might not be my favorite place, but Oregon is beautiful.

"It sounds wonderful."

"Oh, it is. The coastline is just stunning. Not to mention, we have fourteen hundred lakes."

"Isn't there a state with ten thousand lakes?" Annika turns to her husband as he speaks.

"Minnesota," I put in. *The show-offs.*

"But now you live in London." Lukas reaches for his wine glass and swirls the blood-red liquid around the bowl. "It must be a little different to where you're from."

"Oh, just a little," I reply with a laugh. "But I've lived here a year now." And I love it, though I guess I'd be happy to be anywhere that isn't Mookatill.

"Chelsea, did you say?"

I nod. "I'll join the family in the morning. It's just a cab ride away."

The family I work for, I mean. Not that anyone would guess I wasn't born to squander a trust fund in super cool hotel bars because I'm dressed perfectly for the part. Skinny jeans, a white vest, and a Balmain blazer; the designer must-have. *The blazer's a dupe, but it's a pretty convincing one.*

I was supposed to go straight from the airport to the house, but when I'd switched on my phone after landing earlier, I found a text from Martine, my boss, telling me she'd booked me into a hotel in the city. Something about the decorator not finishing on schedule. As you can imagine, I wasn't about to complain. The pair could fluff cushions and reposition artwork until their hearts' content because what kind of idiot would complain about an extended vacation?

"I imagine you need to be back early tomorrow," Lukas murmurs, placing his glass on the table between us.

"No, they have a driver for the school run." I'm basically a tutor and social secretary to a couple of American tween-agers. It's a pretty sweet gig, unlike driving in peak-hour London traffic, which would probably give me a heart attack.

"It sounds like a very good position."

"It's the best. Especially when you consider half term isn't far away, and we're off to Ibiza for the break." Working for rich people is amazing; cast-off Prada handbags and bougie vacations are just the start of it. "And then it's off to Rome and then Lake Como when summer rolls around," I add.

"What is the saying?" Lukas asks with a small smile. "It's a tough job…"

"But someone's got to do it!" And I'm super glad that someone is me because I, Holly Harper, love my job. In fact, I love it more than I love hanging out with old(er) people.

Because I get to spend time with the two most polite and well-behaved tween-agers in the world, who belong to the nicest couple in the world, all while getting to travel the world.

"How fabulous! It sounds like you're getting to see lots of Europe."

At Anna's interjection, Lukas turns to his wife, all soft, loving looks as he takes her hand. Though the pair are from Sweden, Annika looks more Mediterranean than Scandinavian, her hair as dark as his is fair, small and curvy to his lean sharpness.

"It certainly feels fabulous." Sometimes, I have to remind myself that I'm just the hired help. The nanny technically, for an ex-pat American family. Though I have a degree in education and enough experience working in the US schooling system to know a job like this is one to hang on to.

"Do you like living in London?"

"Oh, I do. It's so cosmopolitan. I love the history of the place. The quaint street names, museums, and palaces. Yet at the same time, London is kind of edgy."

Take the boutique hotel we're sitting in. It's all moody, dark wood and steel, situated in a quiet, leafy corner of the city. London is full of secret spots like this. One minute, you're being jostled on the sidewalk by tourists and commuters, and the next, you stumble across a pretty cobblestoned lane or courtyard. There, you might find a cafe, its window boxes bursting with colourful flowers or maybe an ancient looking book shop with mullioned windows and a crooked front door. Every spot is like a tiny oasis of cool. And perfect fodder for my Instagram feed.

"We also love London," Lukas adds. "Also Paris."

"And Rome." This from Annika, albeit a touch wistfully.

"Have you visited Amsterdam?" I've already been to Paris and Rome a couple of times. "I really want to visit." A tingle of excitement rolls down my spine at the prospect of ticking another destination off my list. Instead of Amsterdam being in Holland, it'll be the other way around! Though I go by Holly, Holland is my name. So, yep, I've already thought up my Instagram post!

Once upon a time, I was the girl whose fridge was covered in pictures torn from honeymoon brochures of places I'd never been. While my original travel plans didn't come to fruition, I'm now making travel memories all of my own. And I like to post those high spots on Instagram. The way I see it, the social media platform is the new postcard, and I like to be sure the folks back home know I'm enjoying myself. *Even if the folks back home are the last people on earth I'd ever mail postcards to.*

My sister says it isn't *folks* I'm trying to prove a point to but myself. But she says a lot of things that make no sense.

"We've visited Amsterdam many times." Annika languidly flicks her dark hair over her shoulders, highlighting high, luminous cheekbones. She has the kind of skin most thirty-year-olds would kill for, though she's certainly older than that. Exactly how old is hard to tell. Not that it matters; they both possess the kind of vitality that's super attractive. I don't mean the *hubba-hubba* kind of attractive, though I guess they are. What's more attractive to me is the life they've lived. The stories they have to tell. "What is it about the place that appeals to you?"

You mean, apart from being named Holland? I crack myself up sometimes.

"It just looks so pretty," I answer with a shrug. "The first thing I'm going to do when I get there is rent a cute pink bike with a basket on the front." Which I'll fill with bunches of tulips because I might be a little addicted to the 'gram. "Then I'm going to go exploring"—after I've taken the perfect image of me with said bike and said tulips—"and ride along the canals with the wind in my hair until my cheeks hurt from smiling and my legs feel like Jell-O."

"Annika and I also enjoy a ride." Despite Lukas's even delivery, there's a sudden note of something in his voice that makes me pause. "And a good ride is something I always strive for because it also makes Annika's legs, as you say, turn to Jell-O."

Riiight.

And why is his hand rubbing her thigh now?

"Darling, don't embarrass our new friend." My head jerks up at Annika's playful chastisement. "Just be sure to take a raincoat," she adds smoothly, amusement sparkling in her gaze as she takes in my burning cheeks, no doubt.

I blush at the slightest provocation, which is a pain in the butt, though I try to remind myself it saves me from buying actual blush.

Every cloud has a silver lining and all that.

Willing the color away, I bring my wine glass to my lips as I try to brush off the sudden weird vibe. *It's probably jet lag*, I tell myself.

"No matter what time of year," she continues blithely, "in Amsterdam, you can always guarantee a soaking."

Jet lag definitely. We're talking weather, and there's nothing sketchy about that.

"Well, that's the one thing *we* can always guarantee," Lukas says in that tone again. "No matter where in the world we are. Right, darling?"

"I do so love getting wet in Amsterdam," Annika purrs, linking her fingers over her husband's to still his wandering hand. "But it isn't all summer showers and canals."

"No, of course," I agree, immediately back to being weirded out again. "I look forward to visiting museums and soaking up a little culture. And then there are windmills and tulips and—"

"And sex." *What the what what?* Lukas's eyes widen salaciously. "Amsterdam is such a sexual city. And so much fun." And then he snorts.

Except... no, that wasn't him. He's still too busy groping his wife.

I sit straight in my seat at the realization that the masculine sound almost certainly came from the man sitting at the table behind Lukas and Annika. *The hottie,* I mentally amend. I saw him arrive. I mean, I'm pretty sure anyone with a pulse was aware of him and his friends as they'd walked in. They were a total thirst trap. Which, if you ask me, should be the collective noun for groups of hot guys in razor-sharp suits.

But it wasn't just their impeccable tailoring or how they looked like they'd just stepped from the pages of a magazine that made me stare. It was their air. Their presence, I guess you could call it. You know the type of men I mean; masters of all they survey. But the trio is down to one guy now. Fair of hair, broad of chest, and superhero-ed of jaw. *Or whatever.* A real city gent. A snorting city gent, one who seems to have found something amusing in Lukas's words. Or maybe in my predicament. Either way, Lukas doesn't seem to have noticed because he's still talking.

"It is such a liberating city. We love to visit. To take in the sights. To stimulate the senses."

I don't think he's talking about the coffee.

He carries on talking, but I barely hear the words, distracted by the suit-wearing hottie. He's not listening to Lukas, not precisely, but he's definitely paying attention. I can feel the weight of it almost like it's a physical thing. Or maybe this is just wishful thinking, given the way he appears to be immersed in the newspaper outstretched between his hands.

Almost as though hearing my silent accusation, his eyes appear over the top of the broadsheet, twinkling in their delight. Thick lashes provide a perfect contrast to brilliant blue. I find myself quickly looking away at the rise of one very expressively taunting eyebrow.

So you caught me looking. So what? You started it, Mr. Mystery Snorter.

"But you don't have to wait to visit Amsterdam to sample those delights."

What? Oh, no. Please don't take the conversation there, Lukas.

Something tells me the guy isn't about to offer me a pink bike with a basket full of tulips. My glass clashes with the edge of the table as I hurriedly set it down. *Time for a quick getaway*, I decide, sliding my hand between my chair and thigh and tightening it around my much loved purse.

"You know what? I'm good. I can wait until I get there. For a visit. Get to Amsterdam for a visit, I mean. Anticipation is part of the pleasure and all that."

"Anticipation has certainly been part of the pleasure of your company this afternoon." Lukas's gaze courses over me with a gleam. "What do you say, darling?" Without looking her way, he takes his wife's hand again.

"I say she's perfect," she answers breathily.

And I'd say she, being me, needs to leave. "Well, would you just look at the time!"

"Come now, there's no need to be coy." Lukas's other hand suddenly curls around my knee. "We've enjoyed one another's company so far, haven't we?"

His smile is one I can't return, my gaze unconsciously sliding over his shoulder to find the hottie with the newspaper no longer there. A ball of something like disappointment settles in my gut. With him listening in, the situation didn't seem so sordid but almost comical. But I'm not laughing now, even if there is now one less person to witness to my embarrassment.

It's not like I was expecting him to save me or anything.

"Why don't we move this conversation upstairs?"

How the heck did I get myself into this?

"We could get to know each other a little better," Annika declares.

"A lot better," her husband adds. "And without the restriction of our clothes."

Help!

2

HOLLY

I DO LIKE OLDER PEOPLE, BUT I DON'T WANT TO SCREW THEM, no matter how attractive they are! I don't have daddy issues. Or mommy issues. And I haven't even managed sex as a twosome in eighteen months, so a threesome is out of the question.

Universe, I think you might have your wires crossed. This was not on my wish list!

"I think we've shocked you a little," Captain Obvious says. *Okay, Lukas says. How about no shit Sherlock.* "Annika and I love to travel," he continues, "and when we travel, we like to take a little holiday from monogamy and spice things up."

"That is..." That is TMI, right there. Just *too much information* for me. I'm happy to share a bottle of wine or a cheese platter, but that's where I draw the line. I can't even share a water bottle with my sister without feeling a little unsettled by the *my mouth where her mouth has been* thing.

Am I giving some kind of unconscious DTF vibes because, seriously, I am so *not* down to f—do *that*.

A threesome! What the fluff?

I lean back in my seat as Lukas moves forward in his, like a snake about to strike. *Or a deranged car salesman with a crazy sales pitch. This is a car I'm* not *going to ride.* But then a large hand appears in the space between us. A large hand attached to a strong wrist which, as I look up—and up—appears to be attached to the devil in his Sunday suit. Or his Wednesday suit, which looks just as fine.

I know those eyes. I've met them before. Over the edge of the *Financial Times* just a few minutes ago. Who knew the devil had such cool-colored eyes, amusement dancing there instead of fire and brimstone?

"It is *you*," his deep voice intones, its buttery warmth catching me off guard. I find myself pressing my hand into his, and he pulls me to my feet and almost into his chest. His hard, unyielding, could-rent-the-space-for-advertising chest.

I exhale a breathy, "Yes," because, up close, boy, this is a lot of man. A wall of man, you might say. Older, sophisticated, and so dang sexy. *I like older people*, a little voice inside me squeaks. And then I realize I'm just staring at him. "I-I am me," I stutter. "I mean, yes, it *is* me! And it's you..." You handsome devil, you.

He stares playfully down, one eyebrow quirked almost in a question mark. Up close, his eyes seem a deeper shade of blue. Maybe it's the contrast of his dark blue suit that makes them seem so. Whatever the reason, the result is striking, especially coupled with those extra thick lashes, the kind that is God's joke on womankind. Oh, and some serious crow's feet. I don't mean serious as in *Botox needed, STAT!* More like serious might be his default face. Which would be strange, considering his gaze feels like a hook daring me to play along.

"It's Cousin Lyle!" I belatedly tag on. Fictitious Cousin Lyle, or as he was previously known to me, the hot snorting man who just recently vacated the seat behind the kinky duo.

"How are you, *Olive*?" His mouth quirks in the corner, his tone a tiny bit sour.

I try not to laugh; is it the name he's christened me with or the one I've given him? *Both probably.*

"Olive?" Lukas begins, though neither of us spares him a glance. "You said your name was—"

"Who were you this time?" The stranger sighs and stares balefully down at me. "It was Candy again, wasn't it?"

"If your parents had named you Olive, you'd be making up names, too," I counter happily. Oh, my. I do love a man who can think on his feet.

"But you'll always be Olive to me." Fake Lyle's reply is smooth as silk, or at least the synthetic kind. *For all our insincerity.*

"Lyle, you're such a tease," I murmur, finding my fingers on his chest somehow. "So, how are tricks?"

"Tricks are tricky." If temptation had an expression, I'm looking at it.

"And you need my advice." I deliver my assertion with just a hint of fake sympathy as I turn to grab my purse. "You've got boyfriend trouble again, haven't you?" I waggle an admonishing finger his way.

"You know how it is," he answers, that sour note resurfacing again.

Oh, God, I love that he's playing along, even if I seem to be the only one having fun.

"I'm not sure I do," I answer, sweet as saccharine.

"Come now, you know a hedonist rarely resists pleasure."

The sound that leaves my mouth is more breath than an actual laugh as his purring response twists and coils and blooms in places it has no business visiting. The man has big dick energy—wrapped in a silky, seductive coating of high sexual energy—and I think I'm getting a contact high from the fumes.

"Thanks for the invite." I turn, quickly addressing the kinky duo on the couch, who seem a little too stunned to respond. "Raincheck? I'm sure you understand, family should always come first." And with that, I take the arm my stranger doesn't quite offer and get the hell out of Dodge.

I almost drag him from the bar, not able to move away from the situation quick enough. We're out through the stylishly minimalistic foyer, down the front steps, and into the afternoon spring sunshine all before you can say "straight acting Cousin Lyle to the rescue".

"Oh my God!" I turn wide-eyed to my would-be savior as we round the corner. "Can you believe that just happened?"

"I can't believe you made me leave my cup of coffee."

"I'd say sorry except... I didn't make you."

"No? It must be my good nature to blame." His lips quirk with amusement.

"Well, I, for one, am pleased you did. I can't believe that just happened. I mean, I know it's Wednesday and all, but..."

"I'm not sure what the day has to do with the situation." The man's head tilts as though to study me.

"Hump day?" I offer ridiculously, though not in invitation. Not yet, at least. But he just stares back without offering anything more. "Come on, Lyle, it's not even three o'clock!"

"I'm also not sure what the hour has to do with it."

"Are you telling me you're regularly propositioned weekday afternoons?" My hands suddenly find my hips as I warm to my theme.

"Perhaps not to a threesome," he concedes, rubbing a

hand across his chin. But I see the beginnings of that smile still. *Boy, it must be some gene pool he's been swimming in.* He's too masculine to be pretty, and plain old handsome just doesn't do his looks justice. Brutally good-looking might be a better description. It's like the man has an air of Viking about him.

I suddenly feel like I might need a good… conquering.

But then his smile fades as he seems almost to come back to himself. To himself, the moment, and, judging by his change in manner, the ridiculousness of the situation. He straightens not only his shoulders but also the cuffs of his shirt. Cartier cufflinks, I note. The kind that say: classy yet understated and high rolling rich. Not that rich does anything for me. In fact, no man, rich or otherwise, has ruffled my truffle, so to speak, in more than eighteen months.

Rich might not do it for me, but that accent? That accent is doing things to me.

"I trust I was in the right, intervening as I did." He's suddenly all business; crisp consonants and sharp diction and brows that pull together where before they did not. *It looks like I was right about that serious face.*

"My God, yes!" I exclaim. Way over the top, I know. "A thousand times yes." One minute, my hands are in the air, and the next, they're planted squarely on his chest. Don't blame me. The damn thing is like a magnet. "Thank you for saving me, Lyle."

"That's *not* my name." His hands cover mine, lowering them to my sides, his small smile somehow a demonstration of his amusement and disapproval at once. "But I'm happy to have been of assistance."

"Well, Lyle did Olive a solid." *Come on, smile a little more for me.* "I literally had no idea how to get myself out of that."

"Raincheck seemed to cover it." His eyes narrow once more as though regretting the comment. Or maybe he's remembering how I made him my fake gay cousin.

"I was being polite! Trying not to make them feel uncomfortable. I have no plans of taking them up on their offer, now or in the future."

Something flickers in his expression, almost like he's reached a decision. He inclines his head and murmurs that it was nice to meet me. The soles of his shoes scrape against the pavement as he begins to pivot away.

"Wait!" I call out, not ready for the exchange to be over. Not only have my hands developed a fondness for his chest but he's like a puzzle I haven't finished deciphering. A Rubik's Cube I haven't finished messing with yet. "Where are you going?" The words are out of my mouth before I can stop them, my hand too.

"I'm sorry?" His gaze slices up from where my fingers are currently curled around his forearm, cool blue eyes matching his tone.

It's true I never was any good with a Rubik's Cube, not that it ever stopped me.

"Tell me you're not leaving me here." Which is clearly what he's about to do. "Lyle, you can't leave! I've got nowhere to go but back in there." I point back the way we came. "I'm staying in *that* hotel."

"I don't quite see—"

"If I go back in there, Mr. and Mrs. *Let's Get It On* might think I've changed my mind about that three o'clock appointment."

"You could always go somewhere else," he offers, arranging his features into something that looks like polite confusion. But I'm not buying it.

"Somewhere else?" I repeat. I'm not worried about going

back to my hotel room alone. It's more that I don't want to. I also don't want to wander around London today. It's no fun when you're by yourself. And I would know, having roamed the city lots of weekends, killing time while waiting for Amelie and Aurora, the kids under my charge, to finish up at birthday parties and playdates. I've visited enough bougie cafés and drunk enough coffee to sustain a third-world country's GDP. I've strolled around museums and parks, and designer window shopped 'till I've been ready to drop. These are all things I have no plans on doing today.

Not when Mr. Viking here is intriguing the hell out of me.

"But I might get lost." The words fall out of my mouth without even a flicker of remorse. Or the itch to hitch my *liar-liar pants* higher.

"I beg your pardon?" he asks, his diction razor-sharp.

"I'm on vacation." It's not technically a lie. "Today is my last day in London, but my first away from the tour company, and I've already gotten lost three times looking for a CVS." As he frowns at me, I weave my lie a little tighter. "A pharmacy? I have the blisters to prove it. Want to see?" Tightening my grip on his forearm, I tentatively lift my foot.

"That won't be necessary," he answers with a worried frown. "I really don't—"

"Honestly, I'm amazed I found my way back to the hotel." Oh, woe is me. I'm just a poor damsel lost in the big city and laying it on a little thick. *Did I mention I majored in drama in college?* "I have such a terrible sense of direction. Oh!" I add as though struck by a sudden thought. "Why don't I buy you a coffee?" I add.

At the exact same time as he says, "Perhaps, I can... escort you to the nearest coffee shop?"

"Deal!"

"I'm sorry?" He shakes his head, a little dazed, I think.

"I can buy you a coffee as a thank you and replace the one you left behind." I slip my arm through his and lean on him a little, but his feet aren't budging.

"I'd really rather not." He looks surprised, almost as though the words had escaped from his mouth.

"Oh, do you have to go back to work?"

"No, but—"

"You have somewhere else you need to be?"

"Not exactly." His frown deepens. I'm guessing regret, maybe because he's not as good at lying on the fly as me. *What can I say? It's a talent.*

"I guess I overstepped the mark." I pull my arm reluctantly from his. "I forgot I was in a big city for a minute." I frown and bite my lip for good measure, my brow creasing. "I can't imagine the folks back home turning away a stranger. It'd probably make the evening news." I look up at him, all sad doe eyes, throwing in a hint of teary glisten. "Come to think of it, it might even make the evening news here. Especially when I wind up lost. Or dead."

Okay, so I'm not laying it on a little thick but a lotta thick. Why not? *I just want to see what I can get away with* is my recently adopted motto for life. I just want to see how far I can get. I mean, it's mostly a case of me faking it until I make it, attitude-wise, but so far, it's worked out pretty well.

Look at me, hanging out in London. YOLO!

Something tells me Lyle would be good company, as well as excellent eye candy. And he was nice enough to save me from the terrible two-some threesome people, which proves he's a gentleman.

But no ordinary gentleman, my mind supplies.

Whatever. Being with him will be way more fun than

staring at the hotel walls. I might even get a covert photo for my Instagram and caption it:

Hanging out with hotties in London, living my best life!

Suck on that, people of Podunk-Mookatill!

"Do you have a wife?" While this is important, if he answers yes, I'm calling bullshit because that hand isn't usually home to a wedding ring.

"I don't have a wife. Why would you ask?" His eyes narrow slightly.

"I just don't want you to get the wrong idea. I'm not making plans for your body." Even if it is a *really* nice body.

A glint suddenly replaces his narrow look, though not like the one he'd shot over the top of his newspaper earlier. That look hadn't made my insides feel like a ribbon curled on the edge of a pair of sharp scissors. Kind of fizzy but a little afraid. Not the boogeyman kind of afraid. More like the kind you get when you reach the top of a roller coaster and anticipate what's to follow.

Feels a little like an omen. An omen for a thrilling ride?

I give myself an internal shake. I'm not looking for the kind of entertainment that comes without clothes yet.

"I-I'm just being courteous," I stammer as he does that wicked eyebrow thing again. "I just mean that if I were your wife or girlfriend, I wouldn't like to loan you out."

"Just to be sure I have this right," he begins, "you think it's my civic duty to take responsibility for you as a visitor to the country? But only if I don't have a wife or a girlfriend."

"I mean, isn't that what you just did in there?" I gesture back towards the hotel.

"I gather you thought you were in danger?"

"In danger of combusting into flames of embarrassment, yes. And now, according to the rules of my people, I should thank you. With a hardy handshake." The heat in my cheeks feels like a contributor to global warming as I take his large hand and pump it ridiculously. "And a cup of coffee." I pause. "Lyle, you're looking at me like you know what crazy is and that I'm it."

"I wouldn't say crazy exactly." He frowns in an effort not to give in to a smile.

"Sure. I mean, it's not like *every* man on earth claims to have dated that one girl who turned out to be certifiable." Just most of them would be my guess. "Relax. That's not what this is. I promise I'm not going to get you drunk on pink cocktails before chaining you to my bed. I just have twenty-four hours to kill."

"Twenty-four hours?" If I'd tried to anticipate a reaction to go with his slightly wary tone, I probably would've chosen dread, not the almost speculative look that he slides over my body.

"I'm not even going to ask what that was all about," I mutter, ignoring how my skin reacts as though his gaze were a physical thing. The tingling flare between my legs is a little harder to disregard.

He doesn't offer a reply, though the look he gives me is all innocence, which should look ridiculous on a man of his age, but he somehow works it. I'd say it's been a while since that blazing blue gaze was anything but innocent, something that's confirmed as his expression turns almost calculating. *I just want to see what I can get away with* suddenly feels like having a tiger by its tail.

Time to redress that balance.

"*I* have twenty-four hours until I leave," I reiterate, bringing my hands to my chest. "You..." I reiterate, touching his very nice chest again—is it any wonder that my hands are there again when his jacket hugs him so beautifully? Tight, but not the kind of tight that speaks of ill-fitting, but enough to reveal the very obvious ripple of muscles beneath the fine fabric. *Obviously custom-made.* And so soft under my fingertips. *Soft fabric. Hard male. All male.* Where was I again? Oh. "...You could keep me company for an hour or two."

"A lot can happen in a couple of hours," his low tone rumbles.

For the second time in our short acquaintance, he removes my hands from his chest. Only this time, he reaches his long arm around me, pulling me to his side.

3

ALEXANDER

> Where the fuck are you?

> What kind of man doesn't turn up to his own birthday bash? Bad form, Alexander. Bad fucking form.

My jacket already discarded to the back of the bench, I place my phone back against the table, screen down, and ignore the last in this series of Matteo's texts.

I've never been one for spontaneity. Never been the kind of man who takes off on a whim. Plans are to be adhered to. Responsibilities are to be acknowledged and met. And when your friends have plans for a birthday dinner, you're obliged to attend.

I know all this. Believe in it, even. Yet here I sit, ignoring both my phone and my responsibilities in favor of... well, I don't know what this is. I only know I'm enjoying it more than anything in recent memory.

"Don't keep me in suspense," my oddly compelling tablemate demands, her delicious dimple peeking out. With dark hair and darker eyes, she has an earthy kind of beauty. Deliciously ripe and round in all the right places, and nothing like my usual type. There's her age for a start. She's much younger. Too young, perhaps.

Despite first impressions, I'm pleased to find her not the least deranged, though she's certainly made me feel a little out of my element. *Possibly even a little unhinged.*

"What does it taste like?"

I'd like to know how she tastes. Feel the almost indecent fullness of her bottom lip between my teeth. But that's not what we're doing right now, even if I can't help but imagine it. Instead, I inhale a deep breath, exhaling an equally deep sigh. Then against my better judgement, I aim to answer her question by lifting the glass to my lips.

"Not like that."

I don't think anyone has ever rolled their eyes at me before, have they? She prods the straw in the direction of my mouth, her slender forefinger adorned by a thick silver band.

"It came with one of these for a reason, *Lyle*."

"My abject humiliation?" Because the straw the drink was delivered with is in the shape of a penis. A pink penis.

"Don't be so uptight."

"I tend to be tense when someone is trying to shove a penis in my mouth."

"You're a riot! No, don't do that—you heard the server," she adds with an infectious giggle. "You're not allowed to use your hands."

I went to a party with the same rule a long time ago. There were fewer clothes, as I recall.

Fingers poised over the straw, I narrow my gaze as though what I'd like to use my hands for would be to throttle her when, in fact, I'd be more inclined to use them in other much more satisfying ways. But she does look delighted as I settle my mouth over the straw. Then she's not *quite* so much as I clench it between my teeth and drop it to the tabletop with a grimace. I may be enjoying her company, but that is the limit to this experience.

"Biting? Really?"

"Yes, biting."

Her gaze dips to the abandoned straw. "Did it really taste that bad?"

"Worse." I try and fail to suppress a shudder. Syrupy and sickly sweet, the concoction has the artificial aftertaste of a childhood medicine, thanks to a maraschino cherry garnish. But it was worth it because as I lick the sticky coating from my lips, I note her eyes following the path of my tongue. Eyes that I'd thought were green but are actually hazel. *Green-rimmed, tawny at the center*. "Remind me, what was it called again?"

"Oh, no. No action replays," she replies with a dirty laugh that is countermanded by the stripe of pink that instantly brands her cheeks. "You're not getting me to say *that* again."

Understandable, really, because my cocktail is called a *suck, bang, and blow*.

"Do I need to point out that I wasn't the one who ordered it?"

"That kind of backfired on me," she answers, wrinkling her nose.

"I don't know. I certainly enjoyed hearing you do so."

"You get to order the next round of drinks," she blusters, her eyes darting away.

"But you ordered it so delightfully. And with only the hint of a stutter." And bonny pink cheeks.

"Oh, my God." Her words fall in a rush as she leans

across the table, her fingers grasping my wrist to look at my watch, providing me with a perfect view of her cleavage. Like my jacket, her blazer is draped over the back of the bench. I'd almost swallowed my tongue when she'd slipped it off, her tight sleeveless T-shirt revealing not only toned and tanned arms but also the perfect handfuls of breasts. "Are your two hours up yet?"

"You said one or two hours." My attention flickers down to my Breitling because it doesn't do to stare. Before she can pull away, my free hand makes a manacle of her wrist. "I make it two hours and twelve minutes, and though I've suffered the pink drink, I've still yet to see a hint of those shackles."

Allowing a stranger to strap you to any surface might be a very bad idea, but I'd be lying if I said I wasn't tempted by the experience right now. Almost as though I'd said that aloud, her breath hitches as her eyes take on the appearance of midnight. Dark, seductive, and full of promise.

I'd watched her covertly in the hotel earlier, stealing glances over the top of my newspaper after Matteo and Van had left. It was hard not to watch. She was so effusive and clearly enjoying both her company and the conversation, so much so that her face seemed almost lit from within. Until she wasn't enjoying it anymore, and I sought to intervene. Strange. It had been a long while since I'd cared enough to study the nuances of an expression, never mind offer assistance to a stranger.

We'd spent an hour in a coffee shop, which was only strange and stilted for the first few minutes. I'd begun to think I could make my excuses and leave. But then a series of demanding texts blew up my phone, and I'd realized I was having too much fun to attend to them. Coffee cups drained, she'd suggested a drink, reasoning the longer she stayed out of the hotel, the less chance there'd be of her being accosted by the predatory couple. It had nothing to do with enjoying my company, she'd assured me. Nothing to do with wanting to get me into bed.

Ah, the lies we tell ourselves.

She'd been so delightfully flustered at the offer of an afternoon threesome, I'd almost considered watching how the scene would play out. But when I had, and she'd gripped my arm outside of the hotel, the contact had been... affecting. The sight of her slender fingers pale against the dark cloth of my jacket, the thin strand of silver circling her delicate wrist. Something almost primeval had stirred inside me, drawing the very fibers of my being taut.

She'd be so tiny under me. So malleable. So sweet. Yet spirited.

Thankfully, by the time I'd raised my gaze, I'd managed to master my expression, if not my thoughts. Instinct had won over intellect, and here we are, ensconced at the end of a shared table in a less than salubrious bar off Friday Street. Latin music, garish deco, and crowded banquet tables set out like a school dining hall.

"You know, I'm sensing you agreed to come along not because of your sense of civic duty but because you think I'm cute."

The way her gaze dips belies her feisty tone. While *cute* isn't a word I'd ordinarily reach for, *lovely* had sprung to mind. Fuck it, if a man can't take a pretty girl for a drink on his birthday, when the hell can he? And if we happen to find ourselves in the vicinity of a bed sometime following? Happy birthday to me.

It's not like I'm chasing her. Yet.

"Maybe that's the reason *you* came along with me," I counter. "Because you think *I'm* cute. How did you end up sitting with that couple, anyway?"

"Who? The threesome people? I thought they seemed nice. And I like old people."

"So there's hope for me yet," I murmur as I catch the attention of the server with a beckoning nod and order a couple of single malts.

A tiny smile catches at the corner of her mouth, though she turns her head to conceal it. "I don't like whisky."

"That's only because you don't know better."

"Oh, and you think you know what's good for me, do you?"

"I'm certain there are a great number of things I could introduce you to. Things you might assume you won't enjoy at first."

"Because *that* wasn't brimming with innuendo." The color in her cheeks deepens.

"I can't be held responsible for the murk of your mind."

"Even the murk of my mind knows I don't like whisky."

"Trust me. You'll like this kind."

"Lyle, you're not that cute."

Squirrels are cute. Kittens. My sister's Labrador, even. Cute isn't a word a man aspires to, though I find I don't mind. Because she isn't wrong. I am cute, just the canny kind. The cunning kind.

"You know, now that you mention it," I answer almost airily, "you do remind me of a Yorkshire terrier."

"Because I'm small and adorable?"

"I was thinking more... unrelenting." I do hope she bites.

She narrows her eyes playfully as she gives my shoulder a gentle push.

"Violence, Olive, as well as threats of tying me to your bed?" As I make my reply, the server reappears with the whiskies I'd ordered. It's obvious by the way he's trying not to smile that he heard what I'd said. Brightly tattooed arms reach out, placing a couple of amber-filled glasses on the table and one more with half a dozen chunks of ice.

"We don't get many people ordering the good stuff." He places a small jug of water and another of ice down next. "Sounds like you're in for a good night. On more than one count." With a wink, the server leaves.

"You totally did that on purpose," she says, watching him go.

She's right. I do like to see the color in her cheeks.

"For the record," I reply instead, "if there are any knots to be tied, I used to be a Boy Scout."

My God, her expression. I begin to laugh, the deep sound almost a shock to my own ears. And this is the moment I decide, truly decide, that I must have this woman. It isn't her adorable expressions or because I'd like to know how deep her blushes run. Something tells me a woman like this, a woman with an appreciation for the absurd, would be a joy to bed. A sheet-ripping, limbs-thrashing, loud enough to wake the dead kind of delight.

"Drink your whisky, Olive. Behave yourself." To my delight, she does. "Go on, you can admit it. I was right about the whisky, wasn't I?"

"It's not bad," she concedes with a careless flick of her shoulder. "It's kind of smoky, not sharp. I like the way it warms as it travels."

She moves her hand down her neck, her fingers trailing just a little farther south. My own gaze follows as though invited, my head filling with all the ways I'm going to warm her. Make her hot. Heat her blood like a shot of good whisky cannot.

"But I am so *not* an Olive." She folds her arms against the table, leaning down onto them.

"Shows what you know. Olive suits you perfectly."

"Don't you want to know my real name?" She slides her glass to the side, her eyes following the motion rather than meeting mine. "Or is it that you don't want to tell me yours?"

Despite her playful delivery, I consider her words as I also consider the lush valley of her cleavage again. It's an unconscious motion on her part, I think. Not a ploy or a play for me. As for her question, I reach a decision. No harm can come from her knowing my Christian name, and given that she's leaving tomorrow, I'm not likely to see our names linked in the tabloids.

Reaching out, I wrap my fingers around her wrist and encourage her closer with a gentle tug. She slides herself from the other side of the table and along the end until our shoulders are almost touching.

"I already know your name." Despite the dissonant noise in the place: the music, the hum of voices, the rattle of glasses, and the jarring cackle of laughter from tablemates nearer her age than mine, I keep my voice low. Like I've a secret to impart or some intrigue that requires her to lean closer. "Holland." I draw out her name as though it's a sentence all of its own. I'd thought it an odd name at first. Why would any parent name their child after a region of Europe? Now I wonder if it was excellent foresight on their part because she is truly as unique as her name.

She releases a tiny breath, her lips slightly parted and her eyes darkly glistening. "How?"

I watch her lips form the word, wondering how I'd never noticed how delicate an action it is. *How.* Pouting and soft, and delightfully inviting. Not for the first time this evening, I imagine what it would feel like to press my mouth against hers. We're sitting so close, almost leaning into each other at the corner of the table. It would take nothing to make that connection. But I'm not at all sure I'd be able to stop at one kiss given I've been thinking about her mouth since she dragged me out of the hotel. She isn't like anyone I've ever encountered before and certainly not like any of the women I would ordinarily involve myself with.

Not that I get involved these days.

But getting back to her question, my knowledge of her name isn't magic or kismet. Just observation. And a little novelty on my part.

"It's printed on your credit card." Though her thumb had covered her surname. Not that I feel the need to learn it. "I saw it when you paid for the coffee."

I don't believe a woman has ever offered to pay for my coffee before, but to insist otherwise turned out to be futile. She was so determined to get me there, then so insistent it was "her shout".

She huffs out a tiny incredulous laugh.

"But to me, you will always be Olive."

"Could that be because you think I'm just a tiny bit salty?" she surmises, measuring a tiny space between her thumb and forefinger.

I don't have an immediate answer. My mind and body are reluctant to join in as an image flashes quite suddenly in my head. *Flashes through my head, then flickers through my body.* The heat of her under me, her slick skin against mine as I taste the salt from the indent above the heart-shaped bow mouth.

She's too young for you, my mind whispers. Fuck it. I've likely already booked my seat to hell. What are a few more sins to add to the tally?

"Salty." The word, when it comes, sounds ragged around the edges and stretched taut with a sudden need. God, yes, I'd like to taste her.

"You know, like the attitude?" She leans forward, her

forearms pressed against the table, drawing my attention to the soft rise of her breasts. Once might be an accident. Twice...? I don't think so.

The gentleman that I am, I glance away, and though the sight was fleeting, it leaves a lingering aftereffect. Who am I fooling? The whole two hours and however many minutes we've been together, I've been cataloguing her movements. How she holds her glass. The way her mouth moves as she speaks. She's just so fucking delicious. I want to pull her onto my knee and press my nose into her hair because every time she moves, a hint of her perfume seems to travel my way. It makes me want to grab her and inhale greedily. I'm not sure I'd stop there. I want to know if her skin tastes as creamy as it appears. If her lips are as sweet.

Jesus Christ, I must be having a midlife crisis. My friends have been trying to convince me life begins at forty. They never once mentioned that dementia might set in.

"Have I got something...?" Holland swipes a finger to the corner of her mouth, her brow puckered in a tiny frown.

My gaze lingers on her mouth a beat longer before I reach out and trace my finger across the deep bow of her lip. "Paprika," I lie. There's a tiny dish of chickpeas and pumpkin seeds sitting between us. She'd helped herself to it earlier.

"Am I salty?" Her eyes lift, her voice huskier now.

I find myself staring down at the offending finger before bringing it to my lips. Regardless of whether it was or wasn't an invitation and irrespective of the way she's looking at me, the pit of my balls tighten, and my cock twitches. "Like a Manzanilla olive." I manage to make my voice sound at odds with how I feel.

"I don't think I've ever had one."

They're a little sweeter, round, and ripe. The perfect

accompaniment to a martini and almost the exact color of her eyes earlier in the sunlight. But I don't say any of that, opting for instead, "You look like a girl from Andalucía."

"Like someone you know?" Her mouth twists, unimpressed.

I shake my head. "Manzanilla olives are grown in Andalucía." I only referred to her coloring. Dark hair. Dark eyes. Since when have I been so awkward? Since when have I forgotten to just go for what I want? *Could it be because you have a hard-on for a woman at least fifteen years your junior?* my mind unhelpfully supplies.

"That's just great, Lyle. I remind you of some girl you met in Spain. Is that why you agreed to keep me company?" Her tone is bantering but sharp.

"Agreed to? I wasn't aware I had a choice."

"I'm not holding you hostage."

"Oh, but you are, Holland. Your sparring wit and lovely face have me absolutely captive."

"Even if you haven't offered me your name." She sends me a look from beneath her lashes, part tease, part seriousness. And totally beguiling.

"It's Alexander," I offer reluctantly because she intuited my thoughts perfectly. I would prefer not to give her my name. Alexander *is* one of my names, though not one I'm called in my family circle.

"Alexander," she repeats with a slow nod of her head. "I like it. Do you go by Alex?"

I shake my head.

"Can *I* call you Alex?"

"Not if you want me to answer."

"How about Al?" she continues to bait, causing my mouth to twist with a show of annoyance even though I'm more entertained.

"Zander?"

"I think I'd prefer Cousin Lyle."

"You two are so cute together!" A woman from the other side of the table suddenly offers this as she slides into the seat recently vacated by Holland. "Have you been together long?"

"Oh, we're not dating," Holland replies. "We're family, right, Lyle?" Her gaze slides to me, full of mischief. "Cousins," she further clarifies.

Perhaps the kissing kind.

"Oh, really?" I drag my gaze from Holland's when the woman's eyes meet mine, her attention unsubtly raking over me. "I'm Nikki, and this is Lewis." A languid finger flicks to her right. "Mind if we join you?"

4

ALEXANDER

"You're sure you're just cousins?"

As the idiot arse sitting next to me speaks, I refuse to offer him even a glance as I continue to turn the glass of amber liquid in my hand.

"Only, the way you're watching her, it's not like she's family. Unless you're a close family. Like a *really* close family."

My fingers tap against the tabletop as I try not to bite out my response. "I'm sure if you cast your mind back thirty minutes or so, you'll recall what Holland said."

"I know what she said, and I know what I see," he mutters under his breath. Before I can decide whether I want to answer, punch, or ignore him, he begins to move. "I'm gonna take a leak."

A part of me wonders what I'm still doing here. In telling the other woman we were cousins, did Holland think she was protecting herself? Perhaps she doesn't like me in that way, as childish as that sounds.

That way, I silently scoff. We're not talking a schoolyard romance here. The kind of sweet nothings I want to whisper include coaxing her to slip out of her underwear to bring her sweet pussy over my face.

I stifle a frustrated sigh. I've been turned down before, of course. But it doesn't happen often, mostly because I stick to the same kind of woman. Those aware of my name and my status. Those who are aware of my need for absolute discretion. Those who, for whatever reason, are happy to make do with the part of me I'm willing to give. *Usually my cock.*

No, I decide. It's not that she isn't interested. Her answer was a spur-of-the-moment payback for embarrassing her in front of the server, though I'm certainly the one paying now as I try to decipher her intentions as she dances with... whatever her name was. Is she trying to make me jealous? Trying to or not, I find I am. I'm jealous of anyone taking an ounce of her attention from me. As strange as it sounds and as hard as I currently am watching her sinuous movements on the dance floor, I find I don't want her to come back to the table. Because when she does, she won't be alone given that she's dancing with... Nikki, yes, that's it. A girl who has made it blatantly obvious she'd be happy to fuck me.

Right sentiment. Wrong girl.

Worse, I think her friend might have the same offer in mind for Holland. *Over my dead body.*

I throw back the rest of my drink, wondering if I would've been better served to have left her in the coffee shop and turned up for my birthday dinner. At least until I remember how little I was looking forward to the evening. Which means I'm where I want to be. Where I need to be. Because for the past six months, I've been telling friends and family I wanted nothing for this milestone birthday. But I was wrong because I want her. *God, how I want her.*

The beat of the music pulses through the soles of my

feet as I watch Nikki throw her arms around the fascinating and petite brunette. As she does so, her gaze is all for me. She slides behind Holland, her arms snaking up the other woman's jean-clad thighs. I'm sure it's supposed to be a turn-on. Girl on girl. Isn't that supposed to be every man's fantasy? The thing about realizing fantasies is that it can be a little like opening Pandora's box: nothing is ever the same afterward. Life's miseries visited upon all, as I can attest.

Nikki murmurs something in Holland's ear, causing her eyes to fly comically wide. It doesn't take a great imagination to guess that was a suggestion. *Two salacious invitations in one day, Holland.* I shake my head a little ruefully, biting back a budding smile. I wonder if that's a record. An then how she'll react to a third from me.

I want her on my knee. In my bed. Her cries ringing through the room as I press my face between her thighs.

Even if it is madness. Absolute utter madness.

Which is exactly how being near her makes me feel.

"That was so much fun!" Lost to my introspection, I hadn't noticed the pair's return. "Olive is such a good dancer, don't you think?" The other woman throws an arm around Holland's waist, her long fingernails like crimson spots against the white cotton of her T-shirt. The pair are a study in contrasts. Two pretty faces, flushed from exertion. One full of natural beauty, the other trying too hard.

Holland and I exchange a covert look as Nikki sidles closer, her hand finding my shoulder as she slides into her seat. Or rather Holland's seat.

"Sorry," Holland mouths silently, pushing a wayward lock out of her face.

"You will be," I mouth back, my eyes narrowed slits of retribution.

Holland's eyes fly wide, her shrug seeming to say *what can I do* before she lowers herself onto the seat opposite.

As a general rule, I don't suffer fools. Yet here I sit with people I neither like nor care for while trying to decide how I entice a pretty girl to make this birthday memorable.

I turn back to find Nikki uncomfortably close, her chin rested on her hand. Given that hand is still on my shoulder, she's practically in my face. Her brows lift in anticipation, and though my mind is a beat behind, I remember she'd asked a question. The kind of question that seemed like a segue to an invitation.

"It was fun!" Holland's interjection saves me from a reply but doesn't save me from the woman, who inches inconceivably closer.

"I'm all about fun," Nikki murmurs, her mouth far too close for comfort as she eyes me like I'm her next meal. I slide her hand from my shoulder, pressing it to the table as I lean away.

"Me, too," Holland says. "Remember the time we went to the Festival of Fungus together?"

"The festival of what?" Nikki's head whips around so fast, I'm surprised she doesn't suffer whiplash.

"Fungus. You haven't heard of it? Wow. Back home, it's a pretty big deal. The Estacada festival puts the fun in fungus, right, Lyle?"

"I'm not certain that truer words were ever been spoken," I reply.

"Hey, if you're cousins, how come you two have different accents?"

I'm saved by the bell as my phone buzzes with a text, though not before hearing Holland say that my parents left the cult's compound while I was still small.

I pick up my phone with a murmured apology. Given the

social setting, I wouldn't ordinarily answer, but the diversion seems timely.

> Wherever you are, you'd better be having a good fucking time

reads my text from Matteo, which is quickly followed by a second.

> Because someone (and my money is on your idiot of a brother) has hired a stripper to wish many happy returns to the birthday boy. Only, guess who isn't here?

I begin to chuckle, covering it with a cough. While I'm grateful (so fucking grateful) I'm not there, though I might actually like to be a fly on the wall just to watch how that went down. Like a one-legged man in an arse-kicking contest, I shouldn't wonder.

> And not just any old stripper. Oh no.

> But a scantily clad octogenarian

comes his next text.

> Gyrating. Around the table.

> In a Michelin star restaurant, for fuck's sake!

That is something I don't need to imagine. Griffin will be so pissed I wasn't there, but it serves him right. Without answering Matteo's text, I switch my phone to silent and slide it away.

"I hope that wasn't your wife, Lyle," Nikki purrs. "I don't like competition."

"Lyle doesn't have a wife." Holland stares across at me,

her eyes tawny and full of mischief. I give a slow warning shake of my head, which, of course, she ignores. I begin to wonder if trouble might be her middle name. No, because it would have to be proceeded by *causer of*. "He's not that way inclined," she adds happily, ignoring my silent threats of bodily harm.

I think I'm going to put her across my knee at the earliest opportunity.

"You mean he's…?" The woman's attention bounces between us like a stone skipping across a pond.

"It's just like Olive to spill all my secrets," I drawl, agreeing with Holland that it would be convenient for Cousin Lyle to be gay. "I'm afraid you're barking up the wrong tree." I pat her hand once again, this time with a look of sympathy. "You lack a couple of the essentials." I'm not exactly lying. She lacks being Holland, at least.

"Why are all the good one's gay!" the woman almost wails.

"Oh, I'm sure that's not true. Is it, Olive?" My reply is heavy with sarcasm. Or my unspoken plans for retribution.

"No, because Lyle hits on straight guys all the time," Olive, I mean, Holland, offers, unconcerned. "Of course, they're also usually married."

That's not the direction I'd hoped for.

"Who's married?" Nikki's companion suddenly arrives back at the table. I can't recall his name. *Just his attitude.*

"Lyle is," Nikki whines. Not that I pay her any attention as Holland's smile slips, her gaze meeting mine across the table. I shake my head. I'm not married. I was once, but that was a long time ago. I wouldn't have spent the afternoon with her if I was, and I wouldn't be planning to spend the rest of the evening between her legs.

"Married to her?"

Our gazes break as Holland's attention is snagged by his question. A beat later, she's shaking her head. "No, Lyle isn't married," she says with conviction.

"I didn't mean to say he's married. I meant to say he's *gay*." Nikki's shoulders move up then down in a plaintive and unhappy shrug.

"Oh. Really?" He takes his seat next to me. "So all that staring at Olive was... what?"

"He's very protective," Holland offers.

"Gay." As the man's gaze falls over me, a cold realization sinks in. "I'll drink to that." He raises his glass. "Did Nikki mention I'm bi?"

Holland, Holland, Holland, you are absolutely going to pay for this.

5

HOLLY

Well, shit.

The music fades, then quiets completely as the door to the bathroom closes with an echoing *clunk*. Honestly, I don't know how I get myself into these scrapes. How sometimes *I just want to see what I can get away with* blows up in my face.

"Dammit." Pulling my purse off my shoulder, I deposit my precious Prada to the vanity with less care than I'd normally show it. "Oh, we're not dating," I mutter in a grating falsetto, rummaging through my purse for my lipstick. "We're family, right, Lyle? Urgh!"

Way to go, Holland. Congrats on trying to screw up a good thing! A sure thing.

I eye myself critically in the mirror. My sister is always saying I'm too clever for my own good, not that I feel particularly intelligent right now. And I know I said I wasn't going to sleep with him, but that was before. Before he looked at me like something he wanted to devour. Before I changed my mind and decided I'd be breaking my dry spell sometime and that I wanted it to be with him. I can't remember the last time I met someone, and we just gelled.

But that was before the competition turned up wearing a sparkly belt for a skirt! I mean, I look cute, but it's a look that's more daytime city girl than a vampy *imma-lick-you-from-your-head-to-your*-toes kind of look. There might not be anything I can do about my clothes—other than to keep my jacket off because I know the tatas are high and my butt is tight, and I know he's noticed both of those things—but that didn't seem enough. So, I made him gay for the second time today.

My reflection grimaces back at me from the mirror. *Sorry, Lyle.*

Alexander, I silently correct. It's a good name, and it totally suits him because it's a name that's both strong and classic. Just like he is.

Well, that study in manly perfection is mine tonight. And I know he's thinking the same thing. The way he watched me as I danced made something sticky and sweet flow through me. Every time I glanced his way, his eyes met mine, dark and intense. And when Nikki had grabbed my hips, a very private joke seemed to lurk in the twist of his lips.

Out of the frying pan and into the fire, his expression seemed to say.

And in a way, he's right. Because how could I have foreseen that making Alexander gay would've put him on Lewis's radar?

"Gaydar?" I say aloud, then shake my head. "It doesn't mean a thing. Man, woman, straight, gay, no one is cutting in on me."

I'm not above tripping a bitch. Literally or figuratively. But first, a little common-sense security. Grabbing my phone, I open my Messenger app and select the sneaky photograph I'd taken of Alexander on the way to the bathroom. Cropping out Nikki's hand, I stare at it a little, then press send.

You can do what you like when you're on vacation.
Be anyone you like.
Take a break from your own life.

Or so I tell myself as I return to my search for my lipstick. Pulling it out, I examine my expression again.

He's perfect. I don't mean without flaws because everyone has them. I just mean he's perfect for me. Here. Now. Tonight. Not to mention, the setup is pretty sweet. I'm just a tourist. Here for the night. Leaving tomorrow. On a jet plane. Never to be seen in London again. At least, that's what I've told him. I might as well be leaving because in a city of more than eight million people, it's not likely I'll ever bump into him.

Impatient, I grab my phone again.

> Did you get the photo?

> I already saw your Instagram post

my sister, Kennedy, immediately replies. She means my post from earlier today. It was a piece of London street art posted with a cool filter and some pithy text.

> By the way, it's nice to know you got there. Finally.

> Got here? You dropped me off at the airport. Where else would I be?

> Kidnapped? The victim of a plane crash? This might not even be you, for all I know. Because regular people check in with their loved ones when they get where they're going to.

Ho-boy. This is what I like to call big sister syndrome.

> I'm here. I'm sorry I forgot to report in but if there'd been a plane crash, I'm pretty sure I wouldn't be telling you about it now. Back to our regular programming - pleeease check your MSNGR!!

I turn in the direction of the bathroom door as it creaks open, the thump of the bass reverberating off the tile. A redhead (aka not Nikki) slips into a stall without making eye contact. Girls in bathrooms are like that. Either they want to be your new BFF or they pretend you're Casper the ghost.

> Feast your eyes on the piece of hot Britishness I'm currently enjoying.

No need to mention my idiocy or Nikki the sex fiend, as my mind (clearly a Prince fan) has dubbed her.

> Hold your horses. Nothing has come through yet

> Believe me, it's worth the wait

I text back, but then my phone begins to ring.

"You got it?" I ask, not giving Kennedy time to speak.

"Not yet."

"Is the rug rat playing Minecraft again?" It tends to slow their connection. "Ground that child. The internet is no place for minors."

"If it wasn't for your nephew, I wouldn't know what a modem is, never mind how to switch it on."

This is true. Kennedy is the dumbest smart person I know when it comes to technology. Odd that her kid (and my very favorite small person in the world) is a total techno wiz.

"He also says to remind you he has a name."

"I know he does, but I can't call him Wilder," I complain. "Because that means he's growing up!"

"Can't call him rug rat forever."

"But just for a little longer, okay? At least until the hottie downloads, m'kay?"

The redhead exits the cubical and ignores me as she washes her hands.

"Pretty is as pretty does, Hols. Didn't Nana teach you anything?"

The way I look at it is man is pretty. Ergo, he does pretty things. Hopefully to me!

"Nana taught me lots of things," I retort, purposely ignoring what she means because our nana first and foremost cautioned us often not to turn out like our mother. "Like how to make a gin rickey for her by the time I was eight. So I guess she also taught me to appreciate cocktails as well as the concept of taxation."

"She taught you about tax?" I hear the shock in my sister's voice because our grandmother was the original badass, and taxes were something to be avoided.

"Yeah. Because I always took ten percent off the top." Which she pretended not to notice.

Kennedy harrumphs. "Sounds like you've had more than ten percent tonight."

The bathroom door creaks closed, and I'm alone again. *Except for my sister.*

"I am as sober as a judge. I'm just high on my hottie, and you can't kill my buzz."

"I reserve my judgement."

"Are you trying to diss my taste in men?"

"I wouldn't dream of it," she answers, opting to be kind because we both know what direction a truthful answer would take this conversation. "I'm just saying looks are objective. You might like them tall, dark, and handsome while I might have a thing for sweet dorks."

I snort because Kennedy hasn't had a thing for anyone but her battery-operated boyfriend in a long time. Well, not since she dropped out of college to have a kid. But badgering her about getting some of her own isn't the point of my call.

"I'm about to change your mind. No, I am about to blow your mind because, trust me, this man is every woman's type." The suit. The face. Those knowing looks. The way he made me work for every second of his attention before we were so rudely interrupted.

"Lucky you," she replies snippily.

"Yep, lucky me." I put her on speakerphone before placing my phone on the vanity to free up my hands. "Because he sure looks like he knows the way around a woman's body."

This time, Kennedy snorts. "You make it sound like most men need a compass."

"Come on, didn't you say that guy you dated last year wouldn't have been able to find your magic spot if it was surrounded by neon lights?" Personally, I think she made him up just to get me off her back.

"It's called a clitoris, Holland. You're not at work now. You can use your big-girl words."

"Why, when magic spot sounds so much better? Be happy for me! He's handsome, cool company, British and hung!" I hadn't intended to share that, but when you know, you know. Not only does he have big dick energy, but when I'd dropped my bag earlier and bent to retrieve it from under the table, I'd almost forgotten to come back up again.

"How can you tell? Does he have a funny walk? Wear a sign? Roll it in on a cart in front of him?" My sister may be the straight guy in our double act, but as usual, she has me in a fit of giggles. "Why are we even having this conversation, again? Oh, I remember. Okay, you got me. I haven't even seen his picture, and I'm jealous. Jealous of you living in London. Jealous of your Instagram feed. Jealous of your hot Wednesday date. What are you laughing at?"

"Nothing." She wouldn't understand.

"You win. I'm a loser, and I'm going to overdose on tacos."

"Good. Maybe next time I see you, you won't be skinnier than me." Kennedy has the kind of metabolism that I'll never have, sadly.

"Yeah, but you got all the boobs."

"I'm sorry," I reply sincerely. "That's true."

"Bitch."

"A bitch who loves you," I sing-song back as I uncap my lipstick and quickly coat my lips until they're rosy and glossy.

"Okay, it's loading. Finally," she grumbles. "I need to change service providers before—*whoa*."

"I told you so," I crow as I slide the lipstick back and pout at my reflection.

"Who is he?"

I open my mouth, then realize I don't want to tell her that I only know his first name. In fact, I don't want to tell her anything about our crazy exchange. But it doesn't matter because Kennedy doesn't wait for an answer before words start spilling from her mouth at speed.

"He looks like that guy out of the Viking's TV show. That's not really him, is it?"

"Viking show?" I repeat with a laugh, feeling oddly validated. "No, I don't think so."

"You're telling me regular men look like that over there?" There's more than a note of disbelief in her reply.

"Sure, the streets are full of them. That's why it's called *Great* Britain."

"Smart-ass. You know how to make a man even sexier, don't you?"

"Give him a British accent." But Alexander's accent definitely has a hint of something else.

"Fine. So I'm officially jealous and will be drowning my FOMO with an excess of tacos. Happy now?"

"You know, taco Wednesday just doesn't have the same ring to it. But yes, get fat. Just to please me. But that's not why I sent you the photo."

"Okay." Like only a mother can, she makes her reply sound like the embodiment of suspicion.

"It's to hand to the police if you never hear from me again."

"Oh. Has the pretty-looking man started to talk about his taxidermy interests?"

"Not yet."

"But you want me to have this in case you end up dead?"

"Yep," I reply, noting her indifferent tone. "That's not how I anticipated this conversation going."

"I take it you're going back to his place." She doesn't know about the hotel, but she knows I would never take a random man back to my employer's house in Chelsea. "Or is this going to be an alfresco assignation?"

"You mean, like in an alleyway somewhere?" What is with her today?

"Nothing says special like sex up against a dumpster."

"Bins. They're not called dumpsters here." I don't rise to her tone as I pinch a little color into my cheeks.

"It doesn't matter what they're called," she drawls.

"And why is that?"

"Because to the best of my knowledge, and I have a lot of Holland knowledge as your big sister, you have never had a one-night stand. Not even to get over he who must never be named. So regardless of whether a bin or dumpster or The Savoy Hotel, you're not going to have sex with a man you just met. Flirt with one, sure. I can picture that. But sex? Nope."

"I don't want to hear you've tried to picture me having sex, Kennedy. That's just creepy. Take a look at that photo again," I say, almost bouncing on my toes with excitement.

"Holland..." My sister draws my name out over several long, disapproving syllables.

"Kennedy..." I respond in the same way.

"This isn't like you."

"I know, but this is the first time I've met *him*. And it's not just his looks. It's the whole vibe he's giving off. He started off all cool and remote, but he's got this devilish grin that says he knows things." When he licked his finger and told me I tasted spicy, my God, I thought I was going to burst—explode!

"Well, now *that* makes more sense." I don't get a chance to ask what she means by her announcement as she carries on. "You're enjoying the challenge. The chase." I guess she's not wrong. "The minute you're sure he's interested, you'll drop him like a bad habit."

"I know he's interested. I can see it in the way he looks at me." Not like he'd taste me like he did his finger. More like he'd devour me whole. "I can't explain it to you. It feels right."

"Well, it is time you moved on," she replies carefully.

"I did that months ago." Like eighteen of them. "I just haven't found anyone who was right." Mainly because I haven't been looking. It's been a little like someone switched my sexuality off. "And now suddenly, my hormones are screaming *we want that one, washed and oiled, and brought to our metaphoric tent!*"

"Your metaphoric tent being your underwear," my sister surmises. "Because a one-night stand isn't a risk to your heart." She sounds sad, but I really don't have an answer that will make her happier. "Unless he's about to cut it out," she says, sounding more like herself. "Which is what this call is about, I guess."

But it isn't. Not really. I think I just want someone to share in my excitement. Maybe for my big sister to tell me I won't go to hell. Or turn into our mother.

"Well, I don't know what else to say, Hols."

That has to be a first. "How about *don't* choose the dumpster?" I suggest.

"Stop being a smart-ass. Does this much *older* man have a name?"

"He's not that old, and it's Alexander, if you must know. Just Alexander because we're keeping it at first names."

"Well, just you stay safe. And remember to use condoms."

As if she needs to tell me. Rug rat might be my favorite little person in the world, but I'm not ready for one of my own.

"Wish me luck?" Picking up my purse, I slide it over my shoulder.

"I wish you alive. How about that?"

We say our goodbyes, and I slide my phone into my purse. Then my purse off my shoulder. Then my blazer off my arms. My arms are tan and toned, and my white tank shows off two of my best assets, but I worry I'm trying too hard. Back on it goes again.

"Carpe diem," I say to the mirror. "Or whatever the Latin is for seize the man." It's time to put this derailed train back on the tracks.

Pulling on the heavy fire door, I step out into the dark hallway. And into a great wall of chest.

6

HOLLY

"If I didn't know better, I'd say you engineered this as payback."

"I'm sorry?" Hand still at my chest, the words hit the air a little warble-y. Part laughter at his assumption, part the shock of finding him here.

"Lewis." His delivery, like his smile, is dark and slightly sardonic.

"Oh. Yeah. Sorry about that." I shrug and step away from the bathroom door. Positioning myself against the adjacent wall, I slide my hands to the small of my back, the cool bricks brushing my fingertips. "I didn't think for one minute that, well, you know." My reply is halting and awkward, the words forced from my mouth a couple at a time as I resist the urge to shrug again.

"I'm not sure I do know."

"That he'd be..." Here we go again. "That you'd be..."

"I am not," he replies emphatically.

"No, I know you're not *that way* inclined, but you must get hit on all of the time."

His answer is a disdaining lift of one brow.

"This can't be the first time you were hit on by a man," I bluster.

"It's the first time I've been offered up as bait."

"Oh, Lord. If only you knew." I chuckle, my gaze on my shoes. "Your assumed sexuality was supposed to protect you. It's not my fault you're irresistible."

When he doesn't reply, I look up.

"I wonder if Wednesday at..." As he twists his wrist and glances down at his watch, something flares between my legs. "Twelve minutes past nine is a more suitable time for you?"

"Suitable?" I swallow—it's a thirsty little motion as I try to tell myself I cannot be turned on by his wrists and his hands—before dragging my eyes back to his again.

"Was it the afternoon hour that offended your sensibilities? You said yourself that Wednesday is hump day."

I'd lay a hundred dollars on this being the first time he's ever said *hump*, even if he annunciates it very well.

"Are you asking if I'd be interested in a threesome?" Because *I just want to see what I can get away with* doesn't extend to this.

"I'm merely passing on the invitation issued to me. By Lewis."

"Even though we're cousins?" My words sound like they should accompany the clutching of pearls, though the look he shoots me in return suggests we're not fooling anyone. Shows what he knows. We fooled Nikki. We fooled her good. Lewis, on the other hand, I can't be sure.

"Twice in one day. I should think that's something of a record."

"One I didn't ask for!"

He smiles so freely at my protest that something sweet and sticky rolls right through me.

"Lewis seemed to think you'd be interested. Your gaze did seem to flick his way often."

Asshole. He knows I wasn't looking at Lewis. I was looking at *him*.

"Maybe I was admiring his tattoos."

"You're a fan of body art?"

"I guess you're not."

His gaze doesn't alter, watching me steadily as though daring me to ask. But I'm not asking because, just look at him! He's so pristine and so perfect. He can't even lounge against a wall properly, never mind cover his impeccable self with ink.

"No." I narrow my eyes. I know I'm right. "You're not the type."

"No?" A smile fights to break out though he masters it, the bare flicker of amusement doing something strange to my insides. "You would need to offer me more than a pink cocktail if you want to find out."

I find I'm grateful for the poor overhead lighting as my cheeks instantly heat, grasping to turn the conversation away from me.

"You know I have no interest in Lewis. So maybe this is more about you." I almost cringe as I hear my not so confident response. I didn't mean Lewis. I meant while he watched me dance with Nikki. But my unease is unfounded by his low-voiced announcement.

"I have no plans whatsoever that involve sharing you."

So much for seizing the moment—seizing him—tripping a bitch to make the man mine because the man has other plans.

Like making me his.

And I see that now. See the subtle ways he took control. The whisky and the server, the way he held my wrist.

His gaze pins me to the wall as a current leaps in the air between us, white hot and electric. It feels powerful. And daring. Like it would only take for one of us to reach out, and the whole world would explode. Despite the tension, when my reply falls out of my mouth, I'm surprised at how casual the words sound.

"Is this some kind of weird come-on, Lyle?"

"It's Alexander." There's a warning in his tone as he steps away from the wall. His gaze sweeps over me like a caress sending a tingle down my spine. A pleasant tingle, yes, but it's also cautionary. "And that wasn't a come on. This is."

His hands find my shoulders, one slipping around to cup my neck as he slants his mouth over mine. Maybe the world didn't explode, but the moment is potent, and the first brush of his lips almost elemental. I know I'm not alone in this as he pulls back a little as though to study me. A silent *did you feel that, too?*

"Kiss me again," I whisper hoarsely, my fingers suddenly tightening on his wide shoulders as though to prevent an escape.

"You're bossy for someone so small." His thick lashes cast a dark shadow against his skin as his gaze dips to my lips. I find I'm not the only one smiling into our next kiss.

I've always preferred self-assured over bossy. Just I'd prefer this kiss to never end. Soft and coaxing, this slow, lazy exchange of lips and whisky-flavored tongue makes the blood in my veins sing. Makes me thirst for more, so much so that I find myself pressing up onto my toes to be sure I don't miss one bit of it. *One bit of him.*

"Bossy." This time, his assessment is more growl than word, his hard body pressing me back against the wall.

Small, exploratory kisses test and tease before becoming deeper. Hotter. Wetter. I moan into his mouth because, oh my God, this is—

I don't get to finish that thought as his hand cups my butt, closing the small space between us. My knees go weak as hard meets soft, my body yielding and molding to his as though I'm part of a puzzle that is meant to fit.

"Wait." I lift my head, my breath ragged, and my resolve instantly weakened as his kisses transfer to my neck. "Not here. Someone might see us." Like someone who thinks we're cousins. Wouldn't that just be weird?

"I really don't give a fuck."

His dark whisper coasts past my ear, the images flashing through my brain not flustered but X-rated instead. And there goes my resolve again as he flexes into me, his big hand pressing me impossibly close. Words, reasons, answers, they're all swept away on a wave of need as his warm lips press against my neck and jaw, the brush of his stubble an abrading thrill.

"My God. If this is the way you kiss—"

His deep chuckle is a puff of warm air against my skin as, for the second time tonight, I choose to ignore the part where I said that out loud. Sweeping the hair from the side of my neck, he presses his lips there. "That sounded like a question."

"I-it was rhetorical."

"It was unfinished. Which is exactly the opposite of the way I'd leave you."

The vibration of his words ripple through me, their promise a temptation too great.

"Alexander," I whisper. "I think it might be safe to go back to my hotel now."

His lips slide across mine with a quiet groan. *God, I like this answer.* My hands ball in the back of his shirt as he steals my breath only to feed me his. But this is not the kind of kiss meant for public places but the kind usually reserved for darkened spaces. *For bedrooms.*

"I think you should get your jacket," I whisper. The suggestion of a smile appears against his mouth without quite giving in. I feel like I'm missing something. "What did I say?"

"Nothing." He shakes his head as though deciding against an explanation but then opens his mouth anyway. "It's just a strange British pick-up line. It's been a while since I've heard it."

"Get your jacket?"

"Get your jacket, you've pulled." His delivery is suggestive, but I still feel like that's not the whole story. I guess he must read that on my face. "It means you're claiming me."

"Good, because I am," I assert, even if it feels like other way around.

As we approach the table, I'm kind of surprised to see Lewis still there, though there's no sign of Nikki. I guess it feels like so much has happened since I left, yet it can't be more than fifteen minutes or so.

My grip on Alexander's hand tightens. "I didn't think he'd still be here."

As we draw nearer, Lewis looks to stand. "I thought you'd snuck off without me." His smile has a very short shelf life as Alexander stalls him with a look that's as effective as any hand. He lowers himself back into the chair again.

"Do I strike you as the furtive type?" Alexander's tone is icily unpleasant, and I'll be honest, a bit of a shock to more than just Lewis.

"But I thought when you left—"

"I really can't be held responsible for your thoughts." He says *thoughts* like you might say *cesspool,* as he holds out my blazer and helps me to slip it on. "We won't be taking you up on your invitation tonight." He pulls on his own jacket.

I'm about to make some quip about families when Alexander slides his hand around my hip. "Really, Olive. Like I'd let you leave the bar with a strange man."

"You mean *another* strange man."

"Are you saying you've developed a habit?" Our eyes lock, his dancing with suggestion as he steers us in the direction of the exit.

"No way you are cousins," Lewis calls out indignantly.

"Several times removed?" I offer, my attention unmoving.

"Including continents," Alexander's low voice rumbles. "We happen to be a very close-knit family." His attention flickers to the angry little man. "Very close indeed."

And it certainly feels like it as Alexander's hand tightens. He leads me to the exit and back out onto the cool, dark streets of London.

7

HOLLY

"People will see." Despite my protests, I lengthen my neck to give him access to more of my skin. More real estate for his lips and the tempting rasp of his beard.

"What exactly will they see?"

Maybe they'll see how Alexander has pressed me up against some random hotel room door. At least it's on the right floor. And at least we managed not to maul each other in the elevator. *Thanks to the presence of another couple.* They might also see how his hands seem to own my butt and how I'm trying to ride his thigh like a pony at the county fair.

"They'll see us kissing," I answer much more sensibly. And boy, can the man kiss. And deliver a cutting set down when the occasion calls for it. His talents know no end because he can also do this really cool flex of his muscled chest. Is it any wonder I find my hands there again?

"My room is just along..." He doesn't follow the vague wave of my finger. Instead, he takes my hand in his.

"You just don't know how lovely you are."

"So you're saying it's my fault we're not in my room yet?"

I pout a little, though I'm not sure it does anything to contain my excitement.

"Yes, for being irresistible."

Says the man with a commanding aura and the superhero chest.

At least he doesn't wear jockey shorts on top of his pants.

"Something you're finding amusing?" His gaze turns playful, but there's an intensity there, too. The kind that makes my heart beat a little too fast, an arrhythmic beat I can feel everywhere.

"I was just thinking about your underwear." I might not physically be able to raise one brow—I've tried, and the best I've got is a strange-looking duo waggle—but I've found this tone is a pretty good substitute.

"That sounds promising." Under my fingers, his chest flexes again, muscle and sinew reacting to my touch.

I can't wait to see what's under here.

"There are security cameras," I whisper, spreading my fingers wide and pushing him back as he looks about to kiss me again.

"Then you should stop looking at me like that."

"Exactly how is it I'm looking at you?" I half ask, half taunt.

"Like you're picturing me *without* my underwear."

"I think that's called projecting, *Lyle*. Maybe I was thinking about offering you a very respectable—"

"There is nothing respectable about the things I want to do to you."

I'm not sure if it's the pictures those words create or the delivery of his wicked promise in that very proper accent that makes my knees buckle a little.

"Tea," I respond, surprised I manage to respond at all

and more surprised still at how natural my voice sounds. "I was going to say cup of tea."

"Then I'm about to be very, very disappointed." His serious reply is accompanied with the kind of grin that would make a nun weep into her communion wine.

"Should I save the tea for afterward?"

"You've heard about the deviancy of British men?"

"This smile." I find myself pressing my hand to his cheek, my insides tightening at the brush of his stubble. "I wonder when the devil wants it back." Surely, it can only be on loan.

"You think I have the devil's smile?"

"On such a beautiful mouth, too."

He turns his lips into my palm, pressing a kiss to the meat. His eyes are like twin flames as he turns his attention back again. "I have heard it said that I have the devil's own tongue."

All the tingles. All between my legs.

I don't for one hot minute think this is the kind of man who drinks tea as a post-sex treat. He looks more like the kind of man who'd roll me over, slap my ass, and start again. Yes, please!

And who knew British men had such *aural* game! Let me tell you, if I'd known, I might've dipped my toe in the waters —the waters of eligible men—long before now.

"Oh!" I suck in a sharp breath at the shocking awareness of his teeth pressing down on my knuckles. Delicately at first, then not quite so gently. His eyes watch my reaction, almost feeding from it. Something inside me twists, a sensation sweet, deep, and urgent. It's just his mouth. On my hand. How can this feel like... everything?

"I think we should find this room now." His voice is like velvet. I want to wrap myself in it.

"Yes." Oh boy, yes, we should. I step forward, and he steps back but doesn't let go of my hand. "It's this way." I swing right and take a couple of stumbling steps before catching sight of a sign containing room numbers. *Son of a biscuit, I'm going the wrong way.* I swing around, almost colliding with his chest. *Again.* "My bad. It's this way."

His chuckle follows me along the hallway.

At the door to my hotel room, my hand trembles as I slide it into my purse, but I manage to find the key card. Pulling it out, I swipe it against the door's reading mechanism.

The tiny judging eye remains red.

The heat of him burns at my back, and the shadow his frame casts against the pale door is large and looming. It drowns out my own. A sensible person would say it's no wonder I feel nervous with that hulking body behind me, but it's the experience of that body that I'm desperate for. Desperate to discover the man behind the suit. The muscle and sinew, ridges and dips. The absolute need is one I haven't felt before.

I inhale and swipe it again.

Red. Still. The color of warning. The color to halt. Stop. End.

"These things are so pesky," I whisper shakily, glancing over my shoulder and failing to tempt the green light again. "Dammit!" I fumble, and the thing flips from my fingertips, landing flat on the floor.

Before I can move, Alexander is already straightening, the card balanced between his fingertips. "So very pesky." His words are hot at my ear as he trails the edge of the card up my jean-clad thigh. The skin beneath reacts like a million hot pins; my whole body in fact. I feel wound so tight I can barely breathe.

But no, that's not true as a breath flutters from my mouth. *Ha.* As I luxuriate in the press of his lips at my neck. I arch into him, elongating my neck to give him more skin to kiss, my palm finding the door as I reach for support and—

It opens. The light has switched from red to green.

"Let's move this inside," he whispers, pressing a kiss to the skin behind my ear. "Before we give the whole floor a show." His hand braces solicitously against the marginally open door.

"I—" I turn my head over my shoulder, his darkened gaze falling to my lips. Almost in slow motion, he inclines his head, and our lips meet fleetingly. As his arm comes around me, turning me, everything speeds up again. Lips slide, and tongues clash, this kiss taking on a savage edge as Alexander's arms band at my back, almost carrying me into the room. His presence is encompassing, and his kiss all command as he presses me back against the nearest wall, his body following. A frantic heat swims through my veins, my hands scrambling against him, against his chest, pushing his jacket from his shoulders, unable to get enough of him. Touch enough of him.

"Take it off." I swallow over a rapid breath, drowning in the sight of him. I want to place my teeth against his strong throat and bite. Why is that even a thing I want to do? "Take it all off."

His low, dirty chuckle is like a lick of heat between my legs.

"As the lady commands."

I'm barely able to retain thought as he shrugs his jacket the rest of the way from his shoulders, dropping it unceremoniously to the floor. He's so large, so virile, standing in front of me, the city streetlights casting an arc of illumination behind him.

"Holland," he growls, pulling me closer, allowing me to breathe him in. *Musk and heat and spice and man.* Fabric scrapes against my shoulders, my jacket following his.

"Such tiny hands." Catching my hands in his, he stares down at where we're palm to palm. Our fingers are suddenly linked, and my stomach is twirling and tumbling as he presses them to the wall near my head. "What should I do with you now?" The look in his eyes could burn whole buildings down.

"You could kiss me again."

"I was thinking a little payback might be more appropriate." He slides me a wicked-looking grin.

"Payback? For what?"

"I'm sure I could think of something." His dark head dips, his mouth engulfing my nipple over my bra and tank. I gasp at the contact, then whimper as his teeth graze the instantly tight bud. "How about trying to offload my attentions onto another? *Anothers*," he amends heavily, his eyes flicking up my body.

"That was—"

"Unfortunate."

My insides pulse as he grazes my nipple again. *Grazes. Sucks. Pulls.*

"A mistake," I whisper as his tongue licks long and lushly, tracing the rapid rise and fall of the flesh above my tank. "I was trying to keep you to myself."

It's not a lie but maybe too much truth.

"For more than just a coffee?" he taunts. *Get you a man with a mouth that taunts and teases* sounds like the gold standard of advice that should be given to young girls.

"For at least long enough to prove that you don't have tattoos."

"I suppose that's why you wanted me to strip."

This he doesn't address to my face but to my breasts. As I look down myself, twin damp circles surround my pebbled nipples. *Pebbled and aching for his mouth.*

"Among other things."

"You look so pretty, Holland." He presses a kiss to my jaw, his dark whisper coasting the shell of my ear. "So pretty being held." It might have sounded sinister were it not for the way he pulls back to look at me. Like I'm a treasure, a boon. And maybe it shouldn't, but the pictures his words paint curl sultrily around me.

I arch from the wall with a breathy moan.

"Oh, you like that." As far as theories go, it might not be incredibly inspired, given my desperation to get closer.

"I like—" *it.* But my response goes unfinished as he steals it with a kiss that's nothing short of masterful. A kiss that steals breath and sense, leaving a yearning pulsing in their place as he transfers both my hands into one of his, making a manacle of my wrists before pushing them above my head.

"Kiss me again, Holland." His free hand skims my body, taking in the shape of my breast. "Give me your mouth."

So I do. I give in to the pleasure his mouth brings in words and kisses. Give in to his roaming hands. My body convulses against his, earning me a low growl of his approval, his eyes glittering in the dark room.

"I've been staring at your mouth all evening." His thumb swipes across my bottom lip, gliding through the moisture within. "Wondering how you would taste." Withdrawing his thumb, he lifts it to his lips.

"What's the verdict?" I ask breathily, rolling my lip inward, savoring the taste of salt from his skin.

Like he has a secret to impart, he lowers his mouth to my ear. "Those are mutually exclusive, Holland." Sucking on the lobe, he gives it a sharp tug. "Your mouth is divine. How you taste is something I plan on discovering soon." As he grinds against me, a moan stutters from my chest. "I hope your flight tomorrow is a peaceful one because I intend to keep you awake all night."

My... what? Oh, my fictitious flight.

I send a silent thanks to the heavens for the reminder. Something tells me my wits aren't going to be of much use tonight. Not that it doesn't stop me from trying, a note of teasing in my reply.

"All night?"

"All. Night." He punctuates his reply with a nip and a graze to the soft skin of my neck. "I plan on charting every inch of your skin with my tongue. Learn the mysteries of your body until I know you inside out."

Oh, I am so down for that. So down for that, my insides begin to twist and pulse as he reaches out to the dresser, flicking on the lamp.

"I don't intend missing a single thing."

And he won't. My heart sinks as my attention slides over his shoulder to the room beyond.

Behold, the tools in support of my lie.

My suitcase lies open on the suitcase stand. Next to it, a small armchair cradles my carry-on bag, abandoned like a half-read book.

Clothes spill from both. No, not spill, *explode.*

And the mess isn't limited to these two. Mismatched shoes are scattered across the floor from where I'd tried them on earlier, and towels lay strewn across the pillows of an unmade bed. Makeup and hair products litter the dresser, and for such a short stay, I seem to have used every mug and glass available to me. *So four, maybe?*

Surely, I can't have made all this mess... Except this is *my* room, and those are *my* things. Yet the picture I'd painted of myself today was sophisticated world traveler, not slob!

Alexander seems to register my horror, and a question hovers on his face. A question that doesn't require an answer as I press my hands against his chest, ducking around him, swiping up our jackets as I go.

"I'm not usually so messy," I lie, picking up another damp towel from the floor.

Has there been a Roman bathhouse orgy in this room while I've been out?

Throwing the towel in the direction of the chair, I drop the haphazardly folded jackets onto the bed, shooting him a quick smile over my shoulder. "I, erm, didn't want to trouble housekeeping." Mainly because I didn't wake up until after eleven this morning. And who wants to tidy so someone else can clean?

If I could dare to look at him again, I'm sure he'd be smiling that half-smile of his. Amused but not willing to share it. Amused and a little superior about it.

"Nice pajamas."

At his drawling assertion, I look down at the tank top I find in my hands. More specifically, I look at the slogan emblazoned across the front.

I'M GREAT IN BED

Without speaking, I turn the tank around until the other side is facing him.

I CAN SLEEP FOR HOURS

I slide him a look that earns me a husky laugh, but I guess it might've been worse. It might've been my Minnie

Mouse onesie. My heart skips a beat as he begins to move, stalking across the small space. As he comes to stand in front of me, he takes my pajama top from my hand.

"You won't be needing this."

He drops it to the bed, nudging me around to face away from him.

"I'm sure you can tell I wasn't expecting to bring anyone back here."

The dresser on the other side of the room reflects his neutrality on the subject. Mine, not so much, my cheeks still pink. I try to turn in his arms, not wanting to face my own embarrassment as his arm bands my ribs, drawing my body into his.

Oh, God. He's so hard.

"Life is like that," he says softly. "Unpredictable and beautiful, don't you think?"

My answer is a soft gasp as his fingers tantalize my skin, sliding into my hair to bare my neck.

"One minute you're drinking coffee, idling away an hour, and the next you're looking at someone who takes your breath away. Someone beautiful and unpredictable." I shiver, need blooming deep in my belly. My eyes flutter closed as his lips touch the nape of my neck. "You are a gift." His fingers stir against my stomach, pulling my tank from my jeans. "And I hope you'll look to me as yours."

In the mirror, he drags my tank up and over my head. It drops to the floor and he presses his hand to my belly.

"What are you doing to me?" I whisper, tilting my head to the side to give him more of my neck. My breasts feel heavy from his earlier attentions, and between my legs aches to be filled by the hardness pressed against my lower back.

God, I want him. Want this.

"I'm admiring you," he says softly. The hot puff of his breath on my neck makes goosebumps dapple my skin. His arms tighten before he angles one to hold my breast as the other slides between my legs. He cups me over my jeans, his long finger pressing against the seam, the heel of his palm adding a delicious layer of friction. "Just look at you."

It's strange to see myself as I do, half undressed, all languid dark eyes as I revel in his hold. In his possession. As his arm flexes, muscles and tendons shift and ripple against my bare skin.

"You're exquisite." His reflection rakes over mine, slow and steady. A look that says he owns me. A reflection that confirms as my hips jerk against him, my nipples hardening in response to his fingertips.

"Please, touch me." My pulse races, and my words are a bare rasp as I turn my face from the mirror, looping my hand over his neck. I pull his mouth to mine, though he keeps our kiss chaste. *In contrast to the way he holds me.* I pull harder, opening my mouth fully on his, swallowing his low groan of surprise as he turns me in his embrace. The touch of his gaze dances over the wings of my collarbones, his gaze darkly dilated as it dips to the valley between my breasts.

"You turn pink with arousal," he murmurs absently, tracing the path of his gaze. It's not something I can or want to discount. "As well as embarrassment." He glances up from beneath thick lashes, the look anything but coy. "Who knew there was a perverse kind of pleasure to be gained from watching you turn red. Wondering how far those blushes run."

"And now you know."

"Not quite. But I'm about to find out."

My bra comes loose, spiking in my veins as he bends to trail the flat of his tongue across each of my nipples in turn.

I feed my hands into his hair as his tongue swirls and his fingers tease. He sucks, his teeth graze, his actions rougher than anything I've ever experienced.

Rougher. Better. Real. They match the tide of desperation swelling through me.

"Oh, God!" I tighten my grip on his hair, wanting to share this pleasure/pain, this perfect agony as I begin to move backwards towards the bed.

Or I would if he would let me.

"Not yet."

His hands tighten on my hips as does his mouth on my breast, his body an elegant arch before me.

"I want..." I need so much as fevered sensations swell through my skin, my ragged breaths loud to my ears as his mouth hungrily devours me, his hands and his actions keeping me in place.

"This. You want this." His hands slip to my behind, pulling me into his body, soft meeting hard where he rocks into me, his hands preventing any kind of escape. *Not that I was going anywhere.*

"Yes. Please. You need fewer clothes." Reaching between us, I begin to tug at the hem of his shirt. His chuckle is hushed and hot as I bat away his hands when he lifts them to help. Working from top to bottom, I pull the last tiny hindrance loose and tip up onto my toes to push it from his shoulders. I'm unable to stop myself from swiping my tongue against the flat of his nipple. Muscles tighten under my fingertips, and he exhales a low gasp. There is *so much* of him, and his skin is hot to the touch. I run my fingers over the ladder of his abdominals, relishing both their flex and his moan.

And then I'm hitting the bed with a little bounce, my skin burning under his gaze. Almost instantly, he falls on me, ripping open the button of my jeans. Dragging them down my legs, he whips them off along with my panties.

"You're pink all the way," his low voice groans, his hand at my throat. Trailing it down my body, he follows the flush against my skin.

Pushing up onto my elbows, I watch as his large hands press my thighs open, pushing them wider, his dark head bent, eyes glued to the space between my legs.

"Pink, like a rose."

I gasp, his eyes catching mine, dark and knowing, and he watches my expression as his thumb glides along the wet ribbon of flesh. Teasing, testing, the motion slow and rhythmic, revealing how wet I am.

"I'm going to kiss you here." I arch as his head lowers, my insides pulsing emptily as his lips come to land low on my stomach. *Not where I need them to be.* "And here." They press a little lower, a little closer now but still not near enough. "So soft here." His lips brush across my hipbone.

"Don't tease." My words sound like sandpaper as I arch to fill the space between us as he pulls back, his low chuckle ghosting across my skin.

"Ah, Holland," he murmurs, all silky mouthed and easy smile. "I'm not teasing. I'm being thorough. You know that old saying, if something is worth doing..." His hands trail down my legs and grasp my ankles.

"And I'm worth *doing*, am I?"

I inhale a sharp breath as he tugs, pulling me swiftly down the bed. He drops to his knees in one fluid motion as between the *V* of my thighs, his warm breath brushes over me in a shiver-inducing caress.

As he presses a kiss against the inside of my knee, I push up onto my elbows, determined not to miss one thing.

"You are worth doing..." His tongue darts out in a hot

lick. "Very." Next comes another kiss to the soft skin of my inner thigh. "Very well." To end, or maybe to begin, his half-growled words are more vibration than anything else as he buries his tongue deep inside me.

"Oh, God..." Everything in the room immediately dissolves, melting away beyond him and me. Beyond the place between my legs. My breathing makes me sound as though I've been running, which is ridiculous because I don't run, and he's barely begun! "Oh, God. Yes, like that," I cry out, my body bowing as it chases the sensation.

"I'm sure you can give better direction than that," he says with no conviction at all but plenty of knowing. "I'd benefit from a little guidance. A little *verbal* guidance."

"Y-You should just do that again," I counter, my words shaky.

"This?" His lashes cast dark half-moons against his cheeks as he lowers his head, twirling his tongue around my clit again. And again. And... *oh my God*.

I whimper, my hand finding purchase in the strands of his hair as his fingers press against my opening. *But not in.* It would take nothing for me to lift my hips, to change the angle and make his fingers slide into me, but the way he's watching me, learning me, makes me hesitant.

"Or like this?" The dark amusement in his voice adds another layer of deliciousness as he sucks the swollen bud of my clit between his lips. I almost levitate from the bed, my body spasming in relief as his long fingers part my flesh and drive inside.

"Oh, God, yes!" My hips meet his compelling movements as he continues to lick and lap, not as though I'm a thing to be savored but a thing to be devoured. A thing to be consumed as his fingers thrust harder, driving my hips and my cries higher until I feel almost delirious.

"Such a sweet, sweet girl."

He growls his praise into my heated core, and my hands twist in the bedding as sensation threatens to burst from my skin. It's never happened like this before—never grown this near this quick. The feeling climbs and twines and blooms as Alexander whispers wicked promises, and his tongue pushes me to the brink. But I fight it because experience has taught me that I'm a *one time a night* girl. My orgasms are enjoyable, but they can be a flash in the pan, nice but not quite the full experience. And the full experience? Well, that's likely to make me spread myself across the bed before falling into the kind of sleep that resembles the dead. Which is always the better option, but not how I envisioned losing my one-night stand cherry to this man. Not when I think of all the dirty promises he's made.

Licking. Learning. All the things.

I want the full Alexander experience. Something tells me it isn't to be missed.

"Oh, God. I need—we should—"

"You should stop trying to get away," he growls as his hands push me impossibly wide. "You might give me a complex."

Or you might give me an orgasm before I'm ready for it.

"I can't—"

"Yes, you can." A demand delivered in a honeyed purr. "Come for me, Holland. Let me taste you. Come on my tongue."

My brain shuts off. Shuts down. A misfire in the cerebral wiring, halting my next word, because... oh my. With his fingers curled deep inside me, he reaches that secret part of me that the previous men in my life have never once found. The part of me that makes my thighs twitch and my eyes roll to the back of my head. If I had the wherewithal to be embarrassed, I might regret the keening cry that rings through the room.

"That's better." His masculine groan resonates between my legs, just adding to the deliciousness.

I press the back of my hand to my mouth, gasping like a caught thing. A captured thing. A thing that belongs to him.

"Please!" Please what, I don't know. Please stop. Please never let go as he suck my clit into his mouth, grazing it exquisitely with his teeth. I detonate. Implode. Arch against his mouth's torturous assault, my hands gripping his hair, my body demanding more, through an orgasm that seems unceasing.

But everything ends. And I'm left panting, stretched out across the bed. Or maybe I should say that everything ends, except where Alexander is concerned, everything ends when *he* says so as, in an almost intimate action, he pushes his hands under my thighs and slides his fingers through mine. Fingers that tighten almost reassuringly for a beat. Tighten, then pin my hands to the bed.

"Alexander..." His name is a plea for mercy, my flesh tightening as his plan becomes clear, positioned to his pleasure as I am. Something seems to unlock inside me even before his mouth returns to its torturous intentions, a bittersweet ache rising through me. At the first press of his perfectly despicable tongue, I arch and twist, struggling for freedom, crying out when I find no escape. This is all too much. A sensory overload that I can barely take. But take I do. I take every lick and growled compliment, every graze of his roughened cheek against my thighs.

And I love being restrained. *Who knew?*

I take all that Alexander has to give as he pleasures me with his mouth and fucks me with his tongue. As he laps and pets, stretching and twisting my orgasm into something fierce. Pleasuring me with a chastisement growled into my very center. There is no flowery description for what the man does. Not as he demands I come again.

"Come for me, Holland. That's it. Let me feel you coming all over my tongue."

Something sleek and hot rushes through me. *Gushes from me.* My cries are raw and hoarse as my body begins to convulse, my insides quickening. I'm certain the only thing keeping me from an out-of-body experience is the grip of his hands and breadth of his shoulders pinning me to the bed.

I watch through heavy lids and from some other plane as Alexander rears above me like some mythical deity. His hair is a mess from my hands, and his mouth smeared lewdly with my pleasure.

"How is it you can turn pinker still?"

Those weren't words of criticism, more like wonder as his hand falls to his belt. I feel like I'm almost sinking into myself again, feeling a little full of wonder myself.

"I have never..." *done that.* Come so hard that I saw stars being born. Squeezed a man's head between my thighs to make him stop... or never stop.

"No?" His lips quirk in one corner, not exactly teasing but something more satisfied.

I can relate to satisfaction. Boy, can I.

I wonder if I've been missing out by dating guys my own age. Is this what people mean when they talk about the benefit of experience? Why aren't I curling in on myself, ready for sleep? Because of the man on his knees in front of me. The man looking down at me as though I were something special when it's really the other way around. His skin is the kind of gold that speaks of endless summers, and his body not the kind that was honed in a gym, I think. The fabric of his pants clings to strong thighs, his torso bared to reveal biceps and pectoral muscles for days. Bands of muscle bisect his stomach, a light fuzz of hair meandering from his navel down. His is undoubtably a beautiful body, but he isn't some shredded gym god. More like someone who knows how a body works.

He certainly knows how my body works.

"How come you have a tan?" As I slide away the mass of my hair, my attention dips once more to that delectable happy trail where it disappears into his open pants. "Oh!" My gaze jolts back to his at what I think I just saw escaping from the top of his underwear.

"Is there a problem?"

"No. I…" *must be seeing things.* And I *cannot* hold his gaze. Because then he'll know what I was looking at, even if… it can't be. It just can't!

Alexander stands from the bed, slides out of his suit pants and underwear, and hot damn. Can't be totally can. Totally is! I mean, I knew he was hung, but it looks like Kennedy might be right about the cart. How does that not put his back out?

"And now you're laughing," he purrs.

"No. I'm not laughing." At least, I'm not as he takes that hard length into his hand, fisting at the head. His head rolls back a little as he rewards himself with an experimental tug. A vein pops in his forearm, the muscles in his abdominals flexing at the touch.

Nope. No laughing here.

Just lots of watching. Avidly. My insides pulsing. Longingly.

What was I thinking again? No idea.

No idea how it's going to fit, either.

He aims a roguish smile my way as he produces a tiny foil square, tearing the corner with his teeth.

"Would you like to...?" He glances down meaningfully.

"Oh, no. I'm okay. I prefer to watch." Argh! I hurriedly add, "What I mean is—"

"Watching is good," his deep voice rumbles as he expertly rolls the condom down his length. Who knew there were men like this? Men built like this. As self-assured, as suave of mouth, and as talented of tongue. My heart flutters as he wraps his fingers experimentally around the base, though I jerk back to the moment as his knee hits the bed. "Shuffle up, darling."

"What? Oh." I glance behind me and remember my legs are hanging off the end of the bed. Propping my heel on the mattress, I scramble across and then a little higher up the bed. Like a prowling cat, he follows me, the long line of him stretched across my body, his weight balanced above me as he presses kisses and whispers compliments as he travels, then finally say, "Watching is good. Experiencing is better."

Poised above me on one arm with eyes as dark as midnight, he takes himself in his hand. The muscle in his bicep flexes as his thickly sculpted thigh muscle contracts against my own. Slowly. Deliberately. Deliciously. He strokes the head of his erection through my wetness.

No, not his erection. His cock, my mind supplies. Because nothing as rude and as ruddy could be referred to as anything else.

My hips tilt to meet him when he presses himself against me. His mouth, suddenly pressed to mine, swallows my gasp as he pushes inside.

Swallows my gasp. Feasts on it. Greets it with a masculine groan of his own as he presses deeper. *So deep.* My back arches with a silent plea as he undulates against me, shuddering as I coast my foot along his strong calf.

"Holland." My name is a blessing, a benediction, as he

presses his palms into the mattress, his body above me almost blocking out the light. He growls, his head thrown back, the powerful column of his neck exposed as he savors the moment, the connection, the feel of my muscles contracting around him. His next words are delivered on a long exhale and an equally slow stroke. "Feel how good we fit."

"I had my concerns," I whisper, wrapping my legs tighter around him at his shallow thrust, bringing his body closer still.

"Why, Holland," he purrs, his teeth grazing the skin just below my ear. "Whatever can you mean?" His dark taunt curls around me like smoke, exploding deep inside as he blesses me with a solid second thrust. I cry out, stretching under him, drowning in the feel of him over me.

"You're so big." Maybe later, I'll regret the truism as a cliché, but all I can do now is hang on as he takes my hand in his, dragging it down to where our bodies meet. To where, beneath our tangled fingers, he moves in and out of me, hot and wet.

"Feel. It's like you were made for me." His ragged breath blows across me, and I glance up and see him watching the place where we connect. Watching the slide of his cock and my body accepting it. "That is..." His words shake, his next breath a deeply masculine groan.

I swallow thickly as a familiar sensation begins to move through me, flooding through my veins, unfurling tissue and melting bone.

He drops his head, resting it against my shoulder. His body undulates as he rocks his hips, the motion sending a pulsing thrill through me. He withdraws, and I feel the loss of him immediately, a yearning ache to be consumed by him. Used by him. His next thrust makes me cry out as he plunges inside so deeply, his movements more commanding. Or maybe meeting my body's demands as my hips move with his, the bedding beneath us knotted in my hands. His hand slides under my knee, lifting it higher, opening me. Something inside me snaps, my cries ringing through the room, my fingers lancing the hard muscles of his ass. Alexander groans, a shudder running through his beautiful body. A second later, the tempo changes, and I trade fevered whimpers for solid thrusts, the exquisite tension within me heightening, twisting, building with the collision of skin. The sensation spirals and curls and commands until my thoughts scatter and my body submits. Sensation crashes through me.

Above me, Alexander's strong arms gather me closer, his fingers curling around my shoulders as he thrusts again and again. With a primitive roar, he collapses against me, and I absorb the feel of him as he breaks above me. Around me. Inside me.

8

ALEXANDER

"I was looking forward to being here tonight like I would a prostate exam, but it looks like my feelings are about to change. Not to mention my luck."

I don't immediately turn my gaze from the contemplation of the glass in my hand, but when I do, I try to do so without a scowl. But given it's my brother who has spoken, my half-brother if we're being technical, I'm not entirely successful.

Griffin Middlemass. Half-brother. All annoying.

Why the hell did I think to invite him tonight? Probably because I haven't seen him in three months. It's not a case of distance making the heart grow fonder but distance weakening the memory of how hard I find it to be around him.

"I take it from your avaricious expression that you've either seen a potential client or someone you've fucked." Though judging by the direction of his attention, he seems to be under the impression that he's about to unleash his charm on a member of the catering crew. Unless he's developed a taste for elderly businessmen in the past three months, which isn't inconceivable. Griffin's tastes are wide and varied, though they don't, as far as I know, include men.

"Do you routinely invite members of the criminal fraternity home?" Griffin tilts his chin as though to examine the ornate plasterwork in the high ceiling or perhaps the crystal chandelier hanging overhead. "I suppose you'll know the one or two oligarchs with dubious business dealings. Maybe one or two junior members of the royal family open to a bribe or two?"

"I don't associate myself with the corrupt." Except that one oligarch's son I happen to be old friends with.

"Just the morally corrupt, eh?" he invites, tapping the rim of his glass to his temple.

I don't bite even though the temptation is great. Lately, I've been like a bear with a sore head, so I've been told. The fuse on my temper minuscule. My attention to social niceties non-existent. The general feeling is that my behavior is linked to my recent milestone birthday, and in some respects, it is. It is not, however, the result of a midlife crisis.

"Come to think of it," he continues, "the ruling class? All thieves."

"You forget whose blood runs in your veins."

"It doesn't matter. I'll always be the black sheep, born on the wrong side of the blanket. Brought up on the wrong side of the tracks."

To listen to Griffin would make a person assume he was raised in a tower block somewhere with crack addicts for parents, not in a small manor home in leafy Sussex. But he likes to play the role of hard done by.

"And a silk," I drawl in response. "Appointed by the Queen as a member of Her Majesty's Counsel learned in the law. Or so they tell me." I'm not sure how. Or how anyone would be stupid enough to retain his services, but Griffin is a barrister. Griffin Middlemass, QC, no less. Had I not seen proof of this myself—Griffin dressed in the customary wig and gown orating a perfect character assassination of a witness in the hallowed courts of the Old Bailey—I might not have believed it.

"If you're suggesting I got where I am as the bastard son of a duke, you're way off." Griff straightens his tie with an agitated twist.

I stifle a sigh, unwilling to join in his act of the aggrieved son. It's not like I was ecstatic to find my father had left some half a dozen bastards around the country after his heart attack. But I resent how Griff likes to play both sides. The estate might've paid for his education and later his chambers and staff, but like the popular song, he prefers people to think he's just a poor boy from a poor family. Which just isn't true. Perhaps he should try being the head of the family for a while, then he might see how being in his position has its perks.

"Save me the act. It's not my underwear nor my wallet you're trying to divest me of. And as you're not at work now, there's no need to be such an argumentative ass." Even if that's what makes him an excellent QC. It's probably in the genes. His mother was an actress, after all.

"Arguing is what I do best, and it pays fucking well. Though not as well as being a duke." Slinging an arm around my shoulder, he thickens a fake cockney patois. "And let me remind you, as the head of this family, you're responsible for the bastard son." He straightens. "In that respect, you're wrong. I'm always after your wallet."

"A little louder, Griffin. I believe there are people in the back of the room who didn't quite hear."

"Yes, your grace," he murmurs with faux contrition. "But

getting back to my earlier point, it looks like I won't need to stay here tonight."

"I wasn't aware you were." I wasn't aware I'd extended the invitation to him. Not that it matters. The Belgravia townhouse is almost large enough to house a platoon of Griffins on short notice. I'd just prefer not to.

"It's just such a ball ache getting to my chambers from my place, so I thought John could drop me there tomorrow."

John being my driver. Griffin is just a poor boy who likes to avail himself of the comforts of the family he likes to deny.

"You're in court tomorrow?" I eye the champagne glass in his hand, which I calculate to be at least the fourth, then remind myself my life and liberty aren't in his hands.

"No, but I'm meeting a mate at a private club there. Or at least I was. But now I rather think that little morsel will be bringing me coffee in bed." With his glass, he directs my attention to the other side of the room.

"I will not have you sniffing around the catering staff like a randy dog."

"But I am a randy dog. Ask any of the women of my acquaintance. And by acquaintance, I mean—"

"Be that as it may, I do not need to read that headline in any of next week's newspapers."

"What headline is that?"

"Any headline including your name and the bi-line courtesy of a member of the catering crew."

"I hardly think my sex life is the stuff of tabloid fodder."

Maybe. Maybe not. But mine surely is. Newspaper attention is something I do not need. Something our family does not need. "It doesn't matter," I answer, changing tack. "They're just young girls."

"And I'm suddenly Methuselah, am I?" he says, his attention swinging back.

"You're old enough to know better."

"Just because you seem to have taken a vow of celibacy doesn't mean I'm about to join you," he answers disparagingly. "Isla said you'd turned into a crusty fucker since your birthday. Stepped out of your *dirty thirties* and into your *no more naughty forties*, have you?"

"Isla would've said no such thing." Though I will be asking her just what she said quite soon. So much for family solidarity. If anything, turning forty had the opposite effect. For at least that day. Otherwise, yes, I am a forty-year-old man, a pillar of my community. An employer. A philanthropist. The head of a family that has a lineage going back to the Battle of Hastings. I am the voice of reason. Staid and sober. A duke, for fuck's sake. I do not kiss strange women in public or feel them up in clubs.

Except on milestone birthdays.

"Our family—" I begin, curling my hands around my glass as I try very hard not to point my finger at him.

"Of which I'm just a fringe member."

"Our *family name* does not need to be dragged through the mud."

"Un-wad your knickers," he mutters, "I already know her."

"Who?" *So not one of the catering crew or one of the elderly businessmen?* George, my assistant, is far too good at his job to send out an invitation to any of Griff's conquests. My eyes still scan the guests in the room, a room in the London townhouse that was once used as our ancestors' ballroom. As patron of the charity this gathering is being held for, I could do without the embarrassment of any kind of histrionics.

"That tasty little morsel over there." And with that, he swaggers across the room in the direction of a small group of matronly types. They seem more like sizeable meals than morsels and definitely not girls.

To each to their own, I suppose. *Old, young, small, and tall, they all need loving,* I've heard Griff intone on more than one occasion. His steps begin to slow as he holds his arms wide, his champagne glass dangling from the fingertips of his right hand. Keen to avoid knowledge of any part of his idiocy, I begin to turn away. My movement is barely realized as I register the distaste on those matrons' expressions, quickly followed by their relief as Griffin makes a detour, seemingly following a petite brunette out of the room. My jaw tenses. Fuck, if it isn't one of the catering crew he's chasing, judging by her appearance. White blouse, black skirt, her hair tied back in a neat bun, the strings of an apron tied in a bow at her back.

I don't know why I expected better of him. A case of hope over experience, I suppose as I watch him begin to pick up his pace, chasing someone who is, no doubt, completely unsuitable out of the room.

Fucking Griffin. He likes to maintain he's not family, yet he behaves like the perfect parody of the aristocratic second son harassing the maids. *Like his father and his grandfather before him.* The frilly aprons the servers are wearing certainly lend themselves to the comparison. I make a mental note to remind George to ensure the catering company doesn't use them again.

"Thank you," I murmur as McCain, my butler, exchanges my champagne glass for a fresh one.

"Your grace?" he questions, his gaze following mine.

"The girl. I don't suppose you know who she is?" I ask as something begins to tug at the edges of my consciousness, though what I'm not sure. I feel unsettled, and it's more than just annoyance at Griffin's behavior.

"I can ask the duty manager, if you'd like."

"No, that won't be necessary." I consider the champagne in my hand, trying to push away the feeling. Was there something about the shape of the server's departing silhouette that seemed familiar? Or perhaps it was in the sway of her hips.

I stifle a sigh, pondering how with each passing day, that night seems less and less real. *She* seems less and less real. Of course, I didn't imagine it, but I have perhaps embellished the experience. Gilded the rose, so to speak, because she couldn't have been all that I imagined. Her eyes couldn't have been as mischievous as they seemed, and she was just a brunette, not a woman whose hair reminded me of autumn fields. No, it can't all have been real. And maybe that's why she haunts me in my dreams, coming to me, whispering promises only to make me wake as hard as a steel post and alone.

"If it helps, I do know she sounds American."

The hairs on the back of my neck stand like pins.

No. I'm being ridiculous.

It can't be her. It can't be Holland.

Can it?

Pushing the glass back at McCain, I follow my brother out of the room.

9

HOLLY

"Hey, have you seen Mo?" Stopping in front of a girl dressed in an identical outfit, I block her passage going the opposite way.

"Probs out by the van," Dana replies as she skirts around me, expertly balancing the tray of empty champagne flutes she's carrying up the stairs.

"Damn," I mutter, grabbing the burnished banister as I hurry into the bowels of one of the toniest houses I've ever been inside. *And I've seen the inside of a lot of super fancy real estate in the past two months.* This one is a multimillion-dollar Belgravia address, grand in every meaning of the word. Ceilings high enough to house giants with elaborate Georgian moldings picked out with gold. Crystal chandeliers and walls covered in hand-painted silk, then hung with massive oil paintings that look hundreds of years old.

But there's no time to admire any of that. I've got to find Mo. If she's out by the van, she could be sneaking a couple of bottles of champagne into her duffel, which I've seen happen before. Maybe not Mo, but I've seen other managers on other shifts. Fingers crossed, she's light-fingered too, because that could be my ticket to getting out early. Or at least she might let me hide in the van.

I hate serving, but I hate even more how private catering is a big swindle. Fancy-named companies charge their clients eye-watering amounts per head for nothing more than a glass of bubbles, a few pastries, and one or two limp-looking shrimp. In turn, the supervisor on shift smuggles out the good stuff (usually champagne) already charged to the client. Meanwhile, lower down the food chain, the waiting staff get paid minimum wage and don't even collect tips.

Well, you can't stop me from having one of these, I think, snatching up something I'm told to offer up as "a monkfish croquette with a pea velouté", which, turns out, tastes more like tinned tuna with a hint of grass.

My tray makes a hollow *ting* as I drop it to the commercial-grade kitchen countertop and head for the back door. A few more feet, and I'll have made good on my escape.

"Hey, wait!"

A-hell-no. I'm not stopping. Not even for the kind of deep voice that's haunted my dreams and disturbed my sleep these past few weeks.

I am so out of here.

I'm not even supposed to be here! And I mean that on so many levels.

Alexander. Goddammit, Alexander! In a city of eight million people, we are *not* supposed to see each other again, especially not while I'm wearing a frilly apron with pea velouté stains! I thought I'd made it out of the room before he'd seen me, even if I did squeak and almost drop my tray when I'd spied his magnificence across the room.

Squeaked, almost dropped my tray, and almost peed myself.

And to think these past few weeks I've been complaining that, as a server, I got looked *through* instead of *at*. Why tonight of all nights did that have to change?

I don't really mean that.
I don't want him to see me like this.
I shouldn't want him to see me at all.

"Where are you running off to?" This time, the deep voice is playful. Not so much is the large hand that curls around my shoulder because *that* means business. The business of stopping me.

My heart is beating out of my chest as I stop, trying hard to keep my back straight and my chin high. Fate is certainly entertaining herself tonight; to bump into him now while I'm not wearing my regular armor feels cruel. But what feels so much more punishing is that for two months, I've been telling myself that he wasn't as special as my memories made him out to be. That I'd imagined his brilliance, gilded the experience, as my life in London was flushed down the pan. I've had a tough couple of months, and yes, I've thought of him often as one of the last good things to happen to me this spring. But more lately, I'd begun to persuade myself that the memories weren't true. That as my life turned shittier, I'd somehow rolled him in glitter and made him more than he is. I can't tell you how crushing it is to find that's not true.

So, I do the only thing I can do. I turn, and I fix on a polite smile as my mind scans for reasons to explain my presence here.

I had such an awesome time in London, I decided to move here.

Too random.

The uniform? Oh, I'm just helping a friend.

Ack! What if he asks which friend?

Ich bin nicht Holly. Ich bin Helga?

What if he knows more than the half dozen words of German I know?

"Hell—*Oh*." My fixed-on smile slips.

"I can't remember the last time I ran after a woman." His tone goes from playful to silky smooth, but that's not what's important because, as I look up, I realize that sly smile does not belong to Alexander. I swing from panicked resignation to disappointment quicker than you can say *ich bin Helga*. And my words, when I find them, are borderline rude.

"Hey, how are you...?" Who are you, again?

"Argh!" The kind of cute-not Alexander clenches a fist over the dark lapel of his dark suit jacket. "She doesn't even remember me."

"No, I do," I say on the breath of a laugh. God knows I could do with all the laughs I can get. "You're, erm..." His face is kind of familiar, but that's all I've got.

"Griffin," he replies with no little astonishment. "We met at Martine and Ed's." My stomach gives a little twist at the mention of my former employer's names, my former friend's names, even though I've mentally renamed the pair Judith and Judas Iscariot. "You sat next to me at dinner?" A tiny crease forms between his eyes. It seems someone's ego is feeling a little burned. "One of their kids sat on the other side of me?" he adds, tapping a finger to his lips. "The one without the braces and the lisp."

I roll my lips inward so as not to laugh. "Amalie."

"Right! We talked about ...well, who knows what the hell we talked about, but I remember you."

"I remember you, too." At least, I remember him *now*. In

particular, I remember how Amalie had developed a little crush on the guy. You know, like twelve-year-olds do. And in her haste to be included in the conversation, her braces did make her a little lisp-y. Something else I remember is that I found him a little too fond of his own voice and a lot flirty.

"You're a lawyer, right?"

"Barrister, actually," he answers with a faint smile. A smile that doesn't quite reach his eyes as his hands cup my elbows, moving me from my position in the doorway.

"Cheers," Mo, the supervisor, says by way of thanks as she passes from behind, hefting the large box in her hands higher. "Grab the other one from the van, would you, love? It's still open."

"Sure." I mean, I was running away, though there seems little point now. Alexander didn't recognize me. Or maybe he didn't see me. Or maybe he just doesn't care. Whatever the reason, I'll still do pretty much anything else (catering-wise) to keep myself from being upstairs in that house tonight.

Even if I have thought of him nonstop.

Even if that man bent my body and my mind in ways I'm still recovering from.

"So, what are you doing here?" Griffin says as he follows me out into the garden.

"Working." I throw the word over my shoulder in the tone of *well, duh!* Real mature, I know.

"Moonlighting?" Griffin pulls up alongside me, my hurried steps no match for his long strides. "Come on, I won't tell." As my gaze flicks his way, I see he looks kind of pleased with himself as he slides his hands into his pockets and shoots me a playful look.

But I am *so* not in the mood.

"Nope." I pop the *p*, my eyes fixed on the huge metal gate

ahead. Maybe I can just get to the van, climb in, and drive it away. Escape the memory of the man who hadn't noticed me, as well as the one following me, then plead temporary insanity when pulled over by the police for motor vehicle theft. At least I'd get to escape the topic of why I'm here because it's still so difficult for me to explain. Two months and the bitter taste of betrayal still burns the back of my throat. I thought Martine and Ed cared about me. I mean, I know I was their employee, not family, but I truly thought they gave a damn. As it turns out, not so much.

"You still work for Ed, right? You look after his daughters?"

"I wasn't the au pair," I grate out, yanking on the heavy gate. I'm a teacher. I have a degree in education! I'm not supposed to be offering people tiny bites of food from a stupid tray while they treat me as though I'm invisible.

"Wait up! I know that."

Angry tears begin to sting my eyes. I'm suddenly grateful for the dark out here, a lone lamppost yards away providing the only illumination. I find I'm not so thankful when I trip over a loose cobblestone, fragments of weeds and gravel spraying up from the toe of my ugly yet sensible shoes.

"Careful." Strong arms grab me before I hit the ground, but even as he rights me, I'm asking myself *why won't he just go away*. "You okay?" He turns me to face him, dipping at the knees until our gazes are level. "What is it? What did I say?"

"I don't work for Martine and Ed anymore. They're getting divorced." One hot, angry tear slips down my face. I dash it away with the back of my hand, irritated that it's come to this. It's not even that I'm crying in the back alley behind some rich asshole's house, or that I'm no longer working in a job with the perks of travel, free time, and some level of respect, or that I spend my evenings now serving horrible people and wiping away crumbs. It's because of this—crying in front of some stranger who, despite his worried expression, doesn't give a flying flip about me. I might feel betrayed by Martine, and let's face it, who wouldn't, being told to take a couple of nights in a ritzy hotel because "the decorators weren't finished" only to find later that she'd fucked off back to New York without even letting me say goodbye to the girls. But at this moment, I'm also grateful to her for her warning.

Griffin... whatever she said his surname was, *has no scruples when it comes to getting girls into bed. Watch out for that one, Holly dear.*

"Oh, that's... shitty." His hands tighten briefly on my arms, accompanied by an expression of concern. "And Martine has taken the girls back to the States?"

"Yes."

"You didn't want to go with them?"

"She didn't give me that option," I retort. I mean, even if she had, I don't think I'd have gone with them at that point. One of the reasons I'd taken the job was the opportunity for travel, and I wasn't ready to go back to the States.

But I might be getting to that point now.

I'm registered at all the right employment agencies, and I've had interviews. I just haven't had any offers. Meanwhile, I've rented a room in a house that should probably be condemned. I don't have another choice because living in London is so darned expensive.

"That's a bit shit. Still, every cloud has a silver lining, right?" Griffin's cheerful tone is wasted on me. As is his wicked half-smile. "At least, your pinny is very pretty." His eyes flick downwards.

"Pinny?"

"This," he says, flicking the edge of my white frilled

apron. But then his eyes meet mine, hawk-like. "Ed's still in Chelsea, right?"

"As far as I know." As I shrug, Griffin's hands loosen.

"Good. Right. I might give him a call."

"Sure." Even to my own ears, I sound like a sullen teen. "Just don't expect him to answer."

"Why would you say that?" he asks, his words razor-sharp. "Taking the divorce hard, is he?"

"I've no idea. But the week after you were there for dinner, they had some other lawyer, sorry, *barrister*, over. I heard Ed say you were the bigger risk."

"That cheeky bastard!"

"Look, I've got to get back to work." Swinging away, I pull angrily on the door of the van.

"Holly, I'm really sorry they treated you that way." Stepping next to me, he unhooks the catch on the other door.

"Not as sorry as I am," I mutter, though I'll credit him as looking sincere as the van's interior light illuminates his expression. I shake myself internally because none of this matters. Not anymore.

"I know, but who would've thought they'd treat you so shabbily?" I sigh as I stretch into the back of the van, pulling the lone box closer because obviously, not me.

"Well, what's done is done," I say, my tone thawing a little as I glance over my shoulder. "Are you seriously looking at my ass right now?"

His eyes lift, his expression not at all apologetic. "We should go out for a drink."

"So you can stare at my ass some more?" And I go back to frosty again.

"I mean, I could, but I was thinking a little more

practically. A little more hands-on." He has the audacity, no, the *stupidity* to make grabby hands in the air.

"I'm really not in the mood for jokes," I mutter, sliding the box to the left before slamming the right-hand side door closed.

"Okay, but seriously, I have a lot of contacts. I was thinking I might be able to help you find another job."

"Really?" Hope pierces my chest, but I tamp it down. This might turn out to be his weird version of a casting couch.

"Absolutely. But I'm also a really good shoulder to cry on."

"Thanks, but I'm done crying." My hope plummets again. But come on, what should I have expected given our exchange so far? I don't need a shoulder to cry on. I mostly just need something to punch. I could also do with a sweater as I fold my arms over my chest because I'm pretty sure my nipples are throwing out misleading signals.

"Come on, Holly. I can tell you're upset. It looks like they fucked me over, too."

"So, what you're saying is, we should get even by f— doing each other."

Why are men so predictable? Well, some men. Others are annoyingly persistent and won't leave a girl's dreams alone.

Or at least, one man is.

"You really don't think much of me, do you? Because that's not what I was saying at all." My conscience prickles for half a second until he adds, "Not that I'd turn you down or anything."

He gives a wolfish smile, and the next thing I know, I'm being backed up against the van door, and my hand's in Griffin's, and I'm staring up at him.

"Seriously. Let me take you out." His breath is a little puff of heat in the cold air between us. He begins to slide his hands up and down my goosebump-y arms, his gaze shining with the challenge.

"I'm not good company right now."

"I bet I could make you feel better."

Despite his smooth delivery, I bark out a laugh. "You're persistent, I'll give you that."

"I prefer tenacious."

"I would prefer it if you understood the word *no*."

He scrunches his nose, and I suddenly see what women see in him. I mean, there's no doubt he's good-looking. And self-assured. Plus, he can string a pretty sentence together. But I'm guessing it's this air of boyishness that gets women to his bed. And I've no doubt those numbers are great.

"I don't have difficulty with the word *no*. Not that I hear it very often, which might be part of the problem."

I can't help but smile. Boyish charm for the win? Maybe the small win in the form of a smile because that's all he's getting from me.

"I know. I'm overindulged by the women in my life. A lost cause." The picture of false remorse, he shrugs.

"And there are lots of women in your life?"

"Let me think. Well, there's my mother. And my sister." And all the women he screws on a casual basis, too. "Then my chambers are pretty heavily biased towards your sex."

"Chambers?"

"It's what a barrister's office is called over here."

"So, I shouldn't worry if you ask me to come up and see your chambers sometime?"

"It's on the ground floor," he replies. "And you're welcome anytime."

"I won't be visiting. Something tells me your *chambers* are pretty busy already."

"I'd clear them out for you."

I huff out an incredulous-sounding laugh. "I'm really not interested in becoming another woman dangling from your hook."

"I've never heard it called that before," he quips.

"You are..." I shake my head, lost for a way to describe him. Or maybe it's more that whatever I say, he'd just twist it into a compliment anyway.

"Tenacious," he happily supplies.

"The worst," I amend.

"Harsh, Holly. Very harsh. Come on, I'm really good company. Sometimes, I'm even fun." He does that cute nose scrunch again, and just as I begin to think I might give in, he adds, "I'm also a really great fuck."

"Oh, you almost got me there," I say with a rueful laugh and an admonishing finger waggle. "Almost." And now you never will.

"Damn." His expression twists. "Overshot with the fucking?"

"You think?"

"I mean, it is true. But I don't usually blow my own horn."

"Oh, I doubt that."

His expression is suddenly a little shark-like. "That would be a wasted skill, Holly."

"Because there's no shortage of random women willing to blow it for you, I guess." Barf.

"You're determined to fill my mouth with words, aren't you?"

And you're determined to fill mine with something else.

"Besides," he continues, his tone more conciliatory,

"you're not some random woman I followed out into the cold." At the mention of cold, I shiver, wrapping my arms about myself again. "It's you I'm interested in. Give me your number," he coaxes. "I won't bite."

"Not unless I want you to, right?"

"The rule is, not unless you bite me first."

"Unreal," I mutter, though it sounds more like a laugh as my teeth begin to chatter. I move to brush past him when he stops me. My gaze flicks down to his hand, then up to his face, all traces of levity gone. I'm cold, and now I'm bored, and I just want him to leave me alone.

"I don't have my phone on me."

"I don't remember you being as prickly as your namesake last time we met." I almost deliver a retort when I realize he's pressing a business card into my hand. "Take it." For a moment, his words seem sincere as he folds my fingers over it and then his fingers over mine. "Now you have my number."

"And the ball is now in my court?"

"Probably. Though I also know where you work now." For emphasis, he taps the van over the catering company's logo.

"Because that didn't sound like a threat."

"That's just because there happens to be a very fine line between a threat and a promise," he answers smoothly as his hands find my shoulders, turning me to face him again. "A very fine line."

If this is the part where he kisses me, I might just land my knee in his nuts. Or maybe I'll give in. Maybe I'll let this very good-looking and confident man boost my ego. I mean, he's obviously interested in me, and I could do with a little cheering up. But what's more likely is that I'll stick my tongue so far down his throat, he'll never bother me again. Because my happiness shouldn't depend on a man.

Especially one I'm not interested in.

I tilt my head, still undecided but willing to let fate decide. And she does. Pretty spectacularly.

"Griffin."

As a deep baritone sounds through the darkness, my stomach drops to my feet. One word and I know instinctively who this is. I don't know where to look, where to run, and seriously consider climbing into the back of the van and pulling the door shut. Because I might not be looking at Alexander, but I know I just heard him.

Oh, God. He's here. The man you...

The man who...

A dozen deliciously dirty images flit through my mind. I almost don't notice Griffin huff with an air of long-suffering.

"Excuse me," he murmurs, his tone perfectly matching the roll of his eyes. "How may I assist you?" His back facing me, Griffin turns and ducks a lazy, half-assed bow that I think is meant to be funny.

But I'm suddenly not paying any attention as the man steps into the pool of streetlight, and his eyes meet mine. The knowledge in that gaze reacts like a tiny explosion inside me as though, for a second, I'm reliving my experience with him. Broad shoulders and chest, the amber hue of the streetlight accentuates the hollows beneath his cheekbones while gilding his fair hair.

But, damn, I hadn't imagined how good-looking he is.

"Charles St John has arrived." Alexander's attention moves to the man standing between us. "You said you wanted to have a word with him."

Griffin's posture changes immediately, all business suddenly. He begins to move, then, almost as an afterthought, his head twists over his shoulder. "Don't lose that." I follow his gaze to the card in my hand. "Or else." And then he winks before disappearing back through the garden gate.

For a couple of well-heeled guys, their manners are atrocious.

Where's my introduction?

But then again, we don't really need one.

Loin girding? Well, that's another thing.

10

ALEXANDER

"Hello, Holland."

My heart gives a vicious pang. How many times in the past few weeks have I thought of her, my mind travelling back to that night in her hotel room? *The scent of her hair and the satin feel of her skin.* Too many times to count. Too many times to be healthy, that's for certain. Not that it stopped me.

"You don't have a greeting for me?" My lips curl. Not quite a smile but something more bittersweet. I note she has no smile for me, yet she laughed for my brother. There was laughter and touching, of that I'm sure. And the way he held her looked like it was a precursor to a kiss. Bitter without the sweet, my thoughts turn to damning him. *Why him? Why now? And why the hell is she standing in front of me?*

"Hello, Alexander." Her tongue darts out to wet her lips before she shakes her head almost infinitesimally. Shaking away signs of shock or perhaps contrition? But then I notice the red tip of her nose. Cold or embarrassment? And why the fuck do I care? "I guess you must be surprised to see me here."

Surprised? Yes. Angry? Definitely. Yet strangely grateful

to set eyes on her again. My sanity remains; she is every inch as lovely as I remembered her.

What a night and what I wouldn't give to gain a repeat, to have her one more time. To watch her reactions as she reached that point, the point I'd been driven to bring her to again and again. A night when pleasure was the only purpose—not my pleasure or hers but ours. She didn't offer me what she thought I wanted; instead, she gave me everything. And she took. Feasted. Surrendered to her pleasure under the guidance of my hands.

What a night. With a very amicable and grown-up parting where, as the sun rose the next morning, I'd kissed her once more. A final farewell, or so I thought.

I realize I'd fallen silent while remembering, while staring at her. Her arms tighten over her chest, and for one horrible moment, I consider this her reaction to my gaze. That I've made her uncomfortable. But as she valiantly tries to suppress a shiver, I realize that isn't the case. I know she's as affected by the sight of me as I am her, given her rapid exit, but she's also not dressed for the weather.

I slide off my jacket and swing it around her shoulders. "Here."

"No, you don't have to—"

"Watch you suffer from hypothermia?" I reach out to tug the lapels closer at the same time Holland grips them. My fingers brush hers and are met with an almost familiar zing of electricity. *Just like the first time.* I turn hot and cold instantaneously, my insides fiery and molten even as the chill of the evening air penetrates my shirt.

"Well. Thank you." She hunches her shoulders as a tiny shiver runs through her, the color in her cheeks more from the temperature than embarrassment as her fingers tighten on my jacket. I watch as her gaze dips before she seems to force herself to lift her chin, fixing her attention on some point in the darkness behind me.

Can she be so completely unaware of my attention? My fascination? How I drink in the tiny nuances of her. Her damp bottom lip glistens in the lamplight like a temptation to taste, the escaped strands of her hair dancing in the cool night air. Here we are, almost strangers, yet we're both aware of some of the shades and tones of the other's behavior. How they are in their most private of moments. The sounds they make when at their most vulnerable.

"Aren't you going to ask what I'm doing here?" Oh, so that's what she's waiting for, bracing herself for. "God knows I'm surprised to be here." Not to mention horrified to be standing in front of me, according to the way her shoulders hunch.

"I'd say you're working," I answer gruffly, forcing the thoughts away.

This is Holland the waitress, not Holland the lustful holidaymaker.

My gaze roams over her, my fingers itching to do the same as I recall the curve of her waist and the full softness of her breasts. The feel of her skin under my hands.

A fucking waitress. Should it come as such a surprise, given how she lied so easily that day? We were cousins for a while before we were lovers. I was gay, and she was flying back to America.

As far as lies go, dishonesty regarding your employment status seems harmless. And fuck it. I lied, too. I'm lying now —a lie by omission as I fail to tell her what I'm doing here. Who I am.

No, her appearance has nothing to do with Griffin. She isn't an amazing actress, and this meeting is as much a shock to her as it is to me. Though I'm not the one staring at the dark cobblestones. Embarrassment, likely. Or perhaps she has more sense than me and doesn't trust herself to look her fill. I almost smile at my own ridiculousness. It's a nice thought, but I saw the way she looked at my brother.

"I see you've met Griffin." Despite my best intentions, my words are stiff.

"Who?" Her brows retract, her gaze following mine to the embossed piece of finery she holds in her hand. "You know the lawyer?"

"Better than I'd like to." In so many ways. But we can't choose who we're related to. "And you?"

"Barely at all." Her fingers fold around a business card while we dance around the facts and the occurrences that brought us here. But I'll be damned if I speak just for the sake of words. For the sake of convention. We're hardly old friends catching up.

I want to know what she's doing here.
What she's doing here dressed like a waitress.

"I met him earlier this year," she suddenly supplies, filling the silence between us.

I find myself mastering a smile, thinking she wouldn't be much use in an interrogation. Does she feel unnerved, or perhaps silences make her uncomfortable. She wasn't especially verbose that night, but she was delightfully noisy...

"In January, I think," she offers again. "In Chelsea. At a dinner party."

"Like this?" I indicate her outfit with a lazy gesture of my hand, her gaze flicking down almost as though surprised to see the damn pinny she's wearing.

"No, I was a guest," she grates out, her gaze fiery as it meets mine. "I am allowed a social life."

And there she is. At least, this is a little more like the woman I've known.

Known for less than a day, I remind myself.

"Yes, of course you are." I resist the urge to step closer, to keep a decent distance between us. Not a kissing distance; best to avoid temptation. For her sake, at least. "Forgive me, as I understood it, your social life belongs on the other side of the Atlantic." Though I score a point with words, the way I fold my arms across my chest is a reminder to myself that I shouldn't want her.

"It wasn't strictly a lie," she mumbles, her gaze slipping away again.

"But you do live in London, *not* America."

"So, I might have told one or two lies that night. It's not like I owed you anything. Certainly not the tale of my life story."

"No, but a little honesty would've been appreciated." The mild rebuke is at complete odds with the roar of sensation building inside.

"Are you trying to tell me that everything you said that night was the truth?"

God help me because, against every instinct, I find myself stepping closer as my gaze sweeps heatedly over her. "The important things were."

And she sees it then. Reads my every intention. Hears once more the words I'd whispered as I'd broken her down only to build her back up again. And with that acknowledgment comes an empty longing. My body recognizes hers, mourning our lack of connection. Grieving the space between us, hating the cool of the night air.

"It is a surprise to see you again." I find myself reaching out, my hand ghosting her beautiful face, half in shadow, half ivory in the lamplight. "I thought I'd imagined you." Imagined her that night. Imagined her inside in the ballroom. I watch as she swallows over the matching ball of emotion lodged in my throat. I want to place my tongue there. My teeth. Feel the vibration of her want as I do.

But I don't. Not here. Not now.

For her sake, not ever again.

"I've thought about you, Holland. Thought about you more than I care to admit to myself. Care to admit to you."

Her tongue darts out to moisten her full bottom lip, and she swallows again. "I made an impression?"

"You made a few of them." Something warm blooms in my chest as she fails to stifle a small smile. "Some rather long lasting." I find myself absently swiping my thumb against my bottom lip, almost as though I could still taste her kiss.

Her expression shifts from hesitant to hopeful, and I find I have to slide my hands into my pockets to stop from reaching out.

"Hey, Holly," calls a voice from somewhere behind me. Young. Female. Probably a colleague. "Mo wants to know if you went to Russia to get the caviar."

"Damn, the box," she whispers. "I forgot I was supposed to take it to the kitchen."

"I didn't realize you were *busy*." The young woman's voice leaks with innuendo as, by the sounds of her shoes against the cobblestones, she skips closer.

"Please tell Mo that I've detained *Holly*, and that she will be along shortly."

"A long shortie?" the young woman sing-songs back. But the words are barely in the air when I shoot her a frigid glance over my shoulder. She stops dead in her tracks, recognizing me. "A-absolutely. I'll tell Mo she'll be along when you're done with her. When you're done here. I mean, whenever you're done with what you're doing here."

She seems to shake her head at her own ridiculousness before she scurries—not skips—back the way she came.

"What the heck was that all about?" Holland asks.

I chose to ignore the question as rhetorical.

"Well?"

Perhaps not.

"I'm afraid I don't understand," I offer blandly.

"Her." She points at the gate. "What was that all about because she wasn't struck stupid by your looks."

"You don't think so?"

"Don't try to be cute."

"I thought it just came naturally."

As though testing the hypothesis, her gaze falls to my shoulders and meanders down my chest. "You're too big to be cute." Her lips slam closed with a scowl. "And why the heck isn't she worried about me, standing out here alone in the dark with the devil in his Sunday suit?"

"This is a good suit," I agree, unable to stop myself this time from reaching out, opting to pinch an invisible piece of lint from the shoulder of the jacket she's wearing. "Even if I'm only wearing half of it."

Was that a flinch or a shudder? The latter, as she ignores my provocation, her eyes darting away. It's ridiculous that I feel some sense of disappointment that she's not playing along. *Like she did with Griffin.*

"She should be worried you're trying to talk me out of my appetizers." Her gaze flares belatedly. "I didn't mean—"

"I don't remember needing to talk you out of anything," I purr, even if purring is the opposite of what I should be doing.

"I just meant, I'm at work, and you... you're a punter, I guess."

The word sounds strange on her lips, but it does make me wonder how long she's lived in London. I shake off the unhappy thought, feeling conflicted again.

"Perhaps it is the suit that frightened her off. And aversion to authority?" I hazard.

"I guess she's probably not long out of school." She frowns in the girl's direction.

Not long out of school. A waitress. The words loop through my brain, along with *wrong* and *fucking hypocrite.*

Didn't I just warn Griffin from doing this very thing? Taking advantage of... one of the waitresses. The *younger* waitresses. Meanwhile, I want to pluck this one up from where she stands, throw her over my shoulder, and carry her up the back stairs to one of the bedrooms.

Which only goes to prove I've lost my mind.

Fuck.

I can't do this. I need to leave. Go back to my duty and ignore this clawing demand. But instead, I find myself asking, "How old are you, Holland?"

"No one calls me Holland. I mostly answer to Holly. Sometimes Hols. Sometimes hey you, bring that tray of crostini's over here!"

"I prefer Holland," I murmur, ignoring the rest. That she's evading means... what?

"It's a little too late in the day to ask now, isn't it?"

Jesus fucking Christ, I hope not.

"I'm older than Dana." Her once more gaze flicks behind me, obviously discerning where the question came from. "She's barely out of high school."

And here you are, both doing the same job, the vicious part of my mind whispers.

"I've been legal for a long while, if that's what you're worried about."

"I'm not worried, but I do have questions."

"I'm twenty-four." Her chin lifts as she delivers her edict.

"You look younger." At least, she does tonight. Her face scrubbed of makeup, all that luxurious hair scraped back.

"Well, now you know I'm practically ancient. You can begin to breathe again."

"I'm sorry. It's all just a little much. I don't ordinarily—"

"Oh, honey," she says, her words turning sharp, "I think that's supposed to be my line."

My jaw flexes, my temper flaring.

"How well do you know Griffin?" I try my best to pretend her ridiculous attitude and her cocked hip mean nothing to me, knowing full well I am the cause of it. This meeting, here, now, and the mixed signals I must be giving out. In an ideal world, I could just say it. Say that I want her, that I've been unable to think of much else but her since that night. That she invades my dreams nightly, that the phantom scent of her floral perfume has made me stop more than one brunette out on the street. That night was the best and the worst thing to ever happen to me. I can't ever have her again. Liar or not, she deserves better than to be entangled with me.

"I don't," she grates out. "Like I said, I met him at a dinner party at a time I *wasn't* serving food." It's hard to tell why her attitude deepens. Is she affronted or embarrassed? "I don't normally work as a server." Embarrassment then. "Not that there's anything wrong with being a server, because we should all be allowed to dance to the beat of our own drum."

"Yes. And I imagine you do." The woman is

unconventional. Or at least, I thought so. *Unconventional or a liar.* Possibly both.

"It's an honest way to make a living, but it isn't what I ordinarily do." Her spine straightens, the glint of challenge flaring in her gaze. "I'm just... between positions. Currently."

"May I enquire what it is you *ordinarily do*?"

"Sure. I'm a stripper." She gives an unconcerned flick of one shoulder as I almost swallow my tongue. "With a name like Holly Harper, would you expect anything else?" I don't have time to process this before a bark of laughter breaks free from her prettily mendacious mouth. "You should see your face! Oh my God, that was the kind of laugh I needed!"

"I'm pleased to have helped," I murmur, though the words sound anything but pleased.

"I'm a teacher, you big oaf!" Her hand meets my chest, not exactly in a slap because that would imply her hand meeting my body with some speed before removing it just as quick. Given that her hand is still on my chest, I'm not sure what this is.

I'm also not complaining.

"A teacher." The word is a low rumble as I cover her hand with my own, as though to contain this tiny throb of connection.

"Yes, you know..." Her eyes shine darkly as they meet mine once more. "Classrooms full of little people, though I haven't been inside a classroom for a while." She frowns, her mind slipping to a topic not as happy as this one obviously made her. "I was working for an American family here in London. Tutoring their daughters, getting them from school and their extracurriculars and back again. Part-time tutor, a part-time social secretary." One hand clutches the lapels of my jacket as she pulls the other from under mine, ostensibly to sweep away a wisp of hair that has blown across her cheek. "I wanted to travel. I mean, I love teaching, but I wanted to see more of the world, and working for this family offered me that. I was going to teach at an American curriculum school internationally, but then this job came along. Great pay. Great conditions. Pretty much my own apartment in Chelsea. But... I don't work there anymore. A family split." She encompasses the tale with a shrug. "So that's where the pinny?" Her eyes seek mine, and I nod. "Where the apron comes in. It seems catering ritzy parties is kind of a niche market."

I don't know about ritzy. I would've gone with staid as I watch as she begins to twist the white frill between her fingers. This time, I notice she's holding a business card in her hand. Griffin's business card.

"I'm sorry to hear of your troubles."

"You wouldn't be hearing it now if not for all this." She gestures to the house at my back.

"Yes," I answer simply because none of this seems like the Holland Harper I spent the night with. I'm sorry for her discomfort.

"Things just didn't work out as I planned," she murmurs.

"I find that's generally the way with plans."

"I'm sorry, Alexander." My name on her lips is sincere. Quite beautiful. "Sorry I twisted the truth. We weren't ever supposed to see each other again, and I guess I'm sorry it didn't work out that way."

I am a monumental arse. I didn't offer her my life story, so why should I have expected different from her? But the fact remains, had I known the truth, known there'd be a small possibility of seeing her again, I wouldn't have ended up in her bed.

And what a sad outcome that would've been.

"Don't be sorry. I'm not." That's the truth but not the

whole truth as I pluck Griffin's card from her hand. I'm not going to take advantage of her even though it would be easy to. I'm not going to take advantage of her even though I long to. And I'll be damned if I allow Griffin to take my place. "Is this Griffin's?" I say, turning it over in my hand.

She nods. "We talked about work."

"You don't want to work for him," I assert as her expression morphs into a frown.

"I don't think he was planning on offering me a job."

"No one would employ you to look after children on the recommendation of Griffin."

She rears back as though slapped, and I instantly regret the manner of delivery, though I stand by the truth of my words.

"I'm not sleeping with him, if that's what you're suggesting," she says, her tone sharp.

"I'm telling you that's what people will think. What people who know Griffin will think," I amend.

"Maybe I don't care what people think."

We both know she's not talking about her job.

"Be careful, Holland."

"How about I'll be careful if you don't be an ass?"

"Griffin isn't someone you want to be involved with."

"How do you know that?" she snipes, trying unsuccessfully to pull the card from between my fingers. "Maybe he has a friend with a restaurant. Maybe that's what he meant."

"I thought you were a teacher, or was that another lie?"

"Hey, Lyle," she answers heavily, punctuating each of her next words with a finger to my chest. "Kettle. Pot. Black."

"That's not an answer to my question."

"I'm sorry. Did you think I owed you one? How do you even know Griffin, anyway?"

"How do you know him?" The accusation in my question brings heat to her cheeks and if I thought her eyes were angry before, they're positively glittering now.

"You mean, how *well* do I know him."

"Are you a teacher, or aren't you?"

"Yes, I'm a gosh darn teacher! Degree educated, experienced in the elementary system!"

"Gosh darn?"

"And for the record, I haven't had sex with your buddy, so there's no need to worry about me comparing notes."

"Griffin isn't my friend. He's my brother."

"No way." She looks taken aback, though not horrified. *That has to be a good sign.*

"I'm not certain if that was meant to compliment him or me."

"People who fish for compliments don't deserve them."

"Holland," I mutter, fighting my feelings and my rising temper, swallowing them down like bitter medicine. "I meant it when I said it was a surprise to see you tonight. I'm sorry we weren't more truthful with each other, and I'm sorry to hear you've had issues with your employment. But if you'll just stop trying to goad me for one minute, you'll find that I might be able to help you."

"You mean like your brother wants to help?" she retorts with more than a hint of accusation.

I could, I suppose. Except that she deserves better and that I demand better from myself. My needs are my own, and there are other ways to have those needs met without embroiling the innocent.

"There's no need to be suspicious." Because, unlike some people, I don't act on impulse to the thoughts running through my head. Slipping Griffin's card into my inside pocket, I take out my pen. My jaw clenches as I resist the temptation to ask for her number because I know the temptation might prove too great. I could give her mine, but then she might call. And I might answer. And that sounds like the beginning of a disaster. "Call this number tomorrow." Taking her hand in mine, I jot my assistant's number down on the back of her hand. I try very hard to ignore how small it looks in mine and the delicacy of her wrists. *And how it had looked manacled by my fingers.* "George will be expecting your call."

"What kind of job are we talking about?" As if her expression wasn't enough, her tone drips with suspicion.

"One with children, I believe."

"Teaching?"

"I don't believe so." Because I don't know anyone who owns a school. But between us, my friends and I do own a great deal of businesses, buildings, and estates. And better still, some of them are in very remote locations. The kind of locations that are out of Griffin's reach.

And out of sight, out of mind, I hope.

For both of us.

11

HOLLY

I wasn't going to call.

Yes, I need a job—a decent job—but why would I involve myself in anything to do with those two. Alexander, I know, is too hot to handle, and his brother seems like he could be a handful, too. Singularly, they are trouble. But getting in between them sounds like a health risk.

I *so* wasn't going to call that number inked onto my hand by Alexander's hand. Especially not the way my skin had reacted to the brush of his and how I'd swallowed a sigh when he pressed his palm to mine. Under the warmth and protection of his jacket, I'd inhaled lungsful of his scent, and my stomach had twisted itself into needy and complicated knots. Not that he would've guessed any of that. Not by the way I'd coolly handed back his jacket and walked back to the kitchen without even a backward glance. And who cares if my knees were knocking because I could feel his eyes on me the whole time because I'll never admit to it.

In the kitchen, I'd borrowed a pen from Mo to jot down the number on a scrap of paper. Now that I think about it, it was kind of odd that Mo didn't give me a hard time for forgetting to bring in the box from the van. She just kind of looked at me warily, I thought.

Though I'd washed the ink from my skin that night, I've been unable to wash away the recollection of what it felt like to be near him again.

I was absolutely *not* going to call. Not after being up close and personal with him again. Okay, so maybe not quite as *up close* or even as *personal* as I would've liked—I mean, as the first time we met—but close enough to smell his cologne again. *Spice and earth and all kinds of wonderful.* And I can't believe I got all handsy with his chest again. The damn thing is like a magnet, even when he was being all formal and stiff, the cause of which was probably the way his ass was pinching around that stick he seemed to have shoved up there. He was so different this time. Frosty and aloof. Okay, not all the time, but it's not like he let his guard down intentionally. More like the thing exploded.

I've thought about you, Holland. Thought about you more than I'd care to admit.

Even now, the memory of his voice makes me shiver. I've thought about him, too. Lots of times. Mostly at night with my hand sunk into my pajama pants.

"Are you even listening to me?"

Ah, heck.

I push the phone back up against my ear at the sound of my sister's voice, my cheeks burning even though she's not here to see them. "Yeah, I'm here. I think the call must've dropped." I'm not about to admit I was thinking about a naked Alexander again. Yeah, so I wasn't going to call the number, but I did. And I almost swallowed my tongue when a masculine voice answered. For one crazy, heart-stopping minute, I thought it was him—that I was talking to Alexander—and that troublesome, non-beating muscle had floated to the very top of my chest cavity. And plummeted again when I came to realize I was speaking to his assistant.

He didn't give me his number. He was done with me.

It's probably for the best.

"I just don't get where your reluctance is coming from," Kennedy complains. Again.

"Because of *who* recommended me to the agency," I say. Again. Alexander gave me the number. I spoke to his assistant, who set up a meeting for me with a swanky employment agency, and I was offered a job the same day. Suspicious? Just a little bit. How can I even consider it, given our history? Our very brief history, but still.

"So, you spent the night with the guy. Like you said, if the circumstances had been different, he'd still be too old for you."

"That's not exactly what I said." Because with age comes experience. The kind of experience that can make a girl cross-eyed with delight.

"Besides, it's not like he personally offered you a job."

"If he had," I murmur, flicking away a piece of lint from my hastily ironed interview skirt, "I would've told him where he could shove it."

I couldn't work for a man I've slept with. Another break-up, and where the heck would I end up this time? Outer Mongolia, maybe.

"Sure, you would have," she replies softly because my sister not only knows, but she held my hand through that clusterphuck. "But it's not as if that has happened. For starters, you're not in a relationship with him. Second, all he did was give you the number for an agency he thought might be able to help. And then, when you mentioned his name in the interview, it didn't even register in so much as a raised eyebrow."

"I know," I say with a sigh, not that I could've mentioned his full name, anyway. *Given I don't know it.* But I couldn't resist the niggling thought that something hokey was going on, so at the end of the interview, while shaking hands with Sarah Houghton, my interviewer, I'd said something about being grateful to Alexander for putting us in touch. The woman's expression barely rippled.

"Also," my sister interjects, "I say again, it's not even like you'll be working for him."

"Urgh!"

"A job is a job, Hols."

"If that's the case, I already have a job." I don't have to take this much better offer that doesn't appear to come with strings. *Which would make me an idiot, probably.*

"Yes, you have a job. You also have a tiny bedroom in a shared apartment. With a shared bathroom."

"Thanks for the reminder, Dede," I reply, using her childhood name pointedly. Kick a girl while she's down by reminding her she's living in the equivalent of college dorms at the ripe old age of twenty-four.

"If you want to be a server, you might as well come back and work here."

"Ha! No thanks."

Back when the place belonged to our grandmother, I was pressganged into service enough then. I'm not stepping back into that town ever again. Not if I can help it. A familiar twinge of guilt flutters in my chest. I know in my heart that Kennedy doesn't want to live in Mookatill any more than I do, even if she won't admit it. I sometimes think I did her a disservice when I signed over my share of Nana's business. Like I've somehow damned her to a life there. At the time, it had soothed my conscience to think I was doing a good thing because she had the rugrat to take care of. I'd told myself that I wasn't leaving her behind and that her gratitude was genuine. But mothering instincts do a number on a woman. Except where our mother was concerned, maybe. She seems to be pretty much guilt free around the topic of dumping us on her mother's doorstep when her boyfriend didn't want us around anymore.

"It sounds like a pretty unique opportunity. And Scotland is another country to add to your list, little Miss Jet Setter."

Yep. I run around the world while she lives in the town we were born in and pretends not to ignore the nasty looks and the notoriety of our name.

The Harper girls? Why, they're no better than their mother was. The older one went out to a fancy college and didn't come back with a degree but with a baby in her belly. And the younger one? Her fiancé left her a week before their wedding. You can guess what for.

But guess is all they do.

Meanwhile, I've been offered a job running the education center of a historic castle in the Highlands of Scotland, supervising programmes for kids visiting from local schools as well as devising fun stuff for little tourists. Horrible histories and murderous mayhem made fun. The castle and grounds are a historical visitor attraction, plus they're also hired out for movie shoots. I'm told this is another big tourism draw, given parts of some of the most popular kids movies were filmed there.

I stare out of the café's rain-slicked window. It is a unique opportunity, but something is holding me back. I mean, I love London and I'm not sure I'm ready to leave. It's not some spooky, woo-woo sense of foreboding that's holding me back, but I feel a reluctance just the same. Maybe it's just that I don't want to owe either Alexander or

Griffin—whatever their surname is—anything. Not that I think they'd ask me to pay, in kind or otherwise, because it's not like any of us left a forwarding address. Besides, this job doesn't seem to have anything to do with either of them. Maybe I'm worrying about nothing.

"So? What are you waiting for?" my sister demands. "You're over there because you want to travel and experience new things."

"I know." I really wish I knew why I was feeling so resistant. The pay is good, accommodation is included, and Scotland is on my list of places I want to visit. I should already be packing my bags, not staring out into the wet street, feeling stuck.

"And Scotland has kilts. And men who look like Sam Heughan. Do it for the *Outlander* fantasy, if nothing else!"

"Well, I guess there is that."

"Find you a man who'll call you *Sassenach*," she adds excitedly, warming to her theme, though her Jamie Fraser impersonation is pretty lame. "The way I see it, you have three options. Stay where you are and hope something else comes along—"

"Which won't happen until at least the summer." When other professional American families begin to relocate to London, or their current nanny ends their contract, usually at the end of the school year.

"Or you can take this new job, this new opportunity, with the bonus of men in kilts."

"I don't think they all look like Sam Heughan."

"Or," she says, ignoring me, "you can come back home and be content with staring at men in baggy-ass jeans and New Balance sneakers."

My stomach twists at the thought of moving back to Mookatill, home of the cheese and men with low fashion standards. Moving back to snickers behind hands and sly, calculating looks. To small-town assumptions and whispers behind my back.

I'd rather share a bathroom *and* a twin bed an ogre than deal with that.

"I saw Denise Thomas at the market on Sunday." My sister's airy delivery does not fool me.

"Yeah? How was she?" I answer, imitating her tone. "God, she was such a bitch in high school." I count my blessings she didn't have school-aged kids while I was teaching at the local elementary. She would've had a field day with the fallout. "What's she doing now?"

"You mean, apart from watching your Instagram stories?"

"Ah, you know how to cheer a girl up," I reply with a cackle. "I can't believe she'd even admit to it."

"Oh, she didn't, but she knew you were in London, so…"

"Like I said, she was such a bitch."

"I really don't know why you give a rat's ass about what any of those people think."

"Who said I did?"

"That would be in your reluctance to come visit."

"Hey, if you want to blame anyone, blame Wilder. I asked him if he wanted me to stay with you or if we should go to Disneyland."

"What kind of question is that to ask a kid?" she splutters. "You know what? I don't even know why I'm having this conversation with you. You might've been offering a trip to the sewage plant, and he still would've said yes. You could convince nuns to take a trip to a strip club."

"I think that's the nicest thing you've ever said to me."

"And if I'm going to blame anyone for you not coming home, I'm going to blame that ass of an ex."

But he was more than just my ex. Not for the first time, I find myself wishing that grandma was alive. She would've seen right through him, I'm sure.

"I don't know, Dede. Maybe I should thank him. I always wanted to travel. Maybe his bullshit was just the push I needed."

"I'd like to push him. From a great height. Pity the school is all on one level," she adds in an undertone.

"Shoot him instead?"

"Too messy. And orange doesn't suit me, especially not in jump suits. Listen, I've got to go. It's time to open up and feed that coffee-hungry horde."

"Someone's got to power them through their workday."

"And I am their friendly local dealer. Listen, let me know when you've made your decision. You know you're always welcome home. For what it's worth, my vote is that you stop worrying about being some man's puppet when this is clearly some cosmic coincidence. Go to Scotland, find you a fine-looking kilt-wearing specimen of a man. Then—"

"Put him on Instagram?"

"Nope, bring him back and make *all* the bitches jealous."

"I heard you say a bad word, Mom!" I hear the rug rat named Wilder shout.

"What have I told you about listening to other people's conversations?" Kennedy's words are directed somewhere other than her phone handset.

"That if I'm gonna do it, I need to be smart enough not to let people know."

"That is not what I said, Wilder James!"

"But I'll bet it was the gist of it," I offer with a cackling laugh.

"I can't wait until you have kids," she mutters ominously.

"Don't hold your breath. I can barely look after a houseplant."

"Holly, for the love of God, just take the job—say yes to the opportunity. What have you got to lose?"

I'm still pondering the answer to this question hours after we end our call.

12

HOLLY

DESPITE MY RESERVATION AND THE FEELING THAT I SHOULD BE heading in the opposite direction, I find myself on the first leg of a long train ride a week later. I arrive in Edinburgh first and a train station that, but for the inclusion of a Burger King, looks like it was plucked from the set of a *Harry Potter* movie. Here, in this monument to Victorian architecture, I change trains and travel for another three and a half hours to Inverness in the Highlands of Scotland.

A car waits for me as I step out of the station into the late grey afternoon. An ageing, mud-splattered Land Rover complete with a matching mud-splattered driver. The driver is less on the old side; somewhere in his late twenties, I guess. Beside him sits a chunky-looking Labrador with a sparkly pink collar.

"You'll be the new hire, then?" The man pushes back a tweed flat cap, the kind I associate with country squires and farmers, brushing his hand through a mess of reddish hair. He's tall and built and pretty cute in a ruddy, outdoorsy kind of way. I mean, he's no Alexander—wait, that's supposed to be a good thing.

"How can you tell?" My answer sounds more like a teasing enquiry.

"How can I tell what?" he says, his accent rendering *what* more like *whit*.

"That I'm the new hire. I could be anyone?"

"Gertie, come away," he mutters, trying to rescue me from the floof as she greets me with a lot of excitement and almost as much hair which floats through the air like the fluffy seeds from a dandelion.

"Well, hello there, Gertie." I keep my patting to her head and my feet, and pristine sneakers, away from the reach of her slobbery snout.

"I suppose that'd be the pink suitcases?" The melodic lilt in his accent renders his answer a question, his smile widening as I greet his dog. "That and your accent."

"Well, if you're heading for Kilblair Castle, I'm your girl. If you're thinking about kidnapping and murdering the obvious stranger, that girl will be along shortly."

"Maybe I should be the one making sure you're no' the murderer?" His accent and that last word? A marriage made in melty-girl heaven. All the rolling r's. "Now you're smiling, I see that can't be so."

"Murderers don't smile in Scotland?"

"Not the one's dragging pink suitcases, I'd say. Here, let me take that." He makes to grab the handle of the largest of my two suitcases.

"No, I've got it." But it seems I *don't got it* as he swings the thing out of my hand and into the back of the battered vehicle like it doesn't weigh almost seventy pounds. *One of the reasons I opted for a train rather than flying up here.*

"Holly." I thrust out my hand in anticipation as he slams the trunk closed.

"Cameron," he replies, his warm hand meeting mine.

I breathe an almost silent sigh of relief as I recognize his name as my designated pick-up, confirmed yesterday by email.

"Nice to meet you, Cameron the not murderer."

"In ye' hop," he instructs, pulling open the rear passenger door. For a minute, I think he's talking to me. At least until the portly pooch barrels past me, almost making me spin. He catches my upper arm, righting me with a wry grin. "Ye' can get in the back if you like, but you'll have to wrestle with old Gert for space, and she molts like the devil."

"Oh. Right." I point ahead. "I'll get in the front then, shall I?"

He's still smiling as I pull on the door. "Driving, are ye?"

Argh! "I forgot," I mutter. Stupid British cars with their steering wheel on the wrong side. You'd think I'd remember. It's not like I'm fresh off the plane!

What a terrible impression I must be making.

My cheeks are still burning as I slide into the passenger seat, trying not to wrinkle my nose at the whiff of wet dog. The driver's door *clunks* closed, seat belts *click*, then the engine rumbles to life.

"Inverness looks pretty," I say, staring up at the tall Edwardian-looking buildings and the myriad of shopfronts we pass. *Butcher. Baker. No candlestick maker.* But it seems more like a town than a city. Also, sadly, there isn't a kilt or a Jamie Fraser lookalike in sight.

"Aye, it's no' bad for the capital of the Highlands, though it's no' so big for a capital city, I suppose. Still, it's big enough to keep me out of the place." Turning his head, he shoots me a friendly wink.

"You're not a fan of the bright lights, big cities?" Though there isn't much evidence of either. Inverness seems a little sleepy and very quaint. At least, from the viewpoint of a moving car window. But then we pass a couple of bars and people sitting at tables outside. I find myself suppressing a shiver. It is so *not* alfresco dining weather.

"That I am not."

I know from Google that the journey to the castle should take about ninety minutes. And that's ninety minutes spent taking in the striking landscape and the local points of interest Cameron points out as we travel. And ninety minutes wondering what to expect from a castle with its own website and Wikipedia page, and the family who owns it, of course. An aristocratic family with the kind of internet footprint that lists their failures and triumphs, their marriages and deaths going back thirteen generations. *The debauching Dukes of Dalforth*, I read mention of more than once. It seems like they're a line of rakes, thieves, and bad boys that kind of boggles the mind. Me, Holly Harper, working for a duke. Even if not directly because I guess I'll be the modern-day equivalent of one of the serfs. Way below the butler, but a little above the chambermaid. Do they even have those these days? I guess they probably went the way of the chamber pot at the advent of indoor plumbing.

But I probably won't even need to set foot in the castle as I'll be running the education center, focusing on the younger generation of visitors to Kilblair Castle.

I'm Holly Harper. Let's make history fun!

"You're coming at just the right time now that business has started to pick up." Cameron's voice interrupts my wandering thoughts.

"I did read that the castle closes down over the winter." I'm not sure what that will mean for me, even if I've taken this job telling myself that I'll be moving on to new pastures before this time next year. Warmer pastures, I think as I wrap my jacket a little tighter.

"Aye, but not until the week before Christmas. The silly season is a busy one for Kilblair, though it's a wee bit quieter for my team."

"What is it you do at the castle?"

"I'm the head gardener."

I'd also read about the extensive gardens on the website, available to view at a separate entrance fee.

"Do you live on-site?"

"No, not me. Though a number of us do. I hear you will be, too."

There's something in his tone that seems a little too amused.

"What am I missing here?"

"I'm sure you'll find out yourself soon enough."

"Because that didn't sound ominous." I find myself frowning out at the road as it snakes ahead, the scenery becoming more rural and, if I'm honest, a little bleak.

"It's nothing to warrant a look as dark as yon clouds." His words are delivered in a rough-sounding chuckle. "It's just that your job and wee cottage were promised to someone else."

My head whips around as my stomach twists, my answer a little shrill. "Promised?"

"Well, maybe no' so much promised as expected. But it's not your fault Mari's got herself in high doh. What's coming fir ye will no pass ye by, y'ken?"

"Who's Mari? For that matter, who's Ken." And what the fluff did he just say?

Cameron bursts out laughing, taking both Gertie and me my surprise, judging by her *woof* and my splutter.

"Great. Just great. I haven't even gotten there, and I'm

already making friends. And you know what? I have no idea what you just said."

"It's no' so bad as all that." His guffaws switch down a few gears to a chuckle, his gaze sliding from the road ahead to meet mine. "Mari is your assistant. High doh is like... her knickers are twisted," he adds with a totally cute roll of the *r*. "She's riled, y'ken?"

I find myself shaking my head. The gist I get, kind of like understanding a song without knowing all the words. But that rolling r—*knickerrrrs*—that was something else.

"You'll get there. It'll take you no time at all."

"To understand the accent?"

"Aye. Just don't go asking people to talk slower."

"Why?"

"They're likely just to tell you to think faster."

Just great.

"I'm just pullin' your leg," he says. "We get a lot of Americans visiting during the season, and they get by just fine."

"Well, that's good to know. I guess a lot of them visit because of the movie stuff."

"Aye, and it's not always wee ones that want to take a walk in Tollbride School of Enchantment and Sorcery," he says, using the name of the biggest kid's movie franchise that was partly filmed in Kilblair Castle. "We get a lot of American's coming to visit the home of Rory Roy, the romantic highlander." This is a popular Netflix series, Kennedy tells me. "Maybe you should watch it. You might pick up a bit o' the brogue."

I smile noncommittally.

"You can see the castle up ahead."

The road rises to meet us, darkened heather-covered hills on either side before a coastline appears in the distance. Craggy hills and a stretch of sandy beach, and between the car and coastline, there appears to be a cluster of grey, hemmed in by a wall then wrapped in towering fir trees.

"It doesn't look like a castle." I silently curse myself for saying so, knowing people can be protective of their homes.

"Aye, that's because it's more like a fortress."

Ten minutes or more later, we round an ancient-looking hedge to be met with an equally ancient-looking gatehouse that looks like it wasn't built for show but for fortification. The masonry above the arch is carved with a weather-worn shield and crest, dappled with lichen.

"A fortress?" A nervous sort of anticipation swirls in my stomach.

"Almost." He shoots me a grin as we turn into a driveway lined with huge trees.

"This is some driveway. And this is a lot of garden to keep." Lawns roll left and right, their expanse dotted with trees that mostly look like skeletons, only one or two showing the first bloom of spring.

"This is just the front lawn," he says dismissively. "Wait until you see the formal gardens, the maze, and the orchard. Then there are the family's private gardens and a few other bits to care for."

"How many gardeners are there?" Surely, he can't take care of all that on his own.

"There are three others who work the land full-time, and we get other people in to help from time to time."

"Can I expect to see peacocks roaming about the place? And deer?" It looks like that kind of place. At least, the gardens do.

"Peacocks, aye." He nods. "But there's no deer park.

There are deer out on the estate, though. Mostly red deer. Some roe."

"The estate?"

"It's no' just pretty gardens. His grace owns thousands of hectares of land to the west. Land he has stewardship of. Land that needs to be maintained. Thankfully, that's no' in my remit."

His grace. That's what you call a duke, if you happened to come upon one, or so the internet says. *Hello, your grace. Excuse me, your grace. Let me introduce you to his grace, the Duke of... I'm not even sure. Kilblair Castle?* No, I don't think that's it.

I had time to kill on the train and had googled the current family, including the duke. There wasn't much that came up. Just the date the future duke took over the title, the family's names, and the like. The duke has some long-assed name, let me tell you! Henry Charles Alexander Theodore something or other. Must be a pain to fill out forms for him.

Then just ahead, I spy the place itself. Kilblair Castle.

Before my google search, the name had conjured up images of fairy-tale turrets and buff-colored walls covered in climbing roses. But I can't blame Disney because I'd watched a documentary on TV recently, a behind-the-scenes look at some Scottish country estate. What I'm looking at is far from a fairy tale and far from what the castle's website depicts. Like the man says, it's a fortress. Four stories tall with turrets and battlements, it looks like the kind of place you'd expect to see soldiers pouring boiling oil down onto the heads of marauding invaders. In short, this castle is anything but quaint.

As we drive past the entrance, I notice a round tower with a Disney-esque roof and another entrance that seems to have been bricked up at some point long ago, as well as windows that seem to be set back into walls at least two feet thick. We drive along the building and around another corner, and then I'm looking at a part of a building that's less castle and more palace than anything else.

"We came in through the west gate." Cameron slides me a wry look. "It's no' the best view of the place."

"It doesn't look like one building. More like a few of them," I murmur, mostly to myself.

"Built in different time periods, aye? The foundations go back to the eleventh century. What we just passed? That was built in the thirteenth century and heavily fortified. This part of the castle was added in the 1700s after the family did the king o' England a wee bit of political work. Or so goes the tale. The place has been added to every century in between."

"Even now?"

"The current duke has poured a fortune into repairs after the previous two let it go to rack and ruin. Spent their money on other things. Expensive hobbies, they had." *Debauching must be an expensive business.* For a minute, I worry I might have said that aloud as his brow creases in a frown, but it's gone just as quick. "I reckon I could get a job as a tour guide if I get sick of the gardens," he adds with a laugh. "And in case you did'nae notice, we're here."

By now, it's almost fully dark as Cameron stops the car in a little courtyard. Lights burn from inside buildings to my right, which look like a row of terraced cottages. To the left, the windowless walls of the Castle loom cold and dark.

"The staff cottages," he says, nodding his head in the direction of the lights as Gertie's tail begins to thump.

"But you don't live here." From the back seat comes a disgruntled snort before Gertie's bulky form turns a circle on the back seat before flopping back down.

"No." He pushes back his cap, ruffling his hair, his teeth shining white in the gloom. "I've got a place in the village. It's very convenient for the pub." Then he does that thing that men everywhere seem to have perfected—a sweeping glance that scans the whole of me yet leaves me wondering if I'd imagined his appraisal. "Once you get settled, I'll take you there, if you like."

So, not my imagination, then.

"You mean to the pub." Amusement lingers in my words.

"Oh, aye." It's hard to tell in the light, but I'd swear his cheeks turn a little pink. "Maybe to start, I reckon."

"Oh, do you?"

He's not so shy as I'd first imagined. Plus, he's not bad looking. And the ninety-minute journey has flown by in his easy company. I find myself wondering what harm could come from a drink with him. I might make a friend. Maybe even something a little more, because Lord knows I need to stop obsessing about a certain someone. Because if a certain someone was interested, he would've asked for my number, not given me his assistant's. "If I'm still here in a couple of days, I might just take you up on that."

"You're not worrit about Mari, are you?" Consternation flickers over his brow. "I wouldn't have mentioned it if I thought—"

"No, it's fine. Forearmed is forewarned." Or something. My gaze is drawn to where light suddenly spills from a doorway opening in the cottage we're parked next to.

"Mari won't make a peep. Just you wait and see."

"Will you be keeping the lassie all night, Cameron Stuart?"

At the woman's pointed question, a grin cracks across Cameron's face. He turns as, behind him, the car door creaks open. Cold, crisp air floods in as an antidote to the scent of a damp dog.

"Bide your passion, Chrissy. I was just talkin' to the lass."

"The lass?" I repeat, though not in the same tone.

"You'll be Holly." The woman's smiling face appears at Cameron's shoulder. Pale hair falls in a straight sheet to her jawline, and the hand she thrusts my way is kind of meaty. "Chrissy," she offers. "I'm happy to meet you."

"Hi." I slide my hand in hers, and she treats it to a hearty handshake. "I'm happy to meet you, too."

"I suppose you would call Chrissy the housekeeper," Cameron supplies over the top of our joined hands. "Or maybe the chief cook and bottle washer." He turns to the woman with a grin. "What do ye think? Jack of all trades and master of none? Ow!" The latter is in response to the slap she delivers to the back of his head. But there's no malice in the exchange.

"Cheek," she mutters, pursing her lips. But when she turns back to me, her face is wreathed in a welcoming smile. "Will ye be comin' in, then?"

"Oh, we're here? This is where I'll…"

"Be staying? Aye. Help the lassie in wi' her bags," she instructs. "You might've washed your car before picking the lass up," she adds, though not unkindly as she straightens and Cameron climbs out of the Land Rover.

"What for." *Whit fir*, sounds nearer to his reply. He opens the rear passenger door, and the bulky Labrador jumps out.

"Because it's clarty, that's what for."

"Why wash it only for it to get dirty again?"

So clarty is dirty? The pair continue their bickering, which is more like light-hearted banter over the condition of my transport, as my suitcases find themselves in a tiny hallway off the open front door.

"I've put the hot water on," Chrissy says over her shoulder, disappearing deeper into the cottage. "Come along, then!"

At the doorstep, I turn back to Cameron. "Are you coming in, too?"

"I—ah. No." His boots scuff against the gravel. "I'd best be off home, but I'll see you around."

"Sure." I try to tamp back my smile. I think I'm relieved that he's leaving, oddly. "I mean, I don't know exactly where I'll be, but..." My words trail off as his smile grows.

"I'm sure I'll find you." With that, he turns back to the car. "Or you can ask around to find me."

"They know you around here, huh?"

"Aye, just ask for Cameron, the not murderer."

I duck my head and huff a small chuckle. "Well, that's good to know."

"Better they know me for my finger skills," he says, wiggling all ten of them in the air. I begin to laugh, slapping my hand to my mouth. And I swear, his cheeks turn red. "I mean my green fingers. I'm known for my green fingers, not... not anything else."

It's kind of cute that he's embarrassed, and I'm still smiling as I close the front door.

"He's gone then?" I find Chrissy in the tiny kitchen where she's boiling an electric kettle. Now we're in the light, I can see her pale hair is actually white, and that's she's a little older than I'd originally thought. Upwards of sixty years old, maybe? But they're years she's wearing well, watching the way she almost wrestled Cameron for the smaller of my two cases.

"Yes, Cameron left." I place my bag down on the countertop and stick my hands into the back pockets of my jeans. The air is kind of stale, and the kitchen is worn and dated, but clean. Formica cabinets and cream tiles, dotted every so often with one featuring an urn, overflowing with fruit. I glance down at Gertie the dog, wondering if she comes as part of the job.

"He's a good lad," she asserts, busying herself with a solitary cup. "He has a big heart and he's not too hard on the eyes."

"I can't say that I noticed." My bland look meets her sly one, and we both chuckle. Chrissy and me are going to get along just fine, I can tell.

"Then you'd be the only one on the estate not to."

"Popular, is he?" I know I need to move on, but there's no way I'm getting involved with the local Lothario, treading on toes before I've even had a chance to decide if I'll like it here.

"Like I said, he's a good lad." I guess that was one way of putting me in my place. "You'll have no trouble with him." I sense the female population hereabouts might prove otherwise. Mari in particular.

"Right. The kettle is on, and so is the emersion heater, should you want a bath after your travels." I'm not sure what that is, but I don't want to appear ignorant. *I'm sure there'll be plenty of opportunity for that in the coming weeks just listening to the Scots language.* "There are a few basic staples in the fridge," she says, pointing at the under-counter appliance. "Milk and the like to get you started. I'll leave you the now to get settled, but my house is the last house on the end," she adds, pointing left. "If you're needing anything, just yell oot."

"Okay. Right." I might nod a little manically, not that she notices as she pours hot water over a teabag. Maybe the Scots are like the English in their belief that tea makes everything better.

"Dinnae fash about the morning."

"I'm sorry, what?"

"Dinnae fash. Don't worry about being at work first thing. Lady Isla isn't due until mid-morning, and tomorrow the castle isn't open to the public." Oh, I remember that. It's open to the public Wednesday to Sunday, unless advertised otherwise. And the woman I've been dealing with via email is called Isla. Maybe *Lady* Isla, as in, a member of the aristocracy? Big whoop, I reassure myself. Blue blood or not, everyone puts on their underwear one leg at a time.

"I'm sure someone will come and collect you before then."

"Great." Great that I've been addressing my emails with such reverences as *hi!* and *see you soon!*

A teaspoon *chinks* against the countertop. "I'll be off then, but I'll see you in the morning! Come along, Gertie." She taps a hand to her thigh, and the dog lumbers after her.

Carrying my tea—mainly because the cup warms my hands; I'm not a great fan of hot tea generally—I inspect the rest of the small cottage. A small, square living room with a sofa, a small TV, and an overuse of chintz. A bedroom with a pair of squeaky twin beds and a bathroom that has seen better days. But it's all clean and kind of homey in its own way, and more importantly, mine for however long I stay. Overall, I'm thankful for my blessings, for opportunities risen from the strangest of places. *Not to mention acquaintances.*

Pulling out my phone, I sink into the tweed-covered sofa, intending to call my sister to let her know I've arrived. My fingers fumble, and I clutch it to my chest to prevent it from hitting the carpet. It seems like injustice rather than divine intervention when the screen lights with a photograph I should've deleted months ago.

Alexander, not quite in profile, his face angled away as

I'd snuck the picture on my way to the bathroom in that Latin club.

I should delete it now.

Instead, I study the sharpness of his cheekbone and the color of his hair. This is the kind of face that stops a girl in her tracks. Not that I think he'd notice, not because he's stupid or oblivious—far from it—but it has probably happened so often, he no longer notices it. I mean, look at how hard I had to work to be seen by him, seen as something other than a woman who needed rescuing. And now he's rescued me twice. Once in the hotel and then by putting me in contact with Sarah Houghton, getting me this job.

Yep, this is a face that is no doubt handsome, but there's an arrogance to the man, too. I'd felt it in the way his hands followed the curves of my body and the command of his mouth on mine. But I won't experience it again, and something tells me I should probably see that as a good thing.

I imagine his haughty look if he could see my thumb hovering over the delete button. *The little trash can.* And with one last look, I tell myself it's for the best as I consign his handsome face to the past.

Delete.

13

ALEXANDER

IT WAS EASIER WHEN SHE WAS A TOURIST. WHEN I KNEW ONLY her first name and the vast country she was flying back to. There was some peace in the realization that I would never see her again. That she would be the kind of obsession that lived only in my head. A fascination without the chance of an outlet. But then I saw her again, and the fascination took a more manic turn. Like an addict just one call away from his dealer, it seems I am constantly just one call away from discovering exactly where she is.

Sometimes, I try to satisfy the craving in other ways. I might recall snippets of our night together. Sometimes whole scenes. Occasionally, my imagination takes me elsewhere, like seeing her at the London house, imagining I'd acted on my impulses, whisking her from the frigidly cold lane to my bedroom upstairs. I mostly try to ignore the temptation. To push all thoughts of her out of my head. But sometimes the enticement is too great.

"You're... a Viking." The sound of her lilting accent seems to come from nowhere, my eyes immediately unseeing on

the papers spread out on the desk in front of me. But I don't have time to indulge in idle fantasies this evening. No time to reminisce. Yet my answer from that night echoes in my head.

"*Is it the beard that gives it away?*" Reaching out, I'd curled a lock of damp hair behind her ear, then trailed my fingers down her bare shoulder.

"*I think you look like a modern-day Viking might look.*" Her hand caught the rasp of stubble on my cheek.

"*Are you trying to say you feel invaded?*" She certainly made me feel like a marauding berserker, though it would take a better man than me to conquer Holland. "*In a good way, I hope.*"

"*It was a thorough campaign,*" she'd said with a satisfied-sounding sigh.

Little did we both know I wasn't done at that point.

"*I think Vikings would be bankers in this century.*" All the stealing, I'd presumed.

"*Possibly,*" I'd answered, though perhaps not on the same wavelength as her.

"*Ah, so you are a banker?*"

"*What makes you say that?*"

"*Because you look like a Viking,*" she'd replied with a laugh. "*Or the son of one.*"

"*Almost.*"

"*How can you be almost a banker, or a son of one?*"

"*I meant that you're only one letter out from describing my father.*"

Her brows contracted before she flashed that delectable dimple, a small smile breaking free as she worked it out. *Banker to wanker.*

"*That's a terrible thing to call a parent.*"

She looked genuinely shocked, but God, she looked so lovely. Naked and lovely, the evidence of our recent shower glistening like diamonds against her silky skin. Her halo of dark hair was stark against the snowy pillow, and she'd curled her hands like an angel beneath her cheek. An angel I'd fucked in the shower less than an hour before, but not before bending her over the vanity, whispering that she should watch as I fingered her. *Until her palm met the mirror and her knees buckled.* I'd needed her to see what I was seeing, to in some way share how special she was to me.

A one-night obsession fulfilled. The nights so much emptier since.

"*Not if it's the truth.*"

"*It's very disrespectful.*" But no more than he deserved. "*Respecting your elders isn't done enough these days.*"

"*Is that what you were doing in the bathroom? Respecting me?*" Because she can respect me on her knees anytime.

"*Not to mention, an* awfully British *insult,*" she'd added in a terrible fake British drawl. I thought she'd ignore the rest when she'd cheekily added, "*I just have an affinity for the elderly.*"

I find myself indulging in a small smile at the recollection. I'd show her elderly, given half the chance. I'd get her to sing the national anthem—hers or mine—in that terrible fake accent just to see if she could reach the end as I tongue fucked her.

My smile slowly falls as I realize that will never happen.

I'm never going to have her again.

I clear my throat in the empty room, beginning to shuffle the papers in front of me. I'm a busy man; I shouldn't be idling in the past. But it seems I have no choice as I hear her voice again.

"*So awfully, awfully British.*"

I close my eyes, and I palm myself over my trousers, unable to resist the lure of her again.

"*You make that sound like a bad thing.*" I'd found myself drawing closer, my lips ghosting her silky shoulder, my fingers drawing lazy circles against her narrow back. "*I can't be all bad, can I?*"

"*Says the man with the killer smolder.*"

"*I wouldn't even know what that looks like,*" I'd crooned, the words whispering over her skin.

"*Don't play the innocent,*" she'd chided, even as her body reacted to my touch, relaxing against me, lengthening like a cat in a patch of sunshine.

"*You sound very like a nanny I once had.*"

"Had *being the operative word?*"

"*A gentleman never kisses*"—pressing my lips to the curve of her breast, I'd allowed my next words to vibrate against her ribs—"*and tells.*"

She gave in to a satisfied-sounding sigh, her next words more purr than anything else.

"*From now on, I think Britishness will be synonymous for dirty to me.*"

"*I hope you mean that endearingly.*"

"*I don't think I'll ever be able to hear the accent without blushing. Not after the shocking things you've said in this bed.*"

My God, her blushes. Just thinking about those twists something inside me.

"*Just the things I've said in the bed?*" I'd teased.

"*And maybe the shower.*" She'd ducked her face into the pillow.

"*Water absolves,*" I'd purred, unable to keep from touching her. "*It washes clean.*"

"*It didn't do such a good job with you.*" From the depths of her pillow, one dark eye had peeped open, a little mascara stained and full of mischief, the cheek not squashed into the pillow a delectable pink.

"*This blush.*" Reaching out, I'd traced the path of heat. "*It gets me every time.*"

"*Gets you what?*" Her taunt was telling. So very telling.

"*It gets me hard.*"

"*Want to watch some* Downton Abbey *with me?*"

"*I'm not sure what that is.*" I know what it is now, of course. And the ten minutes I'd watched wasn't nearly as riveting as it was watching her skin be revealed inch by inch. I'd pulled the sheet down her body so slowly, revealing the flare of her hips and the depressions low on her spine, matching the dimple in her cheek.

"*It's like you're from another world.*"

I remember how I'd paused at that point. She'd no idea how accurate her statement was. Another world far removed from hers. Another world that isn't always hospitable to those not from within.

"*I'm an alien?*" And now, after watching an episode of *Downton Abbey*, I'm not sure alien isn't more flattering.

"*I just mean you're not like most Brits I've come across—*"

"*Do you make a habit of* coming *across British men often?*" I'd pressed my mouth against her bicep, a pulse washing through me as I'd felt muscle there. I'd wanted to push her back, spread her out, discover what other layers I might've missed.

"*Do you turn everything into innuendo?*"

"*Only when I'm enjoying myself. But you're talking about the stereotypes, the tea-drinking, crumpet-eating, polite and mannerly bunch. That's just for the tourists.*"

"*To get the tourists into bed?*"

"*Only heathens eat crumpets in bed, Holland. Just think of the crumbs.*"

She'd giggled then, at least until I'd trailed my fingertip down her spine and over the swell of her buttocks. She had such a magnificent arse, as I recall. What I wouldn't give to have it in my hands again.

"*But as a race, we aren't truly polite. We're nearer to the rude as fuck edge of the scale.*"

"*Which sounds all the more so in that accent.*"

"*I don't have an accent.*"

"*Of course not. But you're just trying to distract me from our game.*"

"*I still think there are much better ways to get to know a person than guessing things about them.*" Much more intimate ways.

"*So you've said. But we're taking a break from physical activities. That was your idea.*"

"*A man of my years—*"

"*Has plenty of fuel left in the tank.*" She'd traced a finger up my chest and over my chin, though snatched it back as I'd made as though to bite.

"*You are very... bite-y.*"

"*I think it's more to do with the meal.*" My gaze meandered once more along her curves, just to be sure she was aware of the exact source of my hunger. "*You didn't seem to mind.*"

"*It wasn't a complaint. It was an observation.*"

"*Then observe how I find myself reinvigorated.*" I'd growled as I'd stretched along the bed, a stretch that became one fluid motion as I'd moved onto my back.

Holland's gaze dipped to where the sheet tented over my erection, her eyes suddenly dark. "*So shameless.*"

"*So says the woman staring.*" I'd run my hand over the sheet-covered head with a groan. "*I do so appreciate a brazen woman.*"

"*So, your father doesn't work in finance.*" Her voice was an octave or two higher, and as I'd turned my head, her gaze lifted from where I stood hard.

"*You don't really want to talk about my father.*" Neither did I. Ever if I can help it. "*Not when you're staring at my cock.*" I'd sent her a look that suggested she think less about my position in life and more about my position in this bed.

"*You're... living off an inheritance?*"

I'd barked out a laugh. On my father's death, lots of things were left to me in trust, but of money, there was very little.

"*You run your own business,*" she suggested next, smiling and warming to her distraction tactics.

"*Are you asking or telling me?*"

"*Telling.*" Her gaze narrowed speculatively. "*I can't imagine you taking instructions.*"

"*I can take instructions. When the conditions are right.*"

"*What conditions are they?*"

"*I should've said it takes the right incentive.*"

"*Y-You're not from London.*" Red-cheeked, she'd glanced away while fighting a smile. "*But you live here.*"

"*What makes you say that?*"

"*I guess because there's something not entirely English about your accent. Something that blurs some of your words around the edges.*"

"*A foreign spy,*" I'd drawled, even as I was struck by her attention to detail. She had an unusual ear for accents.

"*Who? You or me?*" she asked.

"*You blush too much to be a spy.*" I'd settled my hands behind my head. I've always preferred, where I can, to be anonymous, so I brought the conversation back to her again.

"*Or do I?*" she said in some approximation of mysterious.

"*Oh, you definitely do.*" I'd pointedly glanced at the inevitable flush of pink highlighting her cheeks.

"It could be part of my disguise." Her reply was a touch defensive as she'd turned onto her side. Heat licked through my belly, my balls drawing tight as her lush figure was bared to me again. At least until she pulled the sheet over her breasts, catching the edge securely between her arms and ribs

"I think the point of a disguise isn't to draw attention." As though anyone would fail to notice her kiss-plump lips or be captivated by her gorgeous coloring.

"Oh. Come look at the pink-cheeked freak?"

"I thought I was the freaky one." That had been one of her mid-orgasm compliments when I'd gotten a little too close to... I push away the thought. I'm never going to get to explore that part of her. Noticing the papers still in my hands, I straighten them, then rap them sharply against the top of my desk. But Holland's voice whispers to me from my memories again.

"Your turn." She'd pushed herself up to sit, her arm still clamped over the sheet. Not for the first time, I'd noticed her gaze skate over the small tattoo on the inside of my bicep. Roman numerals recording the date my life changed forever. A tattoo to remind me of the responsibilities that fall to me under the heavy chains of my dukedom. But she didn't ask for an explanation, and I would never have uttered the truth.

"So, it's my turn to...?" Before the words were out of my mouth, she'd whipped the sheet away from my cock. It settled parachute-like around my shins. The gust of cool air, her expression, and a world of possibilities made my cock pulse. I'd groaned. It was my turn to do whatever the fuck she'd wanted.

"I can't believe you're hard again." Her whisper sounded a little awe-filled.

"You're suggesting there could be too much of a good thing."

"Only if it falls off, I guess."

I might've laughed but for the fact that she was climbing over me. Her knee had twisted in the sheet and she'd fallen forward, catching herself against my thigh. Five hot points of contact branded my skin, the muscles beneath tautening. Under my head, my fingers clenched against the instinct to reach out. To catch her. To touch her. Because I'd wanted to see how far she'd take this even more.

"*How's it looking down there?*" My voice was a low rumble, my muscles taut with anticipation.

"*All present and accounted for.*" Her warm breath coasted over the sensitive crown of my cock, a sudden pulse making it jerk.

"*Lose the sheet, Holland.*" It's not like it was covering much in the first place. My gaze had dropped from her face to the linens banded to her breasts, then still lower to where it cut across her belly, leaving the rest of her gloriously naked beneath. Even now, so long after the fact, my tongue rolls along my bottom lip as though thirsty to taste her. "*Tell me,*" I'd demanded, "*what my turn means.*"

"*You distracted me. I was going to say it's your turn to guess what I do for a living.*"

"*That's easy,*" I'd purred. "*You're a woman on top.*"

With an inciteful look, she'd gathered her hair over one shoulder. "*Damn straight I am.*"

The knot in my belly tightens, my cock throbbing as I recall how she'd bent forward and flicked her tongue across the wide crown. There's always something beautiful about the moment a woman takes your cock into her mouth. It isn't just in the sensation of her lips wrapped around you, whether she toys or plays with you or sets to sucking the essence right out of you. Any of that is beautiful. Gratifying.

Pleasurable in the extreme. But there's also beauty in the moments before, beauty that sometimes sticks with a man long afterwards. The contrast of slender fingers curled around something so rigid and ruddy. The anticipatory breath as she leans closer and the way her soft lips look stretched around something so unyielding. So severe. It's all about the contrasts, I suppose. But it was so much more at that moment, staring into eyes that were suddenly the color of bitter chocolate. Bitter chocolate with flecks of sweet, sweet caramel.

"*At the risk of sounding like a cheap porno...*" Her eyes shone with a mixture of mischief and delight.

"*You can say it.*" Even now, it makes me smile.

"*No, I don't think I will.*" She'd lowered her head, and our eyes had locked, and the way she slid her tongue along the underside of my cock stole my words and thoughts. I'd groaned, the sound deep and carnal as I'd watched my cock slide into her soft mouth.

"*Holland...*" At the agony in her name, her gaze flicked to mine. Desirous. Darkly dilated. "*You are so beautiful.*" Those full lips stretched wide, the sheet falling from her body. Pulling my hands from behind my head, I slid them into her hair, not because she needed any direction but because I needed the connection, needed to see her face as her hair fell around it like a veil. "*You suck my cock so beautifully.*"

Her soft groan was an exquisite layer of sensation, signaling a change of tempo as she began to work me deeper, wetter. Her hand wrapped firmly at the root, stroking where her messy mouth couldn't reach.

"*That's it, darling.*" One hand still twisted in her hair, I'd stroked her cheek as she stared up at me. "*Take me. Take me all the way in.*"

My God. Her mouth. Her tongue. Those dark, shining

eyes. The dark cascade of hair tantalizing my thigh, tautening the muscles there. I could barely stand it. I wanted her so badly. *I want her now.*

"*Get up here.*" I'd slid my hand under her arm, coaxing her higher. "*I need to be inside you.*" Eyes screwed tight, I'd conjugated a few verbs in Latin as a distraction to this feeling tightening my balls. "*Kiss me,*" I demanded, winding my hand around her nape, pulling her lips down to mine for a punishing kind of kiss.

"*I've changed my mind,*" she whispered, her color high. "*It's not your turn.*" Pressing her hands to mine, she'd linked our fingers, and I'd allowed her to press them back against the pillow. For all her strong words, a rapid pulse flickered in the base of her throat right before her mouth came over mine. A press of lips. A teasing swipe of her tongue. Her teeth settling over her bottom lip, hard enough to make me buck under her with a groan.

"*Now who's bite-y?*"

But her only answer was to press her teeth to my jaw. My body reacted under hers, her beautiful curves responding in turn.

"*Am I hurting you?*" she asked, her whisper ending in a playful curl.

"*Harder,*" I grunted as her teeth grazed my neck. My spine arched as she sucked over my pulse, and my cock brushed against her wetness. "*Holland, fuck me.*" My fingers tightened on hers as her kisses pulled against the skin of my collarbones. God, the sweet scent of her hair and the temptation of her pussy made me feel fucking deranged.

She rose above me, lithe and sinuous, her hand sliding between her legs. Her lashes flickered, her eyes rolling closed as she pressed my cock against the warm, wet ribbon of her flesh. I hissed out a curse as my body twisted under hers.

The soft slickness of her acceptance.

The hot grip of her walls.

The surge of her body above me.

I felt like I was truly coming undone, unravelling at the seams.

Heat began to twist inside me, my balls drawing tight as I'd wrapped my arms around her back and flipped her under me. At least, I think that was *my* plan. But not hers. On my knees, one hand braced against the wall, the other bound her to me as my movements became wild and frantic. My mind was a haze of pure red, the need to own her something darker and harder than I've ever felt. Amazingly, she accepted this frenzy, her arms wrapped around my neck and her heels at my back.

"*Oh, my God. I can't believe it's happening again.*" There was a tremor in her voice, her disbelief, the second before her body began to throb around me. And it was in that moment of awe-filled amusement when everything ceased to make sense. Life, the bed, the room around us blurring around the edges.

"*Fuck...*"

With my last remaining brain cell, I'm sure, I'd realized the risk we were taking. The risk *I* was taking. There is no room for a child in my life, let alone a woman.

Lowering her back to the bed, I began to pull out, probably going cross-eyed as Holland's internal muscles clenched around my cock, determined to keep me there. I pressed my lips to hers and took my glistening cock in my hand. Not a moment later, I began to come undone, painting her body's blushes with lashes of my cum.

Back in the room with the clock ticking and the birds

singing from the branch of a tree outside, I drop the papers to the desk as I press my head to my hands.

I've got to stop doing this.

For the sake of my sanity.

For the sake of my throbbing balls.

I sit back with a groan, pressing the heel of my palm against my poor aching cock, looking up as the door to the office opens.

"Did you say something?" Portia asks, her hand wrapped around the door as though she'd like to come in but won't without an invitation.

"No." My voice sounds hoarse, my hand frozen on my crotch. Move it, and I might look like I've been having a little fun alone time. Or as Portia might see it, that I've locked myself in my study to interfere with myself. Emphasis on self.

Why, when I'm here, I can almost hear her say. She'd take it as a personal affront.

"Oh. Well, are you going to be in here very much longer?"

"No. Not too much longer." Why do our conversations seem so stilted?

"You've been gone an age. Bad enough that you didn't pick me up for dinner," she adds with a bright smile, "but then you abandon me in favor of work."

"I didn't abandon you." She turned up here when I thought we'd agreed to meet at the restaurant. "Picking you up would imply this was a date. It would imply we meant something to each other."

That was unkind. Snide even. But must we keep dancing around this? Is she waiting for an offer of marriage or for me to give her the flick?

Portia flushes and straightens her dress, then,

completely ignoring the implication of my words, tells me she'll wait for me downstairs.

As the door to the room closes, I drag a tired hand down my face as I wonder why I'd sought to call her at all. We haven't spent time together since before my birthday. And by that, I mean she'd neither spent the night in my bed nor been fucked. Not by me, at least. *Perhaps she's been fucked by someone else.* I'm unsurprised that the thought doesn't appear to matter to me. Once, I'd thought we'd suit each other. We come from the same backgrounds and understand marriage is often for convenience rather than love. And whatever happened between us, I knew she wouldn't go running to the tabloid newspapers. That she's still here makes me wonder if perhaps she didn't believe me when I said I'd never marry again.

I look up once more as Portia's head appears around the door to my study again, almost as though she's afraid to come in.

"John is here with the car," she murmurs.

I nod, and she retreats. With a weary sigh, I begin to close my laptop. Portia seems to think my recent milestone birthday has left a melancholic, lingering effect. I'm sure my friends think the same. I can't say they're entirely wrong, though they aren't right either because the experience of turning forty might be something that's messed with my head. Nudged my equilibrium. But it isn't the prospect of getting old that fills me with dread. Instead, what has left me feeling out of sorts and perhaps even a little bereft is the knowledge that I'll never turn forty again. And by that, I mean I'll never have the opportunity again to spend the night with Holland.

Pushing back my chair, I stand and slip on my jacket, and slide my phone into the inside pocket of my jacket. I've got to push past this ennui. Maybe a change of scenery would help. Tuscany is always nice this time of year. Or maybe I should do something radical, like propose to Portia. She'd place no demands on my time or my life and help run the estates. Given that we're no longer fucking, it might just be the next logical step.

14

HOLLY

Holy moly. It's cold in here.

I stare at myself in the bathroom mirror, or rather, I stare at the dark circles under my eyes. It had taken me forever to drift off to sleep last night thanks to the unfamiliar bed and the eerie quiet of my surroundings. It's odd to think I'd have trouble sleeping when my previous bed literally rattled every time a bus trundled past my bedroom window. Hooting owls and random creaks shouldn't have been such an issue. But it might've started with the bath after I'd discovered what an immersion heater is: it's something that's complete crap. The faucet (why are there two?) had barely spluttered out four inches of water before running cold.

Most uncomfortable bath *ever!*

Bad enough that there isn't a shower—which will make hair washing fun—without rationing the hot water. And the daylight hasn't improved my accommodation, either. Not only does the heating seem to be on the fritz, but the place hasn't seen a lick of paint since the 1980s. Chintz I can cope with—I just need some heat!

After pulling on more layers than a late spring morning should need, I inhale a breakfast of coffee and toast, making a note to thank whoever provided enough groceries to get me through the next few days. Then I pull a chunky knit sweater over my tank, T-shirt, and black jeans, before slipping on my pristine white Kate Spade sneakers. *Casual but stylish,* I decide. Whatever the dress code usually is, I'm sure this will do for now. It's a little after 10.30 in the morning when I venture outside, figuring I should maybe find Lady Isla, seeing as no one has called yet to take me to her.

Pulling the blue (paint-peeled) door closed behind me, I lock it. I'd found the key on the coffee table last night, resting in a leaf shaped out of glass. Sliding it and my phone into my back pockets, I set off at a purposeful pace because decisive is a good look, even on someone who has no idea where they're going.

Gravel crunches underfoot as I make my way past the row of cottages, each of them a little tidier and homier than mine. Pots sit on windowsills brimming with blooms, mats in front of doors that bid guests a warm welcome. At the end of the row, I slip under an archway. A sign points back the way I came that reads NO ENTRY.

Out in the open, the hills in the distance are the kind of vibrant green that has to be seen to be believed. From a distance, they look like they're coated with a deep green velvet, though darker in the valleys and almost the color of a Shiraz. A grey lacy blanket of cloud enveloping their summits.

I startle as crows caw as I pass a set of honest-to-goodness stocks—the contraption that thieves were kept in. A hole for a head and wrists, like ye olde handcuffs. I'm sure this is a modern-day addition to the castle, built to look the part, but the murder of crows sitting along its edges seems pretty authentic.

If not a little ominous.

Unless they're on the payroll, too.

I push on, following the path as it widens and skirts around the edge of the castle walls heading towards well, I'm not sure what it is, but it looks kind of commercial. I quicken my step as it starts to rain, cursing the fact that I didn't think to bring my jacket as the weather changes in an instant from *starting to rain* to *really going for it.*

"Heckin' hell," I mutter, almost bursting through the first door I come to, adding, "Oh, hi!" when I realize I'm not alone.

"I was just about to come for ye," Chrissy says, looking up from the cell phone in her hand. "Lady Isla is running a wee bit behind, so she thought I could give you a tour of the castle. I know you won't be working here exactly, but it'll be good for ye to have a sense of your surroundings."

"That sounds great. I'd love a tour." Who doesn't love snooping around other people's houses?

"And it'll save you the twelve pounds entrance fee," she adds, her eyes sparkling.

"I'm all for saving money. And staying out of the rain."

"Och, that's no' rain," she says dismissively. "It's just a wee shower."

"The scenery is beautiful," I say, gazing out through the glass doors at the brooding hills.

"Aye. It's bonny, no matter the time of year."

I'm not sure about bonny, but it's certainly striking. "The hills look so purple. Surely that can't just be heather?" It seems far too vivid a color.

"Aye, the color comes from heather growing in the glens.

It seems to enjoy the weather more than most," she adds, her tone droll. "Come along, then. This way."

I follow Chrissy down a stone-flagged hall as she points out the estate offices, storage areas, and the security room. "At the other end of the castle is the entrance for paying visitors, the car park and such like."

"The castle and gardens have been open since April, right?" And the private residence is nowhere I imagine I'll need to know about.

"That's right. The castle and the gardens open at the beginning of April. We get a fair number of visits during the week, but more during the weekend. And school holidays can be very busy." She points out an oil painting of the current duke's father halfway up a very grand (and original, I'm reliably told) staircase.

"Does the duke's family live nearby?" I imagine a ducal family has a lot of real estate to choose from. I can't imagine he'd live here, not with *common folk* wandering around having paid to gawk. I'm sure his ancestors would stroke out at the thought. Or maybe that would be suffer an apoplexy.

"No. Sandy, that is, his grace, the duke," she says with a slight tint to her cheeks, "lives in London mostly. Though he does a lot of business in America and Europe, so I understand. Lady Isla lives no' so far away with her wee family. She has offices in the castle, so we see a fair bit of her. That's not to say his grace is never here. He's no absentee landlord, y'ken. We do see him during the season, though more so when the house is closed to the public over the winter."

I can imagine. Rich or not, I wouldn't like to watch people tramping through my house. "I didn't realize the duke and duchess were divorced."

"Och, they're not divorced," she says with a chuckle.

"They're siblings. Twins, in fact. And a nicer pair you couldn't wish to meet. This is them."

We stop at a painting that's at least one and a half times my height, the frame gilt and ornate. It depicts a pair of fair-headed children, the images as vibrant and as real as any photograph. The pair are aged around eight or nine, the girl sitting on a high-backed chair with a book on her lap and an overweight Labrador lying at her feet. To her left stands her brother in profile, the twist of his lips almost familiar. I guess it must be the look of a sibling about to annoy that I recognize.

"It's lovely." It's hard to guess at the pair's current ages by the painting alone. They might be anywhere between thirty and sixty, given their clothing. A pretty blue dress with smocking and Mary Janes for the girl. Long pants and a white shirt for the boy.

"Aye," she replies with a sigh. "I hope Lady Isla's wee ones turn out to be as devoted to each other as these two."

Ah, so *wee boys* mean the pair are on the younger side. Young enough to have kids, at least.

"Does the duke have children?"

"No." Chrissy angles her glance away. "That is, he's widowed. He and his wife, God rest her soul, weren't blessed with children."

"Oh, how sad." I turn back to the boy in the painting, my heart aching a little for the suffering he would've grown to endure. "Did it happen very long ago?"

"It'll be eight years now." She turns back to me, all business then. "The family's private residence is that way." She gives a vague wave of her hand. "And there has been a Dalforth in Kilblair castle since 1502."

"A Dalforth?" I repeat uncertainly.

"That's the family name," she answers as though

obvious. "Also the name of the dukedom and the land hereabouts. The current duke is the 13th Duke of Dalforth." Bully for him, I guess. "Though the family's fortunes might've risen and fallen over the centuries, and one or two of them might've lost their heads, literally mind, the family still owns the castle. There aren't many aristocratic families who can say the same in this day and age."

"I guess not," I agree, feeling the need, if not the sentiment.

"You know, there's a castle over in Morar where the heir to the Baronial seat—the future baron—sells tickets in the ticketing booth. I've seen him myself with a broom in his hand," she adds in a scandalized tone.

"Some might call that progress." Some being me, maybe. The British royal family seems quaint and all, and they're good for tourism in the capital city, but I just don't buy into the idea of a noble elite just because some ancestor fought for this king or that. Or whored out his wife because the current king took a liking to her.

That's why my ancestors fought for independence, I guess.

Chrissy turns sharply, her white bob as sharp as knives at her jaw. "Not me." She eyes me like one of the crows sitting on the stocks I'd passed outside. "I've served this family for thirty-five years, and my mother before me, and hers before that. This place might not belong to me, but it's as much a part of my family history as it is the current duke, a man of honor and principle, no matter what others might say about him."

That in itself tells me more than I need to know. It's probably best I keep my mouth closed. I don't want to end up in the stocks with only crows for company. Maybe the odd rotten tomato or two.

"That would be the thirteenth duke? My, what a beautiful fireplace." *Maybe flattery will work*, I think, as I stare up at the mantel that is also taller than me. I wonder who dusts the thing.

"Aye, that's right." Chrissy preens like a hen fluffing her feathers, like the duke was her kid, not her employer. "It is himself that turned this place around after it was left to rack and ruin by the duke before him." She gives a slow, sad shake of her head.

"His father." Just checking.

"He was an eejit. God rest his soul," she adds hurriedly, her mouth pinching with disapproval. "The same for his father before him, if truth be told. Between you and me, the twelfth duke didn't leave his son with a pot to piss in. Back then, we were all owed back wages fir lookin' after the place. Meanwhile, he swanned around the world chasing girls half his age, leavin' misbegotten—" She halts quite suddenly, sending me a quelling look like I'd encouraged her to gossip about the people she works for who she may or may not respect. "Anyway, the current duke made his fortune trading on the stock markets. Apparently, he was a wiz at it, straight out of university. Though Lord only knows how much it'll take to bring this place back to its heyday state. Well, Him and the builders."

It looks like Chrissy's allegiance is to the dukedom or maybe the castle, but not the duke. Excluding the current duke because the sun shines out of his ass, apparently.

"When was its heyday?" I ask, glancing at the suits of armor flanking the arch we're walking towards. This place may be centuries older than the cottage I slept in last night, but it's in much better shape. Wood gleams, and the lights sparkle overhead, the scent of beeswax polish and ancient stone permeating the place. It's hard to put into words, but the place smells alive, not dead, no matter when its prime was.

"Probably sometime back when those over there had actual bodies in them," she says, following my gaze to the shiny suits.

Yikes! "Back when boiling oil was a visitor's deterrent?"

Chrissy just laughs, then points out an iron railing to the right of the wall. "You can see the dungeons down there."

I make my way over the small square of railings that stand a little lower than chest height. Leaning over, I release a long breath as I stare down at the square cut into the stone floor. Covered with glass, I see nothing but my own reflection, not that this is enough to stop the hairs on the nape of my neck from lifting.

"That just blows my mind." I can't even imagine living in a place, eating, drinking sleeping, knowing that downstairs, humans once faced horrors beyond my imagination. Imprisonment. Fear. Torture. Speaking of torture, "Chrissy, did you hear the screeching last night? It sounded like a woman was being murdered. I mean, I know that wasn't really what was happening, unless someone was committing a massacre." Because the noise went on and on.

"Peacocks," she mutters, as though this were a curse word.

"Oh." Enough said. Chrissy is not a fan of the peacocks.

"Come along, then," she says, her expression changing from murderous to content in the blink of an eye.

I dutifully (and eagerly) follow Chrissy out of the space, thankful to get away from the topic of peacocks as well as the sad souls dancing on my grave. *As the saying goes.*

As we continue our whistle-stop tour, she points out rooms included in the visitor ticket pass. Though we don't pause long enough for my satisfaction, I'm sure there will be other opportunities. We tread the worn carpets of the long gallery, which looks exactly as it sounds to be. The lengthy room is filled with portraits of the castle's previous inhabitants, depicting faces and fashions from eras long passed. There's a huge room, the stateroom, which features a fireplace I could almost stand up in and carved with the family crest, the walls concealed by faded tapestries depicting battles and hunting scenes. *Nothing says relax and put up your feet like the portrayal of death and destruction.* Next comes a huge dining room set for a formal dinner for thirty, then a lady's parlor, her embroidery still lying on the arm of a chair as though she had only just stepped out of the room. Quickly following comes an opulent salon, then a pretty sitting room. The rooms seem to go on and on.

"The place is huge."

"That it is. And there have been some grand parties held here over the years." She sounds wistful as she stares almost unseeingly at another grand fireplace, this one big enough to roast an ox. "Important families and foreign dignitaries. Even the Queen."

"Wow! The Queen? Was her visit recent?"

"No, it was some years back. Back when Prince Charles wore short trousers. My mother worked here back then. Her granny was in service here before her. Oh, the tales she had to tell. In those days, over a hundred servants were holding this place together."

"How many work here now?"

"Fifteen."

I stop in my tracks. A house this size, not to mention the land, running on a staff of fifteen? I hurry after Chrissy as she turns a corner, then reaches out to push against what looks like a wall. It's actually a door. A door that leads to a passageway with a serviceable green carpet and plain painted white walls. "We call this the backstairs."

"For the servants?"

She nods in agreement.

"Not to be seen or heard, so they just arrive in the room like magicians?" She frowns, and as I don't want to annoy or offend, I return to the previous topic. "How does a house this size survive with fifteen staff? I mean, how does all the work get done?"

"Not by magic," she replies pointedly. "Most of the traditional service roles were done away with by technology. Indoor plumbing made chambermaids obsolete, and electricity and central heating did away with the housemaids. Modern kitchen appliances meant kitchen and scullery maids were no longer necessary. We have a maintenance team of four. You'll probably see them around the place. Then Cameron heads up the grounds staff. I'm in charge of keeping the house shipshape, including the rooms and exhibits. Mari helps me out, as does wee Sophie, and Mari works in the education center, too." Just great. Mari, who wants my cottage and job. "The pair also help keep the private residence in order. Then there are the lot who runs the souvenir shop and the café."

"So, gone are the days of butlers, valets, and ladies' maids." Yeah, so, I might have read a regency romance book a time or two. Maybe more. I'll never tell. And neither will Nana's racy reading selections, even if I had begun appropriating her Mills & Boon bodice rippers from the age of twelve.

"Oh, we still have a butler. Mr. McCain. A proper stickler he is, for all he's only a young man. He travels with himself, that is, the duke, along with the chef, and of course, the duke's personal assistant. He also usually arrives with a few friends," she adds with a tired-looking smile.

"Just three of you take care of cleaning this whole place?" I ask, thinking of the massive staircase and the vacuuming, dusting, and polishing that must need. How can anyone afford to heat a place like this, let alone keep it clean? Which might answer a few questions about why my cottage was so cold last night, not to mention why the hot water was rationed.

"It's no' so bad. We all do our bit, and we also have a cleaning company contracted to keep on top of things."

We make our way along the very plain hallway, then down a much less fancier set of stairs than the ones we walked up earlier.

"And here we have the kitchen," she says, pushing on a modern fire door. "I thought we'd have a cuppa while we wait for Lady Isla to arrive."

"Sounds good." I hope they have coffee. Tea is okay for warming your hands, but nothing says *bing!* like coffee.

The kitchen is something else. One entire wall is taken up with an antique yet pristine oven range. Four double-doored ovens gleam black, and countless copper pots hang from the wall behind, polished to the kind of sheen you can see your face in. The rest of the kitchen is equally as striking but much more serviceable. Burr walnut cabinetry and marble countertops, a commercial range with all the gadgets. A scrubbed pine table, easily twelve feet long, sits under three high fan-shaped windows with an assortment of mismatched chairs gathered around it. Other than the range, the only modern appliance in view is a commercial-sized refrigerator at the far side of the room.

"Is this a working kitchen?" I watch as Chrissy pulls

open a kitchen cabinet to reveal an electric kettle, teapot, and other tea trappings.

"Dougal, the chef, uses it to cater for large groups. Formal dinners, weekend guests, and the like. But when S— when his grace is here by himself or with a smaller party, Dougal usually cooks in the family kitchen. "Tea or coffee?"

"Coffee, please."

She pulls out a fancy-looking French press—*yes!*—as she goes on to discuss how many days a year the castle is open to the public and how popular the gardens are. Every inch of this place seems to make money, the gift shop and coffee shop are weekend cash cows, and the dower house—traditionally used for the widow of the last duke—is rented out for weddings. She also tells me a little about how a couple of Hollywood elites recently stayed while the castle was used as a location for an upcoming blockbuster movie.

"I tell you, that Dylan Duffy is as easy on the eyes as he is on the big screen. And what lovely manners his wee ones have."

"He was here with his family?"

"Stayed in the dower hoose," she says, her accent slipping on *house* as she pushes on the plunger. The delicious scent of the dark roast is just heavenly. "Milk?" she asks, making her way over to the fridge.

"A little, please."

"There was him, his gorgeous wife, who is Scots herself, and their two laddies." Grabbing a glass bottle of milk, she turns back. "They were here for weeks. Oh, I've just remembered, Dougal made some Dundee cake last time he was here. It's in yonder pantry." She puts down the milk, indicating the wall behind me. "Grab it, would you, hen? We'll make this our elevenses."

I push back my chair, resisting the urge to cluck, feeling

a little tickled at her form of address. Elevenses I can handle, especially in the form of cake. "This one?" I ask, looping my fingers around the door handle.

"No, that's the larder. The other wall. Aye, that's it. On the shelf with the bread, I think."

While still wondering what the *larder* might be, I see the pantry is more like another room, lined with shelves along with every baking ingredient, herb, spice, and condiment known to man.

"It's like a supermarket in here," I call back, scanning the thick wooden shelves.

"Dougal keeps it well-stocked." Chrissy's voice sounds like she's very far away. "Just don't mess with his organization, or you'll feel the lashing of his tongue."

"It's been a while since I've had that pleasure," I murmur, though I refuse to indulge in thoughts of Alexander. *You're in another country now. Put that awkwardness behind you.* That would be the awkwardness of seeing him again because the good Lord knows nothing was awkward about his tongue game. "Crackers, biscuits also known as cookies..." My finger trails in the air, following the stacked shelves. "Porridge oats, vanilla pods, rose water, and..." This is a strange filing system. "Ah!"

I pull down a battered enameled tub that looks like something cake might be stored in. As I pull off the lid, the rich aroma of whisky and sugar tells me not only that it is, but it also tells me that Dundee cake is a fruit cake. Caramel-colored, the delicious concoction is decorated with nothing but a daisy-looking circle of almonds.

Get in my mouth!

Turning back to the door, I'm about to call out that I've found it when somewhere in the kitchen, a door slams. The sound is quickly followed by a woman's tearful voice.

"Oh, Chrissy. I've done it! I've left him."

"Och, come here, my love. There, there. You get it all out."

Heart-rending sobs fill the room as I pause at the pantry doorway, not sure what to do. Stay? Go? Either way, I have cake.

"I c-caught him at it, the bastard." Between her sobs, I make out that the woman's accent is English and as smooth and polished as glass. I'm not sure why I expected Lady Isla to be Scottish. That's assuming this is who she is. "W-With the nanny, of all people."

Oh, fudge.

Maybe I'll just stay here, I think, hugging the cake tin to my stomach. But I'm not guilty by association. I'm not even here in the capacity of the nanny. I begin to push on the door, hoping to sneak out when Chrissy catches my eye over the top of the other woman's head, currently pressed into her shoulder. She whispers something into her ear, something that makes the woman's shoulders stiffen.

"I'll, erm. I'll just put this here and catch you some other time." Taking a step into the kitchen, I put the cake tin on the countertop when Lady Isla turns around.

Dark blue eyes stare back at me. The fact that they're red-rimmed and swollen does nothing to diminish her beauty.

"No, really. It's all right." She swipes her fingers under her eyes, laughing unhappily as she uses the back of her hand under her nose. "You must be Holly." I nod as she laughs again, obviously thinking better of offering me her hand.

"Come and sit down, hen," Chrissy says, her hands on the other woman's shoulders as she steers her onto a kitchen chair near the window.

Making myself useful, I pour out three coffees and one tea, just in case, and even slice the cake, reluctant to intrude on the pair's quiet murmurs. The first day at any new job can be awkward, even uncomfortable, but avoiding those red-rimmed eyes will be tough. *I hate being a sympathetic crier.*

"Dougal used more than a dram of whisky in this." Lady Isla's words are filled with a forced brightness, yet not one of us is unaware of how she chews that first mouthful without tasting. The rest of her cake, she mostly crumbles into crumb with her fork.

"Aye, he makes a good cake," Chrissy agrees, having eaten hers already.

"It's very nice." I put down my fork carefully. "Maybe I should go." My eyes dart back and forth between the two, Chrissy seeming to agree, judging by the subtle but appreciative tilt of her head.

"No." Isla takes a gulp of tea the color of red brickwork before putting her mug back down again. "I think I might need your help."

I feel myself frowning, then silently curse myself as words tumble out of my mouth. "But I've only just gotten here?"

"I read the references from your previous employer. Wonderful, really. We're lucky to have you here at Kilblair."

"That's very nice of you to say, but—"

"Please, let me finish." She smiles tightly, balling her hands in her lap. "What you just heard, I'm sure I can rely on your discretion."

"Of course. That goes without saying." And without the protection of a signed NDA. I would never air another woman's dirty laundry in public.

"Thank you." She swallows, her words bright but brittle.

"I have left my husband today. In some haste after finding him in bed with our nanny." A frown ripples across her expression. "I found them in our bed, as a matter of fact."

"That sleekit coward," Chrissy bursts out, her first interjection to the most awkward of conversations. "I knew he was nay good the first time I laid my eyes on him." Her accent thickens as she folds her arms under her chest. "The first time he shook ma' hand, something told me I should count ma' fingers afterwards!"

"I wish I'd had your foresight," Isla offers noncommittally. "Then it wouldn't just be my fingers I'd need to check at this point."

Ack! This poor woman.

"Love makes fools of us all, hen. But I'll give him fingers," Chrissy mutters malevolently. "Right around his scrawny wee neck."

"Holly." Isla draws her shoulders higher, struggling against tears, striving for dignity. "I'll come to the point. I find I no longer need my husband. I do, however, need a nanny. Need one quite desperately at this point. I was hoping we could come to some arrangement."

Oh. Well.

15

HOLLY

I pull back the heavy drapes and stare over the expanse of rolling lawns. It's a lovely view but one distorted by the old-fashioned glass windowpanes. Much of the landscape around the castle is mountainous, the beauty of the land darkly foreboding and very much in line with a fortress. By land or by sea, it'd be difficult to storm this place. I press my elbow to the windowsill and my chin to my fist. I guess the gardens were a later addition, for who had time for pleasure walks when your enemies were at your door? Or sailing boats along your coast.

"Those poor gardeners must spend most of their summer mowing the dang grass," I murmur to myself, my breath fogging the cool glass. "It's just like home." Because it's raining. Again. Just for a change. Very much like the weather in Mookatill, Oregon, the weather forecast in this part of Scotland is surely a variation on a theme.

Rain.

Mist.

Drizzle.

Mizzle. That one is a Scot's word, not Oregonian.

The only variance this week has been the color of the clouds, which has been a veritable rainbow assortment. Thundery grey, secretive silver, ominous black, promising blue, and every color in between. Okay, maybe not every color, but yesterday, we were blessed with some spectacular sunset-dyed pink clouds. It was a beautiful way to end the day.

I sigh again.

Rain, rain, drip-in and a drop-in, I keep hope-in you'll be stop-in.

But I mainly hope in vain.

But at least inside is warm. Not only warm but sumptuous now that I'm an actual inhabitant of Kilblair Castle, and I have been for three weeks. As the new (sometime) nanny of the duke's nephews, I've been given a room that's at least as big as my last apartment, complete with not only an adjoining bathroom but a small sitting room. What's more, I'm getting paid a full-time salary for part-time hours, and that's in addition to what I'm paid for running the castle's education center.

To recap, I might not like the weather, but I'm liking being here!

"Holly!" A little fist pounds against the door to my room. "Holly, it's Archie. Please let me in."

Isla's kids, Archie and Hugh, are six and eight respectively, and more well-behaved boys I have yet to meet. They're polite and respectful and have such beautiful manners. For instance, I've never had a six-year-old open a door for me before, never mind one that insists, *ladies first*. Looking after these gentlemen in short form is a dream. They could teach grown men a thing or two, for sure.

"What's up, Arch?" I ask, swinging the door open.

"You have to come quick!" Reaching for my hand, he begins to tug.

"Friend, I still have my pajamas on." With my other hand, I indicate said pajamas with a flourish.

"Aren't you too old for Cinderella?"

"You're never too old to want to be a Disney Princess. But that's beside the point, it's barely six thirty!" I'm surprised I'm up at all because my bed is *so* comfortable.

"Please, Holly. Come quickly. It's Hugh. He's hurt himself on the stairs and smashed into something really hard."

"Oh, no. What did he do?" I hurry out into the hallway, ignoring the fact that I'm currently wearing the kinds of jammies that most five-year-old's would be embarrassed to be seen in. I mean, I'll defend my right to wear them, but that doesn't mean I want to be seen in them. As the door slams behind me, Archie's fingers tighten on mine as he begins to pull. "Where's your mom?"

Isla—*no need to use so formal an address*, so she's insisted—usually takes care of the boys in the morning. I take over at eight, beginning with the school run.

"She's in her room. She says her contact lenses are making her eyes watery, but we know she's been crying. Daddy called this morning," he adds, his tone morose. But he's still hustling, his blue school shirt untucked and flapping from the back of his pants. "I told him not to do it. I said he'd hurt, and now he's lying at the bottom of the stairs, probably dead!"

"Holy fudge!" I mutter, overtaking the kid as my heart tries to escape from my ribcage. My sock-clad feet skid on the shining floorboards as we race through the long gallery, littered now with a badminton net, a football, and a pair of rollerblades. Past bedrooms and parlors, and out onto the landing, I almost barrel into the banister. Hand flattened to my chest, I give thanks that the kid isn't dead because there, at the very base of the grand and ancient staircase, sits a dazed but smiling Hugh, rubbing his head. Next to him lies a piece of statuary that once stood in a row of them. On black marble pedestals, the whole lot of them would look right at home placed next to the Elgin Marbles in the British Museum in London. Though this one had been in better condition than those antiquities... until it very recently lost its head.

"Hugh, I'm glad you're not dead," his little brother shouts over the banister.

"I'm glad you didn't get mum," he calls back with an impish grin.

"Watch it!" Wrapping my hand in the younger boy's shirt, I pull him back from where his arms are dangling over the burnished handrail, just in case he decides to take a shortcut. "One near death before breakfast is all I can take."

"I'm not nearly dead," Hugh happily calls back.

"Only because I haven't gotten down there yet," I mutter under my breath, setting Archie away from the sheer drop. No wonder families were so big back in the day. With houses like this one, they probably needed to keep more than one spare for the heir. "What happened?" I begin to trip down the stairs two at a time, my heart rate still galloping. I'm relieved that he's talking, but the statue!

"I slid down the stairs on a tray," he answers as though this fact were completely obvious. And maybe it is obvious once I notice the large silver serving tray a few feet away from him. Probably real silver. Almost certainly an antique.

"Oh, my Lord, have you had Pop-Tarts for breakfast? The amphetamines of the breakfast world?"

"We're not allowed Pop-Tarts," Hugh answers, his tone more than a little awed. "They're not healthy."

"And careening down a staircase with your butt strapped to a kitchen tray is?"

"It wasn't strapped. I just sat on it. Do you think that would help next time?"

"Next time? Friend, do you need your head rattled?"

"Nope. I think I already did that this morning," he says, fake shaking it between his hands.

"Why?" I fall to my knees in front of him. Why now? Why with me? I mean, technically, the boys aren't under my charge at this hour, but I am not going to kick their mother while she's down. I might not have a husband, but I know what betrayal feels like. In the three weeks that I've been here, I've seen firsthand the effects of her husband's infidelity. She was slim three weeks ago, but now she looks like a bag of bones. I know she's hurting, and I hate that I know what it takes to come back from it. So no, I'm not passing the buck on this one. Let the woman cry and blame her contact lenses.

"I did it because Uncle Sandy said it was fun. He said he did it lots when he was a boy. I've been dying to give it a try because our stairs at home aren't as big as these."

"Dying to try it? Dying, really? Hugh, you might've gotten your wish! And do your stairs at home have a hallway with badly placed heirlooms?" Despite my grumbling complaints and the now headless Greek-looking statue, my concern is centered on Hugh as I run my hands over the back of his head, then down his shoulders and arms. "Archie said he thought you passed out." *No major lumps or bumps present, thank God.*

"I was laughing. Silently. It was amazing, Holly!" His blue eyes are as wide as saucers, but his pupils are, thankfully, even and not at all dilated.

"Did you hit your head?"

"Nope. Not even a little bit."

"You're sure?" He gives an adamant shake of it that almost makes *my* head hurt. "No headache? Ringing in your ears?"

"I just bumped my knees on this." He taps the tall pedestal the statue once stood on. "Really, I'm fine," he insists with a dazed but happy smile.

"Okay." I blow out a relieved breath. "I'm pleased to see you have all your arms and legs in the right places, though I'm not sure about your brain." I suddenly feel sorry for his mother because something tells me this is the start of his career as an adrenaline junky.

"He hasn't got any brains." Archie giggles as he reaches the bottom of the staircase. "Uncle Sandy is going to flip when he sees what you've broken."

"Maybe he won't." The older boy's smile falters. "Maybe he'll be too busy worrying about Mummy when he sees how sad she is." While his mom is trying hard to protect them both from the truth, Hugh seems to have an eight-year-old's understanding of what she's going through.

"Maybe we can fix it before your uncle gets back." This elusive duke, the absentee overlord, who I imagine to be dark-haired, portly, and the future sufferer of gout. "First things first, we need to hide it." Before Chrissy and the crew start work. Chrissy won't tell, I don't think, but Mari is another story. That bitch has got it in for me. In her eyes, not only did I get her job, but I also got a much better one on top. One that has brought me in from the cottage she'd apparently coveted to the castle itself. "Come on, let's get you up." Hugh grabs my offered hand, and I pull him to his feet. He seems pretty steady, so I turn to the next casualty. "What do you suppose his name is?"

"Unfortunate." Hugh snickers, toeing a chip of marble by his foot.

"It is an unfortunate day when you lose your head," I agree, picking up the decapitated piece. "*Oof.* This one's got rocks in his head."

"It is an unfortunate day when you lose your willie," Archie asserts.

"His what?" My head whips around to what I thought was a stray chip of marble on the floor. "Unfortunate is right," I agree, picking up the offending piece. *Pieces?* "It doesn't look like he had a lot to lose in the first place."

The boys set off laughing. I'm not sure if the sound is infectious or this is the way my body sees fit to rid itself of an excess of adrenaline because, before long, I've joined them and have tears streaming down my face.

"Oh, my gosh. That is enough. We have to clean up this place before we get found out."

"You mean you're not going to tell?" Archie asks, his voice small.

"It's okay, Holly. I did this," his brother says, squaring his shoulders. "I should own up to it."

"Well, that's very noble of you, Hugh. But maybe you want to save your explanations for another day. I think your mom has enough to cope with today with those pesky contact lenses." I send him a speaking look which he seems to understand.

"Well, if you're sure. Of course, I will own up to it. I'll explain to Mother another day."

Mother. How grown-up he's trying to be. I find I'm biting the insides of my cheeks to stop myself from smiling.

"Meanwhile, I'll just hang on to this, I think." I pocket the tiny penis and almost tread on the tiny testicles.

"The man with the broken boaby." Archie chortles.

"Boaby?" I repeat, looking down at the thing in my hand.

"Watch out for his balls!" Hugh calls out, which is something I never thought to hear yelled within these hallowed walls.

So I pocket the balls, along with the statue's unfortunate and tiny phallus (also known as his boaby, apparently) before setting to work clearing up the evidence.

"We need to get this block of rock shifted."

"Actually, that's a marble pedestal."

"Thanks for the clarification, Hugh." I put the decapitated head down by the stairs. "Arch, open that door, please."

Archie dashes over to a door in the wooden paneling that I know houses mops and buckets and other cleaning supplies, swinging it open. Then I roll the marble body out of the path I need to move the bigger piece of marble.

"Won't Chrissy find it in there?" Hugh asks, moving behind to push the thing as I begin to drag the carpet runner, which in turn, moves the pedestal closer to the cleaning closet. *Ingenious, no?*

"Three weeks... and I've never seen anyone... *Urgh! Push, Hugh!*"

"I am pushing!" he grunts back, his teeth gritted, and his cheeks flushed red.

"Hold the door wider, Arch. There!"

We manage to push it into a corner before I drag an old-looking industrial floor buffing machine in front of it. I've never seen anyone use it. Besides, the cleaning crew seems to bring their own each week. Archie closes the cupboard door after I step out, then re-tucks his school shirt.

"Here." I beckon him closer to rub my thumb against the corner of his mouth. "You have a smudge of jelly."

"Silly Holly! We're not allowed jelly for breakfast, either."

"Really? Not even on a little wholewheat toast?" I tease.

He shakes his head earnestly. "Or ice cream."

"Why would you want jelly on toast?" Hugh asked, perplexed.

Jeez. This is what happens when you tell kids they can't watch TV. Po-tay-to, po-tah-to. Or jelly, jam, and Jell-O. Talk about cross purposes.

But getting back to the task at hand.

"Help me with the carpet, Archie." We each grab a side and pull it straight. "Do you think you could manage the head?" I ask, straightening again. He nods solemnly, so I pick up the casualty. I press the decapitated head into his hands, balancing mine under his, just in case. "Got it?" He nods. "Okay, now to get rid of the body." My attention pivots to the other boy. "You and I need to carry the dearly departed—"

"Departed from his head?"

"Upstairs."

Glancing back at the row of statues, I wonder if I should shuffle them a little closer together, but then think better of it. One headless heirloom is enough for one day. I have a better idea. Ducking back into the cupboard, I open a plastic box on the wall labelled LIGHTS. Locating the switch labelled SPOTLIGHTS/HALL, I flick it, and the lights go out.

"That looks a little better, don't you think?"

Both boys shrug. But at least the spotlight isn't shining on nothing.

Between us, we manage to stash the remains in my bedroom, before both boys leave me to get dressed. As Hugh closes my bedroom door, he's still offering profuse thanks.

The journey to school is... interesting. Committing our conversation's words to paper would make anyone think we were mobsters as we discussed the body hidden under my bed and the other body parts stored throughout my room.

"Don't worry, Holly." At the boy's school, Hugh pauses mid climb from the car. "Kilblair Castle has seen much worse things than a decapitation."

"Much worse things we agreed should never be spoken of?" I reply with a wry smile. So much for what happens in Kilblair Castle stays in Kilblair Castle. Though I can't help but wonder if his assurance is, at least in part, for himself.

"Oh, yes. Much worse. That's how Uncle Sandy has a ghost."

"Get out of here." I roll my eyes, then wiggle the shift stick of Isla's Range Rover—which I just *love* driving—readying myself to pull away from the school drop-off zone. "Seriously, get out of here. You'll be soaked before you make it to class." Although, according to Chrissy, there's no such thing as bad weather. Just the wrong clothes.

"It's true," Hugh protests. "My great-great-great-grandmother was pushed down her stairs by my great-great-great-grandfather when he wanted to marry someone else."

"Did she lose her head?" I continue in the same tone.

"No. She broke her neck and then became a ghost."

Wait, what?

16

HOLLY

I park the car at the back of the house. Sorry, *castle*. Given today is Monday, we're closed to the public, but that's not to say there aren't other things to do in the education center. I'm running through my list of tasks today as I hop down from the Range Rover, planting my feet (and my pristine sneakers) in a puddle of muddy rain.

"Ah, for fudge sakes!"

"You need wellies."

I look up from my soggy feet at the familiar voice. "Do you think Gucci makes them?"

"I'm not at all sure what a Gucci is," Cameron answers with a totally cute-looking smile.

"Now that I believe." As I belatedly step from the puddle, I cast my eyes over him in a thoroughly over-the-top fashion. His head dips, following my gaze, as though examining his own clothing now. Wellies, *sorry*, rain boots, a Kilblair Castle branded hoodie, and jeans. And, of course, his ever-present tweed flat cap.

"Something tells me you're insulting my clothing choices," he replies.

"If you don't know what a Gucci—I mean, what *Gucci* is, how do you know we're talking about clothes? And while we're on the subject of appearances, I'm not even sure you have any hair under that thing permanently attached to your head." I circle my forefinger in the air, ignoring the deliberate falsehood. I know he has a full head of unruly reddish-blond hair. *Sex hair*, my mind unhelpfully supplies. Hair that looks fresh from a quick roll around a bed. Or a potting shed.

Okay, brain, enough of your imaginings. You are not Lady Chatterley, and Cameron is a friend. And you need friends more than you need a roll around a bed. Or shed.

"Are you okay?"

"Yeah. Yep. Totally. I just zoned out for a minute." Maybe he'll think my cheeks are flushed because of the weather. I suddenly realize how close Cameron is. *He has brown eyes.* Why do I find that disappointing? And why is he holding a cut flower in his hand?

"Maybe I dazzled you. You've obviously a thing for men in tweed."

My gaze lifts from the flower, tracing up his arm and solid, broad shoulder. He's teasing me, I realize, and I should feel charmed. A cute man is showing me some interest. Instead, it feels... not wrong exactly. But not right, either.

"I thought there was no such thing as bad weather." Chrissy's words tumble out of my mouth. "Just the wrong clothes."

"Come again?" And now, judging by the grin he's trying to rein in, he thinks he's got me all twitterpated.

"It's wet out." For a change. "How come you never seem to wear a jacket?"

Argh! And now he'll think I've been perving on him!

"This isn't rain," he answers, holding up the flower between us. "It's just a wee bit of smirr."

"I don't know what that is." My words are soft as my gaze rises to his.

"It's fine," he murmurs, reaching out to smooth his finger lightly over my brow. "Soft." He clears his throat, his next words a little more strident. "But I'm no' in need of a jacket. We're bred hardy up here. This is for you, by the way. It's one of the early roses. From the garden, like."

"It's beautiful," I answer, ducking my head. Should it be as awkward as this? Shouldn't I feel flattered? "Thank you."

"Well, I better be getting back." He throws his thumb in the direction he'd come.

"Yeah." I thread a chunk of my hair behind my ear. "Me, too."

His upper body twists, though his feet don't seem to be going anywhere as he swings back to face me again. "Fancy coming to the pub on Friday?"

I should say no. Except I don't want to. I can't keep dwelling on the past and what will never be. He deserves more than the brush-off, and I deserve someone who brings me flowers. *Or a flower*, I silently correct, bringing it to my nose.

"As friends?" I repeat his own words from that first night back to him.

"Aye." My heart dips a little. "Maybe to start." He grins, and I find myself joining in.

I'm really overdue for a coffee as I make my way into the basement kitchen. I'd parked at the back of the castle, as I usually do, because coffee. Although Isla had insisted I make use of the family kitchen, given it's closer to my room, I feel a little weird being there for any other reason than preparing the boys an afternoon snack. Besides, the castle kitchen has the coffee I like, plus I know where the French press is kept. The fancy coffee machine in the family kitchen looks like it needs an engineer to work it.

"Here she is!" Chrissy's voice precedes my entrance. "I thought we were going to have to send out a search party."

"Or not." I'm pretty sure Mari just said. Or whispered. Maybe mouthed the words? Whatever, the sentiment was, as usual, unpleasant.

"Good morning, all. Morning, Mari," I say, super perky as I swing to face her. "Did you manage to get the glitter cleaned up?" We had a bunch of six-year-olds in for a recent session, and we made ducal crowns. *Sorry, ducal coronets.* Who knew there was such a thing? And who knew glitter was the herpes of the craft community?

Me. That's who. And that shizz was sprinkled *everywhere*. Including Mari's hair. But I can't take credit for that piece of genius.

"I'm finding the stuff everywhere," she mutters, glaring at me.

I resist the urge to cackle. I might've patted the glitter perpetrator on the head. After all, the enemy of my enemy is my friend. I really don't know why she wants my job. She doesn't even seem to like kids.

"I was just—"

"Gabbin' with Cameron." Chrissy tilts her head in the vague direction of the window. "We saw." Her eyes sparkle with mischief and good humor, her mouth wearing a barely contained smile as she glances at the rose in my hand.

"He was just saying hi." This day just gets better and better!

"We'll need to put in an order to the butcher before the weekend," a masculine voice calls, a white-blond head jutting from the larder's open door. *The kind of white blond that comes courtesy of an expensive hairstylist.* "You must be Holly," he says, stepping out from the larder and holding out his hand. "Happy to meet you. I'm Dougal, his grace's chef."

"Hi. Nice to meet you." Maybe "himself", as Chrissy calls him, is here, too.

"Och, you shouldn't have." As my hand meets his, he takes the spring rose from my other hand. "See this, Chrissy. This is the way to greet someone when they return home. Not with a load of greetin'."

Somehow, those two words don't sound the same.

"I'll give you greetin', Dougal Mac!"

"Aye, and so you did." *Waa-waa!* His mouth silently shapes those sounds as his balled fists make circles in front of his cheeks.

Now I know what *greetin'* is.

"I'll tell ye again, leave that oven in the state you did last time, and I'll skep your arse!"

"I've said I'm sorry." Dougal cocks a hip and brings the bloom to his nose. Inhaling deeply, he then bounces over to the other side of the kitchen and wraps his arms around Chrissy's wide shoulders. "Forgive me?" He shoves my rose under her nose and kisses her cheek.

The man has a lot of energy. A lot of flamboyant, over-the-top energy.

"Can you no' leave a body alone!" she complains, shooing him away. She shakes her head in such a way it makes me think this scene has been played out often. "Just clean up after yourself, and we won't come to blows."

"Darlin', you're not my type." He shoots her a sassy wink.

"Enough of your cheek." As quick as a flash, Chrissy whacks him across the ass with a plaid dishcloth.

"Oh, maybe ye are!" Hands on his knees, he sticks out

his tush for a repeat. But he soon straightens because her expression is less than impressed.

With a sheepish smile, he makes his way back to me, handing me back the rose. "She'll no' be mad at me for long." He gives a diffident shrug. "Not when I make a batch of petticoat tails. Shortbread," he adds, reading my expression. Leaning in, he whispers, "Her tooth is the only sweet part of her."

"Ignore the bampot," Chrissy retorts. "He doesn't know his heid from his elbow."

"She was gonnae say arsehole," he almost whispers but not quite.

"Here you go." Turning from the far side of the kitchen, Chrissy settles a loaded butler's tray on the scrubbed pine table. "I thought ye might like to take this up to Lady Isla."

"Or just Isla, as she's told her to call her," mutters a snippy Mari without lifting her attention from her phone.

"She's in the small study," Chrissy adds, ignoring her.

"Two cups?" One for Lady Isla and one for the duke?

"I've made you a brew as well." She nods encouragingly before her attention flicks down to the tray. "See if you can coax her to eat one of those empire biscuits, would you, hen?"

I love how hen is a term of endearment in Scotland. It makes me feel all fluffy feathered, happy, and content.

"Shop-bought?" comes Dougal's tart interruption to my mini-blissful state.

Chrissy turns her withering expression his way. "Made especially for her ladyship," she replies with a significant sniff. "You don't have to work in a fancy French kitchen to ken how to cook."

Hen *is an endearment, and* ken *is to understand, and not be confused with Barbie's boyfriend.*

I'm almost certain the duke isn't at home, though pause at the closed door to the study anyway. When I don't hear the murmur of voices, I knock on the heavy walnut door, twist the brass handle, then push it open with my butt.

"Chrissy sent elevenses, did she?" Sitting behind a large pedestal desk, Lady Isla looks up from her computer. Her hair is pulled back into a ponytail, and though her makeup is expertly applied, there's no hiding those tear-tired eyes.

As for snacks, something tells me that Chrissy will make sure there's elevenses at eleven before providing a hearty lunch and then deliver some kind of afternoon tea. She's not happy Isla's so skinny these days.

"I think this is more like..." My gaze flicks to the mahogany and gold clock standing on the mantel. It's barely gone nine thirty. "This is more like breakfast dessert." Except she probably didn't have breakfast. I place the tray down on the coffee table as the overweight Labrador I'd met first in Cameron's car lumbers around the desk. I now know that she belongs to Isla, and because of her husband's "allergies", she'd been consigned to the castle staff for safekeeping when Isla wasn't around. That has all changed now that she's living here, though I'm sure she isn't aware of what has been said by the castle staff about her husband's manhood, given that he let a bit of dog hair come between a woman and her beloved pooch.

"Shall I pour you a cup?"

"Yes, please. You'll join me?" I nod, and she pushes back her chair and moves over to the small sofa setting, Gertie settling at her feet. I'm pleased to say she smells much better now that she's back in the care of her favorite person.

"Empire biscuits," Isla says admiringly, lifting an iced cookie from the gold-rimmed tea plate. "These were my favorite as a child." She gestures for me to sit, and I watch as she picks at the glacé cherry garnish, dropping it to the plate. "How were the boys on the way to school this morning?"

"Just fine." The piece of statuary stuffed under my bed, not so much. And I have my own concerns because neither of the boys seems to have much experience with keeping secrets. Which is a good thing, I know, but not for me when I'm sleeping over a headless heirloom Michelangelo, or whatever that is. "Today, Archie decided he's not going to be a veterinarian but a vegetarian farmer when he's grown," I say, pouring out two cups of the dark brew. "Hugh is still set on joining the army, it seems."

"One wants to save animals, and the other wants to kill his fellow man." She absently breaks off a little of the cookie, dropping it to the dog's expectantly open jaws.

"He'll be an officer, which seems to me is just an extension of being the big brother. Bossing other people about."

"Quite." Seeming to come back to herself, she takes a bite from the cookie, cupping her hand under her chin to catch the crumbs. "These are sweeter than I remember." Her nose wrinkles a touch as she places it back on the tray.

"Tastes change."

"Don't they just." She gives a tiny wry smile. "Hugh won't be a soldier but a duke if my brother doesn't hurry up and do something about it." The prospect doesn't seem to make her at all happy. "Though I suppose he should find a wife first."

"And he doesn't...?"

"There isn't anyone." She shakes her head as though to stop herself from going on.

"I imagine it's some responsibility, being a duke."

"Yes, it is. It's a lifetime commitment and one I don't want for Hugh. Sandy hasn't, well, he hasn't had the easiest of times. As the head of the family, he's like the figure of Atlas, but instead of the world, he's balancing all the responsibility of his family and the estates on his shoulders. Is this from the garden?" Slender fingers reach out to stroke the petal of the white rose as she adroitly changes the topic. "It's a beauty."

And so is she. Built on slender aristocratic lines. High cheekbones and deep blue eyes. *Sad eyes*, I think, though that's probably more to do with her current circumstances. "It's one of the first of the season," I say, passing a cup and saucer into her hand. "Or so Cameron says." There's no need to mention who it was originally meant for. Or how I'd taken a moment to rearrange the contents of the tray on the way up here, then took a photo for my Instagram. I'll post it later, once I'm in better range of the Wi-Fi. Stone walls make for a terrible internet connection, so I'm finding.

"My mother used to love her roses." Once again, she rouses herself from her thoughts. "And speaking of family, my brother will be at the castle this weekend."

"Oh? Well, I'm sure you'll be happy to have him here."

"Yes. And no." She tries to temper a smile and fails, though she tries to conceal it as she begins to doctor her coffee by adding milk and a raw sugar lump. "Like Hugh, Sandy is a bit of a force of nature."

Good. Maybe he can take some of that energy and use it to beat up his brother-in-law. Not that I get the impression Lady Isla would let him ride roughshod over her. And while I'm not usually an advocate for violence, I've (accidentally) heard (okay, eavesdropped) some of the vile things he's said to Isla over the phone. And siblings can be protective. Just ask my sister. The chatter in the kitchen yesterday touched on how Isla's ass of an ex threatened to come to the castle but that he didn't turn up. Word was he probably thought better of the plan when he remembered the place has stocks. And a dungeon. Not to mention a rifle room and a wife who is, so they say, a crack shot.

"I met his grace's chef earlier."

"Dougal." She sort of grimaces, then lifts the cup to her lips, the matching saucer balanced in her other hand. "His cooking is better than his personality, though I will say he's extremely meek when Sandy is within earshot."

I hope my smile looks more sincere than it feels because that makes the man sound like he's an ogre. "Will he be staying long?"

"I shouldn't imagine so. Not while the tourist season is in swing. He says it's like living in a goldfish bowl. He's a very private person, you see."

I smile again, but this time, it's genuine. He must be extremely private because when I was researching this job, not one photograph of him as an adult appeared on my internet search. I imagine that's because Isla got all the good looks, leaving him with a face like a gargoyle. A face for radio, my granny would have called it.

"I should imagine he'll be here for the weekend, at least. And he'll bring friends." And his butler and personal chef, laa-di-daa. "The castle will also be closed this weekend."

"Closed?"

She nods. "To the general public. I'm not sure if you're aware, but the castle and some of the grounds were used as a location on an upcoming Hollywood blockbuster. Or so we all hope. And Sandy is hosting a dinner on Friday night for the director and some of the stars. I believe a number of them will be here for the weekend." A deep sigh overtakes her. "It's been a while since we had a house party."

The only house party I've been to are the kinds that serve Cheetos as hors d'oeuvres, use red Solo cups, and offer an aperitif in the form of cheap keg beer. I mean, I've been to parties, sure. And dinner parties, but house parties conjure up visions of my college days.

"Should I grab some paper to take notes?"

"Oh. No." She waves my offer away. "McCain will have it all under control, along with Chrissy. They know the form of old. Holly, I just wanted to say that I appreciate all your help, taking on extra work, helping with the boys, and so on."

"Honestly, it's my pleasure. They're such great kids, and they're going to grow to be the best kind of men." Maybe I should've kept that to myself as her eyes fill with tears almost immediately. "I'm sorry, I didn't mean to—"

"No." She dabs at the corner of her eye. "Thank you. That means a lot to me."

"It's only the truth." I shrug a little uncomfortably, suddenly wishing I had a little of Isla's poise and dignity as she leans forward, setting the cup and saucer onto the coffee table.

"With the castle closed, you'll have the weekend to yourself."

Which is the polite way of saying I'm not wanted, I think cynically.

"Would you like me to move back into the cottage?" Urgh, please say no.

"There's no need for that," she replies evenly.

"You won't need the room for your guests?"

"What do you think?" Her eyes twinkle with mirth.

"That you have space for a battalion or two," I reply, "but—"

"The battalion will be housed, and you will keep your

room in the family apartments. Feel free to come and go as you please. Perhaps you'd like to join the party for dinner on Friday night? Meet some of Hollywood's leading lights?"

"That's very kind of you, but"—that sounds like a nightmare evening— "I already have plans." I'm hardly a seasoned fancy dinner party guest. I mean, I'm not exactly a heathen, and I know a fork is supposed to be held in your left hand, but what fork do you eat soufflé with? Or do you eat it with a spoon? I've examined the table setting in the formal dining room, the one set out for the tourists. The number of china, silver, and glassware pieces was enough to create an anxiety spike. So, nope! Nope, thank you! "But thank you for the invite."

"I completely understand. But if you change your mind, do let McCain know as soon as you can."

"That's the butler, right?"

"Yes, though he's more like Sandy's sergeant major," she says with a small laugh. "The boys adore him. And their uncle, of course."

"And you won't need my help with them over the weekend?" Say, to hide more damaged heirlooms?

"Thank you, but no. You enjoy your weekend."

"I'm sure I will."

"Doing anything interesting?" Her question is accompanied by a smile that seems to say, *come on, girl! Spill the tea!*

"I might have a date." My smile is a reflection of hers and comes without the tingle of anticipation I know I should feel. *It's only natural*, I tell myself. But it really is time I moved on.

17

ALEXANDER

With my phone in hand, my thumb hovers over my assistant's number for the second time in as many minutes before I drop it to the arm of the chair. Pressing *call* would only add selfishness to the list of my shortcomings. Because I wouldn't be calling to issue him with some task. I'd be demanding Holland Harper's number before instructing him to clear my schedule. For three months, at least.

Would three months be enough?

I'm sure I could give it my best shot.

Three months of fucking Holland to get her out of my system.

Or die trying. The corner of my mouth hitches because what a way to go.

Of course, it would also work the same the other way around. Three months for Holland to grow heartily sick of me. Three months of staid conversations outside of the bedroom, of her wondering why I'm so withdrawn. Of her tiring of my sullen face and preoccupation of all things not her.

Or three months for us both to fall in love.

In the mirror on the opposite wall, my tiny smile turns cynical. Three months is a relationship shelf life for me. I don't own my own life. As the thirteenth Duke of Dalforth, I'm wedded to the name, my free time stolen, all thoughts of *self* growing dusty on a shelf marked *self-indulgence, do not touch*.

Oh, but it's fun being the head of this dysfunctional family. I thought the dysfunction might've ended with my parents, a pair who married despite seeming to hate each other. But my mother has long since passed, and my father has been food for the worms for some ten years or more. He had no say in leaving the dukedom to me, but I'm sure he delighted in the fact that he was able to bequeath the kinds of debts that would ruin a small country. Along with more bastard offspring than I can count on one hand. Bad enough that he dipped excessively into the family coffers to fund these half-siblings and their mothers, but he also passed on the responsibility to me. Without telling me, while he was living, that he was doing so.

He left me a noose. And a title. He left my poor sister nothing but nightmares.

Throwing back the remains of my whisky, I glance down at my phone in my hand. The temptation to embroil Holland in the clusterfuck that is my life seems to constantly burn at the pit of my stomach. I deserve a break, don't I? Something of my own? I'd almost forgotten what desire felt like until her. Until now. And now I can't seem to think of anything but how she felt under me and how her fucking smile made me feel. Sometimes, I even think I can smell her perfume—feel the silk of her skin like a memory turned real.

Perhaps this is an early onset of senility.

My grip tightens on my phone before I thrust it into my

inside jacket pocket. I need to move the fuck on. Indulging in thoughts of that night is like suffering a fever dream. I haul my body up from the leather wingback chair. Now that I'm here, I might as well get on with what I came here for.

Passing by the kind of staircase built for debutantes to glide down, I push on the heavy oak doors and make my way through a room that was once referred to as a ballroom. At least, until I bought the place. Thornbeck Hall, once the country home of some baronet or other. Now the high altar to carnal pleasure with the kind of privacy protections that once suited the son of a duke trying to keep his reputation.

As I push past the crowd, acknowledgement ripples through its attendants. I feel so far removed from the club's purpose that I can hardly believe I once owned this den of sin. It seems so long ago, back when I was hell-bent on living up to the Dalforth name. While I sold my shares long ago, I still hold a membership, though it's been a while since I felt any desire to attend. Desire is not a sentiment that brings me to Thornbeck tonight. I'm here for business, not pleasure.

Like the waves for Moses, the crowd begins to part, allowing me to pass. Their sense of excitement almost palpable. I wonder if my distaste is likewise as I pass all the pretty faces. Pretty faces, painted faces, faces adorned in lace domino masks. Evening suits and cocktail dresses, lingerie as delicate as tissue paper, heavy-duty bondage wear. A usual Friday night for the club, so I see, a den of dark, sensual undertones.

It excites me... not. I am patently too old for this. Too jaded. Too weary to fuck anyone who doesn't engage more than my cock.

"Dalforth. What are you doing here?"

"I was just asking myself the same question," I say,

turning to find Matteo, one of my oldest friends, coming out from the throng behind me. "I have an appointment with Van," I add meaningfully, though Matteo's expression doesn't change. Instead, he kisses the cheek of the blonde currently vying for his attention.

"I'll find you later," he murmurs to her.

"Don't be too long." Her cat-like eyes flick to me with interest before she melts away.

"Don't even think about it." My friend laughs, flinging his arm around my shoulder to lead me through the room, hopefully to Van's office. A man who knows I'm here but has yet to surface himself.

"I wouldn't dream of it," I reply evenly. "As I said, I'm not here to fuck—"

"Play," Matt corrects.

"Fuck. Play. It's all the same."

"Not in the eyes of the law."

"That is not my problem anymore. As I said, I'm here to see Van. The current owner of those kinds of problems."

"And he's being his usual elusive self." Matt doesn't look surprised.

"So it would seem. I've been trying to connect with him all week."

"And he's dangled himself like the proverbial carrot until tonight," he asserts with a cynical hitch of his lips. "Any idea why?"

"A very elusive carrot." Annoyed, my brows draw together. "Apparently, tonight is the only time he can spare me an hour."

"Alexander, he's playing games. Tonight is the only time that suits his purpose."

"One night is as good as any other. Days are much the same."

"Except tonight is the first of the cabaret nights." He places an ironic-sounding emphasis on *cabaret*. "He's fobbed you off to secure your appearance for the opening night. Your attendance always used to help." He presses his palm against another door, pushing it open to reveal a sitting room with leather chairs in dark corners, claret-colored velvet sofas, and parlor palms.

"You mean the debauching duke of Dalforth," I mutter with a cynical smile, lowering myself into one of the leather chairs.

"You must admit, there have been moments when you've fit that mold," Matt replies, doing the same.

"Not for some time."

"Portia must be keeping you happy."

My next smile is a little mocking. "You never were very good at fishing."

He shrugs, sort of *suit yourself*. "Anyway, I think you'll find you're known as the delicious duke of Dalforth these days."

I snort at the ridiculousness of the notion.

"It's true. Van might've dangled a carrot to get you here, but now you'll see you've become that carrot."

It's not a very flattering analogy. Unfortunately, the room proves to be far from private as the doors swing open and bodies begin to spill in.

"Surely not," I mutter, doing a comic double take as my gaze catches on my brother. "Who authorized his membership?"

Matt's glance follows mine, his expression unconcerned. "Weren't you just saying this place wasn't your concern anymore?"

"There used to be standards," I mutter, watching as Griffin caresses the cheeks of a tall brunette—not the cheeks of her face—who appears to be wearing little more than high heels and body paint. *With any luck, the paint will stain. Him, at any rate.*

"That was when the place was run for fun, not as an enterprise. I've heard your brother is making friends in high places."

Half-brother, I silently correct. "You can't have heard correctly," I reply, taking a glass of champagne from a passing server dressed as a French maid. Her frilly pinny makes me think of Holland, and I shake my head against the highly inappropriate places that thought might take me. "Griffin prefers to make friends in places much lower than you're used to."

"How do you know what I'm used to? You're barely around these days."

I sit back in my chair and rest my weary head against the chair. "I know."

"All work and no play makes Alexander a very dull boy."

Don't I know it. "Come up to Kilblair this weekend," I offer—demand—suddenly sitting straight.

"Isn't it the tourist season?"

I almost laugh as his expression crumples as though smelling something offensive.

"I've closed it this weekend," I say, waving off his concerns. "We've got some of Hollywood coming to play."

"Play?" Matteo tilts his head in suggestion, and my gaze follows his in a scan of the room. I wonder when I became inured to sights such as these. Naked flesh, heavy petting, hands kneading and stroking. In short, the beginning of an evening of a sexual free-for-all.

"No, not like this." Perish the thought. "Just the usual pursuits. Grouse. Whisky. A little stalking."

"Deer, or something else?"

"And dinner with some of Hollywood's elite," I add, ignoring his teasing.

"Yeah, why not," he replies. I don't know who is more surprised by his answer. "It'll be good to catch up. To get away from the city."

As I spot Griffin heading our way, I resist the urge to settle lower in my chair, hoping he won't see me. "I really don't know where he found the funds to cover his membership," I mutter. He's always pleading poverty.

"I hear Griffin has been chosen to head up the legal team of the elusive oligarch."

"Van's uncle?" I ask. Matt nods. "But Griffin practices criminal law, not corporate."

"And Van's family is not particularly law-abiding. Didn't he once describe them as law adjacent and his oligarch uncle the worst of them?"

"I believe he said a despotic, money laundering, drug trafficking overlord," I reply.

"I didn't expect to see you here." Without waiting for an invitation, Griffin settles himself into a seat between mine and Matt's.

"Expectation implies thought, doesn't it?" My gaze bounces between the pair with an air of bewilderment. "I thought you saved thinking for billable hours." The rest of the time, I'm almost certain he thinks with his balls.

"Hilarious, as always, big bro. What's wrong with your face? Have you got cummy ache?" he asks with a childish pout. "Blue balls?"

I send him a withering look in reply

"You two would've gotten along famously as kids," Matt mutters, straight-faced.

"As we do now," I mutter, tightening my grip on my glass.

"That reminds me, I've got a bone to pick with you." The

dark liquid in Griffin's crystal tumbler ripples as he points his finger at me around the glass.

"Oh?"

"Holly, the cute server from your charity night."

I frown as though confused. "Is the name supposed to mean something to me?"

"It means something to me. It means you are a cockblocker."

Matt snorts, tactfully turning the noise into a cough.

"You know I was into her, so you sent me on a wild goose chase looking for some knob who wasn't even there."

"You can't mean Charles St John, surely?"

"Was he the goose or the knob?" Matt asks, amused.

"He wasn't even there," Griffin replies, his gaze boring into mine.

"He was when I left the ballroom." I take an unconcerned swallow of my champagne without a flicker of conscience or concern. "To look for you." Holland deserves better than to be used by him. Besides, if anyone in this family gets to fuck her, it should be me. Ah, see. I win already, I think smugly.

"What are you smiling about?" he grunts. "Admit it—you chased me off because you knew she was into me."

"You're delusional." And I'll break your arms if you so much as touch her.

"And you just wanted to get your hands on the American bit."

"American bit of what?" Matt interjects, clearly entertained. I glance his way, hoping he has enough sense to stay out of this.

"You should see her, Matt," Griffin replies, warming to his theme. "Cute as a button and as feisty as fuck. She's got this arse..." With a look that I'm sure is meant to convey his rapture, he shapes globes in the air between us.

I'm not biting. Though I am silently correcting him because her arse isn't round. It's more like a heart that's shaped upside down. She has dimples in her back made for my fingers and the noises she makes when—

"She was like a siren."

"Sounds more like she was a false alarm," Matt retorts, "if Alexander was able to whisk her from under your nose."

"I tell you, Matt. If he's fucked her," Griffin says, ignoring my friend's teasing, "I'd be tempted to suck his dick. Just for a taste."

"Griffin Middlemass QC, ladies and gentlemen. My half-brother. The other half must surely be Neanderthal."

"There's a joke in there somewhere. But surely, your grace, you aren't maligning my mother," Griffin says, a hint of warning in his tone.

I'm sure the joke is our shared blood. "I wouldn't dream of it. She has already suffered so much in raising you."

"Now, now, children," Matt interjects with a grin. "You're not telling me this woman would rival the brunette you just had your hands on, are you, Griffin?"

Griffin's gaze flicks to the woman in question, appearing to give the question some thought. "She is gorgeous, but she's more plastic than skin. Plus, she's a working girl." One of the changes Van sought to implement when he took over. High end escorts for those who prefer that sort of experience. "Holly is real. Soft in all the places you want a woman to be. There's something about her." Griffin shakes his head and I find myself almost commiserating as he presses his elbow against the arm of the chair, leaning forward as though about to impart something of note. "Her blow job lips are one-hundred-percent natural."

Bastard. In more than one sense of the word.

"And how would you know," I find myself drawling, my hand tightening on my own chair arm. I don't like where this is going. Fuck it, I don't like the fact that he's been within three feet of her.

"Because I had her in my palm," he says, spreading the fingers of his hand wide before he balls it into a fist.

"And you thought her so wonderful, you put the prospect of money before her."

"Did you fuck her?" Griffin asks sharply.

"This is getting a bit heavy for me." Matt rises from his chair. "I'll call you tomorrow." His hand rests briefly on my shoulder, and then he's gone.

"She hasn't called you, so the natural logic is I must've fucked her." I want to be smug but see the wisdom in keeping my tone neutral in the face of Griffin's heated glower. There's no need to make this a competition. Because I've already won. Even if this victor won't be enjoying the spoils. Not anymore.

"Something chased her off. I called the caterers, and they said she no longer works there."

"You went looking for her? Chasing her? Isn't that a little..." Over the top for him?

"I told you, there was something between us and now I can't fucking find her, and you were the last one who saw her."

"Should I call my lawyer?" I drawl.

"If you've fucked her—"

"For God's sake, I just gave the girl a number to call. A number of an employment agency. That was the whole of our conversation."

"Why?" His brows pull down. Distrust or confusion?

"Because you left me in the dark lane with her. She said

she needed a better job than one that left her outside with strange men."

"That had to be you she was talking about."

"Of course, because no one would find you strange."

"Did you fuck her?" he repeats.

"You're not in court now. I've just told you the extent of what happened that night." This kind of lie the least of my sins.

"How would you have the number for an employment agency with you, your grace?" The latter he adds as a very pointed afterthought.

"I didn't. I gave her George's number. What happened after that, I've no clue." And that, at least, is the truth. I set down my barely touched drink. "You're staying?"

By contrast, Griffin takes a deep drink from his, his manner and expression changing almost immediately. "Yes," he murmurs as his gaze flicks around the room. "I'm staying for the changing of the guard."

My face must reflect my confusion because the changing of the guard is a military procession performed with much pomp and circumstance at various residences of Her Majesty the Queen. Not in a lifestyle club where clothing is optional.

"You're out of touch," he retorts smugly. "Either that, or you've never been on one end of a posh threesome."

Uncivilized? More like deranged.

"My lord?" At the high and breathy voice, I turn without bothering to correct her form of address because I don't plan on being here again. The face of an angel stares back at me. Blue eyes and pink cheeks, waves of burnished copper tumble around her shoulders. She may have the face of an angel, but judging by her clothes, or lack of them, she has particularly devilish habits. "Did I get that right?" she asks, her eyes wide and guileless. She's a good actress, I'll give her that much. *And nothing else.* Depravity paid for by the hour really isn't my thing.

"Can I help you?" I ask pointedly.

"Van sent me." She trails her hand along the back of the armchair. "He wondered if you might like a little company."

"That's very kind of him," I answer, laughing under my breath, because this isn't a gesture of kindness on his part. More like a provocation. "Thank you, but no." I've never held an interest in fucking the help.

"You can keep me company, if you like." Griffin makes a grab for her hand, lifting it to his lips. "I'm not a lord, but I'm better company than him."

So much for his pining for Holland.

"Are you now?" One step and the girl stands in front of him, running her fingers through his hair. She giggles as Griffin pulls her into his lap, and he looks like the cat with a canary between his teeth. "If you're not a lord," she purrs, beginning to loosen his tie, "what are you?"

Not wealthy enough to afford a night with you, I think sardonically. I wouldn't have thought Griffin would be the kind who paid for sex, either. Perhaps he doesn't know the only bulge in his pants she's truly interested in is the one from his wallet.

"Why don't you guess?" he suggests, settling himself back in the chair.

This is a scene I require no part in, so I stand.

"Tinker, tailor, soldier, sailor," she murmurs, stepping her fingers up his chest. "Rich man, poor man—"

"Either of the following two suit him nicely," I assert, striding away.

Beggar man. Thief.

After leaving Griffin to his diversions, I take the rear stairs to the room that was once my office. A room, were it not dark, would afford expansive views over the gardens. I open the door without knocking, surprised to see the décor hasn't changed. Original wood paneling, Persian carpets, and the original fireplace. Even the desk is the same. The wall of TV screens showing footage from a number of security cameras *isn't*.

"Aleksandr." Van places a theatrical emphasis on the pronunciation of my name. His heritage might be Russian, but he's never spoken with anything but an Oxbridge accent. The bar he stands at is new, set into an alcove on the far side of the room. But it isn't vodka he's pouring. "Coffee?"

"No. Thank you," I reply, taking a seat on the opposite side of the desk than I once sat. Van carries his coffee across the room, perching himself on the edge of the desk. In his hand, the demitasse cup looks like it belongs to a child's tea set. "Thank you for the invite," I murmur pointedly.

"You never need an invite to visit, Alexander." With a smile, he inclines his head, then lifts the cup to his lips. Turkish coffee as black as night, as I recall.

"I must say, I'm flattered." Settling back in the chair, I cross one knee over the other. "If you'd wanted me here tonight, you should've said."

"So you could bring your A game?"

"Fucking in public is no longer my forte." I flick invisible lint from my trouser leg. "I'm too long in the tooth these days."

"That must be why you didn't turn up to your birthday party."

If I didn't know better, I might worry he knows exactly

how I spent that night. Van is a friend, but it doesn't do to let him know too much. In his family's line of work, they're always looking for influence. Leverage, I suppose. Not that I'm at all certain exactly how that would pertain to me. I have nothing he needs, unless he wants a castle with a crumbling roof. Truthfully, I can't even give him that because the entailed property isn't mine to give.

"I'm suffering a midlife crisis, so I'm told."

"By Portia?" He almost sneers. The pair aren't fans of each other.

"I've been too busy to see much of her of late. She probably thinks I'm avoiding her."

"That's not a bad strategy," he murmurs, setting the tiny cup and saucer down onto the desk.

"We're not all interested in girls almost young enough to be our daughters."

Wrapping his fingers around the edge of the desk, he leans forward. "There's a girl downstairs you would love. She's studying for a PhD in medieval history. Beautiful, very cerebral. A little cold on the surface, but she likes to be manhandled. Just how you like them."

"As I said, I'm not—"

"Living for yourself. Alexander, there's something to be said for the company of twenty-five-year-olds."

Twenty-four-year-olds, too. As for the woman he just described, I'm not going to bother telling him that his tastes are just that. *His own.* Mine are mine alone, as well as none of his fucking business.

Van holds up his hands as though warding off my words. "I know, we're all far too jaded for love. For fucking? Never. And just the whisper of your visit will be enough to drive this month's numbers up."

"I'm happy to oblige," I reply, curt. "But I'd appreciate it if in the future you just be honest with me. We're supposed to be friends, aren't we?"

"Friends make time for one another," he says rather regretfully.

"Yes, you're right." Of course he is. "Things have just been *precarious,*" I add hesitantly, unwilling to share my burdens. The ongoing battle with bankers and those of my investors, of how my personal fortune is whittled away daily, dripping into the abyss of entailed properties that are little more than financial black holes of ruin, properties in need of millions of pounds for repairs. Perhaps a sensible man would gift them to the National Trust, a charity dedicated to preserving such history. Unload them and move on, but how could I when it feels like giving in? And what of my heir? Offloading them from under him feels little more than theft. So, I'll stay the course and trust that by the time my nephew inherits, the dukedom won't be such a mess. I press my fingers against a building throb in my temple.

"Matteo and I, we're your friends. We can be relied on to lend an ear... money, if the need arises."

I laugh unhappily. If anyone would have the money to help it would be Van, not Matteo. Matteo is wealthy, but Van's father is as rich as Croesus. Or perhaps I should say the family is. Read into that what you will.

"Thank you," I reply. Van smiles knowingly. He'd no more borrow from me than I would him. "It is money I've come to speak with you about, actually." At this, his expression reacts in shock, but blink, and I would've missed it, such is the skill of his poker face. "My sister, Isla. You remember Isla?" A telling pulse begins in his jaw, though I know he'll offer only the blandest of responses.

"How could I ever forget her?" I find my brow reacting as though yanked up by a string. "I've seen her at the castle many times," he blusters, and I find myself wondering if I've ever seen the man so unguarded. "Is she well?" His blonde brows beetle as his fingers tighten on the edge of the desk.

"She's fine."

"And her sons?"

"They're well, too. They're staying at the castle at the moment." Isla had given me some bullshit about repairs on her own home. Add to that I've been unable to reach Chrissy, the woman who is the string that holds the castle together, by anything other than email, and I'm beginning to suspect all is not as they'd have me believe.

"And her husband?" *Bland, so bland, Van. Yet not quite bland enough.*

"No. He's not with them. He came to see me last month, and it seems he's overstretched himself in an investment. A distillery on one of the Hebridean islands, I believe." Along with an ill-fated golf course. "He was looking for a partner." More like someone to bail him out.

"And you turned him down."

"I did."

"Business and families can be a difficult balance."

"I have no allegiance to the man. He's Isla's husband and the father of my nephews. If he can't take care of them, I will. But I'm not adding him to the list of my responsibilities."

"I see." He smiles wryly, his gaze turning to the wall of TV monitors. "I think you have enough of those."

For a moment, I assume he's talking about the house, the estates, but as my gaze naturally follows his, I find myself warding off the sight. "I don't need responsibility for that, so don't think to send me his bill." Because there on screen, I catch an unfortunate glimpse of a half-clothed Griffin, along with the angelic-looking woman from downstairs. The pair aren't alone, another woman crawling up the huge bed.

"The bill? I'll send it to my uncle. I believe he has him on a retainer."

Something else that doesn't interest me. "Sufficient unto the day is the evil thereof."

"English, sometimes, makes little sense," Van mutters, straightening from his desk. "So you think Isla's husband…"

"Thomas," I supply.

"Will come to me for money to invest?"

"You met him at Christmas two years ago, and he's tried to bring you up in conversation numerous times since. The oligarch's son."

Van nods knowingly. "What are Russians known for if not vodka and money?"

Not to mention their dubious business dealings.

"So, am I to invest in this distillery?" he adds.

"Absolutely not."

"I didn't think so." He smiles, shark-like. "But there's no need to bite off my head, old friend."

"I have a feeling that things are getting desperate for him."

"Should I meet him or not? Perhaps I can bring him here?"

To what purpose, I'm about to ask when his head turns quite deliberately to the TV monitors.

"Give me a couple of days to think on that." It's not like I have any reason to ruin my sister's marriage, apart from abhorring the man she chose. "I'm going up to the castle next weekend. I'll see how the land lies then."

"Of course."

"You're welcome, too. It's the tourist season, but the place will be closed for the weekend. Isla and the boys are there."

I'm not sure why I add the latter. I know he has always been attracted to her, despite his attempts to hide it. Besides, for a man who owns a club that allows people to fuck indiscriminately, he's always been quite honorable himself. And my sister is as faithful as her elderly Labrador. *And a lot less trouble.* But the words are out there, and there's no taking them back. Not that he's likely to say he will.

"Yes. I believe I'd enjoy the break."

I try to hide my surprise. I'm not sure whether I manage it.

Sufficient unto the day is the evil thereof, indeed. Or in other words, this is something I'll need to puzzle out another day, I believe.

18

HOLLY

I CLOSE THE EDUCATION CENTER ON THURSDAY AFTER A FAIRLY quiet day where the highlight was trying to work out why one of the little visitors was steadfast in his belief that he was going to be a golden retriever. I'd passed out the crayons and fun workbooks (made to look like schoolbooks from Tollbridge School of Sorcery and Enchantment, though kind of cheap) when he'd opened that sucker and set to, muttering, "*Watch me be a golden retriever, a golden retriever.*"

I'd had to bite the inside of my cheeks when he'd rushed at me twenty minutes later, just as I'd handed back the magic wand (a small tree branch) to a cute six-year-old girl, demanding I'd take a look.

"*Miss Boo!* (that's my stage name, I guess) *Miss Boo! Look, I've finished.*" He'd tugged so hard on the ankle-length skirt that is part of my uniform, I thought he'd tear the Velcro. Uniform. Yep. That wasn't mentioned in the contract. No way I'm posting evidence of this on my Instagram account.

"*Already?*" I'd exclaimed theatrically (because drama major = old ham) as my eyes scanned the room for his parents.

"Yes! Already! My mummy says I'm a golden retriever."

I'd pondered this for a beat before realizing he meant *overachiever*.

Kids. They crack me up.

Loosening the Velcro on the waist of my skirt, I step out of it and hang it on the peg, swapping my prim high-necked blouse for a long cardigan. I usually wear a T-shirt, leggings, and boots under that get-up, but I do wonder what'll happen when summer comes to Scotland. Will I still need the layers, or will I melt?

Maybe I can get a little weather advice from Cameron tomorrow when we hit the pub. As I grab my Kilblair Castle cotton tote, because this is no place to use my Prada, nervousness washes through my stomach. Not the anticipatory, exciting kind, and, to be honest, I just don't get it. Why am I not more excited about it? He's cute and kind, and he brings me flowers almost daily. From the garden, sure, but I'm not exactly high maintenance. Buy me a beer, tell me I'm cute. Slap my ass when we know each other a little better, and I'll be a happy girl! I don't need hundred-dollar bouquets, diamonds, or wooing. I just need you to like me. And for me to like you. And I do like him, but still, this feels…

I push the thoughts away because I'm going to the pub with him anyway. I'm gonna let him blow away those cobwebs! But not *those cobwebs*. I have no intention of sleeping with him. Not on a first date.

I'm such a hypocrite, I think critically, reaching for the door handle. *It's not like he-who-should-not-be-thought-of even went out on a date with me. We just had coffee and drinks. And amazing sex.* My shoulders sag, my Kilblair Castle branded tote sliding from my shoulder down my arm. *Unicorn sex, and boy, did I ride that man's horn. It was the kind of sex I'd never had before, and wonder if I'll be lucky enough to ever experience it again.*

I give myself an internal shake. No good comes from dwelling. Especially when you're not in the privacy of your own bedroom. Pulling on the door, I step out and lock it behind me, then begin to hurry across the castle's grassy courtyard. Today's weather forecast? A light misting of rain, the kind that clings to eyelashes and glitters like tiny gemstones. The kind that turns hair frizzy and unruly, so it's always best to be armed with an umbrella.

I'm heading for the kitchen to call in on my castle homies, but then I see I've left out the sandwich board I'd so artfully decorated, which reads:

Welcome to Miss Boo's class

Come right in, but please note, unattended children will be given an energy drink and taught to curse during the first lesson.

You can bet I'd posted a photo of this to Instagram, along with one I'd snapped of the old stocks and another of the peacocks displaying their plumage. In fact, I've taken quite a lot of photos on my phone since I'd gotten here. The rain glistening in a spiderweb. Rainbows over the castle chimneys. The dark beauty of the nearby mountains. My sparkly sneakers reflected in a puddle. *I'd used a filter for that one, given how they've become quite stained from stepping in a puddle or ten.*

Kilblair Castle has offered me a wealth of images for an interesting social media, but I've found I just don't post very often. I mean, that's partly because my carrier's signal up here is pretty much non-existent. When I'd asked Chrissy if she got 4G, she'd gotten red in the face and started to splutter. Turns out, she thought I'd said orgy. But at least there's Wi-Fi. Sometimes. If I stand on one leg and hang my phone out of the window between the hours of three and four a.m. At least, that's what it seems like. But it's not just the lack of tech that keeps me from posting. I can't explain it, but it's almost like I want to keep this place to myself. I do share plenty with Kennedy, and I think she appreciates seeing where I am and what I'm doing. Though she has remarked several times about the lack of kilt-wearing Scottish men in them.

Seriously, I've yet to see one kilt-wearing man.

Maybe the whole thing is a myth.

Or just for TV.

Folding the sandwich board, I lug it back towards the door, which I unlock while balancing both board and umbrella. This job is about entertaining the kids, allowing them to experience a little of the magic from the movie. In the mornings, sessions center around the castle and its history. There are outfits to dress up in, long dresses and capes, even fake suits of armor. Then in the afternoon, we switch to "lessons" at Tollbridge School of Sorcery and Enchantment, where we might learn to "fly" a broomstick, though "first-year students" aren't ever allowed to have their feet lift from the ground. Then we take part in a mad scientist–style experiment. We might turn ordinary raisins into magical dancing ones or concoct some witches brew slime. It's a fun job, but it's not day-care, and that's what the sign is all about. The job is entertaining kids that come in *accompanied* by their parents.

I leave the sandwich board leaning against the wall, and I'm in the castle kitchen in minutes.

"Did you see him arrive?" Chrissy asks, her tone awed. "He came in one of them flashy STDs."

"I don't know who you're talking about, but whoever he

is, I'm not shaking his hand. Or anything else." I drop my umbrella, more commonly known as a brolly hereabouts, into the brass stand, dropping my tote to a chair before flicking the switch on the kettle. *I wonder if I can persuade Isla to get a machine. Maybe a Keurig?*

"What did I say?" Chrissy's ample form turns my way, bread knife in hand.

"You said Dylan Duffy arrived with chlamydia," Mari mutters from the kitchen table, her eyes not lifting from her phone.

"I thought his wife was called Ivy?"

I begin to chuckle, though stop abruptly when Chrissy points the knife my way. "She's a nice girl, Ivy," she says, her expression firm. "He'd better not be having no hochmagandy on the side. She'll no' stand for it!"

"Hochama what?" I ask incredulously. Sometimes, Scots really is another language.

"She means a side ho." Mari's words sound a little sneery, but it's hard to tell, given her eyes are still glued to her phone. Honestly, if I hadn't worked alongside her these past few weeks, I might think that thing is attached to her hand. I mean, I like my phone, and I like the 'gram, but I'm not obsessed. *Like some people.* "And he hasn't," she adds. "My auntie's sister's husband works for them over on their estate in Auchenkeld," she decrees, her tone highly patronizing. "They don't live in America all the year-round. Anyway, he says they can'nae keep their hands off each other and that she's expecting another bairn."

Bairn, not barn, which is Scots for child. When I googled it, just to be sure, I found out the word comes from the Danish for child. That's Danish as in Vikings, who raped, pillaged, then settled on this coast long, long ago. Following on from that, I tried very hard not to imagine my recent association with the Vikings. Or rather *Viking.* Okay, so I may have dwelled a little. But, back to Duffy family, it sounds as though Dylan Duffy's wife is pregnant. It helps that I'm getting better at reading between those Scottish accented lines.

"Och, that's braw!" Chrissy announces, ignoring the younger woman's tone. *Braw* is a good thing. And *och* I've come to learn can convey sorrow, pain, resignation, weariness, or as in this case, a pleasant surprise.

I zone out a little as I make my magic brew, wondering what I should wear tomorrow night. I might even bust out my Prada purse, which hasn't seen daylight in weeks. Jeans definitely, I think. Maybe a cute shirt. And a coat because, despite summer being just around the corner, the evenings are still cold. And often wet.

Honestly, for the weather, I might as well have stayed in Mookatill.

Coffee made, I find myself smiling into my cup as the pair talk about the formal dinner tomorrow night in tones of awe. I mean, I get it. Hollywood stars and all. One particular Hollywood star that has a little extra somethin' somethin' in his pants, according to that time he broke the internet a few years ago. I didn't see it myself, but Dylan Duffy apparently had some home movies, of let's say a delicate nature, leaked. Word was the man is *hung.* I guess it made for popular watching, especially when it was announced he'd secretly been married. And then they had kids! Ovaries popping all over the place!

Where was I? Jeans and a cute top. Maybe I'll even bust out a pair of heels unless I've forgotten how to walk in them. I wonder what the pub is like. I know there are two of them in the village. Two pubs, something called a "chippy", which is a takeout joint. There's also a dine-in Indian restaurant, which makes the village positively cosmopolitan.

"Dougal says venison." Chrissy's words somehow register in my brain, bringing me back to the conversation.

"It's always bloody venison," Mari replies scornfully.

"Bloody is how it's served. And why go to the expense of a butcher when you've so many of deer roaming about?"

Can't say I'd ever had venison until I moved to Scotland.

"McCain went down to the cellars and brought up the good wine," Chrissy adds. "Champagne, too. The vintage stuff."

I was right in declining Isla's invitation. This is definitely not my kind of party. Even if I'm more likely these days to be found sipping a cocktail or a glass of (non-vintage) champagne than I am doing tequila body shots.

"Come on, Gert." I stand under the stone portico, the one with the weather-worn heraldic shield carved into the masonry, Gertie's leather lead in hand. Not that she's budging. She apparently has no intention of going for her afternoon constitutional, which I'd volunteered to supervise. It had seemed like the right thing to do because almost everyone in the castle was running around like headless chickens in preparation for tonight. Also, I don't have the school run today because Isla said something about needing to talk to Hugh's teacher.

"We'll do a quick lap around that tree." I work the zipper on my jacket up to my chin and pull on the lead again. Gertie just looks at me balefully, her butt firmly cemented to the floor. I can't say I blame her because it's raining again. *Just for a change.* The Bible might talk of it raining for forty days and forty nights, but that just seems like spring in Scotland. "I can't take you back in until you've done what needs to be done," I say, not feeling *too* dumb for continuing a conversation with a dog. One-sided conversations are sometimes the best kind of conversations to have. "Please? How about you pee, and I give you a treat?"

The look she gives me? A big fat no.

I sigh, listening as the rain falls against the leaves of a nearby tree, the syncopated sound almost musical. I guess I'll be tying my hair up tonight. It's either that or I'll have to rock the frizz.

On the horizon, one of the gardener's ATVs moves over the hills and vales of the vast garden. *It could be Cameron*, I think to myself, waiting for that pleasant little anticipatory twist in my stomach that doesn't come. I really don't get it. Why aren't I more excited for tonight? Maybe my excitement is shy. A late developer. Maybe it'll develop tonight.

At the meaty rumble of Isla's Range Rover, I look down at Gertie. "Now you're in trouble," I tell her. "The boss is home."

The boys tumble out of the vehicle, and I move aside to let them pass.

"Hello, Holly. Goodbye, Holly," calls Archie as he dashes in through the door. A split second later, he's back and throwing his arms around a (very briefly dejected) dog. "Almost forgot," he says, shooting me an embarrassed-looking grin. "Love you, Gertie girl." Hugh is a little more circumspect. Head down, he pats Gertie's head before gracing me with a very short-lived smile.

"What's up, champ?"

"It's nothing I want to talk about," he mutters stiffly before disappearing through the open door.

"Off for a walk?" Isla asks, coming to a stop under the portico.

"That was the plan." I glance down at the mutt. "But it's a plan Gertie wants no part in."

"Bloody kids and animals," Isla says, lifting her purse higher on her shoulder before pointing at a patch of grass next to the left. "Gertie, go pee," she commands sternly. Unbelievably, the elderly pooch shuffles her butt onto the wet grass, cops a squat, and does exactly what's demanded of her. "Good girl," she offers in a mildly begrudging tone as she unclips the lead from Gert's collar and the old mutt trundles indoors. "She does hate the rain."

"Then she's living in the wrong country."

"I'm sure we'd both prefer Acapulco, but one doesn't always get the choice, unfortunately."

Oh, boy. That was some frosty tone. I guess that's me told.

"Look, I'm sorry," Isla offers almost immediately. "Pay no attention to me." She presses her hand to her head. "I've just got a lot on my plate today, and it must be coming up to that time of the month."

"Plus, you have a Hollywood superstar staying with you, not to mention a formal dinner to host and a weekend's worth of entertaining to provide."

"God, I know," she says on a moan. "When all I really want to do is disappear into a bottle of wine about this big." She gestures chest height. "And to top it all, my brother is sodding well late, and then Hugh's teacher insisted she needed to see me today. Like I haven't got anything else I need to do!" She throws up her hands, and I think I see the beginnings of some frustrated tears.

"Come on." Reaching out, I touch her arm. "Let's go

inside. I'll make you a coffee, and we can plot to murder this teacher."

"Coffee would be good."

We don't go to the castle's kitchen because there's too much going on in there today. Instead, we make our way to the family's private apartments and the small but stylish kitchen there.

"I'm so tempted to add a shot of whisky," Isla says as I hand over her cup.

"It's your house. You're over twenty-one. I'm pretty sure you can do what you want."

"Best not," she replies, though not before appearing to consider it. "I'd better keep my wits about me for tonight."

"Do you have a big crowd?"

"Eight people from the film," she says, counting the attendants by tapping her finger against her wrist. "The star and his wife, a co-star and his partner, the director, and a couple of the money people. Then there's Sandy, of course. Along with a couple of his friends, I believe. And Portia." She rolls her eyes exaggeratedly before listing off more names that don't mean anything to me. I've heard of Dylan Duffy and his co-star too, but celebrities don't impress me much. Though I get how stressful this must be for Isla. It's one thing hosting a party for friends and another to keep strangers entertained for a whole weekend. And for her brother to dump this on her plate and not be here seems like an asshole move. If Kennedy dumped this on me, her guests would be lucky to be served McDonald's.

"Those who arrived earlier are currently out clay pigeon shooting. Nothing says, *a weekend in the country* like shooting clay discs propelled into the air." Her gaze slips to the clock on the wall-mounted oven. "I suppose McCain will serve them afternoon tea soon. I should make an effort to join them."

"I'll watch Hugh and Archie. I can take them into the village, or maybe drive them into town to see a movie?" Except I'm supposed to be going out this evening myself.

"Thank you, but no. They should probably come to tea. Besides, they're both in the doghouse."

"Oh." I sit back in my chair, not wanting to pry.

"It's nothing terrible. More ridiculous and a case of bad timing." She looks up from the contents of her cup. "Archie has developed kleptomania, apparently."

"School supplies?" This is an educated guess. In my experience, lots of little kids *borrow* from the classroom, whether they want for things materially or not in their lives. I guess if it was going to happen at any time, that time would be now. They know their mom is upset, even if they don't know exactly why. But they're smart enough to know their dad is the cause of it. That's got to be unsettling for any kid.

"Yes. He's not in trouble or anything. His teacher just happened to mention it. She seemed to think it was funny. I suppose it is, in a way. Archie is clearly no criminal mastermind." But consternation still flickers over her brow. "He'd apparently stolen a sheet of stickers from his teacher's desk drawer. Stickers she keeps to reward good work. Actually, I believe she said the stickers say *good work.*" She slides her hair behind her ears. "Archie has been applying them liberally to his own books, ironically where his work has been *less* than good."

"Enterprising." I try to hide my chuckle behind my coffee cup. "I wouldn't worry about it. What kid can resist stickers? The stationery supplies I lost from my classroom back when I was teaching?" My expression twists. "I can't even tell you. Archie is no thief. I bet the stickers weren't even in her drawer. I bet she left them on her desk. He probably couldn't resist helping himself."

"Like a little magpie," Isla replies. "That does seem more plausible. Though I'm not sure what his plans were for the liter of glue he tried to smuggle out under his school shirt.

"Glue?" I feel my eyebrows bounce to the top of my head.

"Yes. PVA."

"Well, he's too little to have developed a habit. N-Not glue sniffing," I say quickly. "I don't mean that. I just mean he…" *Probably wanted to help glue a statue's head back to its body before we were all found out.* "Probably wasn't paying attention. Maybe he confused it for his water bottle or something."

"Possibly," she replies unconvinced. "If only Hugh's teacher was so easy to deal with. Apparently, today he told one of his friends his new haircut made him look like a lesbian. In earshot of his art teacher, who is, in fact, lesbian."

"Oh, dear." This time, I use my coffee cup as a shield for the *argh!* face I pull.

"It's probably not as bad as it seems. Not as offensive, at least because he didn't mean lesbian. He meant feminine. He's only eight. For goodness' sake, he didn't even know what the term lesbian meant! He knows that love comes in many forms, but we hadn't yet gotten to the point where we'd discussed defined terms. His teacher didn't believe that, of course. She saw it only as a slur. Not one eight-year-old boy teasing another because of a haircut." She shakes her head in disgust. "You can imagine what he asked as we left the classroom."

"Mom, what's a lesbian?"

"Exactly."

"That would've made for an interesting drive home."

"One where I wish I'd had whisky in my water bottle, especially when the topic turned to their father and whether we're getting a divorce. Today of all days," she adds in a tone that I think is supposed to be bright but sounds more fragile. The topic is quickly dropped when Archie appears in the kitchen, apparently *starving*. A very reticent Hugh isn't far behind. Both boys changed from their uniforms into shirts and pants, though neither look like their heads have seen the business end of a hairbrush. Not that I'm going to mention that today of all days.

"Chrissy said that Dougal would make sausage rolls and Battenberg cake for afternoon tea," Archie says, pulling on his mom's hand. "I think we should go and make sure he remembers that he said so."

"We've got guests, remember?" She cups her son's chin. "Perhaps Dougal meant some other time. We can't very well serve Hollywood's highest-grossing superstar nursery food," she says, directing her words my way.

"I'm always down for sausage rolls," I answer with an apologetic shrug. Who doesn't love herby sausage meat wrapped in a buttery, flaky pastry? Apart from vegetarians, maybe.

"But Chrissy said," Archie whines. "She said he'd make them just for Hugh and me."

"Then I suppose we'd better go and make sure Gertie hasn't eaten them all."

Because there are sausage rolls, I tag along. It's been a while since lunch, and this trip to a pub might not include much more to eat than a packet of chips. Or crisps, as they call them here. I've driven past the two pubs in the village (each situated at opposite ends), but it's hard to tell if they serve food or nothing more than packets of the dubious sounding pork scratchings. *I've yet to ask about the provenance of those but I guess they're a little like pork rinds.*

"Is there something missing from there?" Isla pauses as she reaches the bottom of the very grand staircase. With a pensive finger on her chin, she glances left and right along the long hallway. "How odd."

I feel Hugh's attention swing my way as I reach the bottom stair. "What was that?"

"It just feels like there's something not quite right about this space."

My response is to affect a noncommittal shrug, and thankfully, Isla quickly concludes I'm not the right person to ask. Yay for being a newbie here.

"We should tell," Archie whisper-hisses as Isla moves out of earshot.

"No!" My sentiment is echoed by Hugh.

"But how are we going to get it back?" Archie asks plaintively, his arms held wide. "And fixed? I tried to get some glue from school, but I couldn't!"

"Friend," I say, reaching for his hand. "Don't worry about it. And don't borrow anything else from the classroom. Leave it to me." And hopefully YouTube.

"But—"

"No," repeats his elder brother. "Mummy doesn't need anything else to worry about right now."

Not to mention he doesn't need to get into any more trouble. Though, come to think of it, it might be me who'd suffer most. Maybe I'd even be out of a job.

Aiding and abetting? Being a big old liar pants? Setting the children in my charge a bad example? Any of those seems grounds enough for dismissal.

Isla is greeting the dog as we enter a kitchen that's a hive of activity, and the Dougal of today seems like another person. Dressed in chef whites, he doles out orders like the captain of a ship, though as he catches sight of the boys, he takes time to get down on their level, ruffling their hair.

"What happened to wee Archie?" he asks with astonishment. "Did someone stick you in a grow-bag while I was gone?"

"No, Dougal," the boy laughs, rapidly shaking his head. "Tell him, Chrissy!"

"Tell him what, my bonny lad?" Chrissy asks from her position of peeling potatoes.

"Tell Dougal I just got bigger!"

"You must be eatin' your greens," Dougal replies without waiting for her collaboration. "Put it there," he then says, turning to Hugh and holding out his hand. The pair shake, each of them wearing a thoroughly contagious grin. "I expect you've come to check on afternoon tea?" Dougal straightens, his demeanor and tone cordial but deferential as his attention moves to Isla.

"I'm sure there's no need for that," she demurs.

"All the same," he replies kindly.

"McCain said it was to be served at half past three to give the ghillie sufficient time to get our guests back."

I wonder if she knows she's wringing her hands.

"Yes, my lady. And Mari said she saw them comin' up the north drive about half an hour ago."

"Then we should be making our way to the…" Her anxious gaze falls to Chrissy.

"The blue parlor, my lady." There's a note of reassurance in Chrissy's tone.

"Come along then, boys."

"But the sausage rolls," Archie complains.

"They'll be there," Dougal reassures. "I've prepared a

different menu for the wee ones. I'm told there will be two extra children this afternoon."

"Oh, yes. Mr. and Mrs. Duffy have two small boys," she replies, distracted.

"Do they have sausage rolls in America, Holly?"

At Archie's question, I turn from inspecting the baking tray Chrissy has just pulled from the oven. A baking tray full of perfect little golden puffs of pastry.

"Sadly, we do not."

"You should go back and open a shop over there. Sausage rolls make everyone happy."

"That would be a good idea. Except, I'd probably get very fat from eating one too many myself."

"Sausage rolls are my favorite," he says with an appreciative sniff as he's steered out of the kitchen by his mother.

"We'd have snuck them both a wee treat if their mother hadn't been with them," Dougal says remorsefully. "But they'll be eatin' soon enough, I suppose."

Mari and the girl referred to as "wee Sophie" appear in the kitchen not long after, both of them dressed in white shirts, black skirts, and hose, and are shortly followed by an austere-looking man in a grey pinstripe pants. A white shirt and a black tie and vest complete the ensemble. I'm guessing by the get-up, this must be the butler, Mr. McCain. Or to his employers, no "Mr" required. Just like Madonna. Or Beyoncé. I wonder if his personality is as big.

"Ten minutes," he announces in a soft brogue. "Mari and Sophie, you'll be ready."

The girls nod though his words weren't issued as a question.

"And you'll be Holly," he says, turning to me with a smile. A smile that softens his hard edges and lines makes me wonder if the parentheses bracketing his mouth have been caused by the frequency of his smile or the opposite.

I'll be Holly. I usually am, though I like to pretend I'm a little more interesting than Holly Harper. Just look at my Instagram! Sometimes, I even get to pretend to be someone else. Someone called Olive.

I shake off the thoughts and hold out my hand.

"Yes, that's me." We shake hands, then both turn to watch the final touches being laid to the tea trays. Small, rectangular platters are filled with tiny tarts laden with crème anglaise and fresh raspberries, a lemon iced slice, colorful macarons, and scones with tiny dishes of clotted cream and jam as fingers sandwiches, minus crusts, of course, are laid onto plates with military precision, then decorated with a neat pile of arugula topped with tiny lilac flowers.

"I doubt Hugh and Archie will be excited at the prospect of eating flowers for tea," Mr. McCain murmurs lightly.

"They've a hankering for sausage rolls." I turn my head, catching the rise of his brows.

"Much more sensible," he says with a nod.

"Dinnae fash," Dougal mutters. "The wee ones have their own menu." He dips his head in the direction of a two-tiered plate in Mari's hand. Tiny burger sliders, sausage rolls, a pink and yellow checkered cake, which I'm assuming is Battenberg, plus a row of tiny chocolate cupcakes.

"We'd best start moving this lot upstairs." I take a seat at the kitchen table and watch the military operation commence. Hot water urns, ornate solid silver teapots, serving ware, food; the list goes on and on... and then it goes into a rickety-looking dumb server. Meanwhile, I get to stuff my face with sausage rolls. As for Battenberg cake, I can't even persuade Gertie to take it.

19

ALEXANDER

"How's school?"

"Boring," Hugh replies without missing a beat.

"But it's..."

He rolls his eyes dramatically and looks exactly like his mother when he does so. Or at least how she used to look when we were children, living in this monstrous house with only each other for company.

"Necessary," he mutters sullenly. "Because knowledge is a powerful weapon."

"Exactly."

"But sometimes, I'd really just like to stab someone."

Wouldn't we all.

"Anyone in particular?" I ask, keeping my tone bland as Hugh rapidly shakes his head.

"I don't want anyone to die, but I'd really like to kick my art teacher. Hard!"

"I'll see what I can do."

"Uncle Sandy, you can't go around kicking teachers. It's just not the done thing."

"You're right, of course." I stretch out in the chair and

cross one ankle over the other. But the school seems mercenary enough to offer me the privilege for a price. God knows I pay enough in fees already, not that Isla knows. Her husband suggested it was that or he'd be forced to remove both boys and put them into the local state school. *Like my father did for me for a time.* I thought it was for his amusement at the time, but now I wonder if he was trying to toughen me up. I certainly learned to use my fists. But I wasn't about to let my nephews repeat the experience, even if it might give Hugh an outlet for his pent-up feelings.

"When I feel like you do right now, I usually go for a run. Maybe you could take Dirty Gertie out?"

"Don't call her that." He giggles. "You know she doesn't like it!"

"Who doesn't like it?" I reply innocently.

"*I* don't like it," says Isla as she enters the room. I stand to greet her. "Hello, Sandy." I jump up from my chair, and her arms slide around my neck. "Don't call my dog dirty," she whispers as her fingers threaten to tweak my earlobe.

"Then do something about her stomach troubles." I press a quick peck to her cheek. "Where is she anyway?"

"Do you need to ask?" Isla sends me an arch look. A look I'm told we've both perfected. "You know she's swindling Dougal in the kitchen. And just how were you planning to kick the art teacher?"

"Your mother has ears like a bat," I whisper to Hugh. "She was the same as a child. Always hearing things she shouldn't."

"She says all mothers have magic hearing," Archie replies, bouncing into the room, strangely enough, along with a rubber bouncing ball. "Uncle Sandy?" his eyes follow the ball as it shoots up into the air, almost hitting the chandelier before he catches it adroitly on its descent. "Do you know Dylan Duffy is going to be in the new Batman movie?"

Dylan Duffy is, I surmise, the Hollywood actor we have staying this weekend. "How interesting."

"I'm not supposed to know because it's a big lollywood secret. But Fergus told me."

"It's *Hollywood*," Hugh interjects with another roll of his eyes.

"You might need to see an optometrist, Hugh. The muscles at the side of your eyeballs might snap then you'll end up looking at the inside of your head for the rest of your life. That wouldn't be very interesting, would it?"

"Ha, ha! That's because you have an empty head," Archie taunts.

"How interesting," the little shit intones. "That's exactly what you say, Uncle Sandy, when you don't give a stuff."

"Have you been feeding these two raw meat?" I ask, turning to my sister.

"No, I think the Dalforth genes have just kicked in."

I pull a face. Isla and I argued at least four times a day until we were at least sixteen.

"Only eight more years, give or take."

"Give," I reply over the strains of *you're mean* along with the classic comeback of *you smell like Gertie's farty arse.* "Give them away," I say, glancing meaningfully their way. "Definitely."

"That is enough," Isla warns, hands on her hips. I'm almost certain she means her sons. *Almost.* And while the pair don't stop sniping, they do bring the noise level down a decibel or two.

"How are our esteemed guests?" I ask with a grimace. I'm looking ahead to an evening of small talk like I would having a hole drilled in the head. At least Van and Matteo are here. It's been a while since we spent a weekend together. Unfortunately, Portia is also here. She was a last-minute inclusion to the party after Isla said we were a female guest short.

"Fine. The director is very Hollywood, but his wife is pleasant enough. The big movie star, Dylan Duffy, is delightful. His wife is a fellow Scot," she adds reflectively, her gaze almost turning inward. "He seems to love her very much."

"A man being in love with his wife? How novel." But she doesn't answer. "Isla?"

"And their boys are lovely," she adds brightly, almost shaking herself.

"Are you all right?"

In response, she sends a cautionary glance her children's way.

"Later, then."

"Much later. Drinks are at half past seven," she adds brightly. "I'll try not to be late, but I can't make any promises. I need to find a trowel to help me apply my makeup tonight."

"Rubbish," I say, placing my hands on her shoulders. "You are as lovely as ever."

"And you should save your flattery for women you might actually be able to marry."

My answer is a placating smile because I have no intentions of doing so ever again.

HOLLY

I spend the rest of the afternoon hanging out in the kitchen, drinking coffee, and sharing morsels of food with old Gertie. I watch as people come and go, toing and froing, all for the benefit of the Duke of Dalforth and his fancy guests.

I decide Dougal is less like the captain of a ship and more like a regimental sergeant, presiding over a battalion of two, eager with their calls of, "*Oui*, Chef!" Because Dougal orders his minions about in French. *Hearing French spoken with a Scottish accent is a treat, let me tell you.*

Mr. McCain, the butler, has spent most of the afternoon in the dining room, apparently with a tape measure, running an operation called *mise en place*, which I'm told means to *put into place*. So basically preparing the formal dining table. Starched linens, silverware, glassware, china, and so on. Table settings are, so I'm told, a serious business. Posh people are weird, but surely even they can't tell if their water glass is half a centimeter off compared to the next place setting.

Meanwhile, every time I think about going to shower or to start getting ready, I push it off a little longer. And maybe that's where things begin to go wrong.

"Oh, Holly dear," Chrissy exclaims, her ample form bustling into the kitchen. "Thank goodness you're still here, Holly."

"What can I do for you?" My gaze darts around the room, almost expecting to see a fire that needs putting out. *Or maybe an escape route.*

"It's Mari. She's suddenly looking awful peely-wally."

"I don't know what that is," I answer hesitantly.

"She means she's sick," supplies one of the chefs whose names I don't know.

"Och, it's bad," she says heavily, "Very bad. She says she feels sick, and she can't serve if she's going to boak."

"She means vomit," the same young man adds next.

"Oh." I pull a face. "Yeah, I guess you're right. Do you think it's something she's eaten?" I ask hopefully, while mentally calculating when I was last near enough to her to catch something viral.

"I don't know," Chrissy answers, exasperated. "I can't think about that now. We're short someone to serve."

"And you want me to help out?"

"Could ye?" she asks hopefully.

No, I think, but somehow "Sure," comes out of my mouth. "Just let me make a call." I'm sure Cameron will understand. *Maybe not that I'm a total chickenshit, but I'll know.*

"You'll have a white blouse?" she says, almost following me as I open the door to the courtyard. "And a black skirt?"

"Yeah." My heart suddenly sinks. I'm truly giving up a night out with a cute guy to serve. What kind of dipshit am I?

"Idiot," I mutter to myself, yanking my hair up into a high ponytail on the say-so of Mr. McCain, who isn't so cheery this minute but seriously stressed in his white gloves. It's as hot as Hades in here, so he can't be wearing them, and a jacket with tails, because he's cold!

"You've done this before, aye?" he asks, eyeballing me as though to find fault in the skirt and shirt I've changed into. But, come on, I've even ironed them!

"Serving? Yeah."

"For a formal dinner? Silver service?"

"No, but—"

He curses under his breath. "Silver service is an art form. And one I don't have time to teach you tonight."

"I'm sure I'll manage," I reply snippily. "I mean, it's not like I have a college degree or anything."

"It isn't a case of intelligence but practice. So, serve from the left and clear from the right, right?"

"But—"

"Don't engage the guests in conversation," he says, barreling on as he begins to recount a list of dos and don'ts (mostly don'ts), marking off the items against the palm of his left hand. "Do not touch the guests—"

"Not even to cop a feel?"

He glowers back at me but doesn't miss a beat. "We do not stack plates when we clear. We move them over to the sideboard quietly and discreetly. Only the sherry glasses are removed. I'll tell you when. And we do not get excited when faced with a celebrity."

"I've lived in London," I retort indifferently. "You see celebrities there all the time." An exaggeration? Yes. Though I did once think I saw Keira Knightly coming out of a Sainsbury's Metro grocery store. But I can't believe I gave up an evening at the pub, an evening with Cameron, for this.

Note to self: run when someone next expects a favor.

"Stations, everyone," Mr. McCain calls out. "Guests will be gathering in the hall for cocktail hour shortly."

I won't be there because when I look down, I have a snag in my hose.

"Hurry!" Chrissy calls, beckoning me along the hallway, despite the fact that I'm doing just that as I hustle along the busy hallway, people I don't recognize carrying trays of glasses and cartons of empty champagne bottles.

"I didn't want to come down the main staircase," I mutter, trying to untwist the tangled and uncomfortable waist of my hose. Hose put on in a hurry is not fun. "It took a lot longer to get here using the servant's stairway." It was neither the scenic route nor the quickest route.

"The back staircase," Chrissy corrects, handing me a silver tray. "These are Scotch quail eggs with mustard seed chutney," she says, pointing at the platter of tiny golden balls, each skewered with a cocktail stick. "And these are haggis bonbons with a whisky sauce. On ye' go."

"Wait. Which is which again?" Both balls are a very similar color, and they both smell delicious.

"Does it matter?" she says with an exasperated shake of her head. "That lot out there won't know the difference. Not after a champagne cocktail or three."

I take a moment to remind myself that I gave up a night of cocktails of my own for this. *Last time,* I remind myself. *Favors are for suckers.*

"And don't be eatin' them," she says, her reprimand accompanied by a slap on the back of my hand.

"Too late," I mumble around a smile and the crispy morsel. "Oh, these are *so* good. Keep me some?"

"Go on with ye!" Hand on my shoulders, she propels me toward the door, pushing it open ahead of me.

I take a deep breath and center myself before making my way sedately into the hall.

Glide. Smile. Don't touch their butts, and don't talk to them, I intone silently, coming alongside a trio of people on the edge of the room.

"I just loved the one you were in with Meryl Streep."

I register the woman's upper-class accent but not so much the words.

"Can I interest you in a haggis bonbon?" I interject, dipping the tray enticingly. *Haggis bonbons. Get your haggis bonbons here!*

"Thanks, but I think you might've confused me with David Schwimmer," the man replies. Not to me, obviously, because I don't know if David Schwimmer likes haggis bonbons. But as his words begin to sink in, I realize why he looks so familiar. "These look good," he says, his gaze dipping to the tray.

"You're..." *so pretty,* I almost say. Thankfully, I catch myself just in time. "Hi."

"Hey there," he says, eyes barely flicking up from the tray. I don't sense any disrespect in his manner, just a man whose priority is food. And yes, the man is familiar, but only through the medium of my TV screen.

Kennedy is going to be so bummed when I tell her I met Dylan Duffy. And that he's hot with a capital *H*.

"What are these ones?" he asks, his finger hovering over the balls on the other side of the tray. His accent, I note, is American with a hint of something distinctly Scottish.

"Those are Scotch quail eggs, I think." My attention flicks to the stunning brunette standing next to him. She's familiar, too. Though only from celebrity magazines. "Honestly?" I lower my voice as I swirl my finger over the two types of offering. "I can't remember which is which." The brunette begins to giggle, covering her mouth with her hand. Wow. *I think they'd be able to see the diamond on that ring from space.*

"Well, I'll give these a try," he says, grabbing two skewered spheres and offering one to the woman who is surely his wife. Ivy, I think Chrissy said. "Babe?"

"No, you go on with your bad self." She holds up a forestalling hand, her Scottish accent almost melodic, like the tinkling of a bell. "Fill your boots!"

"I think I might," he says, turning back to the tray and grabbing another half dozen. "I'm kind of hungry. You don't mind, do you?"

"Less work for me," I answer happily. "But leave space for your dinner. There are six courses, so I'm told."

"He's got hollow legs," his wife says with a laugh. I'll take her word for it, nobly resisting the temptation to glance down.

"Want one?" he asks, seeming to remember the third of their party. "It was Portia, wasn't it?"

The woman slides me an unimpressed and superior glance, her mouth pursed like a cat's ass. "No. But thank you." Then she does this weird thing with her head, which seems to be the upper-class English version on, "go on—git!"

So *git* I do. At least for another couple of faltering steps until I find myself, tray in hand, standing stock-still in the middle of the room. I feel my cheeks lift, a slow smile spilling across my face. Maybe this is the reason I've felt so much resistance to going to the pub this evening. The universe had other plans for my evening—the universe sent me... kilts!

I was beginning to think they were a Scottish myth, but it looks like I was wrong.

Lord be praised. Kilts are Scottish formal wear!

Blue with white plaid, blue with yellow. Green with red, green with blue, and black, and seemingly every other color in between! Long socks and shiny shoes, jackets with sparkling buttons. Some men wear bow ties, others neckties, and almost all of them wear a vest. It's not exactly a scene from *Outlander*, but it's not something second best, either. The women in attendance look pretty cute, too. Evening dresses in every color and design make me wish I could photograph the scene from above. I bet they'd look like expensively wrapped chocolates in a box.

"Mr. McCain says move it," hisses a passing voice as a laden silver tray moves in the periphery of my gaze. I suddenly recall the weight of the one I'm holding.

Welp, back to work. Best make the most of appreciating kilts and legs because in less than an hour, they'll all be hidden under a tablecloth!

20

ALEXANDER

A NECESSARY EVIL, I REMIND MYSELF AS I SMILE AT SOME anecdote or other the florid man to the left of me is telling. *Hopefully, I'm smiling at an appropriate point.* Was he the director or the producer? I can't recall. Someone important to the success of the film, no doubt. Or movie, as he keeps referring to it. Either way, another blockbuster would be welcome. More visitors to the castle means money to repair the roof.

To my right, Isla forces a tinkling laugh, not that anyone else would see it as false. A subterfuge learned from living with a volatile father and a mother who didn't seem to care enough. My eyes meet hers over the rim of my glass. *Join us*, her gaze seems to insist. *Snap out of this mood and do your bit.* But perhaps that's the issue. Perhaps I'm tired of living for everyone else, living for crumbling buildings and failing lands and ancient titles. Tired of putting everyone else's needs above my own.

Fuck it, there has got to be something to throw off this mood. Maybe I need a holiday. Or maybe I should just get it over with and propose to Portia, leave her to run the estates.

"That sounds like something our father would say, doesn't it?" I register Isla's hand against my arm before her words.

"Absolutely." I force another smile, washing down the insincerity with a swallow of whisky because I can't imagine our guest insulted our father or our parentage. Or insist the only good thing about us is our name.

As Isla's hand slides away, she shifts in the low light, and I notice for the first time how pale she looks. The shadows under her eyes almost like bruises. There is most certainly something going on with her, something more than an argument with her husband.

And, like a colossal prick, I just expected her to play hostess tonight.

A twinge of guilt pierces my chest. When I'd pressed her this afternoon, she'd insisted we didn't have time to talk about it. Even the boys weren't very forthcoming when usually they're bursting to fill me in with their news. Though I sense their reticence has something to do with the missing marble statue from the reception hall.

It's been a strange homecoming. Even the staff seem out of sorts, I consider as I catch McCain's irritated expression from across the room. I expect he's upset because Van thought to bring Griffin with him. Though he's barely fifty, McCain is a butler of the old school where bastard sons are never mentioned, let alone brought into the fold.

Sensing our guest is getting to the punchline, I nod amiably, wondering why he hasn't bothered to see if Isla's hand is stuck up my arse, working me like a puppet. It could be because the man has a deep sense of his own importance and a love of the sound of his own voice. Or perhaps he thinks I'm the idiot product of inbreeding. Fuck, what do I care? Provided the money continues to roll in, I can nod and smile like an idiot quite happily for him.

But what the hell is wrong with McCain? If Griffin is winding up Chrissy again...

I turn my head, following the rapid path of my butler, watching as his eyes widen, his next step a long one as though to prevent—

—an almighty crash, flying glass and metal. Food, too. And my eyes seeing things. Seeing people they shouldn't see. People, or a person, more correctly, who isn't really here.

"Oh, my goodness!" Isla's champagne cocktail spills from her glass, wet droplets clinging to the sleeve of my jacket.

"Are you all right?" I steady the glass in her hand. Actually, no, she's pushing it at me.

"Excuse me," she says, smiling at our guests and ignoring the way my hand catches her wrist, how it tightens on it. *We have staff for that*, I hope it says, not *help me, I'm seeing things.*

Seeing someone I want but can't have.

Seeing her on her knees.

In a frilly apron.

Right here, in my ancestral home.

My gaze follows my sister as she tersely suggests to a very dignified McCain that he might help clear up the mess.

"Come with me." My voice is gruff, my fingers closing around the crook of Holland's upper arm before I'd even realized I'd crossed the room.

I'm not seeing things. And neither is she, though she looks almost stunned as she drops the last of the whatever those balls are to McCain's cupped hands.

"Just a case of butterfingers," I mutter to those who care to hear my explanation as I drag the object of my recent—

current?—obsession from the room without even looking at her.

I can't. I dare not. Not until I get her alone.

What the hell is she doing here? I feel elated. Angry. Unsure which of these is the overriding sentiment.

"There's no need to drag me," she hisses as we approach the threshold of the open double doors.

"Close them behind us," I command of Sophie, the timid young girl who works as part of Chrissy's team. The girl looks terrified, her gaze sliding to Holland as she tries to pry her fingers under mine. Holland, however, doesn't look terrified. She looks gloriously livid. It's an expression that does very little to dampen my cock's apparent enthusiasm for this moment. "Tell McCain," I further direct Sophie, "to push back dinner by half an hour."

A lot can happen in thirty minutes, given a little peace and privacy.

Fuck yes, it can.

21

HOLLY

Just one more kiss. One more time with him.

The air still and slightly musty, old leather and even older books, overlaid by the lingering scent of tobacco. Brass glints in the moonlight, drawing my eyes higher as I realize the room has a mezzanine level. *There must be so many books*, I find myself thinking, but I'm just hiding. Hiding from my thoughts.

How can it be him?

How can it be Alexander?

He steps into an arc of moonlight that slices silver through the open drapes.

"I didn't hurt you, did I?" he murmurs, his gaze falling to where I rub my upper arm.

I shake my head. It's not that my arm hurts, but more like I'm suddenly very cold. Maybe my body has gone into a state of shock. A minute ago, my cheeks were burning hot with shame as dozens of little balls of deliciousness hurtled through the air—I even saw one drop into a champagne glass in a guest's hand. And why? Because my stupid eyes had convinced me of the impossible. No way

Alexander could be here, standing in a kilt. I mean, the man isn't even Scottish. So, I'd dropped to the floor, grabbing up those tiny balls of meat and eggs, rolling around the floor like eyeballs. I'd felt like an idiot, and my cheeks were burning as hot as Chernobyl when one bare, tan knee landed on the floor next to my hand. My eyes took in the dark wool of a kilt and lifted. Then lifted again.

Alexander *was* there.

My eyes *did not* deceive me.

And I am so screwed.

I swallow thickly as the soles of his shoes scuff against the wooden floor. Maybe I should come clean and tell him when I said he didn't have to drag me, I meant what I said.

I'd have gone willingly with him.

Probably anywhere.

And oh, my gosh, he looks so good. The way the moonlight falls across him accentuates the masculine structure of his face, turning his fair hair silvery. There's such a naked longing in his expression and I wonder if this is somehow a reflection of my own face. Or maybe it's just that I can't trust my own senses, which is maybe why I find myself screwing my eyes shut and my hands into fists. I don't know what the heck I'm supposed to do. Throw myself at him? Give in? To myself? To him? Run the other way?

"*Holland.*" There's a wealth of emotion in my name. But like a child hiding from consequences, I choose to shield myself in the darkness. I tremble in the shadows. From the weight of my need. From the fear of it.

One step, then two, his footfalls muffled as he crosses the carpet.

The brush of his breath. The whisky scent of it.

I inhale sharply as his fingers touch my lips, swallow a

longing sign as he traces my mouth, almost as though learning the shape of it. Or remembering it.

Remembering what it was to kiss me.

A breath quivers from my chest as I ache. As I long for something I shouldn't, inhaling a soft gasp as his mouth catches the corner of my own at the same time as the pad of his thumb presses to the tiny indent at the bow. His finger drifts down, snagging my bottom lip as though in order to kiss it. *To take it between his own.* He swallows my next exhalation, a sound that's desperate and greedy and the antithesis of this moment. This kiss. My mouth feels so sensitive. Every brush, every trace of his, reduces me to a puddle of need. It's like my mouth is the center of all feeling in the universe, and his, the source of it.

"This mouth," he whispers. My eyes flutter open, meeting his dark and desirous ones. He begins to walk backwards across the room, my hips in his hands as he pulls me along with him. "These lips." His hands slide around me, swapping our positions to press me back against the wall of shelves.

The next time our lips meet, his mouth raids and plunders with a fierceness, his hand cupping the back of my head, finding the root of my ponytail, he begins to wind it. One sharp tug and I'm staring into inky dark eyes and the fierceness of his regard.

"I can barely believe it." He presses his mouth to my neck, shaping words against my skin. "You're really here."

"Please don't talk." *Please hurry. Please use your mouth just to kiss me.* My fingers grasp the shelves behind me to stop me from reaching out. To stop me from using the darkness as my defense because I don't want to think—I don't want to discuss w*hy* or *how* right now. I just want this.

God, I just want him.

His response is a soft chuckle as his hands find my ass, sparing me the inflexibility of the shelves in exchange for a hardness of his own. His tongue is a hot flick at the seam of my mouth, opening mine on a gasp. His lips working firmly, his tongue penetrating, twirling and twining with my own. One minute, we're chest to chest, and the next, his thick thigh is pressed between my legs, his reaction painted in a deep and masculine groan. I drink in his want, swallowing it down as my hands roam over the firm solidness of his velvet shoulders and arms, sliding around him to grab the globes of his ass. *His kilt-covered ass. Good for easy access.* His chuckle reverberates between us, his eyes silver in the moonlight as I gather the thick woolen fabric.

"Feeling a draught?" My taunt earns me another dark chuckle, then a growl as I find his softly furred thighs. Strong muscles contract under my fingers, my hands slipping higher with a determination to discover what *this man* wears under his kilt.

"No," he purrs, catching my hands in his and pressing them back against the shelves. "Ladies first." His voice is as dark as midnight and like temptation itself.

"Alexander." His name on my lips is no reprimand, no plea for time to think as his fingers and tongue conspire to loosen the buttons of my shirt. I arch from the shelves in a silent plea for haste.

"My God, how I've dreamed of this," he rasps, delivering a sucking bite to the swell of my breast as it's revealed.

"Oh, God..."

"How I've dreamed of you. Touched you so many times in my sleep only to wake, aching for you."

"I'm here." I run my hand through his thick hair as his tongue licks away the slight sting, kissing his way up my neck to deliver the kind of soliloquy that makes my knees weak.

"I want you, Holland. I want your taste in my mouth and your cries ringing in my ears. I want you so damned much it hurts. Tell me yes. Tell me I can have you. Here. Now."

"You have the mouth of a sinner." But that can't be true because nothing sinful could deliver such reverence.

"I have a mouth that only wants to worship you." His expression is so full of heat that it scrambles my brain and liquifies my bones.

"But the dinner," I whisper as my hands tighten in his hair. Not to push him away but to bring him closer. I know his madness. Recognize it. But I also now know why I'm not at the pub tonight. Because this is fate at play.

It has to be.

"You're all the sustenance I need." His fingers free my breast from the cup of my bra, my pebbled nipple perched above the lace. My thoughts scatter as his head descends, and he takes my nipple into his mouth.

With a desperate-sounding whimper, I arch from the shelves, chasing the sucking pull of his mouth.

"You were right that night." His gaze flicks up to mine, his lush mouth playing at a hesitant smile. "I do seem pretty bitey." My body bows as his tongue flicks out. "It's all you, darling. You make me want to devour you whole."

Maybe I'd be running for the hills if his words didn't sound so reverent. As it is, I can do nothing but moan as his tongue coasts up the underside of my breast. But as the coarse pads of his fingers begin to pluck my hose, my sense of practicalities, of propriety, are tugged. I can't go back to work with ripped tights, looking like I've been ridden hard in the library on the down-low.

"But Alexander, people will come."

"That's very much the plan," he says, dropping to his knees. "Let me put my mouth on you. I want to taste you."

Oh, yes...

"But they might come looking for me." And if they find me like *this* with one of the guests...

"No," he murmurs, working my skirt up my thighs. "They know where you are. Sophie saw me lead you in here."

"Sophie?" Her name might ring a bell, but not the alarm-sized buzzing going off in my head right now.

"Later." His fingers slide under my now belt-sized skirt, thumbs hooking into the waistband of my hose.

"No." I press my hands over his. I desperately want this —I want him—but that thing tugging at the edge of my consciousness won't be ignored.

Alexander's fingers relax, his hands curling around my hips instead. His gaze dips, the dark crescents of his lashes like a fan against his cheeks. I watch the deep movement of his throat as he swallows, the effort it takes to contain himself. And all the while, I'm wondering why can't I just give in.

"Holland." My name is a groan as he pitches forward, pressing his forehead to my chest. "Don't make me go into dinner like this." Still on his knees, he moves back, his very obvious erection tenting the heavy fabric of his kilt.

Is there anything about him that isn't breathtaking?

"I want..." Him. This. "Let's do this properly. Can you leave? Fake illness or an emergency? Sneak out?" I run my fingers through his hair, trying to make it look a little less sex-mussed. Or almost sex-mussed as the case may be. I'll feign illness. I'll just tell Chrissy I must have what Mari has. Then somehow, I'll sneak him up to my room. My conscience is pinged at the thought of being so disrespectful towards Isla, but this has to be fate! And if nothing else comes of this tonight, at least I will. Multiple t—

"I can't leave a dinner as the host."

A giddy thrill runs through me. But then: "Wait, what?" My hands drop from his head to his shoulders, curling there. He didn't just say host, did he? Guest of honor, maybe?

"I also can't sit for six fucking courses at the head of that table, willing them all to hell." His accent is so proper, though the words not so much. Words that tilt my reality on its axis.

I push at his shoulders, sliding along the tall bookcases to put a little distance between us.

"What is it?"

Alexander Dalforth? But I thought the duke's name was Sandy. When I don't answer, he stands, the action as lithe as a jungle cat.

"You." I swallow, willing this not to be true. "You're the host?" My question, my accusation, swells at the end as I begin to tug at the undignified positioning of my skirt and apron.

"Yes," he answers, his face suddenly falling into grave lines as he rights his kilt with a painful-looking grimace. "I'm sure there's much we don't know about each other, but—"

"Like the fact you didn't mention you were a duke?" I spin away, not really believing it still.

"It's not something I go around broadcasting," he bites back stiffly.

"Sure." I feel inexplicably crushed as he begins to right the cuffs of his shirt.

"Those who already know me know I am the head of a

dukedom. I don't advertise the fact to anyone else. I learned not to with experience."

"How? You don't even have the accent." But then I realize neither does Isla. Neither do the boys.

"My father used to have this saying. If a cat is born in a stable, it does'nae make it a horse." And wouldn't you know it, he executes his answer with a perfectly Scottish accent.

"I don't even know what that's supposed to mean." I spin away angrily, not sure I need to hear anything else, not wanting to look at him. Not trusting myself to.

Fate had nothing to do with bringing me here, I think bitterly. But maybe he did.

"It means I am Scottish and that I'm the Duke of Dalforth, whether you believe it or not, whether I choose to use the accent or not."

"You didn't say," I whisper almost to myself.

"No." He makes no mention of our other untruths this time. "It's a title I rarely advertise. Became tired of being weighed to the last pound."

I sense he doesn't mean what he weighs. He's talking pound sterling.

"There aren't many of us about. Less still with our own teeth, hips, and knees. It tends to add to the novelty."

"Well, I hate to point out the obvious, but it wasn't your wallet I was looking for when I had my hands on your ass."

"I didn't mean—"

"Is that what I'm doing here?" The catch in my voice is so slight, I take heart in the fact he probably didn't hear it. But just in case, I push on with my offensive. "Did you move me all the way up here just to fuck me?" Offensive and offending and loud, I hate how I shuffle back as he takes a step closer.

"I don't know what you're doing here," he utters, his diction sharp. "Because you're not a fucking waitress."

"Well, I hate to break it to you," I mutter, jerkily slapping the apron to my body and tightening the strings at my back, "but that thing I had in my hand in the other room? That was no heraldic shield. It was a serving tray. And those weird-looking balls? I'm told those are what you people call *hors d'oeuvres*." I answer in the most hick accent I can carry off. "Add in this," I flick my apron, "and I'd say your hypothesis is way off. Also, I prefer server to waitress, thank you."

Chest heaving, I say no more. But neither does he, though his icy glare speaks volumes that I pretend not to understand.

"I really have no idea what you're doing here," he says eventually, his words piercing like an insult.

"I came because I was offered a job," I answer calmly, though I can't resist the urge to fold my arms. "Are you trying to tell me you had nothing to do with that?"

"Do you think I would've embarrassed myself out there," he says, swinging his arm wide, "if I'd known you were here? Do you think I would've waited these weeks? Stayed away?"

"I don't know what to think. You said you'd help me get a job, not that you were interested in me!" But I'm still processing his words as I make my retort.

"You have no idea what it took not to pursue you," he says, his nostrils flaring angrily, his hands balled into fists by his sides.

"I..." I don't know what to think.

"Tell me you haven't thought about me, Holland," he dares, stepping closer. "Tell me that wasn't shock out there but fucking kismet."

"I don't know what that was, Alexander," I lie. "I mean, is that even your name?"

"Of course it's my fucking name," he bellows, the sound echoing through the room.

"Your sister calls you Sandy." I might not be able to cock a brow, but I can surely cock a hip, even if my knees are shaking. This is too much. To want him. To almost have him.

"Sandy is short for Alexander. Ask any Scotsman, and he'll confirm that, seeing as how my word means so very little to you." He closes his eyes, his broad chest expanding and falling with a deep breath. Then he begins again. "I know you think I haven't told you the truth, and I'm sure in some respects you're right, but the fact remains, I made a spectacle of myself out there because I want you. Because I have thought of little else but you for weeks. For months. I don't want to want you, Holland, but God help me, I fucking do."

Such want and such anger leave me feeling crushed and defenseless as he steps closer.

I raise my hand. "There's no going forward, either." Not here. Not now. "You son of a—"

"Son of a duchess, yes," he says, catching my fist. "But she was also a bitch. In her defense, I believe that came from being married to my father. I don't want to want you," he growls, yanking me closer, "because you deserve better than she had."

And then he kisses me again. And I let him, his arms banding my body to his. But this isn't right. I feel it in the pit of my stomach, unease swirling like silt from the bottom of a lake.

"No." With my hands at his shoulder, I push away from

him, taking a few faltering steps before pivoting back again. "Start talking," I demand.

"I'm sorry?" he replies, not sounding sorry at all.

"Tell me what you're doing here. Tell me what I'm doing here?" Tell me this isn't how it looks.

"You've already said you're working." His eyes flick over me angrily. "In my own way, so am I."

"That seems very convenient, doesn't it? I'm here. You're here. Hey, let's have sex! Step in at any time," I demand.

"I'm merely waiting for you to say something sensible before I join the conversation."

"Tell me the truth. Did you arrange this job for me?"

"I don't think I like your assumptions," he responds angrily. "And I definitely don't like your tone."

"Well, I don't like being manipulated, so I guess neither of us gets to be happy right now."

"There was no manipulation. I gave you the number of an employment agency. I had no idea you were employed here."

"So you're saying, you're promising me, you didn't personally plan to park me up here in the wilds of Scotland."

At this, something flickers across his expression. Something that looks a little like guilt.

"I didn't know you'd be on one of my estates," he answers. "I didn't plan it like this."

"So what did you plan? If not this, then what?"

"I was doing you a good turn," he grates out. "I didn't like to think of you destitute and waiting tables in London."

"Destitute?" I bark out an incredulous-sounding laugh. "I'm not poor. Or desperate." Not quite, I wasn't. "And I was not in need of an intervention or your charity."

Both our heads swing to the door at the brisk knock.

"McCain," Alexander explains before the door fully opens, moving almost as though to shield me. "I said I didn't want to be disturbed," he growls as it does.

"He knows." Griffin steps into the room, the door clicking quietly closed behind him. As I step around Alexander's large frame, I notice Griffin isn't wearing an inch of tartan. *Isn't that strange, given they're brothers?* Hands slunk deep into the pockets of his tuxedo pants, he saunters into the room like a groomsman on the prowl or maybe a wannabe bad boy at a school dance. "That's why McCain asked me to stick my head over the top of the trench."

He comes to a stop, almost leaning against the side of a late model desk. Flicking on the desk lamp, he angles it in such a way that the three of us are circled in its weak rays.

"You've delivered his message," Alexander mutters, the heat in his gaze going out like a snuffed candle. "Leave."

"I didn't really come in the guise of a delivery boy," he says. "I will admit I thought I'd be walking in on something a little more interesting than an argument. Hey, Holly," he adds with a bland smile. "Fancy finding you all the way up here." Then he glances his brother's way, almost impressed.

"Yeah, fancy," I reply a touch acidly.

"Oh, do fuck off, Griffin," Alexander drawls.

"I would, but you see, we're all hungry. And Dougal is fretting that dinner will be spoiled. A temperamental lot, chefs." He sends me a look that I'm sure is meant to be cheering. It's not. "Besides, that lot out there are desperate to know what's going on inside this hotbed of intrigue." Griffin glances around the darkened room almost consideringly. "Library of intrigue?" His gaze comes to a stop on me. "Library of hotness?"

"Did you know I'd be here?" I demand, glaring back at him.

Griffin shakes his head slowly, his attention flicking to the other man. "We're not exactly bosom buddies, are we, your grace?"

"He doesn't expect you to call him that," I begin when Alexander pivots quite savagely.

"If you're going to rely on Griffin for information, you're much sillier than I thought."

I inhale audibly, tears inexplicably springing to my eyes. I totally have Griffin's number—I understood exactly the type of man he was the very first time I met him. But Alexander, I don't know what to make of him. Other than he resents wanting me.

Griffin makes a chiding sound, a click of teeth and tongue. "That was unkind, Alexander. To you, not me," he adds, glancing my way.

"Oh, I'm aware. Believe me."

"We're only half-brothers and not really friends. So, in answer, it was a surprise to see you here. But whatever he's told you," he adds, pushing from the desk, "it'll be the truth." He appears to consider his own words for a moment before adding, "Mostly."

"Thank you," I murmur, not really sure why as I glance down at my feet. Was that supposed to make me feel better or worse?

Griffin pauses at the door. Whether for dramatic effect, I'm also not sure. "Families are complicated," he says. "This one more than most."

He has barely one foot out of the door when I brush past him.

"Holland!" Alexander calls.

But I can't get away from him quick enough.

22

ALEXANDER

"What was all that about?" At the end of the busy service hallway, I watch as Chrissy catches Holland by the hand. "Are you okay, lass?"

"I'm fine," Holland replies defensively, her words overly loud. "And he's an asshole."

A frown creases my brow. I think that's the first time I've heard her curse. *Well done, Dalforth. Congratulations on being a complete dick,* I think as I stride along the hallway. And that's definitely the first time Chrissy has sent me a reproachful look. A look that causes Holly's gaze to flick over her shoulder. As our gazes meet, hers quite clearly says *fuck you.*

"Ye can'nae say things like that about a duke," Chrissy chides, purely for propriety's sake because the look on her face tells me she'll have questions. There's no fobbing off the woman who runs this house. There never has been.

But I am still the duke.

"Leave us," my voice booms. I'm not the kind of employer that yells or demands, but there's a certain satisfaction to be felt as the bodies melt into other spaces leaving only Holland, Chrissy, and myself. Didn't I ask for something to throw off my recent mood? My ennui? Well, it looks like I've gotten it. My blood rages hot through my veins, my cock as hard as a tent pole.

"Holland," I call out haughtily, warming to my part. "You have fifteen minutes to get your arse into the dining room. Fifteen minutes," I repeat, allowing my gaze to fall disdainfully over her, "to find yourself something more suitable to wear."

"But this is what the girls always wear," Chrissy replies, stepping in front of the object of my desire. "Mr. McCain saw to her outfit himself."

I do not like the sound of that, though the sordid implications are purely my own. Not for the first time, I want to throw the woman over my shoulder and drag her back to my bedroom. But now is time for the duke to come out, not the caveman.

"Be that as it may, but Holland's attendance is required as a guest at the table this evening."

"You can't make me—" Holland begins, stepping around Chrissy, her colors flying. *I don't think I've ever seen her cheeks so red.*

"In this house, you'll find I can do what I want."

Both women's jaws fall open, and how I manage not to laugh, I've no idea. But then Holland's mouth snaps shut, her eyes narrowing on me.

"Not with me, you can't."

Twisting my wrist, I glance down at my watch. "Twelve minutes now," I utter crisply. Uninterested in the extreme. "Unless that is, you'd like to explain to the local police exactly what happened to the statue of Apollo at the bottom of the main staircase."

It was a calculated guess that pays off dividends.

This time, Holland's jaw falls open as Chrissy throws me a shrewd look. A look that's quickly extinguished as Holland's head whips around, seeking her reassurance. But there are no flies on Chrissy, as the saying goes. She quickly assesses the situation for what it is before offering Holland nothing more than a helpless shrug. *What can I do?* It seems to say meekly. But Chrissy has never been meek in her life.

"I... that is... I don't have anything suitable to wear," she spits out. It's hardly a conciliatory response. More irritated.

I glance wearily at my watch again. "Ten minutes now."

"Urgh! You are going to regret this," Holland mutters, swinging around.

"I had better not," I call after her. "The police station in the village is open twenty-four hours."

Her only response is the stomp of her feet on the stairs.

"I don't know what you're up to," Chrissy begins, watching me sharply. "But I trust you know."

I incline my head in a conciliatory manner. It seems better than answering with the truth.

"I expect you'll come and find me tomorrow to explain what this is all about?"

"I will," I promise, though I'm not sure how I can explain how I need to have Holland *with* me, not serving me. There's nothing wrong with honest labor, and this isn't about where we each stand in the order of things. This is simply a case of my wanting her to be near me, I think. "But for now," I add, "I must brave McCain's wrath by asking him to set another place at the table."

"Oh, you'll have him fizzin' for sure," she answers with a sudden cackle. "He'll not be best pleased."

"No," I agree. But he'll do it, or I'll give him the boot. Right up his skinny arse.

Chrissy wanders off to rally the troops, and I return to

the fray and a room of speculative looks. My gaze coasts over Portia's as though I hadn't noticed her, seeking McCain, who appears in front of me like a wraith come to life.

"Your grace?" Either he had his ear pressed to the door to the service corridor, or he's bloody psychic.

"I'd like you to lay another space at the dinner table," I murmur, without waiting for his response. "Once you've done that, dinner may be served."

"I'll pass on the glad tidings to Dougal," he says with a deferential tilt of his head, which is contradicted by his heavily pointed words. And here I was just thinking the man might deserve a pay rise. But he's not quite fizzin', though I didn't expect him to be effervescent in my presence.

I make my way to Isla, who takes my arm with a serene smile.

"You and I," she says, her expression unchanging as she leaves the group of guests she was attending, "are going to have a very interesting conversation tomorrow."

"I look forward to it." The way I see it, we'll be having several very interesting conversations, beginning with her news.

"Sandy, your superior looks don't work on me. You seem to forget I'm your big sister."

"Fifteen minutes doesn't count." I force myself to curtail a budding smile, choosing to look at no one but her. Because if I allow myself to glance around the room, I'll only be looking for one person. *One person who had better toe the line tonight.*

"Says you," she answers serenely as McCain announces dinner.

Folding Isla's hand into the crook of my arm, I lead her to our guest of honor—the director of the much-hoped-for blockbuster—and exchange my sister's arm for that of his wife. As convention dictates, our guests fall into line behind us as Isla, as hostess, leads us into dinner.

Resisting the urge to seek out Holland, I pull back my companion's chair, then make my way to the head of the table as McCain takes the opportunity to discreetly remind me of our guest of honor's name. A guest of honor who is as unpopular with the butler as I am, though his crime was to make it known he wished to be seated next to me rather than the hostess, as is the custom. As I reach the opposite end of the table, the portly man of around sixty years is already beaming at me. We wait for Isla, as hostess, to take her seat before doing the same. It's in this minuscule interlude that my heart sinks as I notice one solitary chair is without a guest. But then, it soars as a vision in a pale blush pink glides along the length of the table. Her dress subtly glimmers in the low light, as do her collarbones, bared by the cut of the dress. Though obviously a dress, the outfit looks to be two separate pieces, the top swaying hypnotically in time with the hem as she walks.

"I'm sorry," she mutters as she passes Isla who, in turn, shoots me a look so arch, I almost bark out a laugh. Amusement doesn't bubble inside me for very long as I realize the person Holland has been seated next to.

Fucking Griffin.

If that isn't the devil at play, I don't know what is. It's my own fault, I suppose, for not being more specific with McCain.

Finally, Isla lowers herself into her chair, and the evening begins.

"You get your staffing problems under control?"

Perhaps I should consider it fortunate that Mr. Horowitz had requested to be placed so close, given how I'd noticed earlier his fondness for the sound of his own voice. It might give me a moment to gather my thoughts. His wife sits opposite him, Matteo next to her, sandwiched between her and Portia, who sits directly to my left.

Portia is used to being left to her own devices but obviously realizes something has changed. The Duffy's and some others whose names I don't remember fill the chairs in the middle of the table, along with Griffin and Holland, who I note with some pain, sit with their heads close.

I lift my gaze, my jaw clenched.

I'd like to snap his head from his fucking neck.

But then I notice how Van leans toward my sister. I wonder if she has Mr. Horowitz to thank for her sudden discomfort or if Van bribed one of the staff to be seated next to her.

Horowitz's voice pulls at my attention once more.

"I'm sorry, you were saying?"

"The girl—the server you frog marched out of the hall from dropping the tray?"

Is that what my desperation to kiss her looked like?

"It was a misunderstanding," I murmur blandly, wondering what on earth would possess him to bring up such a thing, along with how is it possible he doesn't realize the same girl is sitting at this table, in a dress the color of summer clouds at sunset? Dark, luxurious hair piled on top of her head, she wears no jeweler but a thin chain at her wrist and the thick silver band at her thumb. *A band she twists nervously.*

"Americans," he asserts. "That's who you want working for you. American service is second to none."

"But she had an American accent," his much younger wife offers up in an annoying squeak as she declines the first course with a lift of her skeletal hand. "I'm on Dr Newman's thirty-day reset," she explains with a mildly condescending smile.

"You're sure?" her husband asks, turning a little violently to her before swinging to me.

"Yes, Dr Newman said—"

"The girl?" he demands. "She was American?"

Griffin glances down the table, looking like a bastard holding all the aces. *The analogy probably extends to the four spare ones he'd have shoved up his sleeves.* I force myself to glare back as I picture myself knocking out his front teeth. I sincerely hope McCain's mind-reading skills are sharp tonight because I'm going to need alcohol. Lots of it.

"All of his grace's staff are from the local village," Portia curiously answers on my behalf.

"I'm unsure what would possess you to say so," I murmur, not sparing her a glance. I know I'm being rude, but I can't help it. I feel like whipping up her chair, carrying her down to where Holland sits, and exchanging the pair. Which isn't fair. I make a mental note to add Portia to my list of people requiring an explanation tomorrow.

Isla, Chrissy, Portia, Holland. Not necessarily in that order.

In Portia's case, more than an explanation is necessary. We need to have a conversation about ending things. Though how you end something that never truly began, I'm not really sure. *It's not you, it's me.* But she knew that from the start. I didn't pursue her. Quite the opposite. And I've always told her there was no future in this.

"I just meant—"

"McCain is from Edinburgh," I say, cutting her off wearily. "George is from New York. Should I go on?"

"I just meant at the castle, darling." I stare down to where she presses her hand over mine. Since when have I been her darling? She has certainly never been mine. "Of course you hire internationally," she placates, as though speaking to an idiot. "You merely don't have any American staff here on the estate."

"What about Holly here?" Griffin calls up the table.

As I lift my gaze, my blood runs cold. As Portia's hand rests over mine, so does Griffin's over Holland's, her eyes anywhere but meeting mine.

"I don't think I've met Holly," Portia says, picking up her glass.

"No?" he asks, lifting Holland's hand from the table.

I grit my teeth hard, foreseeing a trip to my dentist in the not-too-distant future. I begin to push back my chair, acting on instinct, not intellect. Portia's hand tightens infinitesimally on mine, halting me in my actions and blessing me with some clarity. Portia would be why Holland refused to look at me. *My hand holding darling*, I think cynically. But she is right about one thing; to leave the table now would be wrong. It would be to play into his hands.

"She's Archie and Hugh's nanny," Griffin offers happily. His gaze swings to Isla with a nod as though to encourage her confirmation. He and I both know he's just making a circus of the whole thing. The server who is a nanny, the nanny who is a guest at the duke's dinner table, sitting next to Griffin so serene and demure refusing to look at the duke who earlier dragged her out of the room. The duke, meanwhile, throws down drink after drink and glare after glare while his bastard half-brother plays at ringmaster.

It's not Holland he's trying to embarrass but me. Not that this makes me feel any less sorry to have put her in this situation. However, it could be that she may need to get used to it because I'm not going anywhere, and it looks as though neither is Griffin.

HOLLY

"Her name's Portia," Griffin whispers, bringing his mouth to my ear. I know why he does it; why he makes the moment between us look intimate. And I know why I don't stop him. I don't like being manipulated, but I find I like it even less when I look up to see the man who, not two hours ago, professed to a desperation for me sitting with another woman.

Another woman with a stupid name.

"Like the car?" I murmur back, counting on Alexander being too far away to understand how confused I feel.

"Like the ride of choice for any middle-aged man with more cash than sense." Griffin gives me a sexy half-smile. Honestly, he must think I'm brainless. I didn't want to be here in the first place, but for him to announce to the whole table that I was the nanny is nothing but low. Not that I'm embarrassed: I refuse to buy in to that. But I am *not* happy with the fact that, dressed as a server, I was almost dragged out of the room by the duke. And now I'm sitting here at the other end of the table with the duke's brother while the duke sits with someone else.

I don't know which of us looks worse.

"They're not married," I murmur. This much I do know.

"I wouldn't be surprised if they end up doing that long walk down the aisle sometime." His gaze flicks Alexander's way. "They're two of a kind." He frowns before his gaze moves back to me, brightening. "Like cyborgs. No feelings."

Those are not my experiences of Alexander. The man I know has so much passion. Anger. Regret, even. And to believe everything he'd said tonight would be to believe he also has compassion. That he cares.

I didn't want to think of you as destitute and waiting tables.
I didn't know you'd be here.

And I believe him because I believe in the things his sister has said to me. And the people who work here, too. I guess a man of his position would be forgiven for having some level of arrogance. Hubris, maybe. But he's not so arrogant as to believe he could have his cake and eat it too, I think. To agree with Griffin would be to believe Alexander would have his future wife and his potential side piece sitting at the same table. I just don't see how that can be true.

Even if, out of the two of us, only one of us knows how to eat snails. Or a soufflé. And, as I look down at my place setting, which one of these four forks is meant for fish.

My stomach turns over, nervousness washing through me again.

No, that's not what this is.

I might not know either of these men well, but I know enough not to trust Griffin at his word. It's more likely he'd be the one who'd use me. And that's not about to happen.

23

ALEXANDER

Dinner progresses through the courses without event, unless I count how easy the wine has flowed. I wonder if I'll manage not to blame myself when I'm unable to stop myself from seeking her out once the table is cleared and this lot has fucked off to bed.

It's little wonder she thinks I'm a dog as utterly unconvinced as she was by my explanation. How could I explain the only hand I had in this whole thing was to send her as far away from Griffin as possible? That I couldn't stand the thought of her being with him, that I couldn't trust myself, knowing where she'd be.

Perhaps my reasons for getting her out of London were somewhat nefarious, I consider, glancing down the table at my brother, who is enjoying this dinner with gusto and naturally, entertaining those around him with brilliant ease. Even Portia seems to wish she'd been seated nearer him, though possibly that might be more to do with wishing she was sitting anywhere else but with me on account of my being unable to behave decently to her, either.

Holland. Isla. Chrissy. Portia. All the women in my life

seem in need of apologies and explanations. Only, Holland wasn't meant to *be* part of my life. I tried so hard not to involve her, for her sake. But that has backfired thanks to fate or some other fuckery, and I have no intentions of letting her go this time.

A point I intend to make clear to her tonight.

"Oh, we just love Scotland. I'm one-eighth Scottish, you know?"

During the meat course—saddle of venison with shallots and baked celeriac, not that I seem to taste it—it became apparent that the remaining seven-eights of Mrs. Horowitz is alcohol. Forty percent proof.

"I tell you, duke, the location scouts did a great job finding this place," her husband says over the top of his wife's snorting giggle. "This movie is gonna be a hit."

"I wish you every success," I reply, with a slight lift of my glass as I remind myself the only reason I'm not with Holland right now is because of my responsibilities. The responsibilities of my family, my name, and all it entails.

"Never mind Tollbridge, tourists and fans will be flocking to this place to get a little Rory Roy!" he exclaims.

"I wouldn't mind getting a little of the man myself." His wife not so subtly glances to where Dylan Duffy sits. "Except the way I heard it, there isn't anything little about him," she adds lewdly.

"Carrie," Horowitz hisses, tugging on her arm. "This liquid diet you're on is no good for you."

"I don't know," Portia mutters under her breath. "I'd say Mrs. Horowitz has the right idea."

"Ideas for the man or the diet?" I ask, feigning interest.

"No, no, no!" My bastard brother's laughter catches my attention. "Falling in love is for those with sadomasochistic leanings. Just ask his grace." All eyes turn my way. "Those are his own words I'm repeating, by the way."

"Such a nihilist!" heckles someone at the fun end of the table. Van, I think.

"It's true," I reply because those are my words, though I don't remember speaking them within earshot of Griffin. "Matters of the heart inevitably bring or cause pain."

"That sounds a little tender. A little heartbroken, even." This from Dylan Duffy's wife.

"My heart isn't broken," I answer with a small smile.

"It's probably still in the packaging it came in," Griffin mutters, catching my eye.

"Romantic love, in my experience, can bring as much heartache as happiness."

"But it's worth the risk," Ivy Duffy argues. "To find someone to love is—"

"Is the chance to feel pain." Parting my fingers, I slide the *V* over the base of my glass before my gaze flicks to Portia. "Or for you to cause someone pain."

Portia almost winces though why, I'm not sure. This is a conversation we had a long time ago. I will never fall in love again. I will never again give that power to anyone.

Not even Holland.

"Only if that's what you're into," Griffin supplies to the guffaws of his tablemates.

Matteo smothers a laugh though Van gives in heartily to his, adding, "I think that says more about our learned friend," he says, using pointed legalese, "than it does his grace."

"Love is gentle. Love is kind," joins in drunken Carrie Horowitz.

"Love hurts," Van counters, sending Griffin the kind of glance that makes me wonder what else played out on the club's monitors the other night. "But some people like it that way."

"To love is to give someone the power to hurt you," my sister interjects quite suddenly. "The flip side is that you too can cause hurt." When I glance up, my gaze lands on Holland's as she looks my way for the very first time. I wonder what she's thinking, what she's seeing in this shit show of a dinner. It must be like watching animals at the zoo for her.

"And somewhere someone is singing an R.E.M. song," announces Griffin, playing up to his audience. "But love makes the world go 'round," he says, sliding his arm deliberately behind Holland's chair, who discreetly leans forward.

"I didn't realize you were an expert on love, Griffin." On sexually transmitted diseases, maybe. "I must've missed your great love affair," I murmur, reaching for my glass.

"You shouldn't make fun of other people's experiences." This comes from Portia, her words as heartfelt as I've ever heard them as she stares daggers Griffin's way. "It's human nature to avoid that which has hurt you. Until you've suffered loss, you can't understand."

"Ah. The lady is quite right." Griffin lifts his glass. "A toast to Leonie, his grace's late wife. God rest her soul. The paragon of perfection and the reason her beloved will never, ever remarry."

They are my words. At least, some of them are. I will never marry again. But what I don't understand is why hearing them now makes me feel so uncomfortable. I glare down the table as our guests murmur an awkward toast. I will never love again, but not because I pine for Leonie. I will never love again because I am married to this life. This dukedom. And because I choose not to share this albatross of an existence with anyone else. No, I don't miss Leonie, but part of me wonders if our marriage was part of the reason for her death. Suicide or accident? I suppose I'll never truly know.

I imagine Holland already knows I was married once. Our staff was very fond of the idea of her, but Leonie never spent enough time here for them to know her. This, I suppose, allows them to see her as the fantasy. The perfect duchess for their noble duke. Not the nightmare revealed to me once we were married.

Yes, maybe her death is on me.

"But you can't spend your life wandering around like some lonely Heathcliff," Griffin adds. "Or would that be Mr. Rochester?"

"I'm glad to see your education wasn't wasted on studying dead white men," I answer coolly, ignoring the turmoil his words have created. "I wouldn't have pegged you as one with interest in the gothic." Which of these tales is supposed to hit a nerve, I wonder? Heathcliff was a tortured hero, driven to madness by longing and jealousy. Mr. Rochester kept his mentally ill wife in the attic. While I can't lay claim to that exactly, we all have skeletons in our closets. The attics at Kilblair are full of nothing but useless stuff. Maybe I should also shove Griffin there.

Perhaps he only means Leonie was unstable, but how would he know?

Fucking Griffin and his cluster bomb tactics.

"As for lonely, how can I be with such family and friends." I raise my glass in the most insincere toast of my life.

"But everyone needs love." My attention slides to Portia, whose gaze remains glued to her wine. "And sometimes friendship can develop into love."

Oh, Portia. We have never even been friends.

And if there's something that my forty years on earth have taught me, it is that love, romantic love, is the stuff of nightmares. The data isn't just my own. My parents, my grandparents, my ancestors. And now, my sibling. We've all chosen poorly or had love slip away. If you believe my grandmother, our lineage is cursed. But back in the real world, which is where I prefer to dwell, it's neither magic nor a lack of luck that is the cause. It's more a case that as individuals, along with our familial responsibilities, make us very hard to love. But that's not an explanation for anyone this evening.

"That's where boundaries come in," I reply, my tone low, so low I'm sure that few people heard. A formal dinner isn't the place to bare your soul, nor is it the place to remind the woman sitting next to you not to build up her hopes. Or to explain to the woman you're obsessed with, the woman you were elated to find under your roof, that you're no good.

"Boundaries?" my sister asks, almost as though she can't help herself and her bat-like hearing.

"Rules, if you like."

Rules that I govern my relationships by. Relationships with women who know they will never come first but rather last in a long list of my responsibilities. Women who know and are comfortable with the fact that I will never again commit. In sending Holland away, I was doing her a service. Having her by my side would be a mistake. It would be to make her into someone else. To bend her spirit. To bend her will. To force her to fit to a mold that isn't hers.

At the thought, I give a rueful smile. These pointless ruminations because she's no longer a one-night blessing. But as much as I want her, I'm not about to fall in love. Lust, however, seems another matter.

"But love doesn't play by the rules," Isla says, returning to trite statements and lines from pop songs as she seeks corroboration from Van. *How strange.*

"You're right." My gaze slices up, meeting Holland's at the other end of the room. "Even when you do the wrong thing for the right reason, if it's meant to be, it will always work out in the end."

And I have to believe that right now.

24

HOLLY

Isla gracefully rises from her chair and suggests we all adjourn to the parlor for brandy and coffee, like we're actors in some scene of an episode of Downton Abbey.

This is my opportunity to slip away without drawing attention to myself.

I almost can't believe I've survived the most uncomfortable night of my life. Tomorrow, I am so out of here. There is no way I'm hanging round to give this pair the opportunity to embarrass me again. How dare Alexander force me out of my uniform—out of my element—and what was I thinking getting dressed and coming down to the dining room in the first place? I should've just locked myself in the bedroom. Told him exactly what he could do if he didn't like it. Maybe I'd have even dug out a few of my big-girl words.

You know the ones: the ones about sex and travel.

Urgh! I feel so angry. I literally had to sit on my hands at one point to stop myself from punching Griffin after he'd pulled that stunt. What was the point of introducing me to the guests as Isla's nanny? Other than making me feel like a fool. And then bringing up his long dead wife—what was that all about?

Head high, I rise from my own chair as Griffin pretends to be a gentleman, pulling it out from behind me. *Too bad you didn't get the chance to help me sit down at the start of the evening,* I think. He could've pulled it out from under me, then they all could've had another laugh at my expense.

You can't trust the man, I remind myself. *Trust your instincts. Trust that other people have told you so.* Namely, my old employer, Martine.

My eyes start to sting as I shuffle forward, hating on myself a little more. Like the guests in front of me, I turn like an automaton in the direction of the door, though I refuse to make eye contact with anyone.

Guests and otherwise.

"Shall we?"

Griffin appears by my side before I've taken two steps, proffering his elbow.

"No, thank you," I reply, summoning my best dowager duchess impersonation as I sweep away. *Heel, toe, heel, toe*; I take pains not to step on the hem of my dress. To fall flat on my face is all I need to crown this evening.

My dress. *The* dress.

I'd picked it up in a consignment store in the US for seventy bucks. An Alex Perry! I thought for sure moving to London I'd get an opportunity to wear it. But the opportunity never arose. At least, until now. I guess it's a shame that this is its debut outing. Not only that but also from now on, whenever I open my closet and see it hanging there, I'll be reminded of how awful I felt tonight, rather than be seduced by the color and fabric into running my hands over it.

I suppose I could sell it, only I know I won't, almost as a point of principle.

I like this dress. Everyone else can shove their opinions where the sun doesn't shine.

"Come on, Holly." From behind me, Griffin's voice seems too close to my ear for comfort. Not to mention, far too self-satisfied as his fingers brush my hand.

"Drop dead," I mutter, snatching it away as I step out into the hallway.

"Hols." This time, my name is delivered on the tremor of a chuckle. One I'd like to punch down the back of his throat.

This isn't me. I'm not violent or mean—not even when I'm hurt. But then again, I'm not just hurting. I'm also seething.

"Alexander, who is that girl in that awful dress?" I'd heard the elegantly blonde stick insect sitting next to him ask.

"No one," he'd answered without even raising his gaze to me.

I'm just no one. No one in a dowdy dress, apparently.

No wonder fire seems to burn in my veins instead of blood.

"Holly?" Isla's gaze finds mine from where she stands, waiting for me, compassion and apology shining in her gaze.

"I'm just going to... to..." I point in the opposite direction to where everyone else is going. "Visit the powder room," I add in a moment of divine inspiration.

"Yes, of course." She nods in acceptance. It might be rude not to join her party, but she gets it. But her sympathy does not fuel my anger. It only fuels my tears and my pace as my walk becomes a trot as I round the corner out of view.

"Holland."

Alexander. *Oh, Alexander. Fuck off.*

"Just... just go away."

The whole night as I'd struggled through polite conversation, through feeling the weight of the sympathy of those around me—Ivy, Dylan Duffy's wife, of Isla, women sensing what I was feeling—I could feel his attention like a brand against my cheek. I just wouldn't, couldn't give him the satisfaction of turning my attention to him.

"Holland, stop." His fingers grasp my wrist, and my feet slow. I guess he already told me what he says goes in this place.

"Haven't you made me look bad enough already?" I growl, swinging around to face him, clocking his arm with my fist. I didn't mean to—I've just had enough. Enough of him. Of his brother. Enough of this day!

"I'm sorry," he begins catching my fist in his hand, bringing both of them to his chest. "I didn't think—I didn't know McCain would sit you next to Griffin. My God, I've wanted to pull my hair out just watching you together."

"Together? Are you crazy?" I heave my arms back, trying to pull them away. I even briefly consider kicking him in the shin, but I guess something must clue him in to that thought as he presses me back against the wall, quickly sliding his knee between my thighs. I grit my teeth, and I ignore the flare of heat this drives through me. I will not feel this way about him. I refuse to be distracted by the energy that jumps between us, raw and powerful.

"Yes, if you want the truth," he replies, all fiery blue eyes and fierce expression, "I think I am a little crazed. And I've you to thank for that."

"Did you do a couple of lines of white paranoia before dinner?"

"Holland, stop fighting me." His voice is husky and

almost hypnotic, and he doesn't rise to my insult, which just gets my goat a little more. "Please calm down."

"Calm?" I cry very much the opposite of that thing he'd like me to be. "You want me to be calm after the stunt you just pulled? How could you, you asshole? Oh, I beg your pardon," I snipe, faking a kowtowing sideways kind of bow. *Without the use of my arms, you know.* "How could you, *your grace*, you asshole!"

"I didn't know you'd be seated next to him."

"I didn't want to sit next to anyone. I didn't want to be there! What if I didn't have something suitable to wear? Did you even think of that?"

"No, I. No. I'm sorry, that thought didn't occur to me. But you did." His gaze softens as it falls over me.

"You humiliated me deliberately," I barrel on, refusing to allow him space to compliment me. "And I will never—*never*—forgive you for that!" All those feelings from before, the ones I thought I'd packed up in a box and slid under my childhood bed, never to be examined again, begin to float so close to the surface that choking them back causes me physical pain. The kind that tightens my chest and throat and makes me want to dry heave. Pain. Embarrassment. Shame. The awareness that people were talking about me, wondering what went on, gossiping about who was to blame for why the wedding was not going ahead. That's what this feels like. Again. I wasn't equipped to deal with it last time, and I'm sure as shit not ready for it right now. I need to leave. Go. Now. "Let go of me."

"I'm sorry, Holland. It was utterly selfish of me, but please, listen to me."

"I don't have to do anything you tell me." I sound like a kid on the verge of a tantrum, so I inhale a deep breath. *Aim for dignified. I will not cry.*

"I'm sorry you didn't want to be there, but I'm not sorry you were. God, you are so beautiful." His thumbs stroke the backs of my hands, and I flinch.

"You don't have to flatter me." *It's not going to stop me from trying to knee you in the balls the first chance I get.* "I'm just the nanny, remember?"

"It isn't flattery when it's the truth."

"An inconvenient truth? See, I heard you earlier talking to Portia," I rattle on as my heart pounds and my eyes sting. "Griffin told me her name." He glowers at the mention of his brother, but I'm not done yet. "He said she's one of your regular lays. You know what else I heard?"

"No, but I have a feeling you're dying to tell me," he murmurs, unmoved.

I heard what she said about my dress, is what I want to say, but that would only prove how much it hurt.

"I heard her ask you who I was. Just so you know, I also heard what you said. And it wasn't that I was beautiful, or even just the nanny, or—"

"Stop saying that." His angry response slices through my words. "You are not just the nanny." He glowers down at me, his expression nothing short of furious and making my heart bang against my rib bones with the finesse of a two-year-old with a xylophone. But I refuse to be cowed. To be fooled.

"I'm not anything. I'm no one," I retort, though the wobble feels less than powerful. "Those are your words, by the way. I wonder if you tell her she looks beautiful, too."

"I'm not in the habit of inviting comments on my life," he retorts. "Nor do I choose to discuss my life with those who mean little to me."

"I'm confused. Are you talking about her or me?"

Calm exchanged for anger, he suddenly looms over me. "You are the most infuriating—"

I almost laugh. "Me infuriating?" Then I'm not feeling so entertained as I begin to struggle again. I'm pretty sure if he wasn't wearing a velvet jacket, I'd bite him. Velvet is nice under fingertips but would give me the heebie-jeebies if it touched my tongue. Kind of like peach skin. *So yucky.*

This is not me. This is not how I behave. I never get bent out of shape or stabby ever. But who knows? Maybe I am really that way; maybe I've been saving all my fury for a particularly infuriating and arrogant duke.

"You're the one I've spent the evening watching. You're the one I want to hold in my arms. Can't you see that?"

"All I know is I'm not the one telling lies."

"*This* time, perhaps."

"I'm not the one keeping secrets," I barrel on. "I mean, you say I'm here by pure coincidence, but I know you're not telling me something."

"You want to know why you're here?" His words come without thought and with a fierceness as his eyes blaze and his jaw sets like granite. "It was to keep you away from Griffin because he wants to fuck you!" His chest begins to heave under my hands, his eyes angrily ghosting over my face. "I couldn't stand the thought of you being with him. And if you couldn't be with me, I was going to make damn sure you weren't anywhere near him."

"Strange how the absolute opposite happened."

"What?" His angry mask slips. "What do you mean?"

"I was with Griffin, and you were with Portia," I answer simply. Maliciously. "You know, the expensive *ride.*"

"Portia is no one to me. Just because you don't believe it doesn't make the fact any less true. The woman was the farthest thought from my mind when I insisted you come to dinner. It was you I wanted sitting next to me, goddammit! And your experience of sitting next to Griffin is a perfect example of why I thought to get you a job out of London in the first place."

"That makes no sense." I retort, but the heat has died from my words. "You say you want me with you, but you don't want me with you at all?"

"My life is not my own, Holland. I'm pulled from left to right, from above and below. I put the needs of this family, our properties, and this estate above everything, and the one time I let my guard down, the one evening I allowed myself to carve out something *for* myself, it was with you." He inhales long and deep, his eyes closing for a moment, almost as though to gather the courage to carry on. "It was my birthday that night. And you were the gift I could never have expected."

He lifts my left wrist to his mouth, pressing it to the pale underside. His lips feel hot, or maybe it's my blood. I wonder if he can feel my pulse galloping. My anger might've drained, but I don't feel calm because at the brush of his mouth, everything inside me contracts.

"I've thought of you so much since that night." There's such an intensity to his words, and he shakes his head as though he can't believe it himself. Or maybe it's that he'd like those thoughts of me to go away. "And then, at the townhouse, there you were."

"But you were angry," I whisper, confused. That cold night in London, his anger was well restrained, but I could see it shimmering under the surface. *Just like I can see it now.*

"Yes, I was angry with myself. I wanted you so much, but if I'd given in that night and done what I wanted to do…"

"What you wanted?" I prompt when it seems like he won't finish. Suddenly, I want to hear what he has to say more than I want my next breath. A breath that seems lodged high in my chest.

"Holland." My name sounds like an ache, sweet and poignant. "I have very little time for myself, and I'm tied to this fucking dukedom above everything else. But God help me, when I look at you, I can only think of myself. Of my own needs. Of what *I* want. And that's why I wanted you at dinner. I didn't think about you, of how being there would make you feel. I'm no good for you, darling, because I can't see beyond the want of you. Every time your eyes find mine, every time I touch you, I want to damn the world to hell just to have you."

The hunger in his eyes, in his fingertips, is echoed by a sudden, solitary pulse somewhere deep inside.

You are a gift, he'd said once. *Beautiful and unpredictable, just as life is.*

I close my eyes, blocking out his expression, but it only serves to heighten my senses. His breath on my face and the want in his fingertips. The cool wall at my back is like a memory turned real. The strength in his hands as he'd pinned my wrists to the bed. The clawing ache between my legs sends my mind spinning.

I hadn't imagined how powerful the experience was with him because it's still twisting me in knots to this day.

My eyes open on a slow blink, though it takes me a moment to grasp our bodies separating by stages. His thigh slides from between mine, his hands unfurling from my wrists to lie by his sides. One last soft brush of his breath against my hairline.

"I'm sorry," he murmurs, cool air filling the space between us. "I can see you don't feel the same. This was a mistake."

But mistakes are spilt milk, bad haircuts, and mixing

green pesto into the pan instead of Thai green curry paste. Regrets, however, are for tomorrow.

My arms rise before me, my hands splaying across his chest like starfish. The light overhead glints like a wink from the ring on my thumb as my fingers wrap around the lapels of his jacket.

"You don't want this." His voice isn't at all uncertain but rather dark and velvety as I begin to tug him closer.

"Don't tell me what I want." *Give me what I need instead,* I think as I curl my hand against his nape and pull his mouth to mine.

The initiation might be mine, but the kiss is all his. His lips crash against mine, hot and furious, his tongue demanding entrance as his hands tighten on my waist. As he presses his thigh against me and a flare of heat presses through me. His fingers begin to unfurl, a harsh breath at my cheek turning to a press of lips. "Darling, I don't want you to regret this."

But my mind has already shut down, my animal self responding to a need so powerful, it feels dangerous not to give in to it.

"How about you use your mouth for something other than talking," I snarl as my grip tightens on his neck, a ferocity sweeping through me.

His lips press to the juncture of my neck and shoulder as, with a pained sounding groan, he rolls his pelvis against me.

"If you don't want me to talk, maybe you should just sit on my face." His seductive tone curls around my ear, the base suggestion blooming and bursting inside.

That is—hot. And nasty. And oh, God, how I want it. I want it all. Want what I shouldn't. Want what I'll take anyway.

"Screw you," I rasp, my hand sliding from his neck to his hair. *Tightening there.*

"Oh, darling, you have," he purrs. "My God, you have."

Then he kisses me, cutting off any response I might have. He kisses me like my participation isn't required nor deserved. My knees give way, but that doesn't matter as he grips my ass, dragging me against him as though he'd fuck me right here in the hallway.

"Tell me you forgive me," he demands, sucking at my throat, his fingers pressing hard enough to bruise. Bruises I want. Fierceness I demand. But as his mouth gentles, his hands cupping my elbows, I realize he's pulling back.

"No," I gasp, my fingers tightening, my need shimmering.

"I want." His words are a hoarse whisper. "I need—say it."

"I don't forgive you," I rasp, pulling him against me, refusing to be seduced by his brutal beauty. By the lush temptation of his mouth. "Not for tonight."

"Then forgive me for the things I'm about to do to you."

His words aren't soft, and they crash through me like a thunderbolt. Though nothing else makes sense, I know with absolute certainty that I want him. *Just one more time,* I tell myself. And like regrets, I'll leave the thoughts of consequences for tomorrow.

25

HOLLY

Our footsteps are muffled by a carpet of deep reds and indigo, worn and threadbare in parts thanks to generations of use. How many dukes of Dalforth had walked these halls, dragging behind them some unsuitable woman he wanted to fuck?

That's unfair, I think to myself. *He would've put aside his want for you.*

You're the instigator of this—you put yourself in the driving seat.

When we don't turn towards the service stairs, I tug a little on his hand, even as I realize why: between the dining room and service stairs will be a hive of activity. I'm sure there's no need to give them anything else to gossip about. The same goes for the guests in the parlor whose voices we can hear as we turn the corner.

"Do we have to?" My eyes seek Alexanders. "I mean, pass by there?"

"Unfortunately. It's there or the back stairs." His expression when he glances down at me is less like a smile and more like a mockery of one.

Okay, I know I asked for this—but I didn't ask for *this*. An outing. The walk of shame in reverse. "Are we going to make a run for it?"

"No need. Judge it right, and we'll pass and be up the stairs before anyone realizes."

"Skulking in your own castle, your grace," I find myself playfully replying. He smiles down at me, and something inside me unfurls. "I do—" *forgive you*, I almost say. *I forgive you because I understand desire makes us do crazy things*. But as his hand tightens on mine, my declaration goes unfinished, my feet beginning to slow along with his.

Then I hear. A door creaking open up ahead. Voices shortly following.

I don't have time to panic as Alexander moves, and as quick as a flash, we're tumbling into a room. Except tumbling would imply we made some noise. But it's hard to make a sound, pressed between a castle wall and a wall of Alexander.

"You left—" Alexander's forefinger presses to my mouth, my whisper going unfinished. *The door open.*

No time, his shrug seems to say.

Muffled footsteps meander along the hallway, a deep chuckle ringing out. In the reflection of the darkened window, I see them appear in the hallway before they turn, their backs now facing the open door. I guess they're admiring the paintings hanging on the wall.

I cast my eyes around the room, looking for someplace to hide, just in case they decide to explore the artwork in here. I've been in here before; this is one of the rooms dressed for public view. Brass stanchions cordon off part of the room, claret-colored velvet rope swagged between them. The tourists don't enter from the hallway we were just in, but the door next to the marble fireplace that leads out to the other side of the building.

"... combined with the collective sense of the sublime," a masculine voice in the hallway recounts.

"Is it?" replies a nasally voice. One of the film's money men, as far as I can tell. Not that I spoke to everyone at the dinner table, but his accent is American, and the money men weren't at all interested in me. *I guess they mustn't have seen me juggling haggis bonbons earlier.* "I can't say I like it," he continues. "It's kind of depressing. Gloomy. I mean, couldn't she have cracked a smile?"

"She's enigmatic," the other man protests. "And a Rubens, I think. Not one of his contemporaries, as Lady Isla said."

"Isla is right. It's not a Ruben." At Alexander's low whisper, I find myself suppressing a shiver. Attuned to my every move, as close as he is, he doesn't miss it.

"The only Ruben I know is a sandwich," I whisper dishonestly. "I don't think they're looking at one of those." Alexander's chest moves against mine in a silent chuckle.

Ack! Why did I say that? It wasn't for the *lols*. I know we're not suited, but I don't have to make myself out to be some backwoods hick.

"I know what a Ruben is," I whisper, ducking my head to hide the twist to my lips. "I saw *Sampson and Delilah* at the National Portrait Gallery in London."

I'm not sure he's listening or impressed as his fingers reach for a lock of my hair. I watch as though hypnotized as he winds it around his forefinger, bringing it to his lips.

"A tale of love and betrayal," he murmurs. His gaze lifts, and I see the intensity there. "I swear I would never hurt you."

The moment is broken by the voices in the hallway.

"Now, there's a looker," old nasally Joe says. "And as my old dad used to say, it's not what you look at but what you see."

"It sounds like his father was a fan of Thoreau."

"I'm surprised he can see anything the way the light glinted from the diamonds in his watch. He's not living life simply."

This time, I hear his smile. Feel it as he presses his lips to the space below my ear.

"How long do you suppose he's been dead?" Alexander whispers.

"Who, Thoreau? A hundred and fifty years, give or take."

"So the same length of time they've been staring at that bloody painting."

I stifle a giggle and whisper, "Patience."

"Is *shot*." The hard *t* makes me shiver. "I want to touch you so much it physically hurts." His declaration is intimate, fierce. They create a deep and captivating ache deep inside me. His fingers trail languidly across my bare collarbone before he lowers his head to press a kiss against my throat. "This isn't a recent malady, Holland. It's not something that began tonight."

Thought disappears, and reason drops away as his kiss becomes a sucking pull, everything happening without real thought or cognizance. *Just instinct*. My soft moan. The way he lifts his head and the way my lips catch the sharpness of his jaw. *Just a soft brush*. His throat ripples with a hard swallow, his gaze sharpening in the dim light. As if he needed further hints, I wrap my hand around the back of his neck, pulling his lips down to mine. I taste the wine on his breath, warm and earthy, the world further shrinking at the sound of his low groan.

Kisses in the dark seem worth ten in the daylight, every

sense heightened, every brush of his tongue nothing short of intoxicating. His fingers grip my hips, pulling me tighter against him like he'd climb inside my skin if it were possible.

"The other door—"

His response is to glide his thumb over my nipple, his mouth swallowing my quiet moan.

"I've been imagining burying myself deep inside you all evening," he whispers, his thumb and forefinger pinching it over my dress.

I bite my lips to keep in the sound, my body convulsing against him, demanding more as I press my breast fully into his hand.

"I want—" his clever hands. His tongue. The feel of him pressed against me.

"Tell me." Before I've even registered his answer, his hands mold my hips, following the line of my dress. My ankles feel the brush of cool air. My knees. My thighs as the fabric whispers up my body.

The conversation continues outside of the room, words indistinct, their whereabouts unimportant. My reckless need reigns supreme as Alexander's teasing fingers draw the soft fabric higher. I inhale a soft gasp as his hand cups over my panties at the apex.

"You're so hot." I close my eyes as he presses the meat of his palm against me, my insides tightening as one long finger presses brushes my cleft. "I want to see."

I close my eyes against the sight of him, the intensity in his gaze, and the way he watches me. *I want to be devoured. Devoured by him.*

Fingers pluck the zipper at my side opening, its teeth the only sound in the room. Fabric skims up my torso before Alexander pulls it up and over my head.

And I let him. Crazed. Dazed. And desperate for this.

Until a burst of laughter sounds out in the hall.

"Relax, they won't come in," he whispers. "They're too busy admiring the art in the hall." His eyes glitter as they fall over me. "My God, they have no idea what they're missing."

His words are wrong, seven shades of them, so why do they make me feel like they do? Standing so close to an open door, so close that the light from the hallway falls over my naked skin, I feel vulnerable. Powerful? Exposed and kind of wrong.

Maybe Alexander sees the conflict in me as he speaks again.

"I would never share you. Not ever. Not with anyone."

Words spoken another night bring with them a sense of truth, his gaze shining like sin in the darkness. I like it. Oh, hell, I really do, as I find myself leaning back against the wall in nothing more than my thong and heels. I choose to revel in the power I feel at this moment. Revel in my power over him.

"What did I do to deserve you?" he whispers as his hands find my hips. The way he looks at me heats every inch of my skin, bloody coursing in my veins, a mixture of excitement and disquiet as the pair continue to converse just a few feet away.

"I think you'll find you saved me from a three-way."

He laughs, pressing a kiss to my shoulder as his thumbs hook under the string of my panties.

"They're hardly worth wearing," he murmurs, beginning to slide them down my trembling legs. As he helps me step from them, my hand falls to his shoulder as I teeter. "But they're very pretty," he adds, dropping them to the top of my dress. His wide shoulders turn as he deposits the garments to a chair to our left. And just when I think he'll drop to his knees as he did in the library, he lifts me into his arms instead. Even as my hands feed around his neck, I fight the urge to protest being carried naked across the room.

Or maybe I just feel like I ought to.

The soft nap of his velvet jacket makes pebbles of my nipples, the coarser woolen of his kilt fabric a tantalizing brush against my butt and thighs as we dip behind a folding screen, almost as tall as Alexander. Painted in the classical style with urns of flowers and little fat cherubs, I know (thanks to Chrissy) these were used to block out draughts when the family gathered around the fireside long ago. Set behind the screen is a lady's desk with cabriole legs, writing paper laid out on the surface aids the sense that she'd just abandoned her morning correspondence. It crackles under my thighs as he lowers me to the desktop and begins pulling the bobby pins from my hair.

"Someone ought to paint this sight," he murmurs, resting his hand against my collarbones, encouraging me onto my back along the length of the desk. "And call it The Triumph of Holland." His hand draws down my body before he spreads my legs, his eyes glinting in the darkness as his thumb dips between them. My body jolts as he brushes the pad across my clit. "You're so wet for me, my darling. Maybe you like the thought of being caught naked and spread out like some bacchanal feast." He bends and quite suddenly swipes his tongue along my wet ribbon of flesh.

"Don't tease," I rasp, bucking up into his mouth, refusing to be drawn into the temptation his words create. But it isn't much of a complaint as I have to bite my lip to stop myself from crying out as Alexander's tongue begins to swirl and tease, painting my clit with my own arousal.

"Let me have you here," he whispers, bringing his body

over mine. I taste myself from his mouth as he kisses me. "They won't see. Not if we're quiet." Which is exactly the opposite of what I am as he draws my earlobe into his mouth.

"Shush." The sibilant sound is a taunt, his smile pressed against my neck.

I suddenly decide one of us is wearing too many clothes and begin to grapple with his jacket, pushing it from his shoulders until Alexander begins to tug it down his arms. I move my attention to his snug-fitting vest, and I don't know which of us is more startled by my actions as a button flies off, pinging against something on the other side of the room. Something that sounds very much like china that then sets to wobbling.

"Sorry," I whisper when it becomes clear there's no following crash. I'm so sorry that I'm already stripping him from his shirt. "But I want to see you." I slide my calf up his leg, catching the edge of his kilt. "All of you."

Alexander gives a satisfied hum, though as my leg rises higher, he grasps it, lifting it over his shoulder.

I swallow a gasp as he pushes his fingers inside, my body bowing as he twists his wrist. As he works me. As he watches. As he presses a kiss to my ankle before dropping to his knees on the floor.

My insides ignite at the position, my back arching, papers crinkling as he sets his lips and his tongue and his fingers to such delightfully wicked purposes. I slide my hand through his hair and curl the other around the edge of the desk near my head as the knot of my orgasm begins to climb and build, as he tastes and teases and tortures, as he whispers such compliments.

You're so fucking wet.

So tight around my fingers.
So wet on my tongue.
I'm going to wear your scent like a cologne.

It shouldn't work, the contrast of his polished accent and the baseness of his words. So why then does it feel like a layer of pleasure that only elevates the experience?

"That's it. Feed me your pussy. Let my mouth make you come."

"That... that's not being quiet," I rasp, biting my lip as I rock into him. It's not helping *me* be quiet.

"This sinner's mouth only wants to worship you."

I think my brain shorts right there and then, blood pumping wildly through my veins, draining to the center of me, growing heavier and heavier only to burst through me like a flame.

I roll my lips in to mute the sounds as my orgasm overwhelms me, my penitent continuing to worship between my legs. My throat hoarse, I begin to pant, tears leaking from my eyes with the effort not to cry out. But it's no good, though I manage to bring my arm over my mouth just in time to muffle the sound.

"You're so fucking beautiful," he grunts, his fingers pinning me in place as his mouth works me wetly, twisting my orgasm, distorting it until it threatens to annihilate me. "So beautiful when you come for me."

And I do. Again, crying out and not even caring if anyone hears me this time.

"Please, no more," I beg, between my legs pounding and my thighs trembling. "I need—" I need him.

"You're beautiful," he rasps as he stands, wiping the back of his hand across his glistening mouth.

As though seeking confirmation of my body's loveliness, he slips his thumb inside, parting me for his view. "You're so pretty and pink, pulsing and trembling."

The intensity in his expression is enough to make my insides begin to pound again, as if it wasn't enough that he's feasted on me like a starving man.

I whimper, but before I have the wherewithal to signal for a time-out, my perfect torturer is leaning over me, and I'm tasting my own arousal from his tongue. His kiss is savage and possessive, a signal of his own need as he slots himself between my legs.

"Yes," I whisper desperately, bunching the dark-colored wool of his kilt in my hands. I want this. I want him. I want his cock inside me. "Please, quickly."

"You want me to fuck you?" his deep voice rasps.

"Yes." More it seems than I want my next breath.

His lips ghost over my face, his forehead touching mine. "Darling," he groans. "I don't have a condom."

"What?" My body jerks under his. "No even in that... that little fanny pack thing."

Alexander dips his head, his shoulders shaking with a chuckle.

"You and I are going to have a conversation," he mutters, and when he lifts his head again, a smile lurks in the corner of his mouth.

"About the fanny pack?" I ask, wide-eyed.

"It's called a sporran." Holy rolling r's, that sounded delicious and more than a little Scots.

"I know what it is," I admit, pressing my teeth to his jaw. His responding growly purr is like a lick of warmth to my stomach. "I've watched *Outlander*."

I also know what it's for. It's because kilts haven't yet evolved to include pockets. Just don't get me started on the way Brits use the word *fanny*.

"Someone wants a good spanking." He narrows his gaze but can't quite carry it off, given he's almost grinning.

"Call me Sassenach, and I might let you," I sass right back.

"My God, I love that dimple," he rasps, pressing his lips to my cheek. "Everything about you is so fucking edible."

I shiver deliciously because that sounded more like a threat than a compliment.

"Spankings are for bad girls," he says with a grunt as he swipes the fat, silky head of his cock against where I'm wet.

"You don't think I can be bad?" I ask, glad he can't see how my toes curl. "And what are girls who strip naked in the equivalent of a museum?"

"Perfect." His crown slides over the rise of my clit, and I think my eyes roll back into my head. "Oh, that's…"

"Yes, it is." His throat works with a deep swallow, and as I push up onto my elbows, we both watch between my legs. How darkly he glistens. How wet I am.

"I haven't," he begins, his eyes sincere as they lift to meet mine. "Not since you. Not since forever."

I try to process what he's telling me, which is not the easiest task when he's teasing me as he is. When he's making my thighs twitch. I think I might also be leaking brain fluid.

"But Portia. Griffin says—"

"I swear on the life of my nephews, the last woman I slept with was you. And the last woman I slept with sans condom was more than a decade ago. I haven't been involved with Portia in that way for some time."

"Really? She's not in it for the dick?" I purse my lips together a little too late.

"I'm not even sure she's in it for me," he answers sardonically. His answer is quickly followed by a groan as he slides his crown along that wet ribbon of flesh again. My legs begin to tremble.

"She's missing out." I tilt my hips, opening myself to the movement. "If you ever need a change of career…"

"Flattery," he growls, "will get you—"

Almost fucked. By just the tip as the weight of his delicious body comes over me.

I'm on the pill, I almost say, but instead, "Wait," comes out of my mouth as I press my hand to his chest. "You said 'last woman'. What about men?"

"Really?" He cocks one very derisive-looking brow.

"It's a valid question."

"In my forty years, I have never fucked nor been fucked by a man, either with or without a condom."

"Can't be too careful," I reply, trying not to giggle.

"I would never risk you or your health," he says with such gravity that I believe him, which either makes me the stupidest woman in Scotland or a woman who's sure she can trust him. But knowing what I know of him, what his family and his people have said about him, I trust it's the latter as I reach out.

Alexander watches the progress of my fingers as I trail them down the firm planes of his stomach. As I close my hand around his hardness, the ragged breath that brushes my cheek is a compliment. I bring him to the heat of my opening, teasing which of us, I'm not sure.

"You feel so good," I whimper, my back bowing in a silent urge for him to thrust.

"We can't," he rasps, "not like this."

"Let me feel you." I arch my back, my core pulsing emptily. "Let me feel all of you, Alexander." Wrapping my hand around his neck, I bring down his head and whisper the magic words into his ear. "I'm on the pill."

His hand splayed next to my thigh, he drops his head.

"Minx," he growls as he slides his hands under me before thrusting forward, thrusting into me.

"Oh, God!" The feeling is... everything as my body accepts his. Everything I imagined as my hands ran over his broad shoulders. Everything I'd remembered as I traced the muscles of his back. Every life-altering, ovary-rearranging inch of this man was built on a scale so majestic, is it any wonder I want him to consume me.

I lower myself against the desk, basking in the power of the man as he takes my hips in his hands and begins to move. Deep thrusts interspersed by shallow jabs of his hips, his expression so fierce, so focused on the moment, his fingers holding me so tightly, I'll probably bruise.

I want him to bruise me. Mark me. Rip me in two.

"I want to see you," he whispers fervently, beginning to pick up the pace. Sliding from base to tip, he switches to shallow teasing movements, his body undulating against me like an unending wave.

"You feel like velvet, Holland. Every inch of you. I can't —" His expression is so fierce he slides his hands under me, gathering me to him. "I feel like I'm about to fucking explode," he rasps, his mouth over my ear. "I just can't get enough."

A pleasure spikes through me, a pleasure so violent it makes me shake. Wrapping my knees around him, I pull him closer, my hands unable to touch him enough.

His hoarse groan vibrates against my neck as I begin to come again.

"Please don't stop," I whisper fiercely. *Is it my body trembling, or is it his?* "Please, please, please." Let this never end.

Until it does. Until he presses me back again. Until the

antique desk begins to rattle beneath us, protesting at the tempo of his powerful thrusts. But we have no time for that, no thought or care as nature takes over, dragging us with it.

Everything inside me draws tight, my spine arching impossibly as wave after wave of liquid-hot pleasure rushes through me, our joint climax finally rendering us a twitching, pulsing mess.

26

ALEXANDER

I'd woken this morning with a jerk, my heart in my mouth. Light streamed in through the open drapes and, I'd thought for a moment that I'd dreamed it all. Dreamed about her splayed out on the desk. Imagined her here in my bed. But as my heart had begun to settle into a steady rhythm, the evidence of last night being real began to sink in.

The way my abs felt like I'd spent the night doing crunches.

The way the duvet lay barely on the bed.

The detritus of my clothing scattered across the floor.

The smell of her perfume and the unmistakable aroma of a night spent fucking.

It was real. So very real, I couldn't wipe the smile off my face.

The only downside I could see was the fact that Holland wasn't with me.

So, I'd shot out of bed, the sheets parachuting behind me as I'd made my way for the quickest shower imaginable, determined to find her this morning. Determined that we come to some kind of understanding of where each of us stood.

Next to each other, preferably. For as long as we both can stand it. If last night did anything for me, apart from reminding me I need to incorporate more abs-centric exercises into my workout, it was to prove that I can't stay away from her. Hopefully, she feels the same way.

I'd headed for the main kitchen, gathering from Archie that she could sometimes be found down there. She wasn't there, though Chrissy was, but I was in no mood for a scolding or an interrogation. I'd promised her I'd return later for the former, once I'd done what needed to be done. As for the latter, no one interrogates a duke. Not even the woman who had a hand in raising him. *No matter how I might've suggested I'd stand for it last night.* My efforts frustrated, and given I had no idea where Holland might be or what room she might be staying in, I'd decided to try the kitchen in the family apartments.

"There's only porridge or toast to eat in here," my sister says coolly, falling into step with me. For much of our childhood, Isla was the taller of us. My father used to delight in saying she'd stolen the nutrients from our mother's body, leaving me the weaker of the two. He'd taunted that she should be the duke, and I'm sure in many ways that might be true. But that's not how inheritance laws work. Besides, I'm sure she's much happier without the Dalforth millstone around her neck. As it was, our father changed his tune the year I turned sixteen, and I grew to tower over her. And him. But I got to disappoint him in lots of other ways, thankfully.

"I'm not hungry," I reply. "I just need coffee."

Breakfast this morning will be served in the dining room, as always after a formal dinner with guests. But I'm not ready to face the horde and their speculative looks, not that I particularly care what they think or feel the need to explain myself.

One of the perks of being at the top of the family tree.

Isla pauses at the entrance to the family kitchen, effectively blocking my way. "Portia keep you awake last night?"

"You know better than that." With a sigh, I fold my arms. Portia was in a room far, far from mine; Chrissy never was very fond of her. Not that she's in her room now because after breakfast, I was informed she'd left Kilblair already but had left a note. The note was, understandably, terse and informed me that after I disappeared last night, she'd asked John to take her home this morning. So her apology, and final goodbye, will need to be postponed for a while.

"Are you going to let me pass," I say next, "because when I say I could kill for a coffee, I'm not entirely sure it's hyperbole."

Her gaze flicks over my face. "You haven't shaved," she announces with a frown.

"I'm aware." I run my hand over my bristled chin. "When in Scotland..."

"Fine," she retorts in an irritable tone as she pivots and thunders her way into the family kitchen.

I might be at the top of the family tree, but that's not to say everyone agrees with me.

"You're not joining our guests?" she asks, or more likely suggests. I shake my head as she turns to the sink, sliding her retort over her shoulder. "Why? Are you worried you might find another of your conquests in there, wearing an apron?"

"That's unfair, Isla." I know she doesn't like Portia, but I sensed no animosity towards Holland last night. And she knows I've never dallied with a member of staff before. It's not a question of it being "them and us". I just respect the status quo and value their help far too much.

Well, that and I'd never met Holland before now.

I wonder what would've happened if we hadn't met in London first.

"If you aren't going down to breakfast, why should I?" she retorts, patently ignoring my rebuke as water explodes from the tap. She begins to rinse a cup as though it owes her money.

"Because you have a much better sense of decorum," I answer carefully as she turns and thrusts the dripping cup at me. Shaking the excess water from it, I slide it under the spout of the coffee machine.

"Fine. I'll show my face at breakfast, but—"

Leaning my hip against the kitchen worktop, I tap my ear feeling a wee bit smug. For something that was so ridiculously expensive, it does (thankfully for this purpose) make a lot of noise.

I can feel Isla practically fuming as I turn my back on her to retrieve my coffee. "I'm sorry. You were saying."

"I'll go down to breakfast," she grinds out. "But you will make time for me this morning. My office or yours?"

"Either." I shrug, unconcerned. "But first, tell me where I can find Holland. I need to speak with her."

"No." Her reply sounds more like *ha!* "And I think you'll find she prefers being called Holly."

"What do you mean, no?" I glower her way, my voice dropping to the tone I use when I'm playing the arsehole duke. The rest I ignore as inconsequential. Holly she may be to others. Holland is how she'll always be to me.

"Oh, get over yourself, Sandy." As quick as a flash, she snatches up a sugar lump from the nearby pot, unceremoniously dropping it to my coffee cup. The dark liquid sloshes, spilling over the edge onto my brogues. "Something to sweeten your mood."

"You should take a dose of your own medicine," I mutter. "Now, where can I find Holland?"

"It's on the continent," she answers, her voice clear and bright. "In between Belgium and Germany, I believe. Shall I pull out an atlas for you, just to be sure?"

"Fine. I'll look for her myself."

"I never thought I'd see you turn into our father," she murmurs, snatching up a teaspoon from the countertop as though to study it.

The barb is well-aimed. Bad enough that I'd thought it myself first.

"I am not having this conversation with you."

She snaps the spoon back where it rattles against the marble. "Don't think for one moment that it went unnoticed when you locked yourself in the library last night. As if that wasn't bad enough, you disappeared after the poor girl following dinner, leaving me to deal with your guests, I might add. I have never been so embarrassed, and I recently found my husband fucking our nanny!"

Ice fills my veins at her news, yet my response falls in another direction.

"Don't say something you'll regret."

"What? Like you're no better than him?"

I'd thought she might say something to the detriment of Holland. She can complain about me until the cows come home, and she has done since we were old enough to talk. But I'm glad I was wrong, even if that means she thinks I'm no better than that feckless fucker. I might have no defense for my actions, but I can't regret them.

And I won't regret tearing him limb from limb.

"I'm sorry Isla, sorry he hurt you. But is that what you truly think?"

"Please don't tell me you've done something foolish, Sandy."

"That's quite a broad definition," I murmur, staring into the dark brew.

"You haven't already… you haven't slept with her." She's not asking, but she is worried.

"Are you concerned about her good name or ours?"

"We haven't got a good name," she huffs out her response, skirting around me crisply as she makes for the door. "My study is closer. There's less chance we'll be overheard."

"You want to do this now?"

"Breakfast can wait," she answers sharply, turning right as she makes her way to our mother's old study. Putting down my cup, I follow her and find Gertie trotting along in my sister's wake.

"I take it you're hiding her from me this morning," I murmur, closing the door behind me.

"No, but I will if I have to," she replies, keeping her eyes on her beloved dog. Gertie waddles off to a well-worn corner of the rug, circles once, then twice, before she settles down. "I hear the Duffy's are expecting another child soon." Isla's head comes up sharply. "Perhaps she can go home with them. Tomorrow."

"Except this isn't 1820." I settle myself onto the sofa in favor of allowing her to place the desk between us. Coffee and Holland were what I required this morning. It seems I'm only to get my hands on one of the two. "I think you'll find Holland gets to decide where she'd prefer to reside."

"And you think that's here, with you on the prowl? I

think you flatter yourself, especially after the position you put her in last night."

Except I didn't put her in any of the positions she didn't want to be. At least, not after dinner. The way she'd looked lying across the desk made me think the image of her should be hanging in a museum, all creamy skin, and languid dark eyes. I thought for certain she'd protest when I lifted off her dress, but she hadn't. And I'm all the luckier for it, though when I'd held out my hand, my fingers had trembled, desperate as I was to touch her.

"I like her, Sandy. And when I look at you, I worry you're going back to the way you were before Leonie."

"That's unfair," I murmur quietly. That period was nothing more than a rite of passage, as strange as it seems. If not for going off the rails a little, I might not have come out the other end. And truthfully, that period never ended with the arrival of Leonie. It actually got worse.

"Besides, she's far too young for you."

I sit forward with a groan. She's right, and I know she sees the comparison between how I behaved last night and how I was back then, but this isn't the same. But I can hardly tell my sister the only woman I've fucked in months is Holland, just as I can't tell her I didn't stop fucking other women when I married Leonie. That my wife actually joined in. Ours was an open relationship centered around Thornbeck Hall. Unfortunately, there's no easy way to tell your sister that was the bargain she struck before I'd promised to love and honor her.

Love, honor, defile.

"Do you know Holland has an Instagram page with over ten thousand followers?"

"No," I answer warily. "What kind of page?"

"Oh, relax. It's not bikini shots and pouting posts. It's

mostly of her travels and quirky observations, as far as I can tell."

"I'm not sure why you're telling me this."

"Because you hate the media. Instagram is social media," she adds unnecessarily. "But also to point out how utterly wrong you are for her."

I note but ignore the distinction. *You're wrong for her, Sandy.* Not the other way around.

"I didn't even know Holland was here," I reply tiredly.

"So you did meet her before. Don't tell me," she adds tartly, holding up her hand. "But I suppose if you had, you wouldn't have brought Portia. What I can't believe, however, is how you still have that woman hanging around."

I press my elbows to my knees as I drop my shoulders, refusing to be drawn into the many cock-ups of my life. "How did Holland come to be here?" I find myself asking. "What was she doing wearing that apron last night."

Isla huffs audibly, though she doesn't remind me there are children nearby. "She was working, clearly. My question is, how do you know her, and how did Sarah Houghton come to recommend her to me?"

"I met her before. On my birthday." Isla falls quiet, digesting this. "And yes, she's the reason I didn't turn up to your birthday dinner."

"Oh." She folds her arms, her fingers grasping her elbows.

"It's a long story." Yet a very short one. "I met her in the afternoon, and by the time the evening rolled around, I had no intention of being anywhere else but with her. But it was only ever meant to be for that night."

"And she didn't know?"

"She didn't know who I was, if that's what you mean." So many lies. And I'm still telling them.

"And—"

"She had no idea what she was coming to, and I had no idea she'd be here. Where are the boys this morning?"

"Out," she answers crisply, reading my intentions.

"Out. The same as Holland, I take it. She doesn't need saving from me." It might even be the opposite way around.

Doesn't she? seems to say my sister's speaking look.

"Look," she begins, taking a seat on the arm of the chair neighboring the sofa. "Last night, Chrissy told me Mari called in sick and that Holland offered to fill in for the girl. That was *after* I'd invited her to the dinner as a guest."

"But she's not a guest, is she? She works here." I swear, if this works out how I hope it will, it's the only way George, my assistant, will keep his job.

"She's been such a big help these past few weeks, and the boys love her company. Quite honestly, without Chrissy and Holland, I don't know where I'd be."

"You'd be here, where you belong," I answer immediately. "This is your home as much as it is mine. More so even, but I think it's time you told me why you've decamped during the tourist season."

"Because I've left Thomas."

At the tiniest of wavers in Isla's voice, I sit straight, then lean over the arm of the chair to take her hand in mine. "When?"

"Don't you mean why?" she asks with a wry smile.

"I assumed you'd tell me when you're ready."

"I've been here a few weeks."

"And you didn't think to tell me." I try to keep the offence from my voice. It's not that she hadn't confided in me that makes me feel this way, but rather that I hadn't felt it. We're twins, and though I would never admit it aloud, there's some truth in the talk of the bond between a pair of children who share a womb. Of course, I knew there was something wrong. I just didn't care to ask. Or didn't think to.

"You already have so much to look after. Besides, I needed to be sure I was absolutely done with him."

"And you are?" I ask carefully.

"Absolutely. Which brings me neatly to my next point. I was in need of a new nanny. Because he—" Isla's words break off in a swallowed sob. My first instinct is to comfort her, but I know better than that. *I like my head where it sits.*

I watch as she swallows once more before pulling her shoulders back straight. When her dark eyes meet mine, they glisten.

"It's as I said." She tips back her head with a delicate, watery laugh. "In our bed."

Her pain is like a spike to my chest. I'd always thought there was something unsavory, something sleazy about the man, but to fuck another woman in your marital bed? That probably makes me a hypocrite. Or perhaps it doesn't count, considering my wife was part of what went on in ours.

"I will fucking destroy him." There is no way she should feel one iota of embarrassment and screw her sense of propriety because I'm immediately on my feet, pulling her flush to my chest. "I promise you."

"Best not to." Her brightly delivered words are muffled against my chest. "He is the father of my children."

"He should've thought about that before he—"

"No." Isla covers my mouth with her hand. "Don't say it out loud. Not now. I don't want them to ever find out. They deserve better parents than we had."

"They have one," I affirm, taking her hands in mine. "They have you."

"Promise me, Sandy. Promise me you won't get involved. It will only ever come down to money for him, not love."

"I'm not going to stand by and let him ruin you."

"Oh, I'm not ruined. Those are my plans for him. I've already instructed the lawyers, and they can take it from here."

"And the boys? Have you told them?"

"Not yet, but I will. They think he's overseas on business."

"I take it because he hasn't bothered to try to see them," I answer, hoping for the opposite. They deserve so much more than we had with our father.

"I told him he mustn't call. Not yet. I don't trust him." Whatever she sees on my face prompts her to demand a promise from me. "Say it, Sandy. Promise me you won't get involved."

"I promise I'll take my cues from you." For now, at least. "So, Holland came to Kilblair as your nanny?"

"No, not even." Isla laughs, dropping to the sofa arm again. "Sarah rang me from the agency. She knew we were looking for someone for the education center."

"We were?" I take my place on the sofa arm this time. If Chrissy comes in, we'll both be in trouble.

Arms aren't for arses, I can almost hear her say.

"Anne went on maternity leave. She probably won't return. Anyway," she adds, pushing a harried hand through her hair. "I employed Holland after Sarah interviewed her and spoke with her previous employers. And then I badgered her into helping me out with the boys."

"In addition to running the education center?"

"Yes, but you're paying her for that. I'm paying her salary for helping me."

"I don't care about that. I don't care about any of it."

"But you care about her?" she asks carefully. "Or is it... something else?" Something else like casual fucking, she means. "Because I need her, Sandy. I won't have you frightening her off."

"A minute ago, you were threatening to send her to live with the Duffy's, and now you're telling me she's indispensable?"

"Yes, she is. And while we're speaking about the children, the school told me Thomas hadn't paid the school fees for two terms until you stepped in. Thank you," she adds simply.

"I didn't take over for him," I mutter uncomfortably.

"No, but he came to you, didn't he? Has he tried to involve you in his schemes?"

"Don't worry, Izzy. It's fine."

"Please tell me you haven't." She presses a hand to her mouth, almost as though to prevent her troubles from spilling out.

"I haven't. I told him I'd pay the school fees, and that was it." And set the wheels into motion to make sure he gets no support from anyone else I know. At least until I found out from Isla what the hell was going on. And now I know.

"Well, that's something," she murmurs, her arm dropping to her side as though it were made of lead.

"What about the rest? Has he asked you for money from your trust fund?" Our mother left her a small trust fund on her death. Money she was able to keep from our father.

"Oh, Sandy. I gave him that years ago. There's nothing left. The mortgage is in arrears, and my Range Rover was about to be repossessed. So getting back to Holland, yes, she's indispensable. She has entertained the boys, taken them to the cinema and for ice cream so I could deal with this mess, visit the bank, and so on. She's basically taken over the school run and homework and all that entails. Meanwhile, I have begun to get my family back on their feet.

Thomas excluded, obviously. His cock-ups are his own. And that's in addition to tweaking some things here and running my own business, I might add."

Isla has a clothing line of Scottish fashion. E-commerce. I've teased her that it's mostly tweed and sheepskin products for middle-aged matrons, but I know it's doing well since it has recently broken even. But she doesn't take a salary, as far as I know.

"You didn't need to do it all on your own."

"I haven't. I've had Chrissy. And I've had Holland. And now I don't even know if she'll stay, so... you'd better get yourself back to London after this weekend."

"What?" Now it's my turn for wavery amusement.

"You heard me. You have to leave, Sandy."

"In case she tells you it's her or me?"

"Yes, and after last night, I wouldn't blame her. Whatever possessed you to strong-arm her into dinner and embarrass her like that? It's unforgivable."

"Holland already forgave me." I atoned between her legs. "But you're right. I am an arse." I look away, not able to hold my sister's gaze. "I just didn't want her anywhere else."

"Well, unless you want to look after Hugh and Archie, leave the girl alone."

"It's nice to know where I stand in the order of things," I answer, amused. On the surface, at least.

"Sandy, you are a duke. And even if you weren't, you'd have women everywhere fawning all over you."

"That doesn't sound like my life at all."

"Then I suggest you smile more and scowl less. I need Holly here. I want you to promise you won't frighten her away."

"What on earth do you take me for? I'm not an ogre,

Izzy." But my childhood nickname for her doesn't warm her to me.

"You're too much for most women. I want you to consider that before you run after a woman not—not of our world," she adds a little uncomfortably. "A woman who is far too young for you."

"That's a little old-fashioned, isn't it? Them and us." And isn't age just a number? I didn't feel too old for her last night, and she felt just perfect.

"Don't play with words. And don't play with her."

"I have no intention of—"

"Of what? Making her dance to your tune? Working her out of your system? Because that worked so well with poor Portia."

"Poor Portia?" I scoff. Isla can barely stand her. "There's nothing poor about Portia. She knew exactly what she was getting herself into. And truthfully, I don't know why she's still hanging around."

"Because she fancies being a duchess, no doubt. But I imagine she didn't count on falling in love, and that's why I feel sorry for her. You won't marry her, and you won't ever love her back."

"I could marry her," I retort. "I've thought about it." Briefly. Very briefly. We'll call it a moment of madness brought on by tedium. Isla is both right and wrong. Portia doesn't love me. She's certainly never said so, and we've never had what you might call a loving connection. Or even a passionate one, despite her sad doe-eyed moment last night at the dinner table. "She is *of our world*. Would you allow me to marry her?"

Even as I'm goading my sister, I'm mentally preparing what I have to say to Portia. An apology is due, and I'll need to set her straight. End what little there is between us.

"Don't be a callous arse," she retorts vehemently. "Just leave Holly alone. I can't imagine she's hung up on you, not when she told me she had a date this weekend."

"Did she?" My answer is mild. Internally, I don't feel so sanguine. "Anyone I know?"

"I wouldn't be surprised if last night didn't drive her into his arms," she says, choosing not to answer my question. Perhaps she doesn't know. "I can only imagine what she must be feeling this morning."

A little sore, I should think. A little achy, I consider as I rub a hand over my abs.

"If I were her, I wouldn't let you within two feet of me."

"It's a good thing you're not her then," I say, pushing to my feet.

Maybe I am my father's son, after all. Debauchery may be in my blood, but I've never behaved this way so close to home. But Holland isn't just a flash in the pan. I'm not sure what she is, but she's old enough to understand my feelings on forever and young enough for them not to mean throwing away her future.

"You see the sense in what I'm saying," my sister demands. "You embarrassed them both."

"That wasn't my intention." But I meant what I said when I told Holland I can only think of myself while she's around. And I have no intention of letting her go. "But I understand you feel they both deserve better than me."

"They deserve not to be played with."

She's right. But the knowledge doesn't make me want Holland less.

Or make me any less determined.

∽

As it turns out, I do find myself a little peckish, so I brave breakfast where I behave like cordiality itself. There are no strange questions or funny looks because I am the duke. And because Griffin and my sister aren't there, fortunately. I even arrive in time to wave our departing guests a fond farewell while suggesting someone find Portia—someone other than me; she's a little lower down my list this morning —and ask her if she'd like to join Matteo, Van, and the ghillie (the man in the know about all things hunting) in a romp through the heather-covered hills this morning, deer stalking. I have very important dukedom business to attend to, of course. Or so I tell them. Once the trio has departed in the ghillie's dilapidated Land Rover, I dutifully report to Chrissy, contrite as any schoolboy. Or rather, I bump into her again during my hunt for Holland. Not that I admit to anything or answer her questions, tacitly suggesting it would be ungentlemanly of me to speak to her about Holland without her knowledge.

Chores complete, I head off in search of the woman herself, hoping to salvage this thing between us. I can't promise her long-term devotion, and I think I made that clear last night at the dinner table. But she liked me well enough before. I'm sure I can rekindle a little more of that sentiment. At least, until she finds out the truth of this family. Of me. But by then, she'll likely be conveniently tired of me.

27

ALEXANDER

"You're very chipper this morning."

My footsteps falter against the worn flagstones at the sound of Griffin's voice. "Well, I was," I reply impassively as, for the second time today, one of my siblings falls into step with me. *If I didn't know better, I'd say I was being watched.* "Did you want something, Griffin?"

"Me? Always." His teeth gleam white in the dim light. We're in the old part of the castle, which tends to be gloomier than the more recent additions to the hodgepodge mess of buildings. "Why, what's on offer?"

Room and board. Old-fashioned entertainments. Hunting. Stalking. Decent wine and whisky. *Not Holland.*

"Why did Van bring you this weekend?" This is more like a thought spoken aloud.

"I didn't realize I needed an invitation. I'm a part of the family, aren't I? The black sheep and all that."

"You've been a part of this family for as long as I've known about you." Not that he needs reminding, I'm sure. Our father kept his and his sister's existence from us, but not the knowledge of Isla and I from them. So while their presence in his life came as a shock to us, I do think we got the better end of the deal. Ignorance was bliss while it lasted. Now it's just one more chain around my neck. As for Griffin and Rosa, our interactions to this day are carried out under this veiled sort of animosity. Understandable, really.

I'd say my father was a conniving cunt, but the description doesn't really do him justice. He fucked all of us over for his own entertainment, and I hope the fact that we're now reconciled, though not quite friends, has him spinning in his grave.

"You don't need an invitation. I just wondered why you travelled with Van." And why he's working for Van's uncle when he's worked so hard to get where he is. I'm sure he wouldn't be the first barrister to become corrupt.

"A private jet is always preferable to the train," he says as we step through the open doors and portico and out into the sunlight. "Where are you off to, by the way?"

"I was about to ask you the same thing."

"That I can answer. I'm coming with you."

Drawing to a stop, I turn to him. "So I say again, what do you want, Griffin?"

"I want Holly. But first, I want to know what she's doing here."

"What is it with the obsession with the girl?" Ironically, it's a question I could be asking myself.

"Obsession is a little strong. Unless it's not me you're asking." When I don't fill in the gap in our conversation, he carries on. "You were a bit light on your loafers last night trying to get at her."

"Get at her?" I repeat, my words dripping with disdain.

"Get to her then." He shrugs.

"If you were watching, then you must have seen how surprised I was to see her here."

"What I saw was her throwing hors d'oeuvres all over the place, then you dragging her out of the room."

It strikes me how those words could paint one of a dozen incidents involving our father. He liked to bully his children, manhandle his wife, flaunt his mistresses around the place. He also preferred to hire pretty staff, usually those young and female. They were easier to bully. To manipulate. Not that Griffin would know any of that.

"And what was going on in the library?"

I find my steps slowing. "Nothing that pertains to you."

"That atmosphere seemed quite charged." He turns to face me, sliding his hands into the pockets of his jeans.

"Practicing your cross-examinations, Counsel?"

"What I don't get," he says, "is why you bothered feeding me all that bullshit about an employment agency back at Thornbeck when you've very clearly brought Holland up here for your own use."

"She's not a ride-on lawnmower," I snarl, pivoting to face him. I'd thought to keep our interaction even, that I'd stay calm, but it looks like where Holland is concerned, I have very little control over my emotions.

Griffin and I are of a height and weight, and while I'd love to teach him the meaning of respect, it would only serve to prove to him that I've done something wrong. And fuck it, I have not. Why is everyone around me determined to make me think otherwise? "We do not use people at Kilblair Castle."

Not anymore.

"Touchy," he crows. "You know, there's nothing worse than a reformed man slut. Especially when they turn all sanctimonious and judging."

"I'll thank you to think and speak of my staff with respect while you're here," I retort, disregarding his taunt. *His threat?* "Even those I had no idea were working here before I arrived. Whether you believe me or not, I had no idea Holland was employed at the castle, that she was running the education center, or that she was filling in for Hugh and Archie's nanny. And by the way, what the hell were you thinking, bringing attention to her as you did last night?"

"I was just pointing out who she was. Introducing her, if you like."

I shake my head at his bald-faced lie.

"There's such a difference between your stations, don't you think? The duke and the nanny. Sounds like something I saw once in a club in Berlin. A spanking scene, I seem to remember."

"And you think the barrister and the nanny has a better ring to it?"

"Maybe. For a little while, at least. Let's face it," he adds, his tone mild. "It's not like either of us are about to make her a permanent fixture in our lives."

Callous. Cold. Perhaps even true, though I flatter myself my reasons are better than his. Maybe that's just it. Maybe it is self-flattery. *He is just like our father*, I find myself thinking. I suppose I should feel sorry for him.

But fuck that.

"What you do with your life is up to you. What you do on this estate is at my discretion. But whatever it is you're telling yourself, you're barking up the wrong tree, because I had nothing to do with her being at Kilblair."

If I say it enough, perhaps I might come to believe it myself. But it sounds more plausible than telling Griffin I intended for her to be out of both of our reaches.

God knows she deserves better than either of us.

He appears to consider my explanation as his gaze dips to his shoes.

"If I'd known she'd ended up here, I would've—" I halt, though my mind races on. If I'd known, I would have been here sooner. I wouldn't have dreamt about her all those weeks. I'd have enjoyed her instead, exactly as Griffin plans to do. Which will happen over my dead body.

"You would've what? Made sure I wasn't here?"

"This is not about you." At least, not now it isn't.

"You're sure?"

I sigh and shake my head. So much animosity. He thinks Holland is a toy I resent him having when that isn't the case at all. Because he hasn't had her. I have. And I intend to hold on to her.

"It's almost serendipitous." For a beat, I think he's still flogging that lame horse; Holland and I, here in the Scottish wilderness. But when he speaks again, I wish he was as my blood runs cold. "I've taken a holiday from my chambers," he says far too carefully as he stares up at the castle battlements, shielding his eyes from the sun. "I thought I might stay here for a while. And well, she's here. I'm here. Who knows what might happen?"

I grit my teeth as I remind myself that punching your brother in the face isn't really an advisable redirection tactic.

"And it sounds like I'd better act fast. It seems she's created a bit of a stir, the way I hear it. She's a popular girl."

Is he suggesting she's promiscuous or trying to lose his teeth?

"In a village of a few hundred inhabitants, that's hardly surprising," I say, deliberately misunderstanding. "An American moving here might even make the local newspaper."

"That's not what I meant," he says with a frown.

"Isn't it? What a surprise."

"Did you know she had a date with one of the gardeners?"

"What?"

"There are likely others. Like you say, Kilblair is a small pond to fish in. That's probably why some of the villagers look a bit weird," the arsehole says meaningfully. "But a barrister has to be a better prospect than a gardener, don't you think?"

What do I think? I think a gardener I can keep in line and my brother can go to hell.

If a barrister is better than a gardener, then I'm sure a duke trumps a barrister.

But I don't say any of that. It doesn't matter who or what I am because it was my bed she spent the night in.

Affecting a bored tone, I reply, "I imagine that all depends on her."

Her. I can't quite bring myself to say her name in his presence. Holland. Holly? I know which I prefer.

"I imagine—"

I know exactly what he imagines, and the thought of it has me suddenly stepping into him.

"Keep your thoughts to yourself."

I know I've made a mistake immediately as he steps back, a stupid fucking grin growing on his face.

"I knew something was going on between you two."

"You don't know what you're talking about."

"Can I assume this is one of those times we're not going to share?"

"That happened one time," I growl menacingly. One time, before I knew who he was. Before I knew who I was, blindly following in my father's footsteps. How the old fucker must've laughed. *The apple doesn't fall far from the tree, does it, boys?* "I swear, Griffin, if you so much as breathe in her direction, I will—"

"You'll what? Have me escorted from the premises, never to darken your door again? Wouldn't that make a good story for the dreaded tabloids? I can almost see the headline: the duke, his brother, and the American nanny. That's the kind of deviant love triangle the masses love. Even if it isn't the truth. At least, it's not like old times."

This time, I manage to ignore his taunt. There is no love triangle. This is purely linear, the line running directly from me to Holland with no stop in between.

"I'm sure being embroiled in a scandal would do your career a world of good," I drawl in response. "Not to mention, bring you to the attention of your newest client. I can't imagine the Russians will take kindly to journalists digging about."

A wide smile spreads across Griffin's face. "Someone's been talking to Van. But I note you didn't say she'd be worth it. Worth the risk, I mean."

Maybe she is, but that's not something I would ever discuss with him.

"What I can't make out is if you've fucked her yet," he says ponderously.

"I didn't realize my sex life was of interest to you." My easy answer is at complete odds with how I feel.

"Yours isn't. Hers, however..." He casually turns, sauntering on a couple of steps before swinging back to face me. "I'm going to say you haven't."

"I live to entertain you."

He sketches a mocking bow before swinging on his heel again. "It's either that," he calls over his shoulder, "or the girl has a magical pussy."

As the twelfth Duke of Dalforth's bastard son ambles away, I hear the words that go unsaid. *Either way, he's determined to find out for himself.*

28

HOLLY

I am so stupid.

But maybe not as stupid as I originally thought after Isla cleared up a few things for me this morning when I snuck into the family kitchen to grab myself something to eat while I thought everyone would be downstairs for breakfast.

She seemed to materialize out of nowhere.

So maybe fate did bring me here. Even if Alexander did interfere in an attempt to keep me away from his brother. It seems as though this has been, as Isla has suggested, one big cosmic coincidence. Which is better than discovering the man you'd slept (twice) with—a duke no less—has bundled you off to Scotland because you were such a good lay, he'd like the opportunity to repeat the experience again.

I know, say it out loud, and it sounds ridiculous. If he'd wanted to have sex with me, he could've said as much in London when I'd bumped into him while I was serving because I'm sure I would've hopped on that train.

Like I did last night.

I can't help that the man makes me thirsty just looking at him!

But coincidence or not, fate or not, it doesn't make the wanting not true. For either of us, it would seem.

God... I press my forehead to the cold window. *Is that Griffin and Alexander down there?* I close one eye and peer down at the courtyard, but I can't tell. The sun is too bright, and they're standing almost directly underneath me. Well, if it is, I hope Alexander is giving him a hard time about last night. *The ass.*

I jump away from the window when a thought hits me over the head.

I don't want either of them looking up and discovering which room is mine because where would I hide then? Though, come to think of it, there are so many rooms, it'd probably end up being like that scene from *Friends*. The one where Joey can't find the hot girl in the apartment opposite. Still, best not to take any chances. They probably both spent a lot of time here as kids.

Not that I can hide out here for too much longer. I can't exactly order UberEATS or keep sneaking snacks from the kitchen. And I also have work next week, but at least they'll both be gone by then. *Yes, to work. Not even to work my notice period.*

Not that Griffin worries me. Alexander, however... he makes me worry for my sanity. I press my hands to my heated cheeks, trying very hard not to think about last night. Maybe, I consider, now that we've had sex again, he might travel back to London earlier than originally planned. You know, like he's worked me out of his system.

It's true. I am stupid.

It's not a case of wishful thinking but a matter of stupid thinking because, in hindsight, last night has done nothing more than feed the beast—feed the beast within both of us.

Oh, God. I'll probably need therapy.

Great sex is so dangerous because despite my intentions, despite the fact that I swore to myself as I crept out of his bedroom in the early hours of this morning that I'd be giving Isla notice of my intention to leave, I've somehow promised her the opposite.

I couldn't really do anything else because when I went to see her earlier, she grabbed my hand and insisted I sit down. Then she'd said such wonderful things about me. She told me she appreciated my help more than words could say, that she thought of me as a friend. That she needed me to stay.

Argh!

When I tried (with much bush beating and many euphemisms) to say I couldn't, her delicate fingers tightened on mine as she'd insisted she'd spoken to her brother. She said she understood that "something of a personal nature" had gone on between us, and at that moment, I prayed to the heavens that she and Alexander weren't too big on sharing. But I guess the fact that she was still holding my hand told me enough.

Where was I?

Oh. Isla made it sound like she'd read him the riot act about his behavior at the dinner table and guaranteed it wouldn't happen again. She apparently told him he put me in a very awkward position.

Ah, positions.

Nothing about his position last night was awkward, especially as it had resulted in the kind of orgasms that curled my toes and my hair.

I ache to devour your pussy.

I almost came right then—on the spot. The man's aural game is something special.

In his bed, I'd kissed my way down his broad chest. How he'd sighed when I'd swirled my tongue around his flat copper nipples. How he'd growled as I'd grazed him with my teeth. I'd taken his hard length into my mouth for the first time since that night back in London, and he'd thrown his head back.

Something inside me blooms darkly as I remember the noises he'd made and how he'd demanded I keep my eyes open. He'd wanted me to watch what I was doing to him, watch him unravel. So, our gazes joined. I'd work him so slowly, long slides and deep pulls, teasing him more than trying to make him come. Surprisingly, he'd kept me at that pace, his fingers tangled in my hair as he'd tortured himself through me.

Almost as though he knew he'd never get to enjoy the experience again.

I'd hummed an encouragement as he'd whispered in a tight voice that he was coming. His thighs shook beneath my fingertips the moment before he'd exploded into my mouth with the kind of masculine groan I think I'll forever hear in my dreams. The sky had begun to turn violet with the approaching morning when he'd pulled me up to his chest. I'd kissed his shoulder and nestled in.

"*I've dreamed about your mouth*," he'd said, brushing his fingers down my back.

"*That sounds...*" familiar. It definitely sounded familiar.

"*Deeply erotic*," he'd said with a satisfied smile. "*But even my wildest dreams couldn't come close to capturing you.*"

In a matter of moments, his chest was moving under my ear with deep and steady breaths. But I couldn't sleep, and no matter what had happened over the course of the previous evening, I knew I couldn't stay.

That had been made perfectly clear in a number of ways.

My family and the dukedom rule my life.

The toasts to his dearly departed wife.

Sounds like I'm gonna need this job for a little while longer to pay my therapy bill.

Alexander will go back to London tomorrow, and I'll stay here for a little while. At least until Isla finds someone to fill both of my roles.

Meanwhile, I suppose I should do less hiding. Go rip off that Band-Aid and tell the delicious Duke of Dalforth that what happened last night will never happen again.

I can't be his side piece, stashed away in his Scottish castle, and I like myself better than to be a sometime booty call.

So I guess it's time to go find Alexander and have an adult conversation with the lord of the manor.

Not the fun kind of adult conversation either.

I have to swallow my pride and take the higher ground. I need to make sure he understands that last night was a one-night-only deal. Anything else would be unprofessional. Not to mention so awkward now that Isla knows what we've been up to. Or at least I surmise she knows some of it.

Alexander will leave today, and I'll carry on working, and by the time he comes back to visit, Isla will have her new hires, and I'll be long gone. Here's hoping that all goes to plan because the truth is, I still want the man, and I can't see that changing. The heart wants what the heart wants. And it seems my heart wants my body and my mind to be bent in all kinds of shapes by Alexander Dalforth, the man I now know as the 13th Duke of Dalforth.

"Hey, Holly. How'd last night go?"

I'm on my way from the education center to the kitchen,

mainly to pull off another of last night's Band-Aids by clearing the air with Chrissy when a nearby ride-on mower cuts out, and Cameron calls out to me.

My white knight on a mower? I don't think so. Even if he is nearer my age.

"I guess it went," I call back, wrapping the sides of my hoodie tighter across my body. So, I guess he hasn't heard the gossip yet. Maybe he won't, given the fact that Mari wasn't there. I can't see Chrissy or Mr. McCain saying anything and the rest of the staff working last night don't really know me. Except maybe Sophie. Wee Sophie. Will she spill the beans about us being in the library?

I watch as Cameron turns off the mower and hops off, making his way over to me in great lolloping strides.

"What's funny?" he asks with a wide smile and windblown rosy cheeks.

I give a tiny shake of my head. Nothing except he reminds me of an overgrown puppy. In a totally good way.

"I'm sorry I couldn't make it last night," I offer again as my conscience tweaks. One man offered to take me out, and another got me into bed. Or maybe that should be the other way around? Either way, it sounds worse than it is.

"Och, no bother."

Okay, so he's not pining for me, which is good, but that wasn't the most flattering of responses. As he begins to shift his weight from one foot to the other, it becomes painfully obvious he isn't going to offer to take me out some other time.

Maybe he does know, comes my immediate thought. *Maybe he doesn't want to tread on his boss's boots.* Not that it matters, I guess. There's no way I could make him the piggy in the middle of this clusterphuck. I can't see how Cameron would stand a chance, even if he was interested in me.

Which he's clearly not. Not much, anyway. I'm not even talking about their stations in life: Cameron, the gardener, versus Alexander Dalforth, the Duke. Or even Cameron the gardener who is the employee of the Duke. I'm thinking more about their temperaments because one reminds me of a Labrador and the other a jungle cat.

I guess I can write off using dating Cameron as a decoy or a shield if the need ever arises. Not that I'd considered this as an option. At least, not until it had occurred to me it wasn't. But there is another possibility. Another someone. But I can't think about that right now.

"Did you still go? To the pub, I mean?" Someone has to keep this conversation going, I guess.

"Aye, it was Friday," he replies in the tone of *of course I did*. "I went with Moses." He pushes back his cap and ruffles a hand through his hair.

"Moses?" I repeat, struggling to hold back my smile. "I don't think I've met him. Does he work at the castle?"

"Nah, he's just one of the guys I went to school with. Before you ask, his family is no' religious. He just wore sandals to school once, and the name has stuck ever since."

"That's kind of brutal," I reply with a giggle. "Especially for a place where men wear skirts." My heart lurches a little as an image flashed through my head of Alexander wearing his. And how little he wore under it.

"You know why it's called a kilt?" Cameron asks, a touch mischievously. "Because that's what happened to the last person who called it a skirt."

"What? I don't get it."

"They were *kilt*," he says with faux menace.

"*Oh.* Now I get it. No kilt jokes in front of a Scotsman." Cameron watches me for a beat, and I get the sense he's considering something. And *something* might just add to my list of current complications, flattery be damned. "Well, I'd better get to it," I say brightly, lifting my gaze to the wide blue sky. There's no rain today, just an abundance of brilliant sky.

"Aye. Me, too, I suppose." He pulls his old man's cap down, twisting the brim a little.

"See you around." I turn with a wave.

"Holly?"

The way he says my name stops me in my tracks, bringing my shoulders up around my ears. What now? I don't turn fully, looking over my shoulder instead.

"Yeah?"

"Did you say Mari was ill yesterday?"

"Yeah. That's why I couldn't go to the pub with you. There are guests at the castle, and Chrissy needed me to pitch in." Which is mostly the truth, I guess. But the rest? I'm not so sure it was fate.

"That's weird because she was in the pub last night."

"I don't know what to tell you," I say with a shrug. Apart from that, Mari has it in for me, I think. "She's not here this morning, either."

"Well, she was there last night, looking hale and hearty."

As hale and hearty as his pink cheeks? Could Mari be the reason he no longer seems interested in me? And if so, what do I care?

About a teaspoon amount, if I'm honest with myself. Maybe even less. I have bigger problems this morning. Sometimes *I just want to see what I can get away with* is just a little too complex for comfort.

∽

When I reach the kitchen, the atmosphere in there is... awkward. It's almost like everyone has taken a vow of silence. Dougal and his crew are busy preparing lunch, so I guess they have an excuse, but Chrissy and Sophie barely glance up as I reach for the French press.

And yes, I'm a chicken. A chicken who needs coffee to face the kind of conversation I need to have.

"Coffee, anyone?"

"No' for me, hen," Chrissy says from her position in front of an ironing board and a pile of table linen. Her response is cordial enough, yet she still doesn't lift her gaze.

Oh, well.

"What's on the menu for today?" I ask, lifting a lid from a cauldron-sized pot as I wait for the kettle to boil. *Phew, that is stinky.*

"That's just stock," Dougal mutters, his eyes on one of his crew as he makes tiny quenelles of chocolate ganache. *Much more appetizing.*

"Well, they look yum." No answer. "Is there another big meal tonight?"

"No," Chrissy answers. "Just a small supper party for family and friends. You can just relax tonight."

Welp, I wasn't offering to help either, I think as I smother a cynical smile. Last night was my limit. "No Mari today?" I ask of no one in particular.

"No, she's still no' well," wee Sophie offers up. "She called in sick this morning, so Lady Isla says."

Ah. And there is the reason for this awkwardness. It sounds like they've all been given a talking-to by Isla. Don't sully the name of the duke. Or maybe be nice to Holland because I need her to look after the kids.

Either way, I preferred the atmosphere of yesterday, I

decide, as I take my coffee to the kitchen table and begin to flick through my phone.

I'll finish my coffee, and then I'll be on my way.

On the way to face the duke.

"Hey, Griffin!" I call out, spotting him across the lawn. I know Alexander isn't likely to be out here, but I think I already mentioned I'm a total chickenshit.

Why do now what you can put off for a little longer, right?

"Do you have a sec?" I add as he lifts his head in acknowledgement.

Crossing the verdant cushion that Cameron and his crew seem to spend so much time tending, Griffin steps up onto the ornamental bridge, the soles of his shoes clipping against the stone.

"For you, I have all the sex," he kind of answers, coming to a stop in front of me.

"You mean lots of seconds. As in time? Because that sounded a little wrong."

"To clarify, I have lots of time for you, Holly. Lots of time to sex you."

"Ha, funny."

"Only if you want it to be." Folding his arms, he presses his butt up against the side of the bridge.

"What?"

"I'm more a fan of the intense kind of sex, myself."

"Oh, I am kind of regretting calling you over here."

"Why did you, by the way?" He shoots me a cocky grin but I'm about to disappoint him.

"Because of the peacock." I point my thumb over my shoulder at the magnificent but bad-tempered bird guarding the other side of the bridge. "I wanted to cross the bridge, but the dang thing wouldn't let me." Actually, I wanted to take a photo of him first, but he seemed to take extreme offence, fluffing his feathers threateningly. Yes, I'm supposed to be looking for Alexander, but I thought I'd take the opportunity to use this bridge that tourists are always hanging around. It is a very pretty bridge, very Instagramable, with its weeping willow and stream, but I'm not about to explain that to him. *Griffin, I mean, not the peacock.*

"Oh, so you did want me for my body?"

"Well, yeah. I could've pushed you into the water as a decoy."

"Holly, Holly, Holly." He shakes his head, though doesn't give up on his grin. "I would've only pulled you in with me. Who do you think would've looked best with a wet T-shirt?"

"Urgh, you should live under a bridge, troll boy," I say, swiping him across the chest with the back of my hand. I start a little as he catches it.

"When are you going to take me seriously?" he murmurs, pressing it flat against his chest. One hand resting on my wrist, he begins to stroke the back of my hand. "We could be good together, you and me. I think I told you once before, I'm really good company. I'd keep you warm on these cold Scottish nights."

"It's summer," I retort, sliding my hand away.

"Every time you reject me, it's winter in my heart." My expression? Barf! Even when he does that cute nose scrunch of his. "You can't blame a man for trying," he says, pushing up from the wall.

"And you are that." Very trying. He's also good-looking, solvent, and in his own strange way, I'm sure he's fun. But I'm not interested.

Griffin shrugs and makes as though to turn.

"Wait, aren't you going to help me?"

His brow creases as he glances past me. "I'm not really into angry birds," he says as his gaze catches mine. "Unless they're the kind interested in a little revenge fucking."

"Seriously?"

He begins to walk backwards as he lifts his hand in a mockery of an apology.

"You're on your own, love. That one's a complete arsehole. I think they must feed him live wasps or something. I heard he blocked a tourist bus from coming up the drive last week, then pecked the paint off a Mercedes in the car park."

"And you're just gonna leave me with him?" How on earth did I think he had an appealing boyish kind of charm? He's more like the kid who'd peel the legs off a spider before flicking them at you.

"I sort of like my peacock where it is," he says, cupping his junk.

Urgh!

Oh, well. Too bad Alexander's nowhere to be found.

I practically skip along some of the castle's gloomiest corridors, my little bag of snacks swinging from my hand. So I didn't best the peacock, but I did snap some awesome pictures. I plan to get to my room as fast as I can, then hang out of the window for a signal so I can post them to Instagram. Hopefully, I can do this without bumping into anyone, and I mean anyone.

As I scoot under an arch and turn a corner, I discover things are not going my way.

"Holly!" Archie calls from the bottom of the grand

staircase, sending me a manic wave. "We've been to the cinema with Uncle Sandy."

"Lucky," I reply, slowing my roll, my little bag hitting my thigh with a rustle. *Slow, slow, slow, stop*, go my footsteps, my eyes glued to Uncle Sandy, though I stop a decent distance from him.

And hot uncle alert.

His dark sweater looks soft. It's probably cashmere. His dark jeans fit his long legs perfectly, some kind of stylish suede sneaker completing the ensemble. Killer kilt, dapper suit, or weekend wear, it seems Alexander Dalforth looks delicious in whatever he wears.

And more delicious still, naked.

"Hello, Holland," he murmurs, a sly smile playing around his lips.

Those eyes are the color of oceans. I could totally get lost in them.

He hasn't shaved.

The realization makes a prickly awareness wash over me. No longer the fair gentleman or the Scottish duke, the fair rasp of his beard makes him look more like a Viking than ever before. But for his lips. His lips, wide, lush, and sensual as always. But there's something about the frame of his beard that makes me think of plunder.

"That's not her name," Archie scoffs, pulling on his uncle's hand. "That's a place."

"Is it?" He glances down at the kid, who nods in response.

"Have you visited?" Archie asks.

Alexander's gaze lifts, the glance he sends me is incendiary. "Not as often as I'd like."

Ho-boy. We need to have that talk now more than ever as I resist the urge to pull on the collar of my shirt.

Is it hot in here, or is it just him?

"Why have you gone red?" Scrunching his nose, the little boy tilts his head. But he doesn't wait for an answer before rushing on to his next question. "What have you got in the bag?"

"Huh?" I glance belatedly down at the thing dangling from my wrist. "Snacks. For later." For dinner, not that I'll tell.

"We had popcorn in the cinema," he says, beginning to jump up and down. "And an ice cream. And a big bag of pick and mix sweeties."

"Your mom is going to be so pleased," I say, my gaze flicking back to Alexander, though not for long. Yep, that's just what Isla needs. Her kids high on a sugar.

"We weren't allowed cola because Uncle Sandy says it rots your teeth."

"Oh, so you do have some limits, then?" I make the mistake of taking a couple of steps closer, which I'll blame on the magnet that is his chest. I've never touched his sweater-covered chest before. I'm not going to either, I have to remind myself as his gaze falls over me again.

"You know how it goes. One person's depravity is another's creativity."

A throb of temptation flickers to life between my legs. Before I can make my rebuttal, or run away, Archie bounces over to me like he's on an invisible pogo stick.

"What kind of snacks?" he demands, his eyes glued to the bag dangling from my wrists.

"No more snacks for you," his uncle decrees authoritatively, and I almost ask if he means the kid or me. If I'm going to be bossed about or dominated, I like it to be—

Nope. Scratch that thought. Shove it under the bed with the headless man.

"But what kind?" the kid insists.

"It's just some fruit and a peanut butter and jelly sandwich." Plus some pistachios and a slice of moist and boozy Dundee cake, and a couple of shortbread cookie tails. *What? I wasn't sure how long I'd have to hide out!*

Archie's expression twists, and he seems to think better of investigating the bag, hopping right on by me. I turn to follow his progress, my stomach swooping as I watch him come to a stop between the row of black marble pedestals, each bearing a piece of statuary. You know the one at the foot of the stairs? Worse still, the little snitch assumes the position of the missing statue, cocking his hip and pretending to hold a cup in his hand. How that didn't snap off rather than his penis, I'll never understand, protruding as it does.

The statue, obviously. Not the kid.

With a prickling awareness, I come to realize Alexander is now standing behind me. How stealthy.

"Uncle Sandy?" Archie sing-songs. "Holly says she has jelly on her toast for breakfast. Doesn't that sound yucky?"

I find myself thinking back to our confusing breakfast conversation. "Jelly is just fruit," I explain. "Like a fruit spread. A preserve? Raspberry, strawberry—"

"So, what's the difference between jam and jelly?" he asks, butting in.

"I can answer that." I shiver as Alexander's low whispered response ghosts my ear from behind. "I can't jelly my cock up your arse."

I gasp—if I had pearls, I'd grab them. That's no way for a man of his station to—

I don't even get to swing around to show how shocked (turned on?) I am as he saunters by to stand in front of Archie.

Turned on by his voice in my ear, I mean. Not the other thing.

The other is... does not turn my knees to Jell-O.

I don't think.

"Hello, little Apollo."

"I'm not Apollo! Uncle Sandy, what was that thing the statue had in his hand? Hugh said it was a can of cola."

Alexander chuckles, his gaze swinging back to me. This is not the look of a man about to call the police, I think. Not that he can prove anything. So it's missing. So it's broken. It doesn't mean it's my fault. At least, not entirely my fault.

"In one hand, he's holding the remains of a bow," Alexander explains. "In the other is the quiver."

"It didn't look like a bow," the kid replies, looking at his own hand.

"That's because it's very old. It broke a long time ago."

"How long?"

"Well, the statue was made by a sculptor called Baccio Bandinelli in Florence, Italy, back in the fourteen hundreds."

Oh, no. I think I'm going to be sick. Maybe he will really call the police.

"That's really old," the little boy says with a thoughtful expression. "No wonder his willie fell off."

Ah, fudge.

29

ALEXANDER

"I thought I could fix it."

Poor Holland. She looks distraught. But my God, how I want to laugh.

"I didn't know it was that old!" Hands on her knees, she tilts her head, her eyes a little green in the light, full of a soft innocence.

The late afternoon sun casts long shadows across the room that was once my father's study and his father's before him, dust motes dancing in its shafts. I assume a somber mien, leaning back against the gargantuan desk. *Pulvis et umbra sumus*, I find myself thinking. *We are but dust and shadows.*

Quoting Horace? No wonder I feel like a schoolmaster, drawing out a reprimand for my own entertainment. *Come closer. Bend over the desk, naughty girl...*

"I mean, okay, so I knew it was old," Holland continues from her position in the leather wingback chair. She looks down at her hands, then up at me again, this time with a touch of pleading. "But not that old!"

My expression twists as though troubled by the

admission. The statue *is* old but not as old as I might've led her to believe. It's a Victorian reproduction, though not to scale. The original stands in the Boboli Gardens in Florence. Not that I need to share any of that at this precise moment.

"I wonder, how were you going to fix it?"

"I don't know." She shrugs a little helplessly. "I thought I might find something on YouTube to help. I was waiting until the guests left after the weekend."

The guests and me, she really means.

Twisting from the waist, I begin to shuffle the stack of papers, allowing me time to fix my poker face. "Is that what you've been doing all day? Looking for answers on YouTube?" Because she hasn't posted anything to her Instagram page. Yes, so I might be stalking it a little. Isla was right; it's not an account dedicated to bikini shots, pouting, and overly made-up faces. It is quirky and quite fun. But it's also a little disingenuous. Like she's trying very hard to impress people.

"No."

"Where have you been?" I ask, turning back to face her.

"I—"

"Did you think you could avoid me after last night?"

"I went to speak to Lady Isla," she says, not answering my question and avoiding my eyes as she twists a loose thread at her knees. Not so much a loose thread as a line of them cutting across the hole at the knee of her jeans. Artfully ripped, I suppose. She catches me watching, her gaze dipping to her sparkly running shoes that look to have had a run-in with a puddle or two.

"Oh?" And why?

"I went to see her because I was going to leave." My stomach constricts intensely and immediately. Her head lifts, our gazes meet, and I see the conflict there. Conflict I understand because neither of us could've anticipated this. "After last night."

"It was that bad, was it?" I try to keep my words light, but fail.

"No, you know it wasn't," she says softly, her cheeks turning a delicate pink. "But—"

"Regrets happen in the daylight…" I allow my words to trail off, hoping she'll fill in the blanks. Cold feet. That's all this is. Nothing to worry about.

"No, I don't regret it. But not regretting spending the night with you doesn't make it right, either."

That, at least, is gratifying to know. Especially if it's not flattery. Flattery I don't need. Holland, however…

Do I need her?

There was a reason I spent the morning looking for her and an afternoon thinking about her in a darkened cinema.

"Alexander, we can't do this," she adds almost plaintively. "Isla is relying on me, and I work for you, and I swore to myself a long time ago that I would never have a relationship with someone I worked with."

There's a story behind the statement, but I park it to one side. For now.

"I take it Cameron doesn't count." My tone is sharp, the words spewing from somewhere defensive, reinforced as I fold my arms. I flex my biceps for good measure, like a child greedy for reassurance.

"What?" She drags her gaze higher, blinking as she does so.

Though the action was juvenile, I find I'm still gratified to see she hasn't changed her mind since last night. If nothing else, she still wants me.

"He's part of the castle team. Could you have a relationship with him? He has asked you out."

"That has nothing to do with you." Her tone is prim, her hands suddenly tightening on her knees. "You have your rules around relationships. And so do I," she adds after a brief pause.

"What are my rules?" I find myself purring almost dangerously.

"Don't play games." Her tone is tart. "I heard what you said at dinner last night. You only involve yourself with women who are okay with you not committing. I guess I must look like the ideal candidate." She makes a flourish with her hands which I suppose is to indicate how she looks, perhaps her age. Granted, she's not the kind of woman I might ordinarily glance at twice in the street. But fuck it, she's more than that, and she's more than just turned my head. Since that strange Wednesday afternoon in London, her presence in the world has threatened to turn my life upside down. Threatened to turn me inside fucking out!

"I have no idea what you mean," I answer coolly, unable to say any of this.

"You think we can just carry on with this thing while you're here, and I'm telling you we can't. It's not right, and it's unprofessional. You can't mix business with pleasure."

"I assure you it can be done."

"Not by me, it can't."

"Fine. You're fired." I adjust my posture, lounging almost.

"What?" Holland slouches back in her chair as though I'd pushed her there.

"Effective immediately. You'll be paid for your notice period, but you no longer work here. Now, can we get back to discussing—"

"It doesn't work that way," she says with a sad shake of

her head. "I've told Isla I'll continue to work here until she finds someone else, and I will. But if you want to fire me, I guess Mari will run the education center. Then I'll just have one job to do. And when Isla finds a replacement, I'll leave."

"And then where will you go?" I ask, suppressing the way my stomach cramps at the thought of her no longer being here. I allow my attention to shift to the fireplace as I attempt to digest my new reality.

"Someplace else," she answers simply, divulging nothing else. Not an emotion. Not a clue. Not a fucking thing.

"Come to London with me," I find myself demanding suddenly, wondering why I hadn't thought of it sooner.

"I can't—why?" Her response is promising, despite her denial.

"Because I want you to. Because *you* want to."

"No." She shakes her head. "It just wouldn't work between you and me."

"How do you know?"

"We're too different. I'm me—and just look at you!"

I look down. "I don't see what the problem is."

"Exactly!" She holds out her hands, her palms facing the ceiling.

"Flattery has no place in this discussion. Unless you weren't meaning to flatter. Perhaps you meant to point out the differences in our ages."

"No, but—yes!" she almost yells, latching on to something else.

"You think you're too young for me? That I'm too old."

"That sounds like the same thing."

"You worry that I won't be able to keep up. Hm." I rub my chin consideringly. "I don't remember any complaints last night. You know, when you were crying out my name as I worked my tongue between your legs."

"That's not—"

"Perhaps you think I'm a grumpy, irritable old man."

"I didn't—"

"Out of touch. Too staid and strait-laced?"

"Says the man who made reference to jamming his cock up my ass!"

"I thought it was jelly? Neither, I imagine, are a suitable lubricant."

Her mouth snaps shut, and she glares at me, unimpressed.

"Holland, I can guarantee you that my flaws are many and varied. And while you already seem to have your mind made up regarding my motivations, I promise you, I am sincere. I want you, Holland. I want you for more than just a weekend fuck."

"No, this is madness. I can't do it. I have the boys and my responsibility to Isla. Besides," she adds flippantly, "I've already lived in London. When I move on from here, I want to go someplace else."

"We can go anywhere you like. Or we can stay here, but I'm sorry, I'm just not willing to let you go." Not yet.

She presses her hands to her face and laughs. "Again, that's not how this works. You might be used to getting your own way, but in the real world, you can't always get—"

"And you think I don't know that?" I ask, suddenly leaning forward, my hands tightening on the edge of the desk. "Do you honestly think I get to live my life for myself? That I regularly do what I want, consequences be damned?"

Her sigh is a weary wisp in the air.

"I like my job here. Having a relationship with you, having sex with you, would change how people see me."

"You're assuming they'd be able to tell. Do you really think they'd say unkind things to you?"

"Of course they'd be able to tell. I can barely look at you as it is without turning red. And if you think last night went unnoticed, you're an idiot."

I certainly feel like an idiot, grasping at straws as I am.

"And no," she adds, "they wouldn't say unkind things to me. They'd say them behind my back. So, thank you, but no. I won't come to London with you, or anywhere else. Remember what you said when Griffin offered to help me find work. Being your *whatever* would be no different. It's not a reference I need on my résumé."

"Do not confuse me with Griffin," I grate out.

"As if I ever could."

"I'm not offering to pay you to come with me. I'm asking you to take a chance on this. To explore what it is between us because I have never—" I halt right there before I say too much and frighten her off. The truth is, I have never felt this way about anyone else. I've never behaved like this before, never mind offered to change my day-to-day existence to be with someone.

"I'm grateful for all you've done for me," she says, stealing away her gaze once again. "Whatever the reasons were, I'm glad I got to come to Scotland. And I'm glad we had last night." As though in prayer, she presses her hands together, slotting them between her knees. "I'm not going to lie, I am so unbelievably attracted to you, and while I'd like to be able to say that I'm a grown-up, that I won't act on those impulses, it seems that I can't trust myself."

"I can't see a problem with that." Especially as it appears to be behavior not limited to her.

"But I won't lose the respect of the people I've met here. I like my job."

"So, we'll get you another. A better one. Somewhere else." And now I sound like the aristocratic arse I just insisted I wasn't. "I have other estates if you don't want to live in London and an apartment in Manhattan. I'm sure—"

"No," she says softly.

"What about somewhere with a cottage? A place where you can do what you want."

"No." Her denial is stronger now, and I know I have to stop because I've gone from denying I'd pay her to making it sound exactly like I'd be willing to offer her the position of my whore.

"I don't want to let you go." And I won't.

"Don't tell me what you think I want to hear because I heard what you had to say last night. You're not looking for a relationship. The truth is, if I hadn't insisted I take you for a coffee all those months ago in London, I wouldn't even have registered on your radar."

"Now you're just being ridiculous," I growl, pushing up from the desk to lean over her—to loom over her—as my hands grip the arms of the chair. "Do you think I fell on you last night in the library because you're not my type? That I trembled like a boy does his first time because you're unremarkable? One of any fucking number? You're all I've thought about for months."

Her inhalation is soft but distinct, her eyes dark now, no longer affected by the light but darkened by some other consequence. By my nearness, by my fierceness. She smells like gardenia and looks like she belongs to me.

She should *belong to me.*

"It'll pass. You'll find someone else."

"You're wrong." I know this for certain. What I feel for her is like being in the grips of an obsession. It's unlike anything I have ever felt.

"You'll find someone more suitable."

"Say that again, and I'll rip off your underwear, and

tongue-fuck you senseless to prove exactly how unsuited we are."

"It isn't..." Her voice whispers soft and silkily between us before her lashes flutter closed. I'd like to think she's imagining it, seeing herself. I reach out to touch her face as her eyes languidly open. Hungry, ravenous eyes, eliminating the need for words.

"Holland." Her name is a plea. "I want you to give us a chance."

I don't get to her answer as the door to my study suddenly swings open.

"Uncle Sandy, it's not Holland that should be in trouble," Hugh announces, almost skidding into the room. "It's me. I'm the one that's responsible for breaking the statue."

"Hugh. This is not how you enter a room. Close the door and knock." So I can ignore you. So I can tell you to come back later. I should've locked it. I would have, but I didn't want to turn to find her climbing out of the window.

"Yes, I will, but Holland shouldn't be here. I should be the one you're angry with."

"I'm not angry," I retort, sounding, well, angry. Thwarted. Annoyed. Sexually frustrated, with a cock as hard as a concrete fucking pole.

"Yes, but I slid down the stairs on a tray."

And I was the one who most likely gave him the idea to.

"Hugh," I begin warningly. "You need—"

"I'm the one to blame," he insists with such passion, anyone listening in might think Holland was for the noose.

"Your honesty is admirable, and I fully intend taking this up with you soon, but for the love of God, Hugh, bugger off!"

"No, Uncle Sandy," he says, taking another step into the

room. "I can't. You see, Holland was covering for me. Mother was upset that day, and she didn't want to make her day any worse."

"Hugh!" My jaw flexes. I regret raising my voice. I regret making him look at me that way. I'll regret it more later, *and* I'll apologize, reassure him that I don't give a fuck about the statue, that Holland isn't in trouble for anything other than frustrating the life out of me!

But as Hugh's head drops, my heart gives a little twist. He'll survive, meanwhile I—

"What is it now?" I shout as the door begins to close, only to open again immediately.

"Ah, there you are, Holly," my sister announces, her expression as bland and as false as any mask. "Do you have a moment?"

"Since when has my study become Piccadilly Circus?" I growl, referring to the amount of traffic it's receiving.

"Because of Eros, I imagine," she answers, her eyes flashing angrily.

I left myself open to that, I suppose. Eros, the god of love, does have a monument. *Piccadilly Circus, not here in my study.* Though I should imagine I currently resemble one of the more vengeful deities than the god of love.

"Holly?" she repeats. "Hand her over."

"She's not a thing," I growl, my eyes meeting Isla's over the high back of the chair. "You can't even see her."

"No, but I know she's in here."

I look down as Holland ducks under my arm, poking her head and a quick wave around the side of the chair.

"Ah, there you are," she announces with a triumphant smile.

"Excuse me." Underneath me, yet not in the way I want,

Holland turns so her shoulder meets my chest, as though she'd nudge me out of the way.

"No. You aren't excused. We're not done here yet."

"Sandy, don't be a dick," Isla scolds.

"Mummy said dick," whispers an awe-filled Archie from somewhere behind the door.

"Mummy is about to say a whole lot more if your uncle doesn't pull his head out of his rectum. From where I'm standing, this looks like a clear case of sexual harassment."

"The chance would be a fine thing in this room," I mutter.

"I'm sure the newspapers would have a field day with that," she answers tartly.

I glower Isla's way, not because of her idle threats but because it's clear Holland and I can't continue with an audience.

"Excellent," Isla says as Holland reaches the door. "I suppose we'll see you at supper," she adds, glaring back at me. As my sister moves to the side to allow Holland to pass, I call out her name, and she turns.

Holland reluctantly turns. "What?"

Her expression is blank. I suffer the sting of it as I settle myself back against the desk in a lounging sort of arrangement.

"You might want to alter your form of address, given your concerns," I drawl. "You said yourself, you don't want to give anyone at Kilblair anything to gossip about." Contempt drips from my tone. How does the saying go? Might as well be hung for a sheep as a lamb?

"You want me to call you duke?" she replies as her mouth flattens into a mutinous line.

"Your grace is the correct address."

My sister's humorless laughter floats in from the hallway. I'm heartened to see none of us is truly entertained.

"As you like, your grace," Hollands murmurs, sliding me a look that perfectly embodies her contempt.

But she's to be pitied. Because I mean to keep her. And if that makes me like my father, then he'd better save me a seat next to him in hell.

30

HOLLY

One Uber. There is exactly one Uber in the village. And apparently, he's on the way to the train station in Inverness, which is a ninety-minute drive away, to pick up his brother. I think this must be what it felt like to live in the 1800s. It's a fifteen-mile walk from the castle to the village, so Chrissy said, but that's from the entrance gate, not the kitchen door. There are cabs, of course, but they come from a nearby town. So I may as well wait until the guy with the Uber comes back. Meanwhile, I guess I'll just order another of these, I think, waggling my glass to catch the attention of the bartender. *A woman of indeterminate age and improbable hair color.*

I wonder if I'd look good with pink hair. I guess it would match my cheeks when I'm around Alexander.

Ah, Alexander. That ass. That frustrating, sexy, solid muscled ass. How did we go from *I want you to give us a chance*, my mind intones in its approximation of his deep baritone to, *you may refer to me as your grace*?

And you may kiss my ass.

I drain the remains of my beer because there's a reason I'm drinking alone in the village pub. And that would be one Alexander Dalforth.

What have you got to lose Holland?

Respect. My self-respect. Other peoples.

And my heart.

"Another, hen?" The bartender, upon closer inspection, seems to be around my age.

I nod half-heartedly. I don't feel like being a fluffy, happy hen today.

"You don't look too sure." The woman's worried-looking eyebrows ride a little on her forehead. I don't mean her eyebrows are especially worrying. I mean, they're fierce, but it's more that she looks a little worried for me. "Stella again, was it?"

"Yeah," I say with a sigh. "I don't have the brainpower for inspiration."

I really don't know what I'm doing here, other than I had to get out of the castle after Isla seemed to think she'd rescued me from her wicked brother's clutches. In a way, I suppose she did save me. She saved me from being tongue fucked senseless.

So I guess she saved me from myself because the good Lord knows I have no self-control when it comes to her brother. Even when his ass-holey attitude raises its head in response to being thwarted.

To me leaving with Isla.

To me not listening to him.

To me not giving in.

We are unsuited in so many ways, yet he's the only man who's ever made me feel like I don't know whether I'm coming or going.

So to speak.

I just need to make it clear to him I'm not interested.

Going. So going. But only temporarily today when I'd hitched a ride into the village with wee Sophie, who was heading home after work. I thought, well, I didn't know what I thought at that point. I just needed to get away. So I'd bought cake and coffee in Kilblair's only café, but when the woman who runs the café started to give me the stink eye, I thought I should find somewhere else to go so she could close up. Which left me the small grocery store or one of two pubs as the only places open.

"A half of wife beater, it is," the bartender says, pulling out a fresh half-pint glass from underneath the bar.

"Wife beater?" I repeat, taking a look at the logo on the draft beer tap. *Stella Artois.* "Because the logo has a white background like a T-shirt?" I know, it's a stretch—like cotton, ha—but it's the only thing I can come up with.

She shakes her head. "Because it's got a kick to it."

"I don't get it."

"The alcohol content is nearly five percent."

"So, you get drunk on it before going home and beat up your wife?" I answer uncertainly.

"Aye, if you like."

"That's kind of…"

"Messed up," she answers for me.

"Yep." I pop the *p* for emphasis as she sets the glass in front of me. "But as I don't have a wife to go back to or a husband, I don't see a problem."

"Ye can gi' me a good going-over," calls the resident bar fly, I'm guessing, from the other end of the bar. Call it an educated guess. "I'd even let ye' have your wicked way wi' me."

"Och, away and boil ye heid, Geordie," the bartender quips. "You've a face like a skelpit arse. No way you've a chance wi' her."

Which I think is her way of telling him to cease and desist. *Go away and boil your head, maybe?* Skelpit arse I get —I've heard Chrissy say this in some variation—the pink-haired bartender just informed her customer that he has a face like a spanked ass. I think that was her way of saying I'm out of his league.

"I love you, Emma," replies the lush with a smile full of tombstone teeth. "Put 'nother in there when you've a minute, hen." He sets his empty pint glass down. "I dinnae have a wife to beat either."

"We don't want to know what you'll be beating later," she mutters with a frown in his direction. "He likes it when I treat him mean," she then adds with a wink. "Isn't that right, Geordie."

The man laughs and nods his head.

"Anyway, wife beater," she says brightly, ringing up my beer on a cash register straight out of the 90s. "I reckon the reason is pure bollocks."

This one I know; bollocks = balls = testicles.

She drops the change to my hand from the Scottish five-pound note I'd handed her. I must admit to being surprised at first discovering Scotland had its own currency.

"I think there's a more stylistic explanation," she adds. "Wanna hear?"

"Sure," I reply, running my finger through the condensation on the glass.

"Well." She smiles, settling her forearms on the bar in front of me. "Marlon Brando wore a wife beater in the film, *Streetcar Named Desire*, did he not?"

"And he shouted *Stelllaaaa!*" I say without any real volume.

"Exactly!" She nods. She knows I get it. "That man could really fill out a T-shirt. Not like this lot," she adds, her gaze falling over the pub's clientele. "There are no decent blokes in Kilblair, in case you're wondering. Especially not on a Saturday night. The young ones will have headed into the next town over."

"I was definitely not wondering."

"It's like that, is it?" And there go her eyebrows again.

"No comment." With a twist of my lips, I raise my glass and take a sip.

"Well, unhappy hour is nearly over," she says. "Hang around and join me and my pal for a drink, if you like."

And so I do…

"What? Because they're wrinkly?" Allie, friend of Emma the bartender says with a skeptical twist to her lips. We've commandeered a corner booth, situated at one end of the long mahogany bar. An older man, the owner, Emma says, polishes glasses as he chats to the lush as a couple of other customers watch the game of soccer playing out on a TV.

"That's not what I said." I shake my head as I laugh.

"Did she or did she not just say she fancies the auld ones?" she asks her friend.

"I'm keepin' out of it," Emma says with a laugh.

"I said I like old people, not that I fancy them!"

"Well, I'd say you're in the right place for it." Allie's gaze roams over the clientele of the pub. "It's like God's waitin' room in here."

"Shush!" I say, glancing around, worried that someone might hear. I was already hit on by the lush. No need to add to my man woes tonight.

"Och, half of them have'nae got their hearing aids

turned on. I mean, look at the puss on that one." She inclines her head, my head swinging in that direction with a kind of horrified fascination.

"Puss?" Surely that's not—

"Face," Emma explains.

"I didn't say I fancied them," I say, trying to defend myself. "I just like older people because they have such interesting stories."

"Aye, usually about their bowels."

I almost choke on my Long Island Iced Tea, made by Emma's fair hand, and bought with her staff discount.

"Sounds like she likes her men like she likes her whisky." Allie slides her friend a look, setting her up.

"Three times her age and from Scotland?"

"I do like my men like my whisky, as it happens," I reply. "Full bodied, smooth and smoky."

"Oooh! Fancy. You're up," Allie instructs, turning to her friend.

"I like my men like I like my whisky. Left in an oak barrel for five years with very little oxygen."

"Oh, Lord!" I don't know whether it's the booze or if this pair are just hilarious. What I do know is I've barely thought about my man troubles for hours.

Oh, Alexander...

"Did you keep your appointment at the salon?" Emma suddenly asks her friend.

"I'm sittin' here with you, am I no'?"

I run her answer though my alcohol-buzzed head, slow it down, and decide that her answer was *no*.

"There's a salon here?" I interject as the word sinks into my alcohol sodden head. "Is it any good?"

"It's the only one for miles," Emma answers with a shrug

before her attention turns back to her friend. "Why didn't you?"

"Because I'm here with you—because the twat called and said he couldn't make it. I was'nae going for a wax after that."

Oh, so like a beauty salon. Good to know.

"But I pulled in a favor to get you that appointment yesterday."

"But, Emma, there's no point peeling a tattie if you're no' gonnae mash it."

"Potatoes?" I ask, completely lost. I've heard Dougal call them *tatties*.

Emma makes a critical noise; a click of tongue and teeth. "She's not peeling the potato if there's no one to mash it. Or in other words, if there's no chance of sex, she's not paying for a wax. It's a good job the poor woman at the salon does more than bikini waxes with that attitude." Emma adds.

"Aye, because I could count the number of times I've had a decent seeing to in this village on one hand and still have enough digits left to finger myself." Allie's expression twists as she indicates the bar's clientele. "The talent around here, as you can see, is abysmal."

"I don't need those kinds of complications," I answer, reaching for my glass.

"What?" Emma asks, leaning in. "The fun kind?"

"She's hangin' out for her older man, remember? The other woman taunts. "With his own teeth and supply of Viagra!"

"I am not!" I take a sip of my drink, giggle, then hiccup. "Oh, man. These are strong."

"Wet your thrapple!" Allie cackles. "Get it down you!"

"Wet my what'll?"

"Thrapple." The woman runs a finger down her throat

before her attention slides over my shoulder and she suddenly sits straight. "Hottie alert. Ah, shite." She slouches again. "He's got a woman with him."

I glance in the direction of the door and smile, sort of expectantly. "Oh, it's Cameron!" But my smile doesn't last long as Mari slides in behind him.

"That was a telling look." Emma eyes me sympathetically. "Is he why you were drinking the hard stuff?"

"This is the hard stuff," I say lifting my glass. Not the couple of small beers I drank earlier.

"Aye, but it's good stuff, too," Allie interjects. "You ken Cameron, then?" She cocks her head in the direction of the bar where the two are standing now. Standing pretty close, if you ask me, for people who just work in the same place.

"I work with him," I answer as Emma's attention follows her friends. "The girl, too. Mari," I add in a perky tone, not wanting to encourage them.

"Are you on a working holiday?" Emma asks, turning back.

"No. Well, kind of, I guess." It's not like I plan on staying.

"You're sure that's no' a bit of working holiday romance?" Allie does this weird eyebrow thing then, if that wasn't hint enough, she makes a circle of thumb and forefinger. With the other hand, she pokes it. "I'd do him."

"Stop!" I protest with a chuckle, pushing her hands away. "It's not like that." Thankfully. *Imagine the complications now,* I think to myself.

"So, you work over at Kilblair Castle." Emma says.

"Now, there's an older man I'd go for." Allie's eyes go meaningfully wide. "If I'm gonnae be shagging an auld fella, I want it to be him."

"Who?" I glance behind me again, but the door hasn't

opened again, though I do notice how Cameron and Mari are snuggled up in a booth together. They do seem very friendly with one another. I wonder how long *that* has been going on.

"The duke. He's some man," she adds appreciatively. "I'd totally do him."

Does that mean—no. *Don't be stupid*, I silently rebuke. I have no right to the flash of jealousy that just flared in my chest.

"As if you'd ever have a chance wi' that one!" Emma says with a cackle. "And he's hardly what I'd call old. He's more what I'd call do-able."

"He is, so why can't I do him?" Allie answers, her tone aggrieved. "Like my granda likes to say, we're all Jock Tamson's bairns."

"Who's Jock Tamson?" I ask, my head beginning to spin, Long Island Iced Tea style.

"It's just a saying," Emma replies. "Jock Tamson is, I suppose, God."

"I think your Bible must be very different." A God named Jock? Why not, I guess. Scotland has its own currency, so why not Bibles, too.

"No, Jock Tamson is sort of everyman," Allie interjects. "Like we're all equal, yeah?"

"I get it." *Oh, I do.* The duke and the girl from nowhere grand. I hide my cynical smile with a tiny cough into my hand.

"So, have you met him?" Allie asks with an avid gleam. "I have, but just the once."

"Did you?" Emma asks skeptically.

"Aye, it was a few years ago when I was working part-time at the sweetie shop. He brought in his wee nephew for a treat. It was lust at first sight, I can tell you. Does he smell really lush, or have I imagined that?" she asks.

Emma groans, pulling a chunk of her pink hair over her eyes as though embarrassed.

I purse my lips together to stop myself from barking out a laugh. How does he smell? Try irresistible.

"I have met him, but I can't tell you what he smells like". Or rather won't. I'm also not about to tell you I'm currently hiding from him.

"He was so good wi' that wee boy," she continues, "it's a crying shame the man doesn't have bairns of his own."

"Aye, but his wife died," Emma says, assuming I don't know. "She was so beautiful, like a fairy princess. Her loss fair broke his heart."

"Do you know how it happened?" Of course it's something I'd pondered, but I wouldn't dare ask anyone at the castle. Especially now. I know it's not right, that I shouldn't pry, but I can't help myself.

"Drowned." Emma gives a sad shrug. "Fell off a yacht in the Med a few years ago now. Her body was never found. The suffering he must've gone through those first few days, wondering. Clinging onto hope."

"Devastating," Allie adds as both girls take a sip of their drinks, their expressions bleak. At least until Allie says, "I reckon I could cheer him up, though!"

"You are such a ho bag!"

The pair bust into a fit of raucous laughter that must draw the attention of the whole pub. Not that I'm looking, as pick up my purse to check the status of my Uber, my heart sinking to my shoes.

"Oh, is that a Prada handbag?"

I enjoy the rest of my evening though I have to try very hard to banish the thought of Alexander's marriage from my mind. I know it makes no sense because he's not mine and he never will be, but I can't help regretting that. Which is the part that makes no sense because we're not suited. From different worlds. We are not meant to be. I recognize that. Feel it in my bones. Yet I can't help but mourn it.

No, I decide, on the way back to the castle in my long awaited for Uber. I'm not mourning the fact that I can't have him. It's just sex addling my brain. It's the sex that I'll miss when Alexander leaves tomorrow, not him. Because you can't miss a person you don't really know. And when I say I enjoy the rest of my evening and I try to push those thoughts away, I do. But the company of Emma and Allie has made me realize I miss my sister. Worse, I know I can't call her until I've pulled my shizz together because that girl is like a truffle hound for trouble. So, yes, I enjoyed my evening while missing my sister and lamenting the fact that I have to give up Alexander's dick.

And how I did that was through alcohol.

"Oh, Cooper. My head is super swimmy," I complain, pressing my head to the cool glass of the car window.

"You're not gonnae boak, are you?" He sounds concerned so I open one eye. "Vomit," he qualifies.

"No." I sigh heavily. "I promise. I'm not drunk, just pleasantly pished. Or, at least, that's the way Emma had explained it." My head is swimmy for different reasons. Heavier reasons, I don't even want to think about. Reasons I'm not at liberty to share. And you probably wouldn't believe me if I told you anyway.

You and the duke? But his wife was so beautiful. Tell me another funny, Holly!

"Emma is a bad influence," he complains. "And she's got hollow legs. God knows what witches brew my cousin's been pouring down your neck."

"Down my thrapple, you mean?" I smile. The Scots tongue is an interesting one, and Alexander's tongue—

Nope. I'm not going there.

Cooper and Emma are apparently related, though not full cousins, she'd explained. But he's cranky and tired, and I can't say I blame him after driving to Inverness and back before being strong armed into taking me to Kilblair. I say strong armed when I really mean sent on a guilt trip by his cousin when she'd called him to complain about what he'd done.

She's a single, good-looking girl, Coop. Is your conscience ready to deal wi' her risking walking back to that castle alone? Will you cry when the police find her cold, dead body and you read the headline over your cornflakes?

I'd begun to feel a little scared myself when Allie had hung up and explained the only risk I'd be in on the long walk back was standing in sheep poop.

Then she's added *probably*.

But I'm pleased I'm not walking these dark, lonely lanes. There are no paths and so few streetlights. As I glance gratefully over at Cooper, I feel a little sorry for him. It's such a small car for such a tall guy, too. He must be so uncomfortable. But his discomfort is soon shared as we begin bumping along a road that makes me wish I'd tightened my bra straps. Thankfully, I can see the outlines of the castle looming darkly against the sky.

"I've never been on this road before."

"It's a shortcut. Do you want to be dropped at the cottages or the front?"

"Do you know where the kitchen is?"

"Aye, I used to work for the local fruit and veg shop. It's where I made the deliveries."

The tires crackle against gravel as Cooper pulls into the courtyard, the whole place lighting up.

"Security lights," I mumble, shielding my eyes as I step from the car. But bright lights aren't my only issue because it seems as though the alcoholic iced teas have made me drunk, but only from the feet up.

"Hang on," Cooper calls, unfolding himself from his tiny car as I stumble. "You haven't been drinkin' zombies, have you?"

"Zombies?" I look up. He must be at least six-two, and is pretty cute, if you're into the man-bun and skinny jeans look.

"Aye. She made me one or five last weekend." He lifts my hand over his shoulder, pressing himself to my side, his hand supporting me at the waist. Seriously, I'm not that drunk but we're already on the move. "Last time, I walked out of the pub like the livin' dead. Woke the next morning feeling like it, too."

"Well, it was Long Island Iced Teas *pour moi*. That's French for—"

"Bringing home guests."

At the sound of Alexander's voice, a series of pleasurable explosions begin to bounce around my insides. When I lift my head, the outline of his body fills the door.

"Hey, your grace!" I add a wave to accompany my thoroughly improper form of address, then tighten my grip on Cooper's from where it has loosened at my waist.

"This is Cooper. Coop, say hi to the Duke of Dalforth."

"Hello?" he answers uncertainly, unwrapping my arm from over his shoulder.

"Cooper?" Alexander drawls. "Were your parents fond of barrels?" His gaze flicks over him impassively, but I can hear the tension in his words. Oh, my God, he thinks—

Oh, this is brilliant! I cackle internally. I can't have him, I can't keep him, but I can totally make him jealous.

It feels like one of those times where... *I just want to see what I can get away with!*

"I don't think so," Cooper answers with a puzzled frown. That totally went over his head. Maybe someone should explain how coopers make barrels.

But maybe not right now. I'm having too much fun!

"Can we come in?" I ask, smiling up at the grump. *We. Ba-ha!* "You're kind of blocking the door."

Alexander's gaze drops to my dimple, then my mouth. His frown deepens as he steps to the side. But Cooper isn't really about to follow me into the kitchen. Whatever. I'm still digging the fact that it bothers him.

"I'll, erm, be off then." Cooper takes a step back and risks a small side-to-side wave. Or maybe that was more a "whoa, not me, man" or whatever the Scottish equivalent of that is.

"Okay," I sing-song. "Thanks for everything." I just about stop myself from yelling, *I'll be sure to leave you a good rating!* because I am enjoying this more than I should as I saunter (very slightly wobble?) into the kitchen. A chair at the head of the long pine table is pushed back, an open bottle of whisky and a glass sitting on the table in front of it. "Dalmore," I read aloud as I pick the bottle up. "Can I have some?"

I try not to shiver as I feel him behind me, his arm reaching around me to take it from my hand. As his touch skims my waist, heat bursts against my skin like wildfire.

"I'd say you've already had enough." Whisky-scented want, his words are soft against my cheek as he sets the bottle back and curls his fingers in the neck of my jacket. He slides it from my shoulders in a move that's more practical than seductive, but I shiver anyway. Then I watch as his hand curls around the back of the farmhouse chair in front of me. We just stand there for a beat, his arm a whisper away from wrapping around me. But it doesn't happen.

I turn, tilting my chin to look up at him.

"Killjoy," I all but whisper. His eyes are so beautiful. Like the sun on the ocean, flecks of gold sparkle within the blue. And while the way he looks at me should send me running for my room instead it sinks hooks into me, anchoring me to the spot. "No kilt tonight? No bow tie?" I flick the collar of his open necked shirt, unable to stop myself.

"Last night was the formal dinner. This evening was a quiet supper with friends where your absence was remarked upon."

"Yeah? By whom?" Check me and my perfect English out.

"Matteo and Van, my friends. And by Ivy Duffy who I think might be under the impression I'm a threat to you somehow."

"I don't know why. I haven't even spoken to her. How's Portia, by the way?"

"I imagine she's fine and back in London by now."

She's gone? Stupid heart, get back to your place, rattling around behind those ribs!

"Who was your friend?" he asks suddenly, and I'll credit him as trying to keep his question casual, despite the muscle ticking in his jaw.

"Who? Cooper? Just some guy I met in the pub."

"Does he have a problem with his laundry?" I tilt my head, not catching his meaning. "I'm assuming that's the reason for his incredibly tight clothes."

I fight a budding smile and lose. "Yeah, I noticed, too.

Didn't you know men who look like that are supposed to wear clothes that look like they're painted on?"

"I suppose regular fitting clothing chafes their soft skin."

"I can ask him next time I see him, if you want."

"You've plans to see him again?" His hand slips from the chair, my body blooming as it lands on my hip. Blooms and falls as he moves me to the side to reach his glass. "Sit down. I'll make you something to eat," he murmurs, turning away from me.

"Maybe I don't want to eat," I say, following him across the kitchen like a puppy desperate for attention. "Maybe I don't want to sit down, either."

"Where is the bread kept in this place?" he murmurs, ignoring me.

"It's in this one." I tap the cabinet next to his shoulder then jump up onto the kitchen countertop next to him. I slide my hands under my thighs as a means of not touching him. *Should've stayed on the other side of the kitchen*, the little angel on my shoulder whispers. Unfortunately, it's the devil I'm listening to. A devil named Olive, it seems who's reminding me that Alexander is leaving tomorrow, and by the time he comes back, I'll be gone.

Once more for old time sakes.

The last chance saloon. Or kitchen.

"I thought I told you to sit down," he grumbles.

"I am sitting," I say, swinging my legs to the side and back again. "See?"

Alexander smiles though he tries to hide it as he pulls out a loaf of bread. "I meant on a chair." He slides open a drawer, pulling out a bread knife.

"So conventional," I scoff. "Whatcha doing?"

"Cooking."

"I'm not hungry." Not for bread, anyway.

"I wasn't asking."

I sigh huffily, my shoulders dropping along with the noise. "Are you always such an ass?"

"I don't know, Holland," he answers, his blue eyes blazing as he turns to face me, knife in hand. "Why don't you tell me?"

"I haven't known you long enough to collate the relevant data regarding your assholery. You are, however, grumpy in the extreme tonight."

His sardonic huff of laughter raises goosebumps along my arms.

"If you must know, I'm making you a sandwich because it's clear you need something to soak up the booze."

"Oh." That's kind of nice, right?

"And to give you something else to do with your mouth," he then adds in that velvety voice of his.

I suck in an offended breath, probably to hide how that totally and inexplicably turns me on. "What's that supposed to mean?"

"That it's clear you've followed me across the kitchen because you want to kiss me."

"I've changed my mind. I do have the data. You are an asshole." My retort sounds like it should finish up with me sticking out my tongue.

"Look," he says, turning to me again. "It seems you're either hiding from me or people are trying to drag you away, so I think we should take this late-night opportunity to talk."

Talking isn't for late nights, unless it's the pillow kind.

For a moment, I wonder if I'd said that aloud as Alexander keeps his eyes from me. Almost deliberately. But maybe it's because he can sense I'm watching him. His shoulders are so broad, and my hands know how the muscles in them are so tightly defined. I swallow as his bicep bunches and the tendons in his forearm tense as he slices through the loaf of bread. All I can think about is how I want to put my fingers there and feel the movement as I ride his hand.

Maybe he does want me to use my mouth to talk to him.

Maybe he isn't interested in my kisses or the ways I'd use it.

Except his eyes tell me otherwise.

For someone who'd been drinking the past few hours I suddenly feel very, very thirsty.

31

ALEXANDER

I FEEL THE WEIGHT OF HER REGARD ALMOST PHYSICALLY. IT takes every ounce of my willpower not to react to it.

To not place the bread knife down.

To not slide myself between those jean-clad legs.

To not sate this need to devour her from the mouth down.

"So what do you want to talk about?" she asks, words spilling from her mouth so fast, they seem to run together. I glance her way and notice how her legs seem glued together from thigh to knee. Glued tellingly together in a very telling kind of position.

Fuck.

She'll be wet, I know. Her body is so responsive. So in tune to her wants.

Turning back, I do place the knife down. Then I take a deep breath and begin to silently count to ten as I attempt to temper the demand swirling through me.

"Did you want to talk about Cooper?"

She really is ridiculous. As am I for acknowledging the flare of jealousy that licks though me. I know logically she's just trying to goad me, but I can't help my first reaction: she didn't answer whether she was seeing him again.

This is such bullshit. The way she was in my study, her mouth full of denials and her gaze full of sin. It's me she wants, not some wanker in drainpipe jeans and a fucking Volkswagen Golf.

My eyes are drawn to her again, and though she's a little more disheveled than she was when she left the study, it means nothing. But as good as she looks sitting on the kitchen counter, I'm not a fucking Neanderthal. I don't have to act on the impulse to fuck her on it.

Shoving the loaf back in the bag, I make my way over to the fridge and pull out the ingredients I need. Gruyere and ham. Dijon from the cupboard next to it.

"Did you want to talk about Cooper?" I throw the question over my shoulder.

"I don't know him that well. But Emma says he's a total bad boy."

I almost snort. Maybe I should hand her a butter knife so she can lay it on a little thicker. As for Emma, whoever Emma is, she isn't important to this situation.

"How so?" I begin to assemble the doorstop thick sandwich, then drop a chunk of butter to the frying pan. Turning the knob, the gas burner roars to life. "He looks a little old to throw tantrums." Even if he looked nowhere near my age.

"What?" The word warbles with suppressed laughter.

"Does he scribble his name on the library walls?" As the melted butter begins to sizzle. I drop the sandwich into it.

"Not everyone has a library, *your grace*. But why do I feel like this is something you might've done?" The hair piled artfully onto the top of her head this afternoon now in disarray, Holland taps a finger to her tempting lips.

"Though I imagine it was a few years before you *had* the nanny?"

"Sorry?" I bark out, my turn to be amused.

"You said back in London that I sounded like a nanny you'd once *had*. Had being the operative word."

"How strange because I haven't had a nanny since,"—I flip the sandwich—"last night."

"You are so bad," she replies, throwing a kitchen towel my way.

I catch it and place it over my shoulder, fancying I look the part. But I'm not bad, not at the minute, at least. What I am is gratified. Pleased she remembers, delighted it seems I haven't been alone in reliving that night.

"For the record, you're the only nanny I've ever had." The only nanny I've ever wanted. *Wanted like a drug.* "As for badly behaved," I add, dropping a dollop of Dougal's béchamel sauce to the top of the sandwich before moving over to the oven. "I've never once defaced the library walls."

"Hey, what are you doing with my sandwich?"

I send her an arch look along with my answer. "Elevating it." At least, according to Dougal, who has made more of these than I can count in the wee hours of the morning after parties and overnight flights. It's a novel experience to be on the other end of the spatula. Actually, I find it quite nice.

"It'll be ready in a couple of minutes," I say, turning back to her.

"What are we going to do for a couple of minutes?" purrs my kitchen coquette.

"Behave yourself, Olive," I censure, leaning back against the counter. I cross my legs at the ankle and my arms across my chest for good measure. *Lord, how I want her.* But not tonight. Not now.

"I can't believe you called me that!" she says with a delighted sounding laugh.

"Yes, because Olive is so much better than Lyle."

"I kind of like Lyle," she demurs.

"More than you like Alexander?"

"Lyle was safe," she almost whispers, ducking her head.

I swallow thickly because she almost proves my point. I've been sitting here in this kitchen since dinner, wondering what she was doing. Waiting for her to come home. Dougal must've thought I'd lost my marbles. Mute and barely moving save for to pour and drink my whisky as I'd contemplated my life. But I hadn't considered how if Lyle was a figment of her imagination, then maybe Alexander was her nightmare.

Maybe Alexander asks for too much.

"Do you regret taking Lyle for a coffee?" I ask carefully. "To your hotel room?"

From the periphery of my vision, I see her shake her head.

If she doesn't regret the night then she can't regret the rest, I decide. But I need to be smarter about this. Wasn't that the whole point of tonight's introspection? Sliding open another drawer, or three, I find the silverware and then a napkin as she makes some comment about only duke's needing a fork for a sandwich. *But she'll see*, I think as I begin to plate up.

"Come on." As I reach for her hand, Holland slides from the countertop, her feet hitting the floor with a quiet thump.

"I'm really not hungry."

"I'll help you finish it if you like. Though I think you'll probably jab me with the fork when you taste how good it is."

"Modest, much?"

"Modesty never did anyone any good. But I can't take the credit, really. It's Dougal's recipe. All I did was assemble it."

I lead us back to the table and Holland takes a chair next to where I'd placed my whisky glass.

"What were you doing in here tonight?" As though she regrets voicing the question, she keeps her eyes on the plate as I place it in front of her. "This smells so good, by the way. And if I forget to tell you afterwards, I appreciate you looking after me. I mean, making it for me, even though I'm not hungry."

"You're welcome." A tiny pinprick of pleasure pierces my chest. I want to look after her. I just have to persuade her to let it happen. That I could be good for her. That we could be good for each other. "As for appetites," I find myself saying, "sometimes you don't know what you want until it's placed in front of you."

I'm not sure truer words were ever said. Certainly, not by me.

I want her. I want to get to know her. I want her by my side. I want to see where this goes. I want to try. And I want her to be open to it. To this. To us.

"You know," she says, picking up her silverware, "I told your sister this afternoon that your moods were pretty changeable." Holland freezes for a minute, her eyes rolling closed as the corner of her mouth tips. "Actually, that's not really true." She twists her head my way, the quirk of her lips still visible. "I muttered something to myself, and she overheard."

"What was it?" I ask, ignoring the prickle in my fingertips and the desire to curl a lock of her hair behind her perfect pink ear.

"I asked myself if you were bipolar." She shrugs tightly

then cuts a corner from one of the chunky triangles. "The changeable moods." She pushes the bread into her mouth.

"Lovely," I say, meaning the exact opposite.

"Oh my gosh, this is *so* good." Her expression isn't quite her orgasm face, but it's a close second as she chews and rolls the morsel around her tongue. "This is the best grilled cheese sandwich I have ever eaten," she adds with such seriousness before she begins to dig into the croque monsieur with gusto.

"What?" she asks suddenly, looking up and watching me.

"You were saying. Mercurial," I prompt, shaking my head. I'd become a little intent, watching her eat. Watching her lips purse and stretch while ignoring how my cock perks up as she opens her mouth. *Yes, just like that.*

"Just remember what went on in that room before she turned up." Her gaze dips diffidently to her plate and I decide against telling her I have, that, in fact, I'd gone on and reimagined it in explicit detail. "Anyway, Isla said you weren't of a capricious nature," she adds in some approximation of my sister's voice. "But maybe she's too close to see how hot and cold you run."

"Holland, my moods are never cold around you." Possibly my words, but only when I'm deflecting. *And that's at least ninety percent of the problem*, I think with a sigh. "You asked what I was doing here in the kitchen. Apart from waiting for you, which you know already without asking. But I was thinking about this afternoon, too. I realized I'd asked too much of you. While we don't really know each other, to me, it feels like you've been in my life for longer than a couple of days." She doesn't answer but I don't think I need her to. "That night, the night in London, you said you were on holiday."

"I know, and I was still on vacation, technically. I wasn't lying, not about that—"

"I really don't care what you said or why. I'm just thankful we had that night." And determined it won't be the start of a very brief fling.

"I'm just saying, I didn't have sex with you because I'm easy," she adds rather defensively, "or because I don't respect myself. Maybe I had sex with you because you looked easy. Maybe it's you I don't respect."

"Darling, you can disrespect me anytime."

"That—that's not what I meant."

"Isn't it? Pity. But it doesn't matter." I try to keep the frustration from my voice, the annoyance that I'd fallen back into the pattern I'm trying to avoid. We've come so far from that night, and I think she realizes that. Impossible as it might seem, so different as we are, we have a connection that shouldn't be denied. "What I'm trying to say is that in a strange kind of way, I was taking a holiday, too."

"A holiday from your life, you mean."

"Yes, I suppose so. From responsibilities and family and all that that entails. It had been a while." I grasp my glass and settle back into the chair. "Eat up before it goes cold." She picks up her silverware and begins to eat again. "I suppose I realize I deserve something for myself, and I want that something to be you." I watch as the progress of the fork slows on the way to her mouth. "But I realize it was wrong of me to throw all that at you this afternoon. You don't know me. But I want you to. I want us to get to know each other. Then hopefully, we can revisit the situation."

"What situation?" she says, laying down her silverware, evidently finished.

"The situation of us. The situation where I want us to be together."

"That sounds not... like the things you had to say at the dinner table."

This isn't a slight or a reprimand and more somehow like she's trying to goad me into a reaction. Confirmed as I reach for my glass and follow the dark dilation of her eyes. *My wrist. My bicep. My shoulder. My lips as I take a sip. My throat as I swallow.*

It's possible she's seeking attention, or perhaps this is our pattern. Either way, I find myself reaching out and delicately brushing my finger against a speck of béchamel sauce at the corner of her mouth. There really isn't any need but the one burning inside me. The one I've been trying to ignore since she walked through the door full of taunts overlaid by a blithe attitude. Before I can take it back—my hand, the action—her hands circle my wrist.

"I told you I wasn't going to share it." Her voice is husky, her eyes bitter chocolate again. "Not even a little bit." Then her pink tongue grazes the tip of my finger. *Fuck.* "If you want some, you'll have to take it from the source."

"The source of all temptation, you mean." I try to make it sound like a reprimand, like I'm unimpressed. Like my cock hasn't been left aching from the tiny throb of connection. As I pull my arm back, Holland travels with it, her thighs coming over mine.

"Holland." Her name is a rasping whisper as I trace the path of her hairline with my finger. Past her ear, her jaw, and farther down her neck. Across one-half of her shirt covered collarbone it goes before ghosting over the first three buttons on her shirt. I want to kiss her, but I won't. Not yet. And while kissing is the least I want to do with her, that's where I'll draw the limit. I have to. I want more than stolen moments in the dark. I want to find her in my bed as the dawn breaks and to be able to kiss her on the cheek at lunch time in full view of everyone around. I want to take her hand as we stroll through the gardens, reach for it over the table as we dine in some London restaurant. And this is what I'll fight for as I settle my hands lightly over her hips.

"Touch me, Alexander."

"You don't really want that." I press a kiss to her jaw and murmur my rebuttal there. "You're just a little drunk and incredibly horny."

And God bless her for it.

"That's not true." She slides her arms around my neck and flexes her hips, pressing herself deeper into my lap. "Not all of it, at least." Her chest rises and falls with a deep sigh.

"It looks entirely true to me." And entirely too delicious. I can't quite believe I haven't thrown her over my shoulder already, but I want more than evenings of stolen moments and days of denials.

"I'm not *pished*." The worst Scottish accent whispers against my ear, my chest moving against hers in a chuckle.

"You're not? Then you must be stoatin'," I retort using both the Scots vernacular and the accent. "Or howlin'. Maybe hammered." The Innuit might have fifty words for snow, but the Scots probably have more for the inebriated. "Sootered. Rat arsed." I tighten my hands on *her* arse. "Ruined."

"Oh, you've been holding out on me." A smile leaks through her words as she rocks over me again. I resist the desperate urge to press up into her as she purrs, "Roll those r's for me."

"You mean like Cooper does?"

"Cooper was my Uber driver."

"Minx." I press my lips to her neck and threaten a bite.

"Horny minx," she corrects. "Not a drunken one."

"You'll regret it in the morning." My hands against her shoulders, I press her back until I can see her face. Flushed cheeks and dark eyes, lips as red and as tempting as Eden's apple.

"No. I won't," she promises, her words ghosting over my lips. As her mouth meets mine, I breathe in her needy, ragged groan.

So much for plans. For connections that are more than body parts. Yet this feels inevitable. So much more as I reach the heat of her, running my finger along the seam of her jeans. Somehow, the way her lips tease mine seems so much more intimate than my finger between her legs.

"I want you, Alexander. I want you so much."

"I know, sweetheart." I draw my finger up her body to the first button on her shirt, twisting it between my forefinger and thumb, working my way from top to bottom before setting the edges aside. Her bra is almost silver and gossamer thin, her nipples rosy and hard beneath the fabric. I want what she wants—what her halting breaths want. But instead, I draw my finger down her breastbone, causing her to move against me with a long, drawn-out breath.

"Touch me, please."

My belly tightens as she undulates above me, dragging me with her along that knife-edge of temptation. Without answering her, I reach behind her, dipping my finger into the glass. I run it across the soft swells of her breasts, following the smoky trail with my tongue. Hooking a finger into her bra, I release her hardened nipple, taking it into my mouth.

"That feels so good." Another flex of her hips, one this time I push up into, desperate to feel the heat of her yet knowing I won't. My balls fit to burst. It takes me a moment to process her next taunt. "Or should that be your grace."

In answer, I use my teeth, groaning as she bucks into me, making my dick ache like nothing else.

"Be good," I growl. So much for deference. She pouts as I cover her wet nipple again. But not for long as I feed my whisky-flavored finger into her mouth. Her eyes are dark as she swirls it with her tongue. As she sucks.

"I don't want to be good," she says as I trail the wet digit down her chin.

"Then you won't get what you need." Against my better judgement, I know I will. I'll tell myself I'm doing it for her, that I'm taking nothing for myself. Nothing but the pleasure she brings. "But you have to follow the rules, darling." And if I want to earn the right to call her darling in the daylight, so do I.

"Oh, that sounds kinky," she says, her eyes lighting up like a child seeing her first Christmas tree.

"Only for the first time." My mouth hitches at one edge because I've never been interested in exploring the kink of self-denial.

"And there's the devil's smile." Cupping my cheek, she brings her smiling mouth over mine again, her kiss wet and messy, liquor and Holland flavored.

"And you know what lurks behind the devil's smile," I answer with just a hint of a taunt.

Her eyes gleam as she answers. "Only my favorite thing ever. Well, with the exception of this." I grit my teeth and groan as she rocks over me again, bringing her lips to my ear. "It's his tongue."

Screwing my eyes tight, I promise myself another time where I get Holland a little drunk. Sometime soon. Sometime I can join in.

"I love this part of you," she murmurs, pressing her mouth over my neck. Over my Adam's apple. "And this," she adds, drawing her hands down my chest. "And this." Her voice drops as she reaches for the outline of my cock, wrapping her fingers around the shape of it through my jeans.

Unguarded Holland is a sight to behold. A treasure I don't deserve, but one I'm trying to earn.

"That's against the rules," I censure, forcing myself to lift her hand.

"There are rules?" She almost shimmies over me, a motion that does wonderful things for her tits.

"Just one," I modify. "You must do as you're told."

"That sounds..." Any protest she might make is drowned out as I tighten my hands on her hips and move her pussy over me again and again. "Oh, God." She tightens her hand at my neck, bringing our bodies so close.

I bring my mouth over hers. Teasing touches, butterfly light, as I take my time. As I work her body over mine until her breathing is labored and her fingers dig into my shoulders. When it begins to sound like she might get off, get off on my cock and the seam of her jeans, I slow it down. Skimming my hands under her shirt, I slip it from her shoulders, then press my mouth over her nipple, sucking through the fabric.

"You're so beautiful, Holland. You make me so hard."

"You're driving me *crazy*."

As she begins to move again, I grip her hips. Sucking harder, tighter, releasing her nipple from the other cup to toy and tease with the pads of my fingers.

"Alexander, please." She twists, all tight breaths and taut words. "I need..." Her hands move to the button of my jeans, but I move them away.

"No, sweet girl. Not today." Not until you let me into more than just your underwear.

"But I want to make you feel good."

"You want me to fuck you," I say with a dark-sounding chuckle. "You can't kid a kidder, my darling girl."

"Yes, but it'd be good for both..." But her words go unfinished as I slip my hand between us and grip her pussy.

"I want this more than you can imagine, but I won't. Not tonight." I press my mouth to her neck to conceal a brief flash of my amusement. God, her expression.

"What?"

"I mean to practice a little self-restraint." I begin to trail wet, open-mouthed kisses down her neck, my words a little hoarse. "At least until you're sure of me."

So, that's my big plan. That's what I've come up with after hours of introspection. Deeds, not words, because my words seem to have no effect on her. If I want more, I have to sacrifice a little. I need to prove to her that I'm not the man she thinks I am.

"But I am sure." Her protest is almost a whine. "I'm sure I want you."

I cup her elbows and draw her away from me until we're face to face.

"And I want you, Holland, but I need you to believe me, to hear what I'm saying. We can be more than just stolen moments when no one is looking. You deserve better, and I want to give you what you deserve." Despite my serious tone, her eyes turn molten, and she bites her lip, her hands reaching for my fly a second time.

"I know what I deserve."

"You're making my ardent overtures very hard." I'd meant the delivery to sound mildly mocking, not the low rumble of words we both hear.

"Hard." She repeats the word as though savoring it, pleasure twisting my insides as she grips me over my trousers. Suddenly, abstinence doesn't seem such a good idea, though I manage to force myself to lift her hands away. Pressing my lips to each of her palms in turn, I raise them to my shoulders before wrapping her tightly against me with a ragged sigh. I'm willing, yes, but not enthusiastic. It had seemed like a good plan earlier, but the hold I have on my libido is, frankly, tenuous.

"Let's go upstairs," my temptress whispers, rocking over my cock again. "Take me to bed, Alexander."

"You would tempt the devil," I groan, kissing her again. All the better to stop her objections, all the better to stop me from giving in. Yet the more we kiss, the more I want to taste her, the more frantic I feel.

Slow. Slow down.

Bringing my mouth across her jaw, I track my tongue down her neck and press my lips to her tripping pulse.

With power comes responsibility.

As I set her body away from mine once more, I realize my mistake. I'm not the one with the power. She is. Her body is an invitation, her softly pouting mouth a provocation. I skim my hand across the delicate architecture of her collarbone as she watches me, her gaze full of heat and unspoken promises. Lower my hand glides, and still, she watches, inhaling a sumptuous sounding breath as I bring my fingers to the button of her jeans. One twist, and it opens, the soft *susurrus* of the zip to follow.

I peel the sides of her jeans open as a harshness begins to hammer in my veins.

Need. Want. Take. Bend. Twist. Crush. Capture. Hold. Violate.

Gritting my teeth, I push the madness away. Push away the violent need for gentleness. There's a tremor in my hand as I press it to the soft curve of her stomach. She sucks in a breath and arches into my hand. My fingers breach the waistband of her underwear, the tiny glittery bow winking in the light.

Holland swallows and licks her lips. Leaning in, I press my mouth to hers in a fleeting kiss as my hand finds the heart of her.

"Yes, touch me." Her hands clutch my wrist as though she means to hold me there. I bring my mouth over hers and kiss her slowly now.

"Shush," I whisper. *She's so wet already.* There is no resistance as my middle finger glides over the soft rise of her clit. I lose a few brain cells as she begins to pulse against the pad of my finger.

"Don't tease." Her admonishment is a trembling breath, but who is teasing who, here? Who is the torturer, and who is the tortured as her hands make a tighter manacle of my wrist?

I push a little deeper.

"Darling, you're so wet for me." My words are pure praise. She is so exquisitely formed, and I can't fathom how I'll go on like this, how I'll fight my own need. So I do the only thing I can. I kiss her. Kiss her as I use my fingers to pleasure her. Kiss her as my heart pounds in time to the pulse of her. Kiss her as I push to stand without moving my hand from between her legs.

"You're so lovely I can barely fucking stand it." I listen to myself, almost as from a distance, reminding myself that she's not mine to take. Not yet. But I can kiss her. *Christ,* how I can kiss her, my body bearing her backwards as I support her, my palm at her back, my fingers working between her legs.

She moans, her hands sliding into my hair as we devour each other with long, lush kisses and whispered need. My hands are still shaking as I pull her upright and wrench down one side of her jeans, one side then the other, her body jerking with the movement so beautifully. Her excitement is painted in the flush of pink across her chest. I close my eyes to the sight, spinning her around, bending her over the table and pressing her down.

"Your skin is like silk," I whisper, pressing my lips to the top of her spine. As a contrast, I begin to tug her jeans and underwear down to her knees. "And your pussy is where I want to make my home."

I thrust my finger back into her so hard, her body bows. My name rings around the room as she begins to thrust back, riding my hand.

"Oh, God, yes!" Holland throws back her head, her hand coming around as though to touch me.

"Stay where I fucking put you," I growl, unable to summon a suitable sense of disgrace as I hold her there by the neck. Especially not as her cries begin to crest. I whisper such filth to her as she presses back into my hand, thrust for thrust.

I whisper how she doesn't get to touch. She only gets to come.

How wet and greedy her pussy is.

I whisper that my darling is so cock hungry.

"Yes," she rasps, her cheek pressed to the worn pine. "I want it, Alexander. I want your cock inside me."

Everything in me tightens. My jaw, my abs, the rock-hard pole trapped behind the zipper of my jeans. It takes every ounce of my strength not to give in, not to give up, because I want more than what she's offering. But Christ, if there's a temptation in the world bigger than Holland, I've yet to find it.

She mewls as I pull my fingers from her, pressing my

teeth to the seam of her ass before sliding her jeans and underwear the rest of the way. Her sparkly running shoes bounce somewhere behind me then I'm on my feet, lifting her arse to the table and taking the wet heat of her pussy into my hand.

"You're so fucking beautiful here," I rasp, pressing my palm against her clit. "Swollen and pink and so fucking delicious."

A low growl rises from my chest as she presses her hands behind her, arching into my hand, spreading her thighs wide. The sight of her... my brain short circuits. I drop to my knees, my palms pressed on her inner thighs. I inhale her. Suck. Finger fuck, moan my want and my desire into the very core of her. The sounds she makes are gasping and hoarse, her whispers senseless. As she tightens her hand in my hair, her thighs begin to quake.

There is no yesterday, and there is no tomorrow. There is only Holland. And my want of her.

32

HOLLY

I AM A TERRIBLE PERSON.

A terrible person who had somehow convinced herself she was staying on at the castle because she's responsible, because she feels for the woman she works for and because she likes her kids. And because she knows what it feels like to be betrayed by a man—solidarity in sisterhood and all that.

But maybe I'm just a terrible person with poor impulse control and no morals, and an unhealthy sideline in self-sabotage.

A terrible, terrible person.

I wrap my arm around the post at the bottom of my bed and press my head against the warm wood. Though not for long because the post is carved and not too comfortable. Alexander Dalforth will be the death of me, I'm sure. Just the thought of his name and, *urgh!*

I jump to my feet and straighten the counterpane, absolutely ignoring how just thinking of him makes my insides begin to pulse and my pulse race. And my head? Don't even go there.

And that's just from thinking his name—nothing else! Not how he has a neck that makes me feel like a vampire, or how my hands react to his chest like metal to a magnet. And don't get me started on the man's aural game or the way he insisted he wouldn't—*that*. Not until I was sure of him.

Sure of what?

Sure he's driving me crazy?

What kind of sadist withholds the D?

Though, honestly, that's not really a valid complaint. More of an observation that I made much later because, at the time, I didn't have enough brain cells to raise a smile, let alone raise an opinion.

I shuffle over to the window to distract myself. I've an hour to kill before I need to step outside of this room for the school run.

Green. Blue. Gold.

Summer has arrived in Scotland this morning with a very poor sense of timing. If there was justice in this world, it would be raining because my ordeal continues. Because Alexander, the duke who could teach the men of the world a thing or two about oral sex as a whole meal as opposed to a prelude, is not leaving today.

Not. Leaving. Today.

As in, he's not getting in his car and driving to the airport. He's not going back to London as I'd thought—as I'd expected when I'd climbed onto his knee last night. As I'd begged him to take me to bed. As I'd silently promised myself this would be the last time. It hadn't even been awkward as I'd come down from my orgasm high to find myself curled against him as his hand moved over my back reassuringly. As he'd crooned such words to me.

How beautiful I was.

How there was no one else like me.

How there was pleasure itself in seeing me come.

I'd felt so warm and so happy and blissed out to the maximum as he'd helped me on with my panties and jeans, then held out my shirt, allowing me to slip into it so easily. He'd poured me a glass of water, passed me my shoes, then held my hand as we'd made our way out of the kitchen and all the way up the stairs.

Maybe it wasn't awkward because I wasn't there. Not really. Maybe I was on some other plane, not ready to come back to earth from my orgasm. Whatever the reason, the steady stream of conversation he'd kept up seemed to help the zero awkwardness factor. And when we'd reached my bedroom door, he'd pressed a kiss to my forehead.

"*This is where I leave you,*" he'd murmured. "*I'm afraid I might have to go and take care of some very urgent business.*" When he'd winked, my gaze had dropped to his crotch. My giggle had sounded like an invitation.

"*I think I've been naked in more places in this house than I've been clothed,*" I'd quipped. Because what else could I say? Want me to take a look at it? I'd already offered, and he, for whatever reason, had declined. "*Which is weird because I'm not even a bikini at the beach kind of girl.*"

"*That statement is so sad, it almost brings tears to my eyes.*"

"*Well, flattery gets you a naked girl, I guess.*" I'd shrugged, embarrassed, thrilled, and sad for reasons I couldn't even contemplate.

"*What, do you suppose, gets me her trust?*" He'd passed me the glass of water, his retracting hand finding my hip. He'd seemed to wait for an answer as his thumb had moved almost hypnotically over my hipbone. Heat began pooling at my center all over again. But I didn't have an answer for him, so we'd just stared at each other, and his hand hadn't moved. Not for a long while. *"Good night, Holland,"* he'd said eventually. *"Sleep well."*

"Safe journey tomorrow," I'd whispered, stepping over the threshold while ignoring how hollow I'd felt.

He'd sort of shook his head like he couldn't believe what he was hearing. *"How could you think I'd be able to leave you now?"*

Which leaves me here. In Kilblair Castle. With the duke I'd very much like to f—

Or, in other words, up the creek without a paddle.

Because he might want me, sure. But I'd end up going the way of Portia. A stage five clinger who'll suffer through any manner of embarrassment just to be seen with him. Maybe he's still in love with his wife. Maybe this is all he's capable of.

Lord, I don't know. I don't know anything!

I slide my phone out from my pocket and flick to last night's text exchange with my sister. Maybe it's not my fault I'm terrible. Maybe it's in my DNA.

> Do you think being easy is a learned behavior? Or could it be in the genes?

Her reply?

> I don't have time for your ridiculousness right now.

Kennedy hates talking about our mother. But that's not the reason behind her harsh answer, so I make a mental note to call her this evening.

But seriously, could this be my issue? Maybe I just didn't realize I had this in me. This disregard for what's right. What's healthy. Maybe this really is just selfishness.

Maybe I am all about the D.

"Holland?" My name precedes a light knock on my door. "It's Isla. Do you have a minute?"

My stomach twists a little as I make for the door and swing it open. Would she be so happy to leave me with her sons if she knew what I'd gotten up to with her brother last night?

"Sure, come in. Is everything okay?" I'd thought this weekend she'd looked less tired than she had before. Which is odd given the whirlwind of guests she'd hosted. Looking at the dark circles under her eyes, I wonder now if she's just a whizz with makeup.

"I've just spoken with Sandy." My stomach flips, even if I can't get used to hearing him called Sandy. It's just far too cute a name for someone like him. His nickname should be something like Thor. Or Apollo. Except, I already have Apollo under my bed and his tiny penis and testicles in my nightstand. *So* not to Alexander scale.

"I'm so sorry, Holland." The sound of Isla's voice brings me back to the moment. She touches my arm before stepping into the room. "I don't quite know how to tell you this," she says, coming to a stop at the tall fireplace.

I know what's coming, but I can't tell her that. Because then I might need to explain that I saw Alexander, and then my cheeks will go red, and then this poor woman will know exactly what has gone on between the two of us. Again.

"I saw Sandy this morning, and he told me he's not going back to London as planned. He's given me some ridiculous reason about needing to be here for some survey or other, which is total rubbish." She gives a frustrated huff, and I get the impression she might like to punch something. "Men can be such arseholes," she fumes.

You're preaching to the choir, sister. Also, now I know exactly which man she'd like to punch.

Spoiler: it's not her brother.

"What I said about sexual misconduct," she begins carefully. "I didn't mean to give you the impression that he might behave in that way."

I wave away her words. "I know. He's not that guy." *But maybe I'm that girl, so if you see him running through the hallways with his pants around his knees, keep an eye out for me coming up shortly behind him.*

"He's not." *He's only responding to the signals I'm throwing out*, my mind unhelpfully amends. And that is the root of our problem. "His opinion is that our family name has suffered more than its fair share of infamy." Detailed on the Wikipedia page, I don't add. Though strangely enough, there's very little available on the internet about the current duke.

"It must be hard," I agree, knowing already what it means to have people talking about your family. How it feels personally.

"He certainly feels it. He would do almost anything to keep us out of the press. Most families such as ours have at least one notorious ancestor. It beggars belief that ours seemed hell-bent collectively on besting their predecessor."

"Except for the current duke."

"Exactly. That's why I know he'll behave with honor towards you because Sandy has broken the family mold." But then her eyes slide from mine. "Though I do worry what my divorce will mean to this."

Oh, so she's definitely made up her mind. Good for her.

"Whatever it means, you know he'll stand by you."

"In front, more like," She smiles wryly. "Although my brother frustrates the life out of me sometimes, and apart from the fact he does have a tendency to think he knows better than anyone else, he is undoubtedly the best man I know. The best brother, the best uncle. The best duke this family has ever known, certainly. But my husband is a very unpleasant man, and he knows exactly how hard Sandy has worked to restore the estates and our name..." Her words trail off, her attention turning inward.

"I'm sure it'll be fine. We'll both be fine." I'm not sure where the reassurance comes from. Maybe it's wishful thinking.

"Fingers crossed, I'll find someone to help with the boys soon." Her brief smile seems a little sad.

"I must say," she adds, "You don't seem very surprised."

Is it too late to adopt an *"oh, no!"* face?

"About your brother staying? I guess it's like you said, he's an honorable man." And I'm just a thirsty bird. And together, we seem to have no restraint. But maybe that's the key to getting through these next few weeks unscathed, my heart and my hoo-ha intact. Keep away from him, I mean—throw myself into my work and hide out the rest of the time. My mind begins to process how, beginning by calling into the village's equivalent of a 7/11 on the way back from the school run. I'll pick up a cheap electric kettle and some ramen. I mean, it's not like the atmosphere in the kitchen is the same as it was before Alexander arrived. If I'm there less, there will be less awkwardness. That's not to say I can't liberate a few supplies from there. I can survive mostly on food that doesn't need to be cooked. I mean, I like ramen. And cake. And bread. I can throw in a little fruit just to be sure I don't get scurvy. *Oh, and coffee. I'll need to grab a jar of Nescafe today, too.*

"Sandy told me you and he met earlier this year." Her words are careful, as though she doesn't want to pry but can't help herself. Resisting the urge to fidget under her gaze, I reach for a china tray from the mantlepiece. I put it down after a quick examination. It seems pretty old.

"On his fortieth birthday."

I almost swallow my tongue. He turned forty that night? I mean, I knew it was his birthday but, forty? That means there are sixteen years between us. Sixteen! Well, nearer fifteen, I guess. I read somewhere that there are seventeen years between George Clooney and Amal. And Jay Z is more than a decade older than Beyoncé. Argh! Why am I thinking this? It's not like Alexander and I are going to have a happily ever after. *No matter what he says.* Plus, Bey and Amal have their stuff together—their own careers and their own money. If Alexander and I were in a relationship for real, people would label me gold-digging ho.

The duke and the girl from Mookatill.

What a joke. People would surely laugh all the way from the Highlands to my little buttphuck nowhere home.

A finger of dread pokes at my chest because I've had enough labels for one lifetime. I don't want to be the nanny he once had, and I don't want to find my name in the press. But these are wasted thoughts—he's not serious about me at all. He might want more than a quick screw in the kitchen, but that doesn't mean anything.

"It created quite a stir when he didn't turn up," she adds lightly. "His friends were furious, not least because he was reading their messages and ignoring them. Then afterwards, he wouldn't say where he'd been. But there was a lightness in him in the following weeks. I'd catch him smiling to himself when he thought no one was looking. I'd hoped he'd met someone, but then, he went back to his usual self again."

I can feel her watching me carefully as I digest her words like a cookie you don't need but can't resist anyway. *A minute on the lips and a lifetime on the hips*, as Nana used to say. And though Alexander says he wants more than a moment, he's not looking for a lifetime either.

Isla can't be looking for a positive reaction from me. For hope or pleasure. I'm not the right woman to be on his arm. She must know that.

"When you came to us, I had no idea you knew Sandy."

"Yeah, I know," I say with a twist to my lips because we've already been over this. But one thing I'm certain of, if I'd turned up and said I'd slept with her brother, I'm sure I'd have been back at the train station pretty darn quick. It's nice that she seems to like me. That she's comfortable talking about her family problems with me, but that doesn't mean anything. And that's something I need to keep reminding myself.

"I had no idea who he was," I murmur, feeling like she's waiting for an explanation as I drop my butt to the arm of one of the hearthside padded chairs. "I know he's a good man because he was a gentleman that night." A gentleman of no ordinary standing. "He helped get me out of an awkward encounter when he could've quite easily left me." My eyes find hers, and I wonder what she sees there. "It was a night I won't ever forget, but I wouldn't have come here if I'd known I'd see him again because some things aren't meant to be real."

"I see."

But she can't. Not really. But then a thought hits me. I think I know where she's going with this.

"Look, if you want me to sign an NDA, I absolutely understand." Because no one should have their dirty laundry aired in public.

"No, Holly," she says with a sad smile. "That won't be necessary but thank you. For everything. Well, I suppose

I'd better go and make sure the monsters are ready for school."

"Sure!" I reply with the kind of perkiness that only comes with force.

Isla pauses as we reach the door. "I have a call this afternoon with Sarah from the agency."

"Oh, cool."

"I'm sure," she says, touching my arm once more, "it won't be long until you're able to move on."

And I should be happy about that, right? So, like an idiot, I smile.

"One other thing." Out in the hallway, Isla turns back to face me. "Griffin seems intent on staying, too. Not that I think that will make much difference to you."

"Nope," I answer. "None at all."

"Uncle Sandy says Batman has invited us over for a party next weekend," Archie pipes up from the back seat of Isla's Range Rover a few days later. "It's next Saturday."

"He means Dylan Duffy," Hugh corrects with an air of long-suffering. "Mummy said the invitation included your name, too."

"It did?" I ask, glancing into the rear-view mirror. Hugh nods. "So, is it Alasdair's birthday or his brother's?" I can't recall the name of the younger boy.

"No, it's not a birthday party. It's a grown-up one, but we were invited because Alasdair is allowed to invite two friends to sleep over the same night. We're going to watch movies and eat popcorn."

"And play Minecraft *all* night!" Archie adds.

"You're not supposed to tell. It's a secret," Hugh chastises.

"Holly won't tell," the younger boy retorts, unfazed. "She didn't tell on you for chopping off Apollo's head."

"It wasn't Apollo. It was a statue of Apollo." Leaning over, Hugh squeezed his brother's knee.

"Enough of that," I say, using my stern teacher voice.

"And she took the blame for it, too," Archie responds, punching Hugh in the arm.

"Do I have to pull over and call your mom?"

"No!" they respond in unison.

"Sorry, Hugh," Archie mutters.

"Me, too. And I'm sorry Uncle Sandy blamed you," he adds, his eyes meeting mine in the mirror again. "I'm also grateful you didn't blab."

"Snitches get stiches," I reply with a laugh. "But that's not true," I add in a much more sober tone. I'm not talking to Wilder the rugrat here, but the little men I'm supposed to be setting a good example for. "You really shouldn't hide things from grown-ups. Not the important stuff, anyway."

"Are popcorn and movie secrets important?" Archie asks.

"Well, friend, I guess that secret won't stay secret for very long. Not when she has to deal with a couple of cranky pants the next morning." Unless she's expecting me to look after them that night and the following day. But I can't see that being the case.

"I wonder what the grown-ups will be doing at their party," Archie ponders, staring out at the fields of sheep we pass.

"Holly can tell us afterwards," answers Hugh.

"I think I'll be eating popcorn with you two."

"No, you're not that lucky,' he answers sagely. "Because I heard her telling Uncle Sandy not to bother you, that *she* would tell you."

"Tell me what?" My brows pull together.

"That your name was on the invitation. That you'll have to wear makeup and high heels and a fancy dress."

"She said all that?"

"No, I was just warning you that's what you'll need to do. It all sounds very boring."

Confusing, more like. Why invite me? But I guess it gives me something to look forward to, apart from Archie and Hugh's upcoming school holiday and the extra work that will bring. I push out a huffy breath, silently acknowledging that I'm just being cranky this morning. But it's been a strange week. As planned, I'd mostly confined myself to my room when I wasn't working. The school runs in the morning and afternoons, donning my long brown skirt and becoming Miss Boo in between. I'd made after-school snacks and supervised homework before handing over the kid-watching reins to Isla and hurrying off to my room. I've barely set foot in the kitchen after the tepid welcome I'd received at the weekend. I'd called my sister a couple of times, but she was in no mood to chat. I'd read and watched TV and basically lived like a hermit. Without the inclusion of a cave.

The week had passed by like any other. Busy, busy, busy!

And frustrating, frustrating, frustrating, because I'd expected Alexander to interrupt it. And he had not. Which leads me to think his attention span was even shorter than I thought.

So much for I want you. I'm willing to wait.

Men. I just don't understand them. Including the two mini men in the back seat who begin to argue over some piece of Batman trivia.

When I get back to the castle, I spot Griffin in the

distance, his ear glued to his phone as he takes part in what seems like a very tense conversation.

Thank heaven for small mercies, I think as my feet hit the gravel. Maybe he won't see me. While I might not have seen much of Alexander, I had (unfortunately) seen a lot of his brother. He seems to pop out of the woodwork when I least expect it, and frankly, I'm bored of being hit on.

I pull my phone out of my back pocket and begin to check my emails as I make my way over to the education center.

"Were you just butt dialing me?"

At the deep voice, I look up.

"Because I swear that arse is calling me."

Against my better judgement, I laugh—in my defense, it has been a slow week—but I carry on walking.

"Don't you have anything else better to do?" I call over my shoulder.

"Well, if you're offering, I could do you."

I ignore him. Of course, I do. While internally flipping him the finger.

33

ALEXANDER

"Holland, there you are."

Her feet move quickly, almost hopping up the first two treads of the staircase before her mind seems to catch up with her predicament, and she stops, her shoulders almost slumping forward. *Caught you, darling girl.*

"Hey." She turns, offering me a brief, close-lipped smile, her mouth working a touch as though she's coming to the end of chewing something. Where the examination ends is, as I'd hoped, my legs. *More specifically, what I have between them.* "S-Sorry, I didn't hear you," she begins to stutter, her face turning bright pink.

I manage to curtail my smile as I draw to a stop at the bottom of the stairs. As Holland is standing two treads higher, our eyes are almost level. Not that she manages to keep them so, because there go her eyes again.

Down.

"I h-had my ear... pods in." Her hand lifts to her ear in a jerking motion, halting halfway.

"Did you?" I try not to smirk because she clearly does not, though I imagine she's been wearing them for the past few days as a perfect excuse for ignoring me. Not that I'd sought her out until now, yet it seems as though it's been a wasted effort. I'd thought a little space might help her try to work out her own feelings about me, especially given our interlude in the kitchen. I'd expected her to seek me out at some point. I thought an admission to having feelings would be a little too much to hope for, but even just to hear she'd missed me would've been nice.

I don't know what else I'm supposed to do. I've been rejected before, of course, but not by someone whose gaze turns soft when they see me. Not by someone who clearly still wants me.

The past few days have been nothing short of hell. I'd found enough to keep me occupied, initiating some minor repairs to the castle and spending late nights on the phone to my broker in New York. I'd taken Isla's boys to the pizzeria in the next town over and even began to teach Archie to ride. Far too late, in my opinion. A failing I place squarely on the shoulders of his father. But whatever I've been doing, physically or mentally, my thoughts haven't strayed too far from Holland. To know she sleeps under the same roof has kept me awake and frustrated well into the wee hours. I want her in my bed, next to me, not in a room somewhere else in the castle.

I just... want her, goddammit. I want her in whatever capacity she'll have me.

"I, erm, thought I had them in." Holland hitches a cotton tote higher on her shoulder, her gaze almost—but not quite—dipping again.

"So, you thought you didn't hear me... but then you

realized you did?" I tilt my head like old Gertie catching the rustle of a biscuit packet, only in this case, what I hear is her planned-out efforts to avoid me. Yet she can't keep her eyes off me.

Relaxing my posture, I hook my elbow over the newel post and lean against it. Holland purses her lips and shakes her head before she ultimately chooses to ignore my goading. *What a shame.*

"I haven't seen you around much this week," she says instead.

Her breath smells sweet. Sugary. It makes me wonder what she was eating. And whether she'd allow me a taste. And while she might not have seen me, I've seen her, even if she has tried to be more evasive than a cat burglar. She's never in the kitchen, not around at mealtimes, and the door to the education center is locked outside of opening hours. Which has left me calling to see her when she has an audience—Hugh and Archie or the kids taking part in broomstick lessons or crafts—or ambushing her in her bedroom, which would be the exact opposite of the point I've been trying to make. That I want more of her. More than just the pleasure found between her thighs.

"I know," I agree regretfully, my gaze flicking to the floor. "I've been busy. Also, I'm not sure if you realize, but I've been giving you some space."

"Oh." Her answer seems more a sound than a question. Might it also include a touch of relief? "I didn't even notice." She makes a careless gesture with her hand, the words delivered as one long string, and they don't sound like a lie at all. Or they wouldn't if you were say, deaf. "I mean, I only just noticed I hadn't seen you. Now that I am seeing you. In front of me, I mean."

And seeing quite a lot of me because there goes her gaze

again. Maybe I should've just ambushed her the morning after the kitchen wearing this get-up. Or maybe I should just tie her to my bed and keep her there until she gives in.

Holland, what am I going to do with you?

What do I *have* to do to make you see we're worth it?

"I'm cut to the quick," I say, clutching a fist to my heart. "You haven't missed me? Not even a little bit?"

"Do the gardeners grow cannabis in the orangery?"

We don't have an orangery. Which she knows.

"I'm just high on seeing you. No white lines or green leaves necessary. Just Holland."

"H-Have you been for a ride?"

At last! These riding boots are always a bastard to put on. I'm pleased the effort wasn't wasted. Very pleased indeed.

"As a matter of fact, I have not."

"What's with the get-up, then?" Her eyes flick across my tight-fitting polo shirt then *down*. Down to my pale riding jodhpurs, more suitable for the polo field than the Scottish countryside.

"Funny that you should ask, but I recently heard that those who take care of themselves, those who are in good shape," I add a tiny flourish, "should wear tight-fitting clothing, lest their delicate skin chafe."

"You are nuts," she says, her laughter seemingly against her better judgement as she shakes her head. But it does my heart good just to hear it. "There's nothing delicate about your skin. You have the hide of a rhino."

"Are you saying I'm old?"

"You're old enough to know better," she says, her words taking a turn for the serious.

"And selfish enough not to care." This time, my heart gives a hollow knock at the way she's looking at me.

Seriously. Critically, even. "But in answer to your question, I was planning to go for a ride this afternoon when I was waylaid by a call from a marble restoration expert." I allow my gaze to flick over to where the plinth and statue once stood. "I wonder why the spotlights aren't working."

"I switched them off," she mutters, her mouth almost a straight line. "I would've gotten away with it too, if it wasn't for those pesky kids. It's a *Scooby-Doo* reference," she elucidates unnecessarily. Suddenly, it seems I'm Methuselah.

"Because Archie is a nark," I reply in kind. "The little snitch who ratted you out."

"Is that your attempt at talking street?" she says in the kind of tone that makes me want to swat my hand over her delectable upside-down heart-shaped arse. She clears her throat when I don't answer. I sense the conversation is about to take a turn. "You know, I was thinking how that statue kind of reminded me of you."

"I hope you're not thinking about chopping off my family jewels and shoving me under your bed." Leave them intact and slide me in next to you, however...

"I didn't do that. They were already lying on the floor when I got there!"

"A likely story, one I'm sure the police would see right through."

Her eyes widen to the size of dinner plates.

"I'm joking." Reaching out, I slide the backs of my fingers down her face to find her almost leaning into my touch. "Why would I call the police when I have my own dungeon? Where are they, by the way? Apollo's bollocks," I qualify. You know, just because.

"In my nightstand," she says, pulling back with a narrow look.

"You've put his genitalia in your nightstand?" I repeat suggestively. "That seems a little…" Well, a little *too little* to be any fun, that's for sure.

"And his head is in the closet," she retorts, not playing along.

"Who knew you had such a gruesome side."

"I had wondered if the statue was modelled after *family lines*." Her eyes dip to my crotch in a taunt.

"It's gratifying to know you've been thinking about my body." As if I needed her goading to add to my already very explicit imaginings.

"I—that. I didn't say that. I meant that you look alike."

I sense she's not referring to my physique. Though she's giving out clues like a Scotsman does pennies or, as the saying goes, a miser, I still hear what she doesn't want me to. She's missed me. She's been thinking about me. Possibly even a very particular part of me.

It's time to up the ante, I think.

"The last tour of the castle began more than an hour ago. We could always revisit the scene of Friday evening's nakedness if you need a reminder."

With a sound that's more a frustrated grumble than anything else, she wheels away abruptly and begins stomping up the stairs.

What else can I do but follow her?

HOLLY

"Where do you think you're going?" I sound very *schoolmarm* of the ye olde variety as I turn at the sound of boots on the stairs behind me.

"Where does it look like I'm going?" Alexander's reply might be cool, but the expression he wears is anything but, and though his ascent is sedate, his pace seems a little threatening. Like a prowling cat.

Or maybe I'm projecting, my brain fuzzy from seeing him in those jodhpurs—jodhpurs that make me long for some very strange things. Like a dress of peacock silk, the kind that swishes dramatically around my ankles. *And a riding crop,* comes my next unbidden thought. Damn Harlequin and Nana's racy reading tastes, and damn Alexander for looking like something from the cover of a bodice ripper.

I don't need a corseted gown because that would just mean it would be harder to get out of it...

Exactly! Because that's exactly what I'm going to do—what I'm *not* going to do, I mean. There will be no nakedness happening this afternoon!

"What's that in your hand?" asks the prowling jungle beast.

I open my palm to find the melting remains of a piece of Scottish tablet, which is kind of like fudge, only crumblier and sweeter. This delicious morsel is flavored with a nip of whisky and chopped nuts, and I was absolutely enjoying the heck out of it until I was so rudely interrupted.

I was wearing my Air pods. Urgh! What an idiot I am. I would've been too, if I hadn't been so engrossed in my treat. The treat I'm currently licking off my hand.

"What are you eating?"

"Mind your own."

"Holland." He makes my name sound like a reprimand. A sexy reprimand. "You can't run away from me."

Something inside me seems to say *wanna bet?* Almost unbidden, my feet seem to pick up the pace as a quicksilver thrill rolls down my spine. His low chuckle sounds from behind me, the cadence of his own footsteps altering.

Ohmygosh, he's chasing me.

Or maybe he's just going the same way, and I'm an idiot. But fight or flight instincts aren't usually engaged because you don't want to share a sweet treat.

How about a kiss?

Breath halts in my chest, a sense of exhilaration shimmering over me as his footsteps seem to time themselves with the thrumming pulse between my legs. This is a long staircase, but I don't think I get to evade him for any other reason than he wants me to, but still, I hurry, and still my heart beats frantically. As I reach the first landing, my excitement reaches a fever pitch—I've made it! Until...

His hands find my hips.

"Where do you think you're going?" he whispers seductively as his arm feeds around me, pulling my body back to meet his like a cat toying with its next meal.

"I-I'm going to my room," I whisper, eventually loosening my tongue. My mind is noisy, full of chidings and warnings, but they melt away like ice cream on hot pavement as the fingers of his other hand circle my wrist.

Do I always want to be caught by him?

I offer no resistance and watch almost out of myself as he lifts my hand. His tongue flicking over my sticky palm, and the sensation resonates between my legs.

"Tablet," he asserts. The second time his tongue touches my flesh, it's with the full flat of his tongue. I roll my lips together, swallowing the sound I want to make. The sound I won't give in to. "You've been to the kitchen."

My face heats just at the name of the place, my brain filled with flashes of distorted images. Him. Me.

"Yes." Such a small word yet so sultry. Like an invitation. A temptation. *Taste me, Alexander. Slide your tongue between my legs again.*

"Why didn't you come to me?"

"I—" Because it would've been stupid of me. Because I can't afford to fool myself.

"*Holland.*" His voice breaks over my name as he turns me in his arms. My tote full of kitchen booty hits the floor with a quiet *thump*, my sticky hand finding its way into his hair. His tongue tastes sweet as he slides his mouth against mine, his hands anchoring my body against his, his big hands firm. Soothing. Both his touch and taste are so reassuring that I tighten my hand, almost curling into him. Our kiss becomes deeper and wetter, and I moan into his mouth. Everything becomes frantic for a moment, teeth and tongues clashing, fingers gripping and fighting to get closer as he backs me up against the wall.

"God, Holland. I've missed you. Haven't you missed me? Didn't you want...?"

Yes. *Yes.* I've wanted him. Wanted to see him. Wanted to touch him. But I'd told myself I can't. That nothing good would come from being with him. There would be pleasure, but pleasure that comes with a cost because I lose a little more of my heart each time I'm with him. All those pieces mount up, and one day, I'll realize I love him utterly and completely, and that he doesn't love me back.

Doesn't. Won't. Can't. The reasons won't matter at that point.

But I can't tell him that, so I do the only thing I can.

Can. Will. Am.

I tighten my grip on his hair instead and try to answer his question with my kiss, recording the moment as a tactile memory.

His lips on my neck.

The prickle of his beard against my hand.
The corded muscles in his arms and the mass of his chest.

His hand glides up my side, glancing the side of my breast. My mind fragments. Thoughts scatter and mean no more as I whimper and twist towards him in silent encouragement. Alexander growls low in his throat, his hand closing on my breast, the sight so lewd and lush that I have to close my eyes.

"Open your eyes." The command in his voice liquifies my bones. "Don't you dare close your eyes to what's happening between us." But for his hands and the wall behind me, I might be a slick pool of Holland on the floor. "This is everything, Holland. More than either of us could've anticipated, but—"

At a childish shout, we freeze. Alexander's hand falls away, and he pivots, setting himself away from me. *In front of me.*

"It's mine, Hugh! Give it back!"

"You'll have to catch me first!" Feet scrabble against the carpet as Hugh's rangy form comes into view. "You son of a monkey arsed—"

Alexander bows forward as Hugh runs smack into him. He catches the boy by the shoulders to steady him.

"Hugh." Alexander's voice is thunderous, drawing an intake of breath from his nephew. "Your timing is impeccable, as always." I think that's the duke-ly way of calling him a little cock blocker.

"Whoa!" Archie shortly follows, his shirt tails flapping, as usual. "I didn't see you there, Uncle Sandy."

"Evidently." Alexander glowers down at the boys. "Remind me, what have you been told about running near the staircase?"

"That Great-Uncle Leo went daft after falling down them?" Hugh offers, clearly not sure.

"He was like Humpty Dumpty!" Archie pipes up. "He fell down and broke his head!"

While the exchange might be entertaining some time other than now, I find myself pressing my hand to my tripping heart. *Tripping, like it's recently dropped acid as it freaks out and dances all over the place.* What if they hadn't been yelling? What if, like (ab)normal kids, they'd walked sedately around the corner? They might well have been on the receiving end of sex education they're not yet ready for.

As Alexander continues his uncle-in-charge duties, I find myself sliding along the wall in the other direction. But before I've even made two steps in the opposite direction, I almost fall over my bag.

"Holland." Alexander's head whips around, his brows beetled as I swipe the tote up.

"Quick," Hugh doesn't quite whisper. "Let's make a run for it while Holly's in trouble."

As a boy-sized thunder of feet hits the stairs, my gaze slices their way, then back to Alexander again.

"Don't do this," he mutters, reading my intention. His face is like thunder as he reaches out for me. "We need to talk."

I skirt around him, and like an errant kid, I also hit the stairs.

"I'm sorry," I say over my shoulder. "But I can't do this." My voice breaks on the last word.

But I can't live like this.

I can't *be* that woman. Be like my mother.

Even when it seems like I am, after all.

34

HOLLY

"Holly, how are you?"

I find Isla in her office behind the mahogany desk.

"Are you well?" She looks concerned as she begins to stand. "You look quite flushed."

Because I've been running, I don't say. Running away from your brother. Running away from myself.

"No, I-I'm fine." My gaze slips behind her to the large window and the grey clouds gathering there. "I was running," I admit, bending to give Gertie a stroke as she lumbers over to me. "To get indoors before the rain." I feel bad for lying, but what's one more on top of the whoppers I've told so far? I imagine my smile looks a little more manic than it does encouraging, but she's far too polite to suggest so. *With words or otherwise.*

"The weather forecast didn't say anything about rain today." She glances over her shoulder before rounding the impressive desk. As she indicates the seating area, Gertie lumbers over, curling at the base of an overly cushioned armchair. The chair that Isla then gracefully lowers herself to. I settle into the couch, kitty-corner. "Oh, but I have news," she announces. "I've found someone to take over the job of looking after the boys. A nanny."

"Oh, wow. That's great." So why does it not feel so great, especially when I'd arrived in her office ready to hand in my notice, effective immediately? I can't claim to be hurt or upset when we both know finding my replacement had become a priority.

A bigger priority after what just happened on the stairs.

"Yes, I interviewed her last week. Not a face-to-face meeting, but over the internet. Her references were excellent, and I've just gotten off the phone with her last employer, who was very encouraging."

"Well, that's just great. Really great. I'm happy for you." Or I'm trying to be.

"The only thing is she can't start for two weeks. Do you think you'll be able to carry on until then?"

"I…" am in trouble, but how can I say no when Isla has enough worries of her own? How can I tell her two weeks' notice is too much unless she wants to take the chance her sons might get the kind of education not available at school? *Dammit.* "Of course." I am so incredibly screwed. "Yes, of course I can." I add what I hope is a bright smile as I blunder on, "but I'm sorry to have to tell you that I'll be moving on completely then."

"You mean, from the education center?" Isla looks visibly shocked.

"Yes." I guess I'm really doing this. "I'm sorry for the short notice, but I really feel it's for the best."

"Things are…?"

"Nothing has changed," I say quietly, folding my hands in my lap. "You can't blame—it's not just his fault." My words hit the air in staccato bursts and probably don't make a lot of sense. "Argh! I hate crying." Though I find myself doing just that as, a moment later, a box of tissues appears on my lap. "I have to go," I whisper, curling my hand around the box like it's a life vest. "I really can't stay. I know this is for the best."

"You don't... like Sandy in that way?"

"I think the problem is I like him a little too much, but please don't tell him I said that." I hide my horrified expression behind a super soft tissue scented with eucalyptus.

"I would never betray your confidence," Isla replies sincerely. "But I will say that I'm relieved it isn't a case of him making it uncomfortable for you here."

"No." I swallow. "That's not it," I murmur, not quite able to hold her gaze. "I just know that if I stay here, no good will come of it." No good can come of a twenty-four-year-old girl from Mookatill and a peer of the realm—a duke, no less.

It's just not possible.

"Sandy will be very upset to hear you're leaving us," she says carefully. "As we all will be, myself and the boys especially."

"That's nice to hear." And bittersweet in the extreme. I'll miss Archie and Hugh and Isla. I just can't contemplate anything else but being far away from Alexander right now. The temptation is just too great. And I know he'll be upset —though at first, he'll be super pissed. Whatever reaction he has to the news will be genuine because it's not like there hasn't been anything between us. It's just that what is between us isn't enough. And it never will be.

"You know, Sandy hasn't shown interest in anyone in—"

I hold up my hand as I roll in my lips. My heart hurts, and my head thunders. I don't need to hear what she has to say because *this cannot be*. I like Alexander—I like him way more than I should—but I don't know him. Not really.

I know the sum of his parts. That he's brutally good-looking, and he looks amazing in a pair of jodhpurs, in a suit, or a kilt. I also know my favorite memory ever will be the one when he's wearing nothing but a sheet and a satisfied grin. *Because the image is indelibly inked onto my brain.* I know he's comfortable in his own skin in a way I'll never be, that he's smart, and he's charming, at least, he is when he wants to be. He can be an arrogant ass, and I can secretly dig it, though I'd never admit that out loud. I also know his tongue should come with a warning label listing side effects ranging from a first-rate swoon to a pleasure coma.

I know he loves his family, that he'd do anything for them. That he looks after the people who work for him. I know that he's kind and honorable and principled, just as a man of his station ought to be. And that's where I come to a stumbling block the size of Ben Nevis. Because I'm just a girl from a worn-looking house in a small town, still trying to find her way in the world. I don't have what he needs, not beyond the physical aspects of our relationship

We're not suited, and he's not serious. Not really.

He wants me, yeah. And I want him. But he'll tire of me eventually, but not because he's a rat or unprincipled, but because he said from the start, he's not the settling down type. I'm pretty sure you don't get to his age without knowing your own mind.

Maybe one marriage was enough. Maybe losing her broke his heart. Maybe there's no getting over that. But that's exactly my point. I don't know the reasons because I don't know him.

And while I might not be so comfortable in my own skin, I also know my own mind. I know he has the makings of an obsession. Of a broken heart. And those are the kinds of temptations I could do without.

Alexander, the 13th Duke of Dalforth, was never meant for me. Not really.

"Well." Isla swallows, and for a minute, I wonder if I should pass back the tissue box. "At least you'll be here for Duffy's party."

I frown a little, then remember the conversation in the car.

"Batman," I offer, and she nods.

"It's apparently Batman's birthday, and his wife, Ivy, is throwing him a party. Quite short notice, but I don't know anything about Hollywood types."

"I think she said she used to be a hairstylist."

"Did she? Well, whatever she did, whatever she does now, I like her."

"Me, too. But I don't think I'll be coming along. I mean, unless you need me to look after the boys—"

"No, not at all. That's all taken care of, and Ivy made particular mention of the fact that she'd like to see you again."

"Maybe you can pass on my apologies. Or I'll write her a card or something." I don't need another repeat of last week's dinner, and I mean, any of it.

"Holly," she says, her posture and her gaze softening. "How many people get to say they've been invited to the home of a Hollywood star, let alone that they were invited to his birthday party—to Dylan Duffy's birthday party? How can you not be excited? This is a first for me, too. It's quite a coup, I understand. I expect my currency will fly through the roof with the PTA mothers."

"I'm not much for parties. Besides, I don't have anything suitable to wear."

"I'm sure I can help."

At this, I laugh. Laughter that deepens as her eyes coast over me, confidence exchanged for uncertainty as her brain catches up with her mouth. Nothing hanging in her wardrobe would fit me. I'm much shorter and not exactly what you'd call sylph-like.

"A dress is an easy fix," she says, joining me in my amusement with a cheeky grin. "The important thing is that you see the invitation for what it is. An opportunity. Who knows what might transpire? Who you might meet? What kind of opportunities might reveal themselves? Work, for instance."

"I don't know. I don't feel like partying, to be honest."

"But you won't be partying. You'll be... What did Griffin call it last night?" she mutters to herself. "Networking!" she adds, in the way of *eureka!*

"Griffin's going, too?"

"By default, I think. He wasn't named on the invitation, but Ivy was kind enough to extend it to include him. To be honest, I'm not sure what he's still doing here. He's never stayed with us this long."

"Doesn't he think of Kilblair as his family home?" He seems to treat it like it is. Though it's kind of ironic I'd be surprised by this. I mean, it's not like "home" represents anything positive to me. Well, apart from the people who live there. *Kennedy and the rug rat are the only things I love in Mookatill.*

"It's not truly his home," she replies, taking the tissue box from my lap. She places it back on the coffee table. "Griffin didn't live here as a child or even visit. He grew up in the Home Counties with his mother and the man he thought was his father. Both he and his sister."

"Oh." Such a small sound with so many implications.

"We were as surprised to find out about them as they were us," she adds brightly. "Possibly just as pleased." Her expression falls a touch. "It all came out in our father's will. It turns out he was quite the profligate."

Which is a nicer word than the one I'd use. It strikes me how Griffin was the one to tell me they were half-brothers back on the night I showered Dylan Duffy in haggis bonbons. Alexander has never referred to him as anything but his brother in my hearing. He'd never made the distinction, at least, not to me. He'd never made him sound any less than family. That says a lot about his character, for sure.

"Yes, well," she begins again, "what's done is done, and Griffin isn't around very often." Thankfully, she doesn't say, but I hear it anyway. "Think about it at least. The invitation, I mean."

I agree that I will when she begins to speak again.

"One other thing, Holly. I don't think I need to say this, but you know we don't stand on ceremony at Kilblair."

"You've been very welcoming," I agree.

"Sandy and I, we don't think of ourselves as any more important than anyone else here. Each of us has a role, yes, but we're all equally important, and I'd like to think the respect we have for each other is mutual." She kind of half rolls her eyes as she adds, "Sandy might have a very high opinion of himself from time to time, but he usually remembers to pull his head out of his rectum in the end."

"I might've noticed that," I answer with a watery laugh. His instinct is to lean towards arrogance, but his heart is usually in the right place. But the rest? I choose not to examine her words. There's no denying the fact that he's a duke and she's a lady of the aristocracy, and they might fool themselves that there's no difference between us, but the rest of us can see it.

I can't help but like them anyway. I like them a little too much, truthfully.

"You've been a wonderful help to us, Holly. I hope you know that. And you're welcome back to Kilblair anytime."

It's nice of her to say so, but I think we both know I won't be taking her up on that.

Two weeks, I think to myself. *Maybe he'll think I still need space? Maybe I can tell him I need time to think?*

Somehow, I know that's not going to work. If anything, after what happened on the stairs, he's likely to go the other way, increasing the likelihood of us bumping into each other. And why wouldn't he when I'm so melt-y and yielding in those moments I'm in front of him?

I need to come up with a plan.

Something to make him keep his distance.

Despite the gathering dark clouds, the rain has yet to put in an appearance as I make my way around the castle, like *all* around the castle, in the quest to get to my bedroom. The early evening is a little cool, and I'm pleased I have my hoodie as I trudge through the longer grass, a little off the beaten path, in an effort to avoid, well, everybody, but especially Alexander.

How am I going to manage to avoid him for two more weeks?

A few days have been hard enough. I wasn't cut out to be a spy. Plus, I'll be so sick of ramen and cake by then. *Okay, maybe just ramen.*

How to avoid Alexander...

Maybe I could accidentally "borrow" his phone and download one of those tracker apps that parents use to monitor their child's movements. Well, parents and suspicious spouses, I guess. But that would mean I'd need his password. What's more, it would mean being near him. And I know how that usually ends.

Me with a smile on my face and less functioning brain cells

Maybe I could tell him I've decided to date Cameron after all.

No, that won't work, not now that he seems to be dating Mari.

Cooper?

Something tells me he wouldn't be interested.

Probably the way Alexander stared daggers at him the night he dropped me off.

I pull out my dog-eared map that isn't really a map, but a sketch of the castle Chrissy had drawn on the back of an envelope for me my first week. According to this, there's another door into the old wing of the castle, and from there, I can make my way, via an alternative route—a long-ass route—to the service staircase and up to my room.

I sigh. On two counts. This is going to be a long two weeks. Two weeks of many steps. And two weeks that needs a plan or an idea to keep Alexander at arm's length.

What does he hate most in the world? Is there anything he fears? What can I use as leverage or a shield to keep him at bay?

I spot a green-painted door about five feet high. I guess they were made shorter back in the day.

"This is ridiculous," I mutter, pushing on it, surprised when it creaks open.

The hallway smells dank and dusty as I take another look at my map, Chrissy's words drifting into my memory.

"*He's taken over the steward's office in the old part of the castle,*" she'd sniffed when Griffin's name had come up in conversation. "*Nothing' so fancy for the likes of him.*"

I find myself wondering what Griffin is still doing here. It's not me, that's for sure. It's clear he doesn't like his brother, and the feeling seems mutual. Isla was very careful about what she said, but I guess Griffin must rub everyone the wrong way.

Me included.

As I close the door behind me, the hallway falls dark. Boy, Chrissy must *really* not like him. Not only is this the ass end of the castle but it's also more than a little creepy.

My footsteps echo against the ancient stone as I trudge along, praying I'm going in the right direction and that I won't end up in the dungeons. Or come face-to-face with any of the castle's ghosts. But then I hear a noise echoing from the end of the hallway. It sounds as though someone is in pain—like centuries of pain—as a long-drawn-out wail echoes along the walls. A fist clamps around my suddenly rapidly beating heart, my feet shuffling to a stop and almost turning in the other direction.

Another moan sounds.

Where the fluff is a crucifix when you want one?

The next moan comes as I pivot on my toes. I'd rather risk bumping into Alexander than whatever lurks down there. But then the tenor changes, and I freeze in place.

Did that moan include the words, *yes, daddy, again*?

Surely, that's not... there must be better places in the castle to have sex on the down low.

Say, the kitchen. Or behind a screen in a display room.

My steps are almost silent as I make my way along the hallway to where the light spills from an open door. I'm not a voyeur, but there's no point in backtracking if I don't have to. And if the "daddy and his baby" don't want to get busted, they should've closed the door behind them.

Nope, not a voyeur, I think as I draw closer. Especially as it might be, say, Mr. McCain and Dougal. Or Chrissy and Mr. McCain. Or maybe all three of them!

Eww. I press my hand to my mouth to stifle a giggle.

"Yes! Yes! Fuck me like that!"

I'll just close my eyes as I pass.

But then, something other than a moan sounds from the open door.

"Okay, so what do you want?"

I freeze again, this time due to the distinct lack of sexual undertone in that question. Weird, considering only a moment ago, it sounded like someone was about to… you know.

I hear the voice again, though the conversation is one-sided and mostly indistinct. It's Griffin, I know that for sure, but who's he with?

I move closer as Griffin growls, "I need more time. You'll get me fucking struck off. Disbarred," he says after a beat. "Then I'll be no use to you."

I take a super quick peek around the open door, my head immediately swinging back before I try a second time once I realize he's facing the other way. But Griffin isn't looking out of the window. Rather, his head is dropped between his shoulders. He's sitting at a desk that looks nothing like Isla's or Alexander's. It's easily as old but less ornate, the patina worn, and the wood scarred.

His laptop is open on the desk, and I find myself

wondering what the Wi-Fi signal is like down here. *Worse, I imagine.* The room is old and full of brown cardboard boxes, the kind that holds box files full of documents. There's no sitting area, tea sets, or whisky decanters down here, and I suddenly feel a little sad for him.

He swings back around in his chair the second I duck back around the doorframe.

Close call. But I can't stay here, and as a roll of thunder sounds from outside, I'm not going back the other way, either.

I'll count to thirty, then stamp my feet a little before appearing to move past the door. But before I get to fifteen, and Griffin sighs the kind of sigh that seems to bear the weight of the world in it, I realize I can't go rushing past.

Twenty-eight, twenty-nine, and...

"Oh, Griffin! What are you doing down here?"

Sounds plausible enough, right?

"Jesus, Holly!" he says, lowering from about three foot above his chair. "You scared the living crap out of me!"

"I'm sorry," I say, not sounding sorry at all. "I thought you must've heard me, all the noise I was making, whistling and humming as I skipped along the corridor."

Once a ham, always a ham.

"Fuck." He presses a hand to his chest as though to reassure his frantic heart that all is well. *There, there, little guy.* "Never interrupt a man when he's deep in contemplation," he censures.

"No?" I reply doubtfully and with a hint of amusement.

"We're gone." He makes a shooing motion with the same hand. "Well, physically, we're here, but mentally, we're not at all."

I don't think I need convincing of that, I think tartly.

"So, where'd you go during this sacred contemplation?"

"To examine the cemetery of our fallen dreams. The dearth of our missed opportunities."

I can literally feel my eyebrows coming off the top of my head. I'm being out-hammed.

"Really? Whenever I've asked a man what he was thinking, the answer has without exception been *nothing*." The latter, I add in a deep tone.

"That's the answer we use when we're thinking about fucking you." His gaze roams over me suggestively. "Ask me what I'm thinking," he adds. "Go on, I dare you."

"Ha. No thanks!" I begin to turn, but the movement is almost done in slow motion as pieces of an unseen puzzle begin to fall into place.

Not Cameron. Not Cooper. Maybe Griffin?

Didn't Alexander say he wanted me out of the reach of his brother originally?

He couldn't stand the thought of us being together.

No, I couldn't hurt him like that.

But maybe it wouldn't hurt him.

Maybe it'd turn him off.

Make him despise me.

Yes, he *would* hate me. But taking me out of the equation, what would this do to them? I guess it's not like I'd be ruining their relationship because they can barely stand each other as it is.

Barely stand might turn to hate.

But what other choice do I have?

I don't know which part of me hurts more as I turn back to face Griffin.

My head. My heart. My stomach.

I watch as Griffin lifts his face expectantly. If I do this, there will be no going back.

"Do you think the castle has ghosts?" I find myself

asking. Maybe I'm stalling for time. "I'm sure I heard a lot of moaning as I came along the hallway earlier."

"There's supposed to be," he answers without a flicker of concern. "The punters love a good ghost story."

"Huh." I tilt my head. "I wonder what those noises were, then?"

"If you ask Isla or my brother, they'll tell you it's the twelfth duke haunting the place. They reckon the devil gives him a few hours off now and again for good behavior. The way they describe him, I expect even Old Nick would find him an ordeal."

The twelfth duke? Not "my father"? I shake my head and the distractions away.

What if Griffin doesn't go for it?

I'll make him think I heard more than I did because he wasn't watching homemade porn. Or at least, that's not all he was doing. Something is jangling chains down here, and it isn't the twelfth duke of Dalforth's ghost.

"I have"—either lost my mind or am truly a horrible person—"a proposition to put to you."

"That sounds interesting." Griffin lounges back in his chair with the satisfied air of someone who thinks they know what's coming.

Foolish man. It's *so* not going to be you. Unless you're using your own hand. And if you are, I hope you have wipes. Those drapes look like they've been hanging there for half a century or more.

"I need you to pretend you're interested in me."

"Didn't I make that clear on the bridge? Remember? You turned me down."

"When you left me with that monster peacock," I splutter.

"And offered you mine. What about that time in

London," he adds, hurrying on when I open my mouth to protest. "Standing out in the cold." You mean when you didn't offer me your jacket, I don't add. "You're the one who didn't call."

He is such a prick.

Maybe I should've mentioned the jacket after all. Unlike his brother, who—

Nope, that is not a helpful thought at all.

"The important word there was pretend." My hand in the air, pinkie out, I make as though to drop the word between us.

"Why make-believe when the real thing is on offer?"

"Because I don't *want* the real thing." I fold my arms across my chest and lean my shoulder into the doorframe.

"You can come in. I won't bite."

"I feel like we've had this conversation before."

"Maybe this time you might be listening."

"No, thank you, Griffin, I don't want to come in. I don't want to date you, and I'm not interested in a hookup. I have two weeks left in this place and I need you to... to..." How do I put this? I think, gazing past him to the darkening sky beyond the window.

I need you to be my shield?

If he was another kind of man, that might appeal to his sense of chivalry.

I need you to do me a favor?

Too ambiguous. Too many sexual connotations. Bleurgh.

"You're trying to keep Alexander out of your knickers, aren't you?" he says with a slow grin.

"Do you have to be so crass?"

"I don't have to be," he says with a shrug. "I just prefer it that way."

Urgh. Do I really want to do this? What's the saying? If you lay down with dogs, don't be surprised if you get fleas.

But fleas can be squished. Poisoned. And I am pretty desperate.

"Why, I wonder?" Leaning forward in his chair, he presses his elbow to the desk, resting his chin on his hand. "Is the big Boy Scout just not doing it for you?"

"I just told you why. I'm leaving soon, and things are complicated."

"It wouldn't need to be complicated between you and me," he replies suggestively.

"I'm aware," I reply in a much snarkier tone. "I'm not interested. You get that, don't you?"

"So, what's in it for me?" He sits forward in his chair like a snake about to strike. "What do I get out of this, lovely Holly?"

"You do the math." Because I don't want to be so tasteless as to point out the obvious. Griffin is jealous of his brother in every way possible.

His gaze bores into mine, corkscrew sharp. But this isn't about me. This is him recognizing an opportunity. "You need me to do this. To throw my arm around you and call you my girl." I roll my eyes so hard, I think my eyeballs suffer a touch of whiplash. "Because, for some reason, you don't want the big bad duke blowing... down your door."

"Something like that."

"But he's already been there. Blown down your... door."

"Fishing, much?"

"Not really," he says flatly. "He told me to stay away from you, so I knew the two of you must've been fucking. But now you don't want to fuck him anymore."

"Think what you want," I mutter, exasperated.

"Oh, this is excellent!" He launches himself back in his

chair and cups his hands behind his head. "I will absolutely fake date you," he announces. "I'll fake date the fuck out of you. But I have a few stipulations of my own."

"I'm going to regret this," I mutter. "Go on, spit them out."

"First, it has to be believable," he says, sitting up, all business again. "I won't be made a fool of."

I don't think he needs much help in that department.

"So no shirking, right?"

"From what?"

"From my touch."

"I'm not asking you to feel me up!"

"Hand holding," he says levelly, "smoothing the hair from your face. The occasional kiss to your cute button nose. That kind of stuff."

"I do not have a button nose, and I don't want you kissing it."

"If you want a fake boyfriend, you will."

"Look, Alexander isn't going to buy that we're suddenly in love."

"Of course he isn't, but that's not going to stop us from being in love, is it? Because love makes you blind to everything but the person in front of you."

"Oh, for—" As if he knows anything about love.

"It's all or nothing."

"Why?" I find myself suddenly asking. "What makes you so happy, so gleeful, for the opportunity to get one up on him?"

"Look around you." His tone is even as though it means nothing to him.

"But Alexander didn't allocate you this room. Chrissy did. I guess you must've done something to annoy her."

"Yeah, like being born."

"I'm sure that's not it. You must've pissed in her cornflakes sometime, and this is her payback." In fact, I'm almost certain this must be the case because Griffin can be charming, but he can also be abrasive.

So abrasive he's making me curse, dagnabbit!

"Let's just say, it's not often I get to best *his grace*. That I have a hard time saying no to someone as pretty as you."

"Okay." *Enough of your bull*, I think as I straighten while hoping this isn't going to blow up in my face. "I guess we should talk about what happens now."

"I'm not finished with my conditions yet."

"What? What else do you want?"

"Just to be the one to tell him."

"Sure," I answer as though this wouldn't be a huge weight off my shoulders. I'm not certain I'd be able to go through with it if I had to stand in front of Alexander and tell him I'm dating his half-brother.

There's no doubt that the dynamic between the two is strange. But while Alexander might not have been very complimentary about Griffin in other ways, he hasn't once belittled their association. I guess that speaks volumes about the differences between these two men.

"Also, and this is my most important condition. I want you to be open to my attentions."

"Ho, no," I say with an unkind laugh. "Didn't we already go over this? I'm not letting you feel me up."

He makes a disparaging cluck of his teeth and tongue. "That's not what I said. I just think you should keep an open mind when we're spending time together. See me as a fake boyfriend that might turn real."

"Even though I've slept with your brother?" I deadpan.

"I have a pretty open mind, Holly," he says in a tone that makes the hairs on the back of my neck stand like pins.

"And I'm thinking maybe you don't know Alexander as well as you think you do."

I bite when I know I shouldn't. "What the hell is that supposed to mean?"

"Just that Alexander has a very open mind, too."

35

ALEXANDER

"Have you got a minute?"

Griffin pulls my attention from my laptop. Not that I was really engrossed in the contents of the screen. I was thinking about Holland again. Two weeks. Twelve days, in fact. And in the past two days, I've been unable to get her on her own. I'd even lowered myself to knocking on her bedroom door last night. She had to be in there, but she ignored me.

Twelve days to find out her plans. To make her see sense. To make her see that there's never a perfect time or a place for something like this. That sometimes you have to trust in that instinct. In that single blinding flash. I'm sure you can find your soulmate in a single heartbeat. In the throb between a lover's legs.

Am I truly talking about love?

Folding my laptop closed, I push the thought away for later examination. Some time when Griffin isn't staring at me like the cat that caught the canary.

Love would be... odd. Unexpected. *Unlikely?*

But it might go some way to explaining this burning sensation in my chest.

One I've been suffering with for days.

Or it could be heartburn, I suppose.

"What can I help you with?" I ask, refocusing my attention as I observe my brother saunter across the room, evidently very pleased with himself.

He indicates the seat with a deference I'm not used to from him, but I nod, and he lowers himself into it.

"Everything all right?" Because I know the reason he's hanging around the castle isn't truly Holland. I've been meaning to put in a call to Van to ask if he knows why Griffin is avoiding London.

"Yes, actually." He rolls his shoulders like a boxer in the ring. "Things are really very good. Wonderful, in fact."

"I'm glad to hear it." While also waiting for the other shoe to drop.

"I wanted to have a word with you," he murmurs. "About Holland."

My heart stops.

"Holland?" Shifting in my chair, I run my thumb along the old-fashioned ink blotter, ignoring how the muscles in my back begin to tense and then clench.

"Yes. Actually, she asked me to have a word with you." Crossing one knee over the other, Griffin opens his hands. It may be a gesture of sincerity and openness, compliance even, but not on Griffin. He's the type of person who makes me want to check for my watch after shaking his hand. "Look, this is awkward, so I'll just come out and say it. She wants you to stay away from her."

"Oh, she does, does she?"

That must be why tiny shivers of anticipation run down her spine at my voice. And why she closes her eyes as though to revel in the tenor of it as I press words against her skin. It must be the reason my name sounds like an incantation on her lips and how, when I'm moving inside her, her moans are powerful enough to move the earth on its axis.

"You don't believe me?" He almost laughs. "You're pulling the eyebrow move you're known so well for." His expression twists playfully as he points at his own brow. "It doesn't work on me."

"I wasn't aware I was doing anything." I lean back in my chair and gesture for him to go on.

"Let me put it this way," he says, opening his hands again and making me want to snap them off at the wrists. "You're making it pretty awkward for her, considering she's agreed to date me."

"To date you." The words come out clipped and slightly incredulous and not at all like a question. *And not just because it's not something I'd like to hear him repeat.*

"Who could believe it? The black sheep of the family. But yeah, me," he adds, his tone hardening. "So, I'd appreciate it if you'd stay the fuck away from her."

"This is all a little sudden, isn't it?" A cold hand clamps around my entrails. This is all bullshit, yet I can't help but suffer the pain of it. The jagged edge of her using my brother to... to what? To keep me from her door? As if I'd put that kind of pressure on her. As if she needs the fucking encouragement herself! She burns so hot in my arms, I'm surprised I don't suffer first-degree burns.

"Sudden? I suppose that's one way to look at it. But if you cast your mind back a few months, you'll remember a night in a cold lane in London. I think I made my position clear then."

"Haven't we already been over this, *ad nauseam*?" I ask, my tone bored.

"Yes, you're right. We have. So no, it's not a little sudden, but it is convenient."

I'll say it is. At least for Holland. I suddenly want to wrap my hands around her but not to pull her to my chest. Not to caress her. I'm more likely right now to pull her over my knee. Spank her properly and not for kicks.

I can't say I won't enjoy it, but that wouldn't be the point of it.

Why must you fight it, my darling?

Doesn't she see that this is the last thing I ever expected to happen to me, either? She hasn't so much unbalanced my world, setting it off kilter, as she has blown up my fucking universe!

"Are you listening to me?"

"I do apologize," I deadpan. "Do go on." Feed me more of your inconsequential lies. "I believe you were explaining how this is convenient."

"Yes." He glances down at his hands. "She's leaving in a couple of weeks, so it'll work out well for the both of us."

"You're sure you won't drive her away before her time is up?" I glance down at my hand on the desk, forcing it to uncurl from a fist. My fingers are stark, bloodless. More like bones than fingers currently. "Isla will be very unhappy if that turns out to be the case." I'm surprised how even my voice sounds. How unconcerned.

"Are you suggesting I can't keep a woman happy, your grace? I think we both know there are no issues on that score, are there? I've only got two weeks. I intend to use them, and her, very well."

I rue the day this man walked into my life. I've tried to like him—I really have. Tried to do the right thing by him. Tried to include him in our family life. But it has all been for nothing because the die was already cast when he walked into our lawyer's office after our father's heart attack.

I realize he's still talking, and I find myself wondering about the length of jail terms for fratricide.

"In fact, now that I come to think of it, the last time we were intimate with a woman in the same room, you were a fair bit younger."

No, I could never like him, and I could certainly never love him.

"I expect you're not long away from filling your wallet with those little blue pills."

I don't reply, though I do glare his way.

"And I completely understand why you didn't want to share Holland. Because now that I have her, neither do I."

An interesting slip of the tongue.

Now that I have her.

Not now that I've *had* her.

Quite an interesting distinction for him, I think.

Of course, none of this cools my heated blood. None of it offers me solace at all as I growl two words in my brother's direction.

"Get out."

"Not until you give me your word you won't try to fuck this up for me."

"I will give you nothing, and I think we can both agree that this will be a first." From ice cold to burning, flames of anger lick at my insides. "Leave or, so help me, I won't be responsible for the consequences."

Griffin rises slowly and shrugs. As he gets to the door, he turns back, but I've already opened my laptop, effectively dismissing him.

I hammer the keys aimlessly, typing out a response to an email as I mentally count to ten, then to twenty. I stand, closing the screen again. Crossing to the drinks trolley at the other side of the room, I consider it has already gone five in the afternoon. Not that it matters. It could be five in the morning, and I'd make an exception right now.

I lift the decanter and pour out two fingers of single malt. The amber liquid burns my gullet on the way down, its potent warmth spreading through my veins. It doesn't help calm me at all, even as I pour and down another.

I knocked on her door last night. Maybe she wasn't there.
Maybe she was with him.

I don't for one moment believe it, even as I hurl the crystal glass across the room.

36

HOLLY

Sometimes, the philosophy of *I just want to see what I can get away with* is the worst philosophy ever invented. Even if it is my invention. But this is the nightmare I've created for myself.

"I can't believe I'm doing this," I mutter, pulling my hand from Griffin's for the second time. "I didn't ask you to rub his nose in it."

"Come on, Holly." Turning to face me, he slides me a bored look. "If you want him to take this seriously, he has to see it with his own eyes. Besides, the kids keep saying they miss you. Didn't you used to eat with the family?"

"Yeah, at the kitchen table," I mutter, unmoved by his poor and blatant emotional blackmail. There were just four of us then—Isla, me, and the boys. And it's not like it happened every night.

"Well, it's only the family dining room, not the fancy one. And I'm hardly wearing a tux."

I don't care, and I don't like it, and I ignore what I expect was his invitation for me to tell him how good he looks. He does look cute, but I'm in no mood for his version of cute.

"Isla is going to hate me," I complain, yanking my hair behind my ears. Next, I abuse the dropped waist of my polka-dotted print dress, twisting and pulling on it. I wish I was back in my room eating crackers.

"What did you expect?" he snaps. "You can't have it both ways." He reaches for my hand again, this time almost dragging me along behind him. "If you want to make an omelets, you've got to smash a few eggs."

The man has no compassion.

And I have few scruples.

And I'm *so* gonna put a peacock in his room before I leave. *Somehow.*

"Holly!" As we round a corner, Archie launches himself at me, wrapping his arms around my waist.

"Hey, friend!"

"Mummy says you're leaving us, but I told her I'm going to lock you in a cupboard."

"That sounds scary."

"No, you can live there like a secret Harry Potter. Uncle Sandy broke his laptop today," he then adds randomly.

"It looked like it was working this afternoon." Griffin sounds smug. Was that when he went to tell—

Oh, man.

"Do you like crabs?" the kid asks next, his attention swinging to Griffin.

"Crabs are *clawsome*," he answers without missing a beat.

Hugh gives a little belly laugh as though the joke caught him off guard.

"Why do you ask? You haven't put one in my bed, have you?"

"No!" Archie laughs again. "That's what's for dinner."

The boy runs off giggling while I hold up my hand for Griffin to high five.

"Good response!" I don't know why I'm surprised he's good with kids, but I am.

"We're on the same wavelength, obviously." Griffin tries to curtail his shy smile as his hand meets mine.

"Wasn't gonna say it." Then his fingers slide between mine, and we're suddenly holding hands again.

"Do you like kids?"

"I couldn't eat a whole one," he quips. "I've got a nephew." I almost correct him by pointing out he has two when he speaks again. "Mo. I've told my sister it's a ridiculous name, but he's too old to change it now. I mean, who calls their kid Montague?"

"There are worse names," I reply. Wow. He really doesn't see himself as part of this family. That's probably why he doesn't feel bad about what we're doing. Not sure how that theory correlates to me because I'm obviously not related to this bunch, yet I feel pretty wretched right now.

Buck up, buttercup, I tell myself. *This is what you need to do to make sure you leave at the end of next week with your heart still intact.*

We follow in Archie's footsteps, turning a corner into the family's quarters. This part of the castle is much less historic, but still very grand with its high ceilings and Georgian paneled walls. We enter a room where a fireplace of black marble dominates, pale colored sofas flanking it. It's quite an opulent space but less fussy and a touch more masculine, I think. And then I remember why. Or rather, I become aware why as I lift my gaze.

Alexander lounges on a chair by the unlit fire, the table lamp behind him casting a golden glow to his hair. *Golden and glowering*, I think as my feet grind to a halt and a flight of vicious birds swoops through my insides.

"Come on." Griffin swaps my hand for an arm around my shoulders, maybe discerning my sudden distress. "Whatcha, Al."

I assume the ridiculous fake-cockney accent he uses must be to get under Alexander's skin. Not that he seems to pay him any mind with his energy focused on me. And not pleasantly.

"Hello, Alexander," I murmur through what feels like bloodless lips.

"Holly." Those horror birds swoop to my throat. So I guess I'm Holly now. Why does that make me want to cry as Alexander inclines his head, tilting the glass in his hand as though in a toast?

But what is he toasting? My new relationship?

Unlikely.

"What are you drinking?" Griffin asks, his arm slipping away.

So much for solidarity. I didn't realize I was one of the eggs we were breaking.

"Ah, the good stuff," the egg breaker says approvingly, picking up a bottle from a black lacquered drinks cabinet in a chinoiserie style.

"Holly!" This time, my name is delivered in a much warmer tone as Isla glides across the room to greet me as though we're old friends. Her hands tender against my elbows, she presses a kiss to my left cheek. "He's in a terrible mood," she whispers, changing cheeks as I lightly pucker my lips to make the appropriate response. "I hope you know what you're doing," she adds in a low tone as she pulls away.

I'm not so sure anymore.

Standing by myself, I suddenly feel adrift, like I'm

floating in a sea of my own stupidity. How did I think I could carry this off? I glance around the room, looking for something—anything—that might serve as a distraction. Anything to keep from looking at *him*. Not that it truly matters because I can feel the weight of his gaze anyway. Grave and brooding, it pushes down on my shoulders as I realize I'm not really adrift. I might feel lost, but I'm not because I'm anchored to the spot by his attention in a thoroughly unpleasant way.

"Oh, but you haven't got a drink!" Isla suddenly announces, turning from her children. "What sort of gentlemen do you call yourselves?" she playfully chastises. "You know better than that." She turns to Alexander. "A gentleman's purpose is to see to a lady's needs. Drinking needs," she adds hastily, her expression turning panicked.

"I think you'll find that's Griffin's job," the duke's deep voice rumbles, though he sounds as though he doesn't care either way.

Isla's gaze moves to Griffin, doubling back as she realizes I'm still standing where he left me. Where Alexander's gaze has cemented me.

Like a damn mannequin.

"Griffin, get Holly a drink, would you?" She takes my arm and leads me to the sofa opposite Alexander.

"What's your poison, Hol?" Griffin calls across the room.

I lick my lips as I refuse to look at my poison of choice.

I've given up things that are bad for me.

"Let's have martinis," Isla announces, answering the question on my behalf, possibly intuiting my pattern of thought.

Martinis are made and served by the butler, Mr. McCain, who materializes in the room like magic. He avoids my gaze as he proffers me my drink from a silver tray. The first one goes down too quickly to notice the taste, but the second is crisp and deliciously dry. The boys are engrossed in their iPads and no help to the stilted conversation as they are completely oblivious to the pre-volcanic atmosphere. Meanwhile, Isla flaps around the room like a nervous bird. At least until Mr. McCain announces dinner.

This is... kind of unexpectedly fancy. The family dining room is set as though to accommodate an intimate dinner party, not a family dinner. A flower arrangement sits at the center of the dining table covered with white linens. Candles are lit, and the lamplight is low.

I know the family doesn't dine like this every evening. Dougal cooks when he's here, sure, but Mr. McCain doesn't stand on ceremony and serve. Seriously, I've eaten with Isla and the kids at the kitchen table on nights when everyone was expected to load their own plate into the dishwasher afterwards.

Griffin holds out my chair, and Hugh valiantly beats his uncle to do the same for his mother before the meal begins. And still, Mr. McCain keeps his gaze from mine as the first course is served. He's disapproving, I guess. I'm sure it won't be long until the rest of the staff hear how I'm "with" Griffin now. They'll hate me, I'm sure, and not just because he doesn't have much of a fanbase at Kilblair. But no doubt they'd hate me more if Alexander had gotten his way.

If I'd stayed on in the capacity he'd wanted me to.

"This is really delicious," I murmur, not lifting my eyes from my plate as I stick my fork—one of three on the table in front of me, and snaps for me because I know what each is for—into the shell of a North Sea crab. The meat of the crustacean has been seeped in koji butter, apparently. Not that I have any idea what that is, but I'm happy to ponder it as a distraction. I heap a little onto a delicate sliver of sourdough and take a bite of the decadent deliciousness, continuing to ignore the weight of Alexander's gaze.

"Oh, Sandy." Isla rolls the deliciousness around her mouth as she looks at the other end of the six-seater table—she sits to my left, Griffin to my right, and the boys facing me—"Holly is right. And I think I might need to steal Dougal."

"There's no need," he drawls. *I can still feel his eyes on me.* "I have no plans to be anywhere else but Kilblair currently."

Was that a threat?

"Are you looking forward to the Duffys' party?" Looking up from the crab shell, I try (not for the first time) to engage him in conversation.

Try for normal. Aim for amiable.

"Not particularly." His words are cool and dismissive, yet the way his eyes roam over me is wholly contradictory.

"Sandy's not especially big on parties," Isla adds.

"On account of him almost being a geriatric, I should imagine," Griffin mutters only for my ears.

"He wouldn't even let me hold one for his birthday."

Griffin uses the moment to slide his hand between my shoulders where he rubs. I have to fight the instinct to rebuff his touch, which is something he seems to recognize. And ignore. "You okay there, babe?" he asks in a tone that's a little too sickly to be sweet.

"I've seen *Babe*," Archie pipes up. "It's a film about a talking pig." He glares across the table at Griffin. "You shouldn't call Holly a pig. It's not very polite." The kid's solemn expression morphs as his attention swings to his mom. "Mummy, why do you think writers write but fingers don't *fing*?"

"Because the English language is a strange and wondrous thing," she answers without missing a beat. "Eat your fish cakes, Archie."

The boys are dining on a somewhat adapted menu. They're missing out because this crab is yum.

"You're sure you're enjoying that?" Isla murmurs, sliding me a concerned glance.

"Yes. It's delicious." I shoot her a quick smile. "I guess I'm not very hungry." On account of every mouthful feeling like a lead weight as it hits my stomach. I wish I could manage it because it really is delicious. Light and delicate, and flavored with dill.

I struggle through the main course of Asian-style vegetables and twice-cooked sticky duck, though mostly just move my food around my plate. I hate that this is my first real meal in days, and I can't even ask for a doggy bag.

"What about you, Holly?" At the sound of Alexander's sudden and voluntary address, my shoulders seem to levitate up around my ears. "Are you looking forward to Dylan Duffy's birthday?"

"I—" As I inhale a jagged breath, my gaze falls anywhere but on him. "I don't think I'll be going."

"Of course you will," says Griffin as though I didn't just say otherwise.

"I'm trying to persuade her," Isla adds.

"Hollywood parties aren't really my thing. Plus, I'm kind of busy. And I really don't have anything to wear." As I reach for my glass, my eyes flit Alexander's way. *He's still watching me.* I swallow nervously, my throat suddenly as dry as the Sahara.

"I'm wearing my Batman outfit," Archie announces as Mr. McCain sets down a square of chocolate cake and ice cream in front of him. "I'll come and show you before we leave, if you like, Geordie?"

"That would be marvelous," Mr. McCain replies with a genuine smile.

I'm pleased to see informal dining is just that. Although, thinking about it, I guess the butler still didn't speak until he was spoken to. Still, Archie's pretty pleased with his response, judging by his smile. It's as wide as half a bicycle wheel.

"You can't be Batman, stupid," retorts Hugh, who has barely spoken all evening. "It hasn't been announced that he's going to be playing Batman yet."

"But he's not going to be Batman if I'm wearing the suit, is he?" Archie answers with a six-year-old's logic.

"You're such an idiot," Hugh mutters as his mom begins to scold him.

"That was unkind, Hugh. Apologize to your brother."

"I'm sorry you're an idiot," he snipes.

"Hugh," she repeats in a warning tone, "we do not get to take our bad moods out on other people. And we especially don't behave this way at the dinner table."

I murmur my thanks as Mr. McCain sets my dessert—sorry, my pudding—in front of me. *When in Rome!*

"You didn't tell *him* off for smashing a glass," he retorts, loud and aggrieved, his arms swinging out in the direction of his uncle. "Why is he allowed to bring his bad mood to the dinner table, and I'm not?"

"Because I'm not taking my foul mood out on anyone else," Alexander answers impassively.

"You took it out on your glass, though, and you didn't clean up after yourself. McCain did. And, if you want the truth, you also keep looking meanly at Holly. So," he concludes, his attention turning back to his mother, "I'm not the only one with bad manners at this dinner table."

"Maybe I should send both you and Uncle Sandy to bed."

"It's okay, Hugh," I interject. "Your uncle isn't really

being mean to me." No more than I deserve. Boy, I wish I was in Mr. McCain's place right now as I watch him almost tiptoe from the room.

"I'm surrounded by idiots," Hugh cries, raking both hands through his hair.

"Hugh!" his mother calls for a second time. Me? I roll my lips inward to keep from smiling because he sounds like a miniature Alexander.

"It's true," he demands, pointing across the table at me. "Uncle Sandy keeps sending her death glares, and she's just taking it. I shouldn't be surprised, though, should I? Because she fell off her chair while taking a photograph of her breakfast last week!"

Isla slides her napkin from her knee, depositing it on the table as she stands. "Out," she demands in a clipped tone. "You and I are going to have a little chat."

The table falls silent as Isla frog marches her son out of the room.

Well, for at least ninety seconds.

"Did you really fall off your chair?" Archie asks, his expression puzzled.

"Yeah," I admit. "Though I was actually standing *on* my chair when I slipped. I thought I'd sprained my ankle," I add in a low tone. "But he wasn't right about it being last week. It was more like three weeks ago."

"Maybe Hugh's right," Griffin says, reaching out to chuck my chin. I consider ducking and biting him, but who knows what I'd catch? Also, there's Alexander's watchful gaze to consider.

"What were you doing standing on a chair?" Alexander asks, his tone even.

"Like Hugh said, I was taking a photograph of my breakfast. And I... slipped."

"You're supposed to eat it, not break your neck for it," Griffin scoffs, reaching for his spoon.

"It looked pretty." I shrug. It was kind of a ridiculous moment but admitting it feels nowhere nearly as awkward as this dinner has been. "Blueberries and blackberries, raspberries, too. And I needed something to post to my Instagram page."

"Needed?"

"It had been a while."

"She tried to take a photo of that psychopathic peacock yesterday." Griffin scoffs as he begins to dig into his food.

Rude. Shouldn't we wait for Isla?

And speaking of Instagram, my fingers are currently itching for my phone, though I'd left it in my room. What did Mr. McCain say this was again? *Chocolate mousse with miso caramel and macadamia.* I'm not sure how I'm supposed to eat the meringue sitting on top of this stack of deliciousness. Not without making a mess.

"Are you going to eat it or take a photograph?"

I look up and catch the tiny quirk at the corner of Alexander's mouth, and my heart gives a painful little ping.

"I was thinking about it," I murmur, staring down at it, "but I don't have my phone."

"Some things are better just experienced in the moment."

A cold shiver runs through me as I glance Alexander's way. His eyes are focused on me in a way that I recognize from our first meeting. The intensity in his gaze making my insides feel like a ribbon pulled over the sharp edge of a pair of scissors. As though he's seeing something I hadn't intended for him to see. I remember being a little afraid, like being balanced at the top of a fairground ride.

A little like I do now.

ALEXANDER

A more unpleasant evening I have never experienced, and I once spent a disagreeable night in a Peruvian hospital after a motorcycle accident. But it has also been enlightening. And gratifying. I've never seen a woman less into Griffin than I have Holland.

Holland, not Holly.

Jesus, the look she gave me when I called her that. It took every ounce of my willpower to keep me in the chair. I wanted to go to her. To pick her up, tell her I'm sorry, and carry her out of there. When I would've probably shaken the living daylights out of her.

But I didn't. For obvious reasons. But I trust her playacting with my shit of a brother will drive her into my arms at some point.

I have to believe that, even if she seems on edge around me, primed like a deer sensing danger.

Am I a danger to her?

I suppose that's up to her.

"I am so sorry." My sister looks shaken as she makes her way into the drawing room. When it became clear she might be a while, I'd encouraged Holland to eat her pudding, though I couldn't face my own. While I'll be sure to tell Dougal it was delicious, I had difficulty tasting anything but betrayal. Dramatic, I know. I know nothing is going on between them, but it still fucking hurts that she'd go to such lengths to deny this.

And why?

To protect herself?

From me?

And what was her reason for going to such extremes to take a photograph of her breakfast? She'd offered the information up so easily. At least, on the surface. But as I'd wondered as I'd watched her pick at the mousse, I realized that wasn't the truth.

The admission had cost her.

Meanwhile, I'd swallowed a little of the mousse while Archie and Griffin ate with gusto, leaving nothing but the pattern on their respective plates.

What a fucking nightmare of an evening.

"How is he?" Holland asks Isla, beating me to the question. "I've never seen him so upset."

"He's sad," she replies eventually, her eyes filling with tears that I know she won't allow to spill. "He's sorry, Holland." Holland begins to wave off her words, but my sister pushes on valiantly. "He's sad, and he doesn't want to see you go. His emotions are all mixed up, and he doesn't know how to process what he feels."

"He's not the only one who's sorry," Holland replies, her gaze dipping to her lap.

"You've nothing to be sorry for. Change is a fact of life we all have to face multiple times through the course of our lives." She touches Holland's shoulder as she passes to the sideboard and the tea tray McCain had unobtrusively delivered to the drawing room. What she doesn't say is that someone at school recently told him his parents are getting divorced. Worse, that his father had been seen holding hands with the nanny. So now he's desperate for Holland not to leave because he's terrified what a new nanny might mean. Child logic, I suppose.

"Archie, look," Isla says brightly. "Someone's sent up hot chocolate. Do you think you might manage a cup?"

"Can Hugh have some?" he asks, his voice small.

"Maybe tomorrow. He's having some time to himself at the moment. There are marshmallows," she adds temptingly. My nephew succumbs, reluctantly nodding his head. She places the child-sized Batman mug on a table next to Archie with instructions to give it time to cool. As she turns her back, he shoves one pink and one white marshmallow into his mouth, leaving him to look like a happy squirrel.

"Coffee, anyone? Tea?"

"Coffee for me, please." Griffin lifts a lazy hand before bringing it to Holland's lap in a blatant attempt to goad me. "It doesn't matter if I'm kept awake tonight, does it, love?" He raises her hand to his lips as though to press it with a kiss, but she pulls it away quite deftly, playfully pushing his shoulder instead.

"Oh... you!" I think that was supposed to be playful, though her expression looks more painful. In fact, she looks like she's imagining his head exploding.

Or maybe that's just me.

"How do you like your coffee, Griffin?"

"Like I like my women."

"Except you don't have to pay for it here." The room goes quiet, and I look up from my glass. Fuck. I said that out loud, didn't I? Much to the horror of everyone.

"Alexander!" This from my sister.

"Jesus, Al." This from my half-brother.

Though there comes no verbal response from the woman I've inadvertently insulted. Just a reproachful look

"I beg your pardon. Present company excepted, of course." I lift my glass to my mouth but can't quite bite back my thoughts. "For her price is far above rubies," I mutter, reciting Proverbs.

31:10, if I'm not mistaken.

Strength and dignity are her clothing, and she laughs at the time to come.

I am an arsehole.

"Coffee, Sandy?"

At my sister's question, I shake my head. As she frowns my way, I shore up my defenses. "I have a touch of heartburn." It's not indigestion, and it's not quite heartache. It's more like an aggravation, burning me from the gullet up.

"You want to watch that at your age," Griffin interjects. Despite being just a few short years behind me, he does like to make age-related digs. "It's like they say, you are what you eat."

Then it would seem that at some point, Griffin has eaten a massive prick.

I keep the thought to myself. Little ears and all that.

"Holland?" Archie asks, looking like a miniature old man, sporting a fluffy white moustache as he sits in the overly large chair. "You're sitting on the same chair as Uncle Griffin."

"Yes, it's called a couch," she explains unnecessarily.

"Sofa," he corrects.

"There's space for you to sit here, too," she says, tapping the empty cushion next to her.

"No, thank you." He scrunches his nose, then wipes the milky froth from his face. "That might mean I'd have to marry you."

"What?" Holland's face turns immediately pink. "I'm not marrying anyone, Archie."

"Are you sure? Aren't you having a baby then?"

"What? No!"

"But Chrissy said that last time she saw anyone eat the kinds of things you do, they had a baby a few months later."

"No, *nononono*. No baby," Holland insists, her eyes moving warily between my sister and me. "*Nuh-uh!*" With another denial that sounds more like a noise than an actual word, she almost jackknifes to her feet. "Thank you for a lovely evening," she adds brightly as Griffin and I both rise to our feet.

"I'll come with you," he begins.

"No, you finish your coffee," Holland insists, sending my sister a grateful look as she almost pushes a cup and saucer at him.

Suddenly, I find myself in front of her, taking her arm. "Let me walk you out," I murmur in complete contrast to the way my fingers tighten on her upper arm. If Griffin protests, I don't notice, basking in the relief her nearness brings to me as the pain in my chest dissipates. Not that Holland seems at all happy about my presence, which is a shame but not an eternal situation.

I love how small she is compared to me. Next to me. And I hate how it takes every ounce of my willpower not to pull her against me. To take her in my arms. Be the man forever at her side. I want to protect her always. Curl myself around her when she's swollen with our child.

My steps falter—where the hell did that come from? Holland appears too annoyed to notice my astonishment.

"It's fine," she says through gritted teeth, swinging to face me once we're out of the drawing room. "I know the way. I can get there perfectly well on my own."

"No one is suggesting otherwise." My cool tone is instinctual, though I have no idea where the words have come from, but I wear this armor well. All I can think is how I want to get her alone. Strip her bare, strip her down to her soul. But a secluded corner of a hallway will have to do as we turn a corner, and I allow her to pull free from my grip.

"What do you think you're doing?"

What indeed as I tip her chin.

"Have you no—"

"Morals? None it seems where you're concerned." I don't hold her in my arms, but I do hold her as I lower my head, heedless of how she tries to pull away. She smells like flowers and looks so fucking incensed. But her shock tastes delicious, her pretense fracturing at the first brush of my lips. She gives in to a soft, quivering moan, her lips a decadent mixture of chocolate and wine.

I want her. Goddammit, I want her here and now as I feel her body shudder against mine, as though a draught had just run along the hallway. It's the moment she gives in, relaxing into my kiss. My whole being is gratified—elated—by the way she responds to me, by the way she tilts her head, allowing me access to the silky skin of her neck. The tiny hitch in her breath and the way her body unconsciously moves with mine, she's like a flower following the rays of the sun.

She makes it too easy for me really, her soft moan signaling the moment she truly lets go.

I force myself to release her. To pull away.

She is so beautiful. The way the light falls casts a shadow across her cheekbone, highlighting the moisture against the soft, fullness of her lips. Her lashes lie like dark crescents across her pale skin. She is everything I've ever wanted and never thought to dream of. As if I'd never see her walk past me on the street. As if I'd ever be able to resist her. Too easy, yet so regrettably hard as her eyes flutter open. I see the confusion there and suffer such a pang of regret.

"What...?"

"Yes, exactly. What are you doing?"

"Working my notice?" A crease forms between her brows. She looks more hurt than annoyed.

"No, Holland. What are you *doing*. Here. With him. And don't give me any of that bullshit about dating him. You can barely stand to sit next to him."

"You don't know that."

"I know a lot more than you give me credit for. I know you're scared. I know that you think it's me you don't trust, but it's more that you can't trust yourself."

"You know nothing about me," she says, her gaze flashing.

"I know he doesn't kiss you the way I kiss you. I know you don't bloom like a flower for him or spread yourself wide on the kitchen table and beg for his touch."

"You're a pig." She raises her hands as though to push me away, but I catch her arms.

"And you're like a miser with a pocket full of pennies. You're just not willing to part with the necessary, darling. Especially not with him." She winces, and I realize my fingers have tightened, but fuck it, I won't let go.

"I'm with Griffin now," she retorts, her expression hardening. She tries to pull free from my hold. "Let go. You're hurting me."

"I know, you're just a delicate little flower," I find myself growling.

"I didn't say that."

"A delicate, fucked-up, horny little flower." I enunciate the words so clearly while she looks at me as though she'd happily punch me in the face. "A little flower who, if she isn't careful, will end up being fucked by my brother."

"You don't know what you're talking about."

"A little flower that lies."

"I don't know what you're talking about."

"Face the facts, Holland. Your little act didn't fool anyone tonight. But the longer you keep it up, the more danger you're in."

"Just because I won't let you feel me up!"

"Wouldn't you?" I drawl, despite my heart beating out of my skin. She'd have to touch me to know it, which isn't going to happen this evening. *But soon.* "It didn't seem too much of a stretch a few moments ago."

"You are… despicable."

Uncurling my fingers, I press my shoulders against the wall behind me. I might look like a bored aristocrat, but the cool plaster grounds me. Reminds me of my purpose as I slide my hands into my trouser pockets.

"This from the woman who would have the world believe she'd jumped from my bed to my brother's while the sheets were still warm."

We'll call this an artistic liberty, and not just because we seem more suited to tables and walls. Not just artistic but also cruel, I decide, as, with a pang of regret, I watch the heat leave her eyes. *Like a candle blown out.* I brace myself, expecting some retort as she inhales deeply, her shoulders rising along with her chin. But no, she treats me with more grace than I deserve and possesses more dignity than a queen as she turns her back on me without speaking a word.

She begins to walk away, and I do the only thing I can for now.

I let her go.

37

HOLLY

I feel like something that was chewed up, spit out, then trodden on by a heavy boot this morning, but I guess I brought that on myself.

From my bed to his while the sheets were still warm...

Alexander's words continue to haunt me as I find myself wandering through the long gallery, the solemn faces of Isla's and Alexander's faces staring down at me... along with Batman and Spiderman, I see, as I pluck the plastic figurines down from the bottom corners of a particularly thick and ornate frame.

"Well, you are no oil painting," I murmur, looking up into the austere countenance of the portrait in the gilt frame. "But I respect your fashion choices." He was probably rocking it back in the day with his baby blue silk embroidered coat and white satin high heels.

"I see you're admiring one of our ancestors."

I turn to Isla's smiling words.

"One of the fam?" I throw my thumb in the painting's direction. "I was just telling him Cher called. Apparently, she wants her wig back."

Isla releases a surprised-sounding laugh as she comes to stand next to me. Shoulder to shoulder, we examine the painting together.

"He's not exactly bringing sexy back."

"This is Henry Algernon Benedict Talbart-Dalforth, otherwise known as the first Duke of Dalforth. And no, you're right. He wasn't very easy on the eyes. This is his wife, Isobel," Isla adds, indicating a looker in a russet ball gown.

"He was punching above his weight." Because Isobel was truly beautiful. Or at least, she was painted so. "I guess she got the raw end of the deal."

"Well, no one married for love in those days. They married for money, for power, and for allegiances. The first duke was no exception. He married for money, and his wife married probably because she was told to."

"Tough break, Isobel. I'm sorry for you."

"It might've been worse," she adds, pointing at another painting on the opposite wall. "She might've been born a generation later and ended up married to him. He was also a bit of a beast, by all accounts." The fashions may have changed in this portrait, but the look of superiority has not. "He took another man to his bed and expected his wife to say nothing about it."

"And did she?"

"What could she do? A woman was nothing more than a chattel. His lover was an earl, no less, who abandoned his wife and family for this strange three-way existence."

"I thought that kind of behavior was a big no-no back then."

"Yes," she says with a sad but brief smile. "For ordinary people. No matter the age, it seems if you've enough money, you can get away with almost anything. Take him, for example, the next of our illustrious ancestors. He wanted to divorce his wife, but that was frowned upon. So he pushed her down the stairs instead."

"That's one way to get rid of your wife, I guess."

"Yes, quite an extreme way. He also went on to fatally wound his paramour's husband in a duel after that. He fled the country and never returned. Then we have his grandson, who became a highwayman for kicks, was disowned, and then hanged. Next came an opium addict. Then we have my great-great-grandfather who married this beauty."

We come to a stop in front of a portrait of a young woman in cornflower blue. With slim shoulders and a proud, haughty chin, she wears the kind of evening gown that would necessitate a dozen skirts underneath. Her skin is pale, her dark hair pinned simply in stark contrast to her extravagant clothing. The pearls at her throat and wrist and the jeweled fan she holds closed on her lap. But the most striking thing about her is her violet eyes. They seem to follow me as they move.

"She is stunning." And kind of familiar, I think, as my gaze slips to Isla's profile. They look like one another. I wonder if she realizes that. "Please don't tell me hers was an unhappy marriage."

Isla turns to me, her expression wry. "Aren't you seeing a pattern?"

"What happened?" I ask, my heart sinking just a little.

"She tried to divorce him on the grounds of cruelty and desertion, but the petition failed. But she'd fallen in love with another man, and they planned to run away together." She turns back to the painting with a sigh. "He locked her in the castle's highest tower. And she threw herself from it not long after."

"Oh, my God. That's terrible."

"At least she didn't see her son, my grandfather, live to grow into such infamy. He was indiscriminate in his affairs, from ladies of rank down to street sweepers. Men and women alike. By the time my father became the duke, the affairs of the estates were in a terrible mess."

I don't say anything because this is a tale Chrissy had already told.

"I see you've heard of him." Turning to me again, she smiles properly this time.

"There must've been good dukes of Dalforth? Dukes without notoriety."

"Oh, I'm sure there were. Those who died before reaching their majority."

We walk a little farther along the gallery before Isla comes to a stop.

"Here he is. Our illustrious father. The man who left his only son to sort out three hundred years of purgatory."

The portrait features a man in his thirties, dressed in the uniform of the fox hunt. White pants, shirt and cravat, polished high-top boots and a scarlet jacket. Fair-haired and pleasant-looking, he has a twinkle in his blue eyes I almost recognize. He looks… friendly. Not like some ogre who ruined his children's inheritance.

"What about Griffin?"

"Slip of the tongue." She waves away her explanation, ignoring the tactless nature of my words. I guess it makes it sound like I was defending him, which is what a girlfriend would do.

I hope you know what you're doing, she'd whispered last night. Maybe this will help convince her of my lie. The lie I feel awful about.

"But Griffin wasn't handed any of the responsibility. It all fell to Sandy, even the responsibility for Griffin's education and the start of his career, but that's another story." She turns back to the portrait. "I'd like to think our parents married for love. She didn't come from the kind of money needed to get the family back on track. But my father couldn't stay faithful. So, they loved, and then they hated, and my mother drank herself into an early grave."

"I'm sorry." So sorry for them both. I mean, I had a less than idyllic childhood, being pushed from mother to grandmother and back again. At least until the last in a long line of boyfriends decided Kennedy and I were more a burden than anything else. But at least we had Nana.

"That's kind of you," she murmurs blandly, turning back to face me. "Did you have a happy childhood?"

"Yes, I did." Mostly. "I was mostly raised by my grandmother, who was a character and a half." I smile in remembrance. "My father died when I was very young, and my mother wasn't much in the picture. But, yes, I had a happy childhood."

"Sandy didn't. Our father was very charming when he wanted to be. Usually when he wanted something. To women, he was a delight. Until he was done with them, I suppose. But he was hard on Sandy, and he left him nothing but trouble. But I'm not telling you this as gossip or a history lesson. I'm telling you because I think you might like to hear it. Sandy isn't like our father, no matter what anyone says. He's loyal and just and puts his family and his land above everything else.

"Do you know the meaning of the name Alexander? It means defender or helper of man. I know his manner can be cold. Superior, even. And I know he can seem like such a superior snob. But he isn't. He's a good man."

"I know." My voice is small. He's a good man who can't

seem to help himself. I don't mean it as a slight. It's more an observation. *An affinity, maybe.*

"I did tell him to stay away from you, and now I'm beginning to wish I hadn't. Griffin is—"

"Please." I shake my head, unwilling to get into this.

"You're a good person, Holland. You deserve better."

"How come there's no portrait of him? Of Alexander?" I ask, trying to change the subject.

"There is." I begin to follow her across the room, realizing what we're heading towards.

"This is us," she says, pointing at the portrait Chrissy had shown me my first day here.

I find myself smiling up at the boy in long pants and the girl in the blue dress.

"You know, when Chrissy told me about 'Lady Isla's wee boys', I thought you were married to the duke."

"The Dalforth's aren't quite that bad," she says with a laugh.

"What about the later duchess?" Like a scab I can't help but pick, I find myself glancing around the room, wondering where her portrait is.

"We don't have one. Just this." Her shoes echo as she walks to the far end of the room. I hesitate, wondering if I should follow, but I can't seem to help myself. A dozen silver-framed photographs stand on a credenza. Some sepia. Some black and white. Some color. Isla reaches to one at the back, lifting it before dusting the sleeve of her blouse over the front. "This is Leonie," she says, passing it over. "I'm not even sure Sandy realizes it's still here."

"He doesn't like the reminder," I assert as I stare at the image of the Duke and Duchess of Dalforth on their wedding day. He seems so young, and she resembles a fairy queen. They appear so happy. So happy I can't look at it, so I hand it back.

"I suppose that's one way to look at it," she replies cryptically as she sets it back on the credenza.

I know it's not right or even sane to be jealous of someone who isn't living, but that pain in my chest tells me I am. Which, in a way, tells me I'm doing the right thing. I need to remember how Alexander looked on his wedding day to help strengthen my resolve. To remind me Leonie had Alexander in a way he'll never be available to me.

The tattoo on his bicep. Was that to commemorate the day they married?

Whether it was or not, this little walk through the Dalforth past has been a useful reminder. And maybe he's right. Maybe I am despicable. But sometimes you've got to be cruel to be kind. Especially to those you love.

38

HOLLY

"You brought this on your own head," I mutter, slapping jelly ferociously onto a slice of bread. "If you hadn't acted like Griffin had leprosy, he wouldn't have known, and then you wouldn't have had to go through this whole stupid charade."

"You've not eaten your snacks already, have ye?" Chrissy asks, bundling into the family kitchen with a pile of laundered kitchen towels. "Were you talkin' to yourself?"

"No," I retort, slapping the bread onto the top of another before swinging around to face her. So she caught me in the pantry last week. Big whoop! Saw me and helped me fill my little tote with delicious nibbles to take to my room. And fruit. And now she thinks I might be pregnant, so she thought it might be a good idea to say that out loud?

I was so embarrassed. In fact, I think my cheeks are still burning now.

"What's got your knickers in a knot, then?" She puts the neat pile of towels down and turns to face me, pressing her fist to one generous hip.

"Well, funny you should ask, Chrissy." I turn back to the

jelly sandwich, slice it viciously, and swing back again. "But last night at dinner, Archie saw fit to announce to the family that you think I might be pregnant."

Hers is not the reaction I anticipated.

Basically, she laughs. She laughs like it's the funniest thing she's heard in weeks.

"The wee bampot," she says, wiping a finger under her eyes. "He'd have me hangit, I'm sure!"

"He'd have you what-it?"

She makes a fist above her ear and sticks out her tongue.

"He'd get you hanged?"

"Aye, and I'd die innocent!" she says with another incredulous chuckle. "I never made any such suggestion. I only said you had the eatin' habits of an expectant mother. Strange, like. It was, I thought, better than announcing you were trying to stay out o' reach of himself." She slides me a very eloquent look. One that says, I see you. I know what this is.

"Oh. Well. Sorry."

"Not as sorry as you will be," she mutters as she bustles past me, yanking on the dishwasher door.

"I'll be sorry why?" I ask, following her progress, perplexed.

"Because that man is no good." She almost throws a cup onto the top shelf, making it rattle.

"I know," I protest, aggrieved. "Well, he's no good for me, but I have been trying to stay away from him."

"Not Sandy," she says in a low hiss, the dishwasher door clunking closed. "I'm talkin' about—"

"There she is." My shoulders tense at the sound of Mari's voice. I really could do without this. "I told you you were wrong about her," she says to Chrissy. "First, she sets her sights on Cameron, then goes after *himself*. And now, she's with his brother. What does that tell you about her?"

I turn very slowly in the direction of Mari. "See this outfit?" Like a cheesy game show hostess, I do a little flourish, indicating my denim cutoffs. "Giving a fuck doesn't really go with it."

So worth cursing just to see her face.

"Mari, you apologize," Chrissy chastises.

"I'm only saying—"

"You're only saying something that's moving you this close"—I hold up my finger and thumb, the digits almost touching—"to a smack in the jaw." Cursing and a beatdown. Guess she picked the wrong day to mess with me.

"Holly!" Chrissy censures.

"You're just a silly girl who knows nothing about anything," I add, incensed. "A silly girl who's projecting, as far as I can see." I whip around to Chrissy as I say, "I saw her in the pub with Cameron last weekend, the same man who told me she was in the pub last Friday when she called in sick."

"I was sick," she retorts. "And then I felt better."

"You know what, I don't care. I'm not chasing anybody." I throw up my hands because I don't know what else to say. Except maybe I'm the one being chased. But they wouldn't believe me anyway.

"You." She points a finger Mari's way. "Go and hoover the stairs."

"But that's the cleaning company's job," she complains petulantly.

"Today, it's yours. Go to the cupboard at the foot o' the stairs and get out wee Henry."

Oh man, Mari's face! *Wee Henry* is a little red vacuum cleaner—the actual brand is called Henry; Henry the hoover—which has a little black bowler hat and a cheerful face. Yes, a face! It's the cutest vacuum cleaner I have ever seen, but the castle's model is pretty old. It spits out more than it sucks up. A bit like Mari around me, I suppose.

"It'll take ages!" she protests.

"Good," Chrissy retorts as she folds her arms across her ample chest. "Off you go, now." With a scowl, Mari huffs and stomps out of the room. Chrissy's attention turns back to me.

"Sorry," I blurt out before she can say anything. "You know I don't curse as a rule, but that girl would make a saint lose his temper."

"I prefer it when you don't sound like a fish wife," she says with a sniff. "And I'll tell you somethin' for nothin'. I see what's going on between you and Sandy."

"Nothing is going on."

"I'll no' say I believed it at first. Now don't get yourself all twisted. I just meant I didn't believe he'd behave like he has. He's always been so good."

"He's still good," I whisper. "I think we just bring out the worst in each other."

"Or maybe the best?" she asks expectantly.

"No, I got it right the first time."

"But Griffin, he's no good. You hear me?"

"He's not that bad," I mutter.

"He's not that good, either. Just you watch yourself with him. And Sandy? He'll no' take this lying down if I know him. And I do know him—I've known him as man and boy."

"Chrissy, I think we can both agree that I can't stay here."

"I can'nae see why not," she begins.

"Because the man is a freakin' duke! And he had a wife who he loved, and he hasn't been serious about anyone since then!" As far as I can tell.

"So?"

"I can't stay here and fall in love with him. I won't be made a laughingstock." Not again.

"So you don't like to take risks? Is that it?" Chrissy pulls a kitchen chair out from under the table, lowering herself onto it. "That seems like a very boring life for a lassie as young as you."

"Risks? I like risks." *Calculated ones*, I silently amend. "I took a big risk in moving to London and another moving here." Even as I say this, a prickle of unease creeps up my neck. Am I being dishonest? And to Chrissy or myself? "Look, you've worked for this family for a long time, right? And your family before you?"

"Aye."

"Can you think of one instance where a Dalforth has gotten himself engaged or taken a wife from somewhere other than his own sphere? His own world?"

"Aye. The tenth duke," she says a touch smug. "He married an American!"

"An heiress, I'm guessing?" My love of historical drama and romance novels pays off yet again.

"Well, aye, but—"

"Someone bred into the role, not a teacher—a nanny." I tap a finger to my chest. "Not a girl who works the checkout at a grocery store, or a nurse, or a—"

"It doesn't matter who you are. Not these days."

"I don't think that's true."

"I think the Duchess of Mreeth might disagree. She lives with her former gardener after she divorced the duke."

"Really?" I feel my expression twist.

"Aye, and Mr. McCain was saying as how the king of one of the Asian countries married his bodyguard not too long back."

"Well..."

"O' course, Dougal did say it was maybe because the king was frightened of her, with her being the bodyguard and all. She might've strong-armed him."

"Have you all been talking about this? About me?"

"We only want to see him happy," she says, pulling a thoroughly unimpressed face. "And if you make him happy—"

"No." I hold up both of my hands. I'm not having this discussion. Even if it would be easy to love him. I mean, I'm sure he wouldn't make it easy. He'd probably drive me insane, and—*no*. I'm not going there. "We aren't suited. That's all there is to say."

"Maybe that's all you have to say about it," she says half under her breath. "I dare say he'll have a fair bit more to say on the subject just yet." She glances back at me innocently. "Well, he's nothing if not dedicated."

If by dedicated, she means insulting, annoying, and just plain persistent, then maybe she's right. I turn back to the task I'd begun before she came into the kitchen.

He also looked hurt as well as annoyed. I push away the thought.

"That looks like a wee picnic," she says, coming to look over my shoulder.

"Yeah. I'm taking the boys down to the stream." Isla had suggested I close the education center early, and I'd offered to hang out with the boys after school. I won't get many more opportunities to do so. I don't want to leave with Hugh still upset. "Or at least, that's the plan. I guess it depends on what the peacock is up to."

"It'll be packed wi' tourists down there." Her expression twists doubtfully.

"We could go somewhere else, I guess. But the maze and

the formal gardens will be busy on a warm day like this, too."

"Go to the family gardens. Have you been into the secret garden?"

"Well, no," I admit. But part of the point of this outing was for me to be seen with Griffin again. *If he turns up*, I think, glancing at the digital clock on the wall oven. I don't particularly want to have tourists gawking at us, but I do want to be seen. Seen by someone, in particular, I mean.

"It's up to you," she says. "If you change your mind, the key is downstairs in the castle kitchen, hanging inside the pantry."

What am I thinking! Chrissy knowing where we're going is enough to make this a topic of conversation for all in the castle.

"You know, I think the secret garden might be nice after all."

"Oh, good!" Chrissy beams. At least until Griffin saunters into the kitchen, souring her mood.

"I've come prepared!" he announces, brandishing a bottle of champagne.

"Me, too!" Swinging open the fridge door, I pull out a couple of juice boxes.

"Mimosas?" he asks, looking slightly confused.

"For us or the kids?"

"What?" He slowly lowers the champagne bottle. "What am I missing?"

"Hmm?" I keep my expression bland while internally cackling. I'd invited Griffin on a picnic. The picnic I'm taking Hugh and Archie on. I just didn't tell him his wasn't the only invitation. The fact that he's arrived with a bottle of champagne confirms that keeping quiet was a good plan. Poor Griffin. He probably thought he was looking forward to an afternoon of champagne and canoodling on a cashmere rug. Not Frisbee and a couple of rowdy kids.

"Holly!" Archie, as usual, comes bounding into the room. "Can we climb trees and chase the peacocks?"

"Do you have a death wish?" I tilt his chin and smile down at him.

"Why? Will they peck out my eyes?" he asks, pulling down his cheeks and making himself look grotesque.

"If the wind changes, you'll stay like that," Chrissy says with a laugh.

"What's he doing here?" Hugh asks, following his brother at a more sedate pace.

I turn my attention his way. "Griffin? He's coming on the picnic with us."

"Wonderful," the kid drawls, sounding a lot like his uncle.

"Yeah, right back at you," mutters the supposed adult. "I didn't realize we'd have an audience."

"To have an audience, you'd need to have something to show, laddie." I try not to laugh at Chrissy's barb as I notice she's tucking a tube of sunscreen and some linen napkins into an honest-to-goodness wicker picnic basket labelled Fortnum & Masons. *As in the bougie London department store.*

"Whatcha got there?" I ask, peeking over the lip as she slides in a few more containers.

"Chrissy always packs the best picnic," Archie announces, trying to get a look at the goodies she's adding, container after container.

"Did you bring the Frisbee?" I ask Hugh, ignoring Griffin's less than impressed expression. *That's the only action you'll be getting, my friend.*

"It's in the hall, along with the picnic blanket and a cricket bat."

"And my football!" Arch adds.

"Cricket is a game I don't know. I guess you'll have to show me." And with that, we set off for the castle kitchen to look for the keys.

The strap hinges on the old oak door creak as it's pushed open, Hugh pulling the barrel key from the lock.

"Oh, my gosh! I can see why this place is kept secret," I murmur as I step into a garden that's a profusion of color. The smell of lilies planted along the wall is almost overwhelming, a velvety mossy path leading through flowers and plants of every shape and color.

"Isn't it amazing?" I say, turning back to find Griffin grinning at me. Well, after he brings his gaze up from my ass.

"I don't think you've looked any more American than you have today."

"Like people in the rest of the world don't wear denim shorts," I retort with a scowl. But he's not spoiling this for me.

"We don't all wear baseball caps."

"Excuse me, but this is a trucker's cap." Glancing back at him, I tug on the bill. "And it's Prada, thank you very much." *Or at least the nice man at Camden Market assured me it was. Which means it isn't. But whatevs. It cost me less than twenty bucks.*

Griffin chuckles, probably resuming his view. Meanwhile, mine is soaking up all this loveliness.

The wall around the garden is at least eight feet high and looks, in part, to have supported something like a greenhouse at one time, plants twirling and twining over the bones of the derelict frame.

Foxgloves, pineapple flower, lady's mantle, chamomile, and feathery ferns run along the edges of a gravel path that leads to a patch of meadow grass surrounded by an array of trees. Something about the setting is magical. It's more like an enchanted woodland, the kind of place fairies would choose to live. We reach the meadow grass where paths spill out in all directions, some bordered with hedgerows like a miniature maze, another leading to a pond with actual water lilies. Bee's buzz and birds sing as Hugh and I pull out the picnic blanket, which might actually be cashmere, and throw it up into the air like a parachute.

"It's so beautiful in here." I stare at the view where the garden dips to provide an almost never-ending view over the rolling lawns and landscaped gardens. "So pretty." Dropping to the blanket, I stretch out my legs and turn my face to the sun, soaking up its rays like beams of sunshiny happiness. I decide the rainy weather during my first weeks was worth suffering through if it went some way to creating this spot.

"What kind of tree is that one?" Archie asks, pointing at a twelve-foot-high spiky-looking tree. Hugh, meanwhile, heads off with a soccer ball. A football?

"That's a monkey tree."

"Do you think monkeys live in it?"

"No," I say with a chuckle. "At least, not in Scotland. Haven't you visited this place before?" I ask as I begin to unpack the food. It looks like Chrissy has packed us a feast, which certainly puts my hastily constructed PB&J to shame.

"Yes, but not since last year. And last year, I was only five, which isn't really old enough to appreciate something like this." Sometimes this kid sounds like a little old man. A little old man with a hungry stomach, judging by the way he watches me as I empty the contents of the basket, his eyes lighting up as I pull out container after container, pulling the top from each as I do so.

Eco-friendly bamboo containers. No Tupperware for these kiddos.

Crackers. A wedge of Scottish brie. A tub of preserved figs. Raspberries. Goat's cheese tartlets. Herby sausage rolls—

"Yum! Eww, is that fly graveyard?"

"Is it what?" I ask, turning the container around and staring into it. Inside is a pastry slice with sugar sprinkled on the top.

"Fly graveyard," Hugh says, dropping his knees to the edge of the blanket. "I love that stuff!" His hand sneaks into the container, whipping out a corner of the pastry and shoveling it into his mouth.

"But why is it called fly graveyard?" I ask, peering into the container and swatting away a curious wasp. And why would anyone want to eat something that sounds as unappetizing as that?

"Because of this, see?" Speaking through a mouthful of pastry, Hugh holds out his index finger where a single currant and a few stray crumbs sit. "It looks like a dead fly, doesn't it?"

"That's gross, Hugh!" I complain, though I'm less grossed out by the currant on his finger than I am about the pastry and fruit he's swilling around his mouth.

"Disgusting," Griffin agrees, popping the champagne cork over the nearby flower beds. "Who names a cake something like that? Bloody mental Scots," he complains.

"Hey, I'm a Scot!" Archie shouts... sounding anything but Scottish. "And that's littering!"

"Nah," Griffin answers. "Cork is biodegradable."

"You're half Scottish, too." Hugh glowers Griffin's way.

"Scots. They're a temperamental bunch." Griffin splashes champagne into two (not plastic) glasses, the effervescent bubbles sparkling in the sunlight. He reaches over to a tub of raspberries, plucking a few between his fingertips before dropping a couple into each glass. "That's half temper and half mental."

"You're really just calling yourself," Archie says sagely.

"Can we play Frisbee now, Holly?" Archie asks around a mouthful of sausage roll.

Griffin declines an invitation to play Frisbee in favor of stretching out on the blanket with his glass of champagne. I kick off my flip-flops before leading Archie and Hugh to the meadow grass, where we stand in a triangle and begin our fun but sedate game. Isn't that usually how Frisbee starts out? Nice, easy glides of the disc, aiming for each other's hands. But before long, squeals and giggles are rising through the air, the boys' throws becoming longer and increasingly sillier, leaving us diving in the long grass and pulling the disc out from tree branches and flower beds. I can't say it's *all* at the boys' instigation. Though I blame the champagne for my poor aim. I kept popping back to the blanket for a sip. It's thirsty work!

"Time out!" I shout, sliding the Frisbee under my arm. "Don't you know the aim isn't to try to chop off your opponent's head?"

"But it makes it much more fun," Hugh retorts with a grin a mile wide.

"I think it's time for refreshments."

"Your champagne is getting warm," Griffin calls.

"You mean my magic glass of champagne that never seems to fall an inch below the rim?"

Griffin is completely unabashed as I lower myself to the other side of the blanket. "It must be the magic of this place," he offers.

"It is pretty magical, isn't it?" I reply, ignoring the way his eyes roam over me. For a minute, I thought we had an affinity for the setting, not that he was being his usual suggestive self.

"It'd be even more magical if you were over here." He pats the space next to him. "Come over and let me top up your glass."

"Oh, I think you've topped it up enough already." I feel pleasantly buzzed, which is enough warning to make me change to water. "Besides, this is where the cookies are... were? My gaze slides to the most obvious culprit. Archie had returned to the blanket almost as many times as I did to my glass. *A girl's got to keep hydrated.* "Who ate all the chocolate chip cookies, I wonder?"

"Ninjas," Archie replies, as quick as a whip.

"I didn't see any ninjas about."

"Of course you didn't. They're ninjas. You're not supposed to see them."

"Here," Hugh says, proffering another bamboo tub. "Have one of these instead."

"These look like Oreos." I examine the sandwich cookie that both smells and looks better than the real thing. But I guess homemade always wins, especially when you have your own in-house chef. "Taste pretty good, too."

"Dougal made them." Archie's eyes gleam a little mischievously as Hugh offers the container to Griffin.

"Well, I helped," his big brother answers. "Would you like one, Uncle Griffin?" he asks in a tone much sweeter than I'm used to hearing from him. "Dougal only made a few of them, so there's only one each."

"Sure." Griffin reaches into the container as I take another bite of mine. "Thanks," he says before stuffing it into his mouth. Whole.

"*Gofdefek!*" Griffin heaves to his side and begins spitting out his Oreo with a hacking kind of cough. Meanwhile, the boys are rolling around with laughter.

"What did you two do?" I ask, trying to use my serious teacher voice.

"We just made Oreos with Dougal," Hugh playfully protests.

"Yes!" agrees Archie. "Then we licked the filling out and filled it with toothpaste!"

"*Bleuk!*" Griffin hurriedly reaches for his glass. I think he might mutter something uncomplimentary, but it's hard to tell with all that white foam coming from his mouth.

"Toothpaste doesn't foam."

No," Hugh agrees between guffaws, "but it does if you mix a bit of Alka Seltzer in."

Griffin eventually stops foaming. And fuming. And after the least sincere apology ever, he settles back into a somewhat easy-going mood. Though that might be the hip flask of whisky he's brought along.

"It's a little early, isn't it?"

"It's always five o'clock somewhere in the world." Legs bent in front of him, he rests his elbows on his knees. He offers me the flask in a negligent fashion.

I shake my head. "Are you okay?" I ask, thinking back to the phone call I'd overheard and his dejected tone. Despite the porn-worthy moans, I don't think it's girlfriend trouble.

"I've got a spot of trouble at work," he replies, not meeting my eye. "Nothing I can't handle."

"Anything I can do to help?"

A slow grin grows across his face.

"Yeah, anything but that."

"This is seeming very one-sided, Holly. I'm meeting my side of this bargain, but you're not doing as we agreed."

"What exactly did we agree?" I fix my attention on the boys currently kicking a soccer ball around.

"That you would be open to my attention. To my wooing of you."

"Woo?" My head swings back, my reply a touch incredulous. "I mean, have you started? I guess I must've missed it."

"I didn't realize you were expecting grand overtures."

I clamp my lips together because my first instinct is to tell him he'd never best the master of overtures. Of gambits. Of smoldering looks. Of exquisite touches.

"I obviously need to up my game."

"I never said I'd be open to anything. I'm leaving soon, remember?"

"I'm not after your hand in marriage, love. Just your knickers in my hand when I leave your room."

"I never said—"

"Whoa! Hold your horses. I'm not the villain here." He chuckles, pressing his right hand over his heart. "I wasn't expecting you to lie back and grit your teeth as a form of payback. I'm not that desperate," he adds witheringly. "I just expected you to be a little more open to the attraction between us."

"Griffin—"

"Or what the hell am I doing this for?"

"To annoy your brother, I guess. To get one up on him."

"Oh, Holly." He presses his palms behind him, leaning back and tipping his head to the sky. "Do you really think he believes our little charade?" He turns his head and opens one eye. "If anything, I just look like a bigger prick than usual to him right now."

"If you think I'm the kind of woman who'll sleep with brothers—"

"You wouldn't be the first."

"It'd be a first time for me!" I protest.

"But not for Alexander," he seems to mutter.

"Is that what this is between you two?" I ask suddenly. "Did he sleep with a girlfriend of yours? Is that where the atmosphere comes from?"

"No." He tilts his head to the sky again with a deep exhalation. "Forget I said anything."

"May I have some juice, Holly?" Archie settles himself next to me and shoots Griffin a wary smile.

"How about water, instead?" It's not really a suggestion as I hand him a bottle of mineral water. "You're going a little pink." Reaching behind me, I grab his Batman bucket hat and pop it onto his head.

"Do you know, I love trees," he says, wiping away droplets of water with the back of his hand. "They're so... majestic."

"That they are," I agree. "Especially the very old ones."

"Uncle Sandy says some of the cedar trees on the front lawn are more than three hundred years old. That's really old, isn't it?"

"There's a yew tree in Wales that's said to be five thousand years old," interrupts Griffin."

"Wow!" The little boy's eyes widen like saucers. "Did you know trees are good for us, Holly? And not just because they made us happy and give us wood."

"I do love things that give us wood." Tilting his dark sunglasses, Griffin stares suggestively over the top at me. "Wood makes me very happy."

"Then you must love trees, too," Archie says.

"He wasn't talking about that kind of wood," Hugh mutters disapprovingly, coming to sit next to his brother. His fair hair is damp with perspiration and sticking to his head in some places and standing up in tufts in others.

"Hugh, what kind of bird do you think that is?" I ask, pointing at one swooping overhead. If in doubt, distract.

"You're not supposed to know about stuff like that," Griffin mumbles.

"I am almost nine," the boy retorts.

"And he goes to an all-boys school. And as we know, boys are, by and large, gross."

"I'm not gross." Archie's little face is a picture of indignation.

"Of course you're not. I meant other boys, obviously. And Griffin."

"Take that back," the man growls, launching himself at me, flattening me half against the blanket and half against the grass. I squeal and kick out as he grabs my hands in one of his and begins to tickle me viciously. Let's face it, tickling is always vicious. All those poking and pinching fingertips and being made to laugh against your will. *Or better judgement.*

"This is what you get for laughing at me earlier," he growls, clearly entertained at his form of payback.

"I. Didn't." My head flails from side to side, my words breathless.

"I think I've changed my mind about you lying back and gritting your teeth," he murmurs darkly. I gasp as his attentions move under the hem of my T-shirt. "I quite like the view from here."

I can hear the boys complaining, and I think Hugh might even go as far as to pull on Griffin's belt loops in an attempt to pull him off. But I can't help—I can't do anything but gasp and wheeze and flail.

"Get. Off!"

His eyes suddenly gleam, intent on mine as he pauses for the first time in his torture. "You've changed your mind."

"What?" My chest heaves between us. It doesn't go unnoticed by him.

"You want me to get off? Right here? Over you?"

"Eww! You know that's not what I mean." I pull on my arms and buck up from underneath.

His groan is a little less than PG despite our audience. "You know that's what I do for a living, right? Get people off. I'm really good at it."

"You're really—"

"Aaaarrgh!"

"Oof!" Suddenly, I'm Griffin-less, and the sun is beating down on me once more. My gaze cuts right at the sound of a terrible groan.

Griffin's face is the color of pickled beetroot. Well, from what I can see from where he's curled in a fetal position. His hand cupped between his legs, he groans again.

"Because I'm a ninja!" yells Archie, waving the cricket bat above his head.

"No," Hugh hurriedly adds, his gaze darting from Griffin to me. "He means he saw a wasp."

39

ALEXANDER

"If you want my advice—"

"Which I don't recall asking for," I retort. Switching my phone to the loudspeaker, I'm decidedly uninterested in what Van has to say on the matter.

"But you're getting it anyway. Free of charge."

I lean back in my chair and stare at the office ceiling as I begin drumming my fingers against the surface of my desk.

"Are you trying to deafen me?" Van drawls.

"Would it shut you up?" I sit forward again and glare at my study door. "Because where women are concerned, your advice is like verbal junk mail."

"And you're such an expert. Do I need to remind you who called whom?"

"I asked you to get me a woman," I growl, my attention flicking to the partially open door as I wonder if those were footsteps. *Unfortunately, no.* "I didn't invite you to comment on my life." Where the fuck is he getting his information, anyway?

"You want me to *get* you a woman."

"That sounded worse than it is." Even if he does keep high-end call girls on staff.

"But in essence, that's what you asked for."

"I don't need a woman to fuck, Van. I need a pretty ornament for my arm." Because I'll be damned if I have to watch Holland and Griffin's great romance pretense without having a shield of my own this coming Saturday. What's good for the goose is good for the gander, or should that be the other way around?

"According to Isla, you haven't sat the girl down to have a proper conversation with her. She says you've just been chasing her around like a randy dog. Trying to hump her leg and feeling her up in dark corners."

"Since when have you and Isla been bosom buddies?" I find myself frowning down at my phone. While it answers where he's getting his information, it opens up another can of worms. A can of worms I don't have the bandwidth for.

"Because she's worried about you."

"I'm sure I've given her cause for concern many times, but I don't recall her seeking your advice."

"And the Duke of Dalforth sees himself as God," he intones as though narrating the soundtrack to the story of my life. "Omnipotent. All-seeing. The supreme being rules over us all. Or so he likes to think."

"Van, answer the question. Are you and my sister—?"

"Do you think if the answer were yes that this would be how you would come to know? That I'd tell you over the phone?"

"No. I suppose not." Van would have the balls, the decency, to come to me first. Probably. "Although Kilblair does house a weaponry."

"But it's mostly ancient."

"An ancient mace works as good as a new one. Probably

better. And there are any number of guns. We might have us an old-fashioned hunting accident."

"Not with a mace." He chuckles.

"No," I agree. "There are tidier ways to kill a deer."

"And a friend? But back to your woman troubles."

"I don't have woman troubles. Or I won't. Not if you bring me one." Van has his employees sign airtight NDAs. I wouldn't risk asking him otherwise. I certainly wouldn't go elsewhere. "Just be a good friend."

"And procure you a woman? What's wrong with Portia?" he adds in a rare sign of frustration.

"I need someone who can act. Someone who can pretend to like me."

"That does exclude her. She did only like your title."

"Are you done playing, or should I bend over so you can really fuck me?"

"You're not my type. But you know who just might be?" For a moment, I think he might say Isla. And then we'd really have a problem. "Holland."

I manage a dry laugh even as my lunch turns to cement in my stomach. "Very funny."

"Isla says she's worth ten of your usual type. That she's genuine."

"Isla says, does she? Of course, she must be right." I rake a hand through my hair. I didn't expect the conversation to go this way. "So what sage advice did my sister issue? That I should just get on my knees and profess my ardent admiration? Let me tell you, I have been on my knees"—I fucking worshipped her—"and it didn't help."

"Perhaps you need to use your words, not just your mouth."

"Let me handle my own life. You're going to the Duffy's'

party, so bring me a girl in a fancy fucking dress. I promise I won't even touch her."

"If you're paying for her, you can touch her."

"But I don't want to touch her," I explain patiently. Or snap.

"Paying for it will be all that's left if you do this. Women don't like being played."

Neither do men. Neither do dukes.

But that hasn't stopped Holland.

"You're going to fuck this up and let this girl slip through your fingers. I guarantee it."

"I don't need relationship advice from a degenerate."

"At least I know how to enjoy life, and I'm not frightened to live it. To take chances."

"You live in an ivory tower. Rarely do you deign to join the rest of the world."

"More and more lately, I find myself doing so. Living, I think it's called. Taking a little something for myself."

"I don't need this existential bullshit." Almost jumping from my seat, I stalk over to the window for the fifth time this afternoon. When Isla had let it slip that Holland had taken the boys for a picnic, I'd expected to be able to see them from this window. A bucolic scene from a bygone era. A picnic rug under the shade of the cedars, Holland in a sundress, and my brother lounged out like some petulant aristocrat. There would be no footmen in striped waistcoats or tea served from silver pots, but there would be a show. After all, Holland was to be its director.

But there has been no sign of them. Perhaps Holland came to her senses and decided an afternoon with my brother was a fate not worth the payoff. But if it's all pretend, why am I so agitated?

Because she's not yours, my mind whispers, *because Holland is a prize you want to keep, not spoil.*

And you don't trust him.

"Existential. Exactly," Van replies, bringing me back to the phone call. "I have found myself to be out of touch with the world, which is why I've sought to re-join it. So, who knows. Maybe I will find out for myself." His tone is like an incitement.

"Find out?"

An incitement to violence, judging by his next words.

"What all the fuss is about." The heavy pause allows my mind to fire up a dozen scenarios, and none of them pleasant. "Why your sister speaks so highly of her. Why you're so keen not to tie yourself to her."

"You don't know what you're talking about."

I've tried—I have fucking tried.

"I hear it's likely she'll return to London. I could look her up when she gets here. You know, when she slips through your fingertips."

I say nothing because I've just decided she won't be moving back to London, not even if I have to bribe someone in the immigration department to cancel her visa and send her home. If I'm not good enough for Holland, there is no way on God's green earth Van is.

"I could be her shoulder to cry on. Did I ever tell you I have a thing for crying girls?"

Pressing my forehead against the cool glass, I try to ignore the goading of my degenerate friend. My mind takes that inopportune moment to remind me of how Holland looks, though not when she's crying. How she looks breathless with laughter, her head thrown back, thoroughly immersed in the moment. Or perhaps it's the reminder isn't so much about how joyful she looks but rather how it made me feel, knowing her joy was my responsibility. That I had made her feel that way.

As for her tears, I never want to see her cry because of something I've done. I never want to look at her face and see tears of recrimination.

But that is inevitable if she's ever to become mine.

I find for the first time, I really don't give a damn.

Because the truth never stays buried forever. Like all rotten things, it eventually bloats and comes bobbing to the surface.

~

HOLLY

"He is such a pussy," Hugh mutters, kicking a patch of longer grass at the edge of the path.

"I'm going to pretend I didn't hear that." Mostly because I've had enough of men this afternoon—big and small men. "But, I promise, if I hear anything like that from your mouth ever again, I'm gonna tell Chrissy. I hear she has a special soap for washing potty mouths."

Oh, man, my head aches, and it's not the aftereffects of the champagne.

"It's not fair. Archie wasn't supposed to hit him in the nuts. I thought he might've hit him on the butt!"

Well, he didn't. And now Griffin is back at the castle with two ibuprofen and a cold compress between his legs, which, if he's to be believed, should be on his throat because that's where his testicles are currently lodged. What's more, I almost had to carry him back there myself. No wonder my arms ache as I struggle back to the castle like a pack mule balancing the majority of the picnic stuff, including the basket and the empty bottle of champagne.

I should probably chastise Hugh for using nuts in that context. To heck with it, I choose not to pick this as one of my battles right now. Bad enough that I had to lump that great oaf back with a tearful Archie tagging along behind us, but then I had to explain the whole thing to Isla, and then go back to the scene of the crime and lug back all this stuff!

"Archie is six," I say, swinging to face the kid, almost dropping the cricket bat in the process. "You shouldn't have told him to hit Griffin with the cricket bat, and then you wouldn't be complaining because there would be no punishment. And anyway, why am I carrying the weapon? Here!" I thrust it at him. "You carry it."

"It still sucks."

"If you do the crime, you've got to be prepared to do the time."

"But I didn't mean—"

"It was your idea, Hugh."

And the punishment was their mother's. Archie is currently banished to his room "to think on his behavior and summon a suitable apology". Hugh, meanwhile, has been sentenced to an afternoon digging over Chrissy's weed-plagued vegetable patch.

It was Hugh's idea, wasn't it? Only he doesn't look so contrite. Aside from the Oreo prank, which I thought was very funny myself, Hugh is pretty upstanding for a kid.

"You did say you told Archie to hit him, right?"

"No. I mean, yes. But Uncle Sandy said—" The kid's mouth clamps immediately closed. Then with a superior look I've seen adopted by a much older inhabitant of this castle, he hikes both cricket bat and picnic blanket higher in his arms and picks up his pace, speeding past me.

"Uncle Sandy said what?" I say, hurrying after him.

"Nothing. I misspoke."

"I wonder if Chrissy has soap for little liars, too."

"Uncle Sandy didn't do anything. I told Archie to hit Griffin."

"You brought up his name, not me," I say, getting in front of him. "Did he tell you to hurt Griffin?"

"No!" Hugh comes to a sudden stop, the indignation in his tone telling me that this is probably the truth.

"What about the Oreos? Whose idea was that?"

"Mine." He tilts his chin higher, like the little lordling he is. "I saw it on YouTube. And he deserved it. He's nothing but mean to Uncle Sandy."

"Uncle Sandy is big enough to fight his own battles."

"That doesn't mean I shouldn't stand up for him, especially as he does so much for me—and Archie. He taught me to ride my bike and a pony. He takes us on outings and holidays. He lets us ride our skateboards in the portrait gallery, he doesn't tell us to be quiet when we want to speak, and he never looks at us like we're a nuisance, like he wishes we were never born! He likes us, Holly. Likes us more than our father does." As Hugh speaks, his bottom lip trembles, words spilling with such emotion. "So, if he had asked me to hit Griffin with the cricket bat, I would have. I would've hit him hard because Uncle Sandy is a good man and... and..." He drops the blanket and bat and makes as though to bolt past me when I catch his arm.

"Hugh, it's okay."

He ducks his head, unwilling to let me see the sudden spill of tears as I pull him against me and wrap my arms around his trembling shoulders.

"It'll be okay. An afternoon digging weeds isn't such a

harsh punishment," I murmur, smoothing my hand over his back.

"It's not about the punishment," he mutters between halting breaths. "Uncle Sandy asked us to keep an eye out for you, to make sure you were safe. And Griffin was behaving like my father, ignoring us when we told him to move. You told him to get off, too, and he didn't listen, and w-we were supposed to be looking after you." Through a tangle of words and worries, Hugh presses his tearful face to my chest, letting weeks of emotions tumble out.

Hugh's sobs calm to little hiccups and those little hiccups to sniffles eventually. We drop the blanket to the path and cop a squat for an impromptu chat. He knows his parents are heading for a divorce, and that's a lot to process for a kid of eight years old. I tried to do what I could. I told him that his parents would always love him and his brother and that though things might be changing, that never would. I agreed Griffin was a bit of an asshole, which at least raised a smile. But other than that, I'm not sure he took much else onboard. Then once he'd dried his tears, he'd pretty much clammed up like a shell.

Men!

40

HOLLY

I SEND HUGH ALONG AHEAD OF ME WHEN MY PHONE BEGINS TO ring with a call from Kennedy. Poor signal prevents the call from connecting, and after a half dozen variants of "Hello? Can you hear me? Dang phone." and "I can't hear you." I hang up and send her a text.

> What Scotland lacks in phone signal, it makes up for in beauty. Everything okay?

> Yep, just checking in. I'll try again later.

comes her immediate reply.

> Yeah, like on the weekend you next remember.

Kennedy has a terrible memory.

> You can call me, you know. The thing in your hand makes outgoing calls, too.

> Also, Wilder says please send more shortbread.

I'd sent a tin of the Walkers shop-bought stuff, which isn't nearly as yummy as the kind made in the castle kitchen. But I won't tell her that because it would be cruel.

> Tell rug rat roger that.

I'm just about to slide my phone into my pocket—and pick up my mountain of picnic stuff—when I notice a bank of clouds coming over the hills. In the shadow of silver and grey, the heather seems to take on an almost eerie appearance. Wild but also kind of magical. This part of Scotland is certainly all those things and more. And talk about four seasons visiting in one day, I think, as I peel away hair suddenly glued to my cheek. Clouds and the wind picking up? Maybe we're due for a storm.

I pull out my phone and snap a couple of images of the rolling clouds, the drama of the weather demanding not to be ignored. I shiver as the cool air whips across my bare legs and consider how there's little wonder in the fact that whisky is so popular in these parts and how I could do with a *wee nip* right now to warm my bones. Swooping down to gather the picnic things, I start.

"Here, let me get that."

"Oh!" Hand flat to my chest, I stand and meet the brilliant blue eyes of Alexander. "You gave me a fright. I didn't see you there." Although my words sound a little harsh, something inside me blooms. I know it's wrong, but I can't be held responsible for my body's responses. My hands go to the back of my head instinctively. I must look a mess. My trucker's cap is Lord knows where, lost in the ruckus of Griffin's swollen testes, leaving my ponytail half falling out and as low as a founding father's.

And we all know they weren't what you'd call fashion-forward.

"You were too busy taking a photograph... of the hills?" The expression he's wearing is one I haven't seen on him before. Is that caution I'm looking at? "Sorry, I didn't mean to disturb you, but I just saw Hugh. He thought you could do with a hand."

I don't think Hugh was in any mood to think of anyone or anything when he left me, but it would be petty of me to say so. *He could probably do with a little time alone to process, the poor little guy.*

"Thank you." Maybe I shouldn't be speaking to him at all, given what happened last time we were alone, but I can't seem to bring myself to be angry. "I was taking a photograph of the hills, thinking how beautiful they are when the weather is like this."

"*Beinn a' Bhathaich Àrd.*"

"*Gesundheit,*" I answer with a quizzical smile.

"It's what the big one, the mountain is called." His smile spreads through my insides like that *wee nip* of whisky. "It's not the most impressive mountain in the Highlands, but it's beautiful nonetheless."

But he's not looking at the mountain now. He seems to catch himself then, bending to gather the picnic detritus.

"Let me help." I reach for the cricket bat as he slides it deftly under his arm.

"You can get the bottle, if you want." He means the empty champagne bottle. "I see Griffin must've talked McCain into loaning him the key to the cellar."

"If he shouldn't have—"

"Did you have a pleasant afternoon?" he asks, changing the subject. His tone is uncharacteristically mild. "Is something funny?"

"No, nothing." I duck my head, hiding my lingering smile. For some reason, I feel like skipping. Maybe just because he's here. Or maybe because of the way he's behaving, like he's making some concession. Or trying to, at least.

I know it's ridiculous. Except for the bit about him trying. Because Lord knows the man is trying.

"Yes, I had a very pleasant afternoon, thank you. Although it did turn a little disastrous toward the end."

"How so?"

"Hugh didn't tell you?" My gaze slices his way. "You haven't seen Griffin?"

"No?" The way his brows twitch together suggests he's telling the truth. Plus, I guess Hugh wasn't exactly chatty Cathy when he left, and Griffin is probably still rolled in a ball somewhere.

"Well, I'll just let them tell you all about it."

"Was the photograph for your Instagram page?" he asks, directing the conversation back to me. "Isla says you have quite the following."

I find myself immediately on the defense. "I haven't posted anything about the castle. Nothing to link me to being here."

"That's not why I'm asking, Holland. It's true I don't relish the idea of finding my face on your Instagram page, but—you're laughing again. You don't think I'm photogenic enough?"

"No, that's not it." I try to fight my amusement, thinking about the one photograph of him I did take back in London. *Where this madness began.* It seems like a lifetime ago. "I promise, I haven't posted any photographs of you. Or your family."

"An interesting distinction," he murmurs. "Posted versus taken."

"Huh. So you do know social media." If my words sound arch in their delivery... well, good.

"I'm not a relic." His mouth quirks, his gaze slicing my way at the same moment as a huge drop of rain splats against his cheek. He lifts one laden arm, wiping the tiny stream of water away with the back of his wrist as he glances up at the sky. "We'd better make a run for it," he says, his eyes widening in surprise. "It's about to really come down."

"But—" That's as far as I get before a crack of thunder sounds. then the heavens open, and rain begins to lash down. I squeal a little as raindrops seemingly the size of golf balls begin to hammer my head and jog after Alexander.

So much for him doing the gentlemanly thing.

"I told you we were about to get a soaking." His eyes dance as he glances over his shoulder at me. "Come on, this way!"

While never the best thing to run in, my flip-flops are more flip-*flaps* at this point, the moisture making it increasingly difficult to get any traction. I kick them off, grabbing them up from the ground, and continue in Alexander's wake. Sweeping the fallen wet strands of my hair, I watch as he cuts across the grass, heading to what looks like an abandoned building built from grey stone and kind of ramshackle from this vantage point.

"Oh, my!" I'm breathless and shivering as I step between a row of columns that support a rickety-looking roof. "How is the rain so cold? It had to be nearly eighty degrees out this afternoon."

"The clouds will have come in over the North Sea." Alexander puts down the basket, pointing vaguely over his shoulder. "Norway is just that way."

I fail to overpower a shiver as I place the bottle down and fold my arms over my chest. *And not just to hide my chilled nipples.* "What is this place?" I swing around, feeling his eyes on me and liking it more than I should.

"It's a folly, I suppose you'd call it. Romanesque. Or at least, that's what the intention was. You're freezing." He comes up almost silently behind me, his hands resting on my upper arms. "I don't have a jacket to offer you this time."

You could offer me your shirt, I don't say as he begins to slide his hands up and down vigorously.

"I have an admission to make." I keep my eyes ahead. Turning to face him would only make trouble. "What we were talking about before the rain. I might've snapped a quick pic." I take a cautious glance his way. "Of you, I mean."

He doesn't answer, though his hands slow.

"That night in London. I took it while you weren't looking. It was to send to my sister just in case, in her words, you might've had it in mind to practice your taxidermy skills on me."

Alexander's laughter reverberates off the stone walls, his hands falling away. Judging it safe to do so, I turn. I don't want to miss this because the man is pretty when he gives in to spontaneous amusement.

"And if you say anything about stuffing," I add, "remember I have an empty champagne bottle."

"I wouldn't dream of saying such a thing."

"Uh-huh." I just about manage to refrain from mentioning his jam/jelly moment comment, obviously. Besides, he's not hitting on me but instead being companionable.

Like friends?

I ignore the pinch in my chest, forcing a bright smile to my face.

"Don't get bigheaded. I deleted it afterward."

"You didn't keep it? To remember me by?"

Is it still a lie if you don't speak? I did delete it. And not five minutes later, I moved it out of the virtual trash and back into my saved images.

But I'm not admitting that.

"Well, I know it didn't appear on your Instagram page."

I narrow my gaze. "You've seen it?"

"I may have visited."

I don't know whether to be happy about that or not.

"It has a very attractive aesthetic," he says consideringly. "Though I must admit to not quite knowing what the purpose of Instagram is. I see the benefit for business, of course. And for those who want to share their life with their friends, but you're not in your posts very much. Obviously, the words are very you. But there's a distinct lack of images of Holland Harper."

"There are some."

"If there were more, you might have even more followers."

My cheeks begin that telltale sting as I bluster on. "Well, people like the platform for all kinds of reasons. It can be very pretty."

"True. But so are you. And I don't desire sharing you with the world." My heart makes a little pitter-pat. So maybe we haven't moved on quite as much as all that. "What's your aim?" he asks suddenly. "What is it you aspire to? A million followers and a deluge of free stuff?"

"Like sponsorship?" I scrunch my nose. "I mean, who would say no to free stuff? But that's not it. I just like it. I guess I must be a very visual person." His eyes seem to track over my face, and I find myself hurrying on, not sure what I'm saying but the words spilling anyway. "The beauty of the visual. And I aspire to travel more. And yes, I like owning nice things, and if they're free, then I'm not going to turn them down."

"You want people to envy you." He stares down at my bare feet, a frown marring his brow. "For women to covet your life. For men to desire you?"

"Now who's making assumptions?" I answer brightly, spinning away and opening my arms. "Everyone has Instagram. Facebook. Some form of social media."

"Not everyone."

"The castle has social media," I retort, turning to face him again but from a distance. "Maybe I'm just vain. Maybe I want people to know I'm in Scotland and having a fabulous time."

"And are you?" he asks almost haltingly. "Having a good time?"

I find his concern strangely endearing, which I guess should be weird, given his recent behavior.

"Instagram doesn't have to be about the truth," I hedge. It's certainly not why I post. I tell people I left Portland because I wanted to travel, but the truth is, I needed to be as far away from there as possible. So here I am, far from home. A whole different person with the Instagram account to prove it.

"I've been thinking," he says. His eyes are so blue as he lifts them to study me. "About a lot of things, but particularly about what you said in my study the other day."

When he threatened to tongue-fuck you senseless, my mind whispers, causing my insides to tighten in a thoroughly treacherous way.

"You said that you would never become involved with someone you work for."

"Yeah, I did," I answer, forcing myself to hold his gaze. "What about it?"

"It made me wonder about your past." He takes a step to the right, which is really a step closer, resting his shoulder against the stone wall, sliding his hands under his arms. It's such a casual stance, though something tells me that's not how he's feeling at all. "Did something happen to you? Where you worked before?"

"Maybe that's just a rule I have. You have rules too, remember?"

"Holland." He drops his head with a deep sigh, the rumble of my name almost disappointed. "My rules went up in flames the night I held you in my arms. The second night," he qualifies, his head coming up sharp. His eyes burn blue in the gloaming light. "Rules are, after all, made to be broken."

"Not this one." I can't believe I'm saying this when my body aches for his. I find it so hard to tear my gaze away, but I force myself to do it anyway.

Because what choice do I have?

"Am I allowed to ask why?"

I could tell him a beautiful lie. Or I could tell him the ugly truth.

"I fell in love with the wrong man." I shrug. It sounds so ridiculous. How could I ever have loved someone like him? "And yes, that's why I left Oregon. Like the saying goes, a tale as old as time."

"You worked for him?"

"Not like this." Not as a nanny or whatever I am here at the castle. It didn't feel like this either. This all-consuming experience. I'd never once feared I'd be burned back then. "He was the principal of the school I worked at. When we broke up—actually, no," I say with a hard-sounding laugh.

"When he dumped me a week before our wedding, I not only ended up alone but I also ended up jobless."

"You were going to be married?"

"Mm-hmm." I thought that's what I wanted.

"And he fired you?"

I shake my head. I could've looked for a transfer and moved to another school, but none of that seemed far enough away from the looks and questions. From my humiliation. It's strange because I've been over him for a long time. What I'm not over is how the experience left me.

"I couldn't go back to work the next week as though nothing had happened. Never mind about my dress or the venue or that my sister had to call around and tell everyone. I was supposed to show up in class and smile at him over the coffee pot in the staff room? Nope. That was never going to happen."

"So you left. You left your family and your home."

"I couldn't stay after that. So, yeah, I guess I ran away." It all sounds so simple. I ran away from the man who jilted me. But it was running away from more than just him. I was running away from myself, from the failure I saw as my own. I could barely stand to be around me, and I certainly couldn't stand the thoughts rolling through my head. My family has always endured some level of trash talk, and I hated how I'd given the gossips something else to talk about. I didn't want to be around to see their fake pity, knowing all the while I'd given my family more airtime.

I knew it wouldn't last.

He was too good for her anyway.

Like mother, like daughter.

Well, screw all that.

"I'm sorry you had to go through that."

"I guess I lost myself for a while, and I didn't want to be

the person people thought I was. But I wasn't heartbroken, so I know he did the right thing." Alexander continues to watch me. I fall quiet, wondering why this has only occurred to me now. I was using him as a shield. Someone to hide behind. Someone to make me seem like someone else.

"Holland." Alexander reaches out, his fingers ghosting my bare arm as though he's afraid to touch me right now. The sky is so dark and the wind so wild. I wonder if the land possessed the personality of its owner or if it was actually the other way around.

"I'm fine," I protest. "He did me a favor because I've seen so much more of the world than I ever expected to. I went to London to..." *Have some fun*, my mind says. Though my mouth says something much worse. "To reinvent myself."

"The Holland I know is perfect."

"Which just goes to show you don't really know me at all." I glance down at the grass stain on my left knee and absently swipe my hand against it.

"I'm trying to know you. I want to."

"Don't." I study the chipped nail polish on my big toe. If I can't keep the principal of a rural middle school, how the hell could I keep a duke? "Please, just... don't."

Don't tempt me.

You'll only break me.

And my heart couldn't take that.

"I think this is the most honest conversation we've had," his low tone rumbles.

"Ours hasn't been a connection of words." I wince immediately at how that sounded and glance out at the hammering rain so he can't see my lie.

"I wish I'd done as Isla suggested, insisted really, when I'd discovered you here."

"You mean you wish you'd left." I don't know if that

would've been better or worse. But when he nods, my heart gives a painful pang, and I discover I already know.

"I don't mean how you think. If I'd left, I could've come back periodically. Weekends perhaps. I could've given us time to get to know one another better. Perhaps you would've been surer of me then." His eyes drink me in, but somehow, the set of his mouth seems reflective. "It might've worked for you," he adds, "but for me, there was only one way to go once I found you in my path again."

As the saying goes, the only path is through.

To push through until we burned to an inevitable end, I guess.

"Something else that's been bothering me about what you said. That you aren't my type." Our eyes lock, and I watch as his expression seems to flit through a range of emotions—annoyance, disbelief, disappointment, and ending in something that looks like pity. "You're so wrong, you know."

I open my mouth to protest—to remind him how he'd looked at me when I'd gripped his arm outside of the hotel in London, or maybe to say how he'd managed to resist me, not to tell me any of this, standing in that cold lane, him in his tuxedo and me in my white-frilled apron—but I don't get the chance as he sweeps my feet from under me.

"You see, Holland, your difference has been beautiful to me all along."

41

HOLLY

"I spy with my little eye, something beginning with *quwa*."

"You mean *q*," Hugh replies with the kind of superiority only an older sibling possesses.

"No, I don't," Archie protests. "I'm allowed to spell it frenetically, aren't I, Mummy? I'm only six, remember."

"It's phonetically," Isla corrects patiently, glancing at her progeny through the rear-view mirror. "And, yes, I think an allowance might be made for Archie's age, Hugh."

"Are you sure I can't have my iPad back?" he complains.

"The thing has been glued to your hand almost the entire way. Just play with your brother for a little while."

"*Fine*," he grates out, muttering, "Quality time," aggressively.

"That's the spirit," his mother replies, not sounding too impressed at his sass.

"No, that's my guess." He huffs out a hard breath. "Oh, never mind."

"The joys of travelling with children." Isla glances at me briefly as the car slows at a crossroads, and she flicks on the turning signal. "It could be worse. You could be stuck in the car with Griffin. I've heard he has a liking for classic rock."

No way was I travelling to the Duffys' residence for this birthday party with Griffin. Apart from not being in the mood to deal with him, I wasn't about to give him the opportunity to get all handsy. It's not like there's been much need to keep up the charade, but it hasn't stopped him from making those overtures. Or uttering more innuendo than *The Great British Bake Off*. I can't believe I'd been persuaded to come at all, but I guess Isla is right. It would be a shame to miss out on whatever opportunities might come up.

Besides, I wasn't about to stay behind and mope around the castle by myself. Especially when there's every chance Alexander might be there. *I can look without touching,* I tell myself.

"Griffin and classic rock," I repeat. "You're sure he's not more of a K-Pop kind of guy?" Isla's chuckle is short-lived as I ask, "What kind of music does your brother like?"

Urgh!

"Sandy?" I choose not to examine the ripple of delight in her expression. "He has quite eclectic tastes. You might find him listening to The Beatles or Simple Minds. The Strokes."

"Sometimes, he listens to boring classical music," Hugh complains. "All pianos and sadness."

"I caught him listening to The Cardigans last week." She pulls a distasteful expression as she turns the steering wheel to the right. "'Lovefool', of all things. I suppose love does make fools of us all," she adds in a tone I'm probably not meant to hear.

"I like it when he plays the song about the crying clown."

"I don't think I know that one, sweetie." Isla glances conspiratorially my way, and like a well-played guitar,

Archie launches into a tuneless rendition of "The Tears of a Clown".

Who knew? Layers. The man has hidden layers. And I am hiding my amusement with a slow shake of my head.

"He can dance too," she says.

"Yeah?" Of course he can dance. Alexander Dalforth has *all* the moves.

"I mean, he can waltz, obviously." Yeah, *obviously*. "We were forced to learn," she adds quickly by way of explanation. "But in general, he can dance. He's an excellent salsa partner, so I'm told."

I don't want to know exactly who told her and make a vague noise in answer.

It sounds like he's been holding out on me. And how did we get from the topic of my fake boyfriend's taste in music to that of the man I'm supposed to be weaning myself from?

Oh. I remember.

Me.

I blow out a long, trembling breath. Anticipation, I think. The big Hollywood birthday party. People. Happiness. Humbug. But it all pales in comparison to how I feel about seeing Alexander again.

"Are you okay?"

"Yeah. I'm just tired." I shoot her a reassuring smile. "I stayed up late last night to call my sister." And only got to speak to my nephew.

"Is everything well?"

"Yeah, fine." Apart from the thing he said about her arguing with some man. No, he said the same man. An Australian man. Which led me to think about her first year in college when she'd call home. There was a time she positively gushed about an Australian guy she had classes with. But then she came home for good, and he was never spoken of again.

A coincidence? I think not.

The boys return to their game of I Spy as Isla turns up the radio a touch before her attention turns to the long stretch of road ahead. The radio DJ drones on about something I have no interest in as I fix my eyes to the side window, watching as fields of sheep morph into heather-covered hills, tall thistles beginning to line both sides of the road. It's been a strange few days, and I feel out of sorts. Emotional, I suppose, which I've been putting down to my time in Scotland coming to an end.

Yep, that's what it is.

Nothing to do with... anything else.

As the familiar introduction to one of my nana's favorite songs spills from the Range Rover's fancy speaker system, I huff out an unhappy-sounding laugh.

Thanks, Nana. Just what I needed. I send my ironic thanks heavenward as the plucking strings section comes to an end and the late great Buddy Holly begins to croon about perfect weather and raining hearts.

My nana always did have a caustic sense of humor. And to say she swore like a sailor was an understatement. It was more like a naval fleet.

Okay, so it's been raining in my heart since the day it last rained on my head. With my sad-looking ponytail and my knees stained green and, as it turned out, more blades of grass stuck to my ass than my wet feet, Alexander told me he sees me in a way I've never been able to see myself. He saw through my bravado and pretense and told me he likes me anyway.

It's such a stupid cliché—but clichés are a thing for a reason—because it's been raining in my heart since then.

Raining in my heart and, in my private moments, raining from my eyes, the deluge of tears pouring down my cheeks.

No one has ever said such beautiful things to me, but maybe that's not why I'm crying because he didn't stop there.

"*As Chrissy likes to say, what's coming for you won't pass you by,*" Alexander had said as the rain hammered on the roof of the folly, cascading over the edges onto the grass below. He went on to say that what is meant to be will always be, regardless of what anyone wishes for. He was talking about fate. There was no avoiding the inevitable, but that it can't be forced either. He said he feared that's what he's been doing.

"*Our connection has been physical, yes. But it has also been a joining. I truly believe ours has been a meeting of both body and soul, Holland. I'd argue that our hearts have clashed, too. So, I have to trust that if you're meant to be mine, you will be. That you have your path to follow, and I should look at mine. So, to that end, I'm going to go back to London for now because I can't be here and not touch you. I think we've seen the proof of that. But I also can't be here and watch you leave. I need to look the other way and trust that if we're meant to be together, we will be someday.*"

Maybe he has the devil's tongue in more than one way.

Because it says the things I want to hear, but I'm not sure I can trust.

"Are you sure you're all right?" Isla's tone carries a world of concern, though at least it snaps me back to the moment. Tears me from the sincerity in his eyes and the feel of my hand in his.

"Yep, I'm great. Just peachy. I just have something in my eye." Rain. I have rain in my eye, that's all. I swallow over the ball of emotion swelling in my throat and turn to look at the boys in the back seat, hearing Hugh's continued bored tone.

"I have to agree with Hugh, Archie. I've been looking for something beginning with *quwa,* and I can't find it either."

"Is it outside of the car, Archie?" his mother asks.

"No, inside," he offers up, puffed up that he's besting us all. "In the front, more pacifically."

"Specifically," drawls his older brother.

"That's what I said. I bet you'll never guess it. Not in a month of Mondays!"

"Sundays," his brother says.

"But a month of Mondays sounds much worse."

"Oh, I give up," Hugh mutters harshly. "You *f-flipping* win."

"Yes!" I smile as Archie pumps his fist in the air. "I knew you'd never get it."

"Well, tell us what it is, sweetie," his mother coaxes.

"Quirky bird!" he exclaims with a big grin.

"That's not a real thing," his brother complains.

"Yes, it is," he protests. "It's what I heard Uncle Griffin calling Holland to Uncle Sandy last week."

"That sounds quite endearing." She shoots me an unsure but encouraging smile. I know she's not at all convinced about my relationship with Griffin, but she still plays along. I'm not sure why we're still doing it, to be honest.

"He also said she had a spectacular arse," the little boy adds with a grin.

"Sounds like Chrissy needs to get out her potty mouth soap."

"No! It doesn't count if you're just repeating it," Archie protests, all vigorous arms and indignant face.

I have to turn my face back to the windshield to stop him from seeing me laugh.

"I think Holland meant for Uncle Griffin," Isla says.

"Claish Castle up ahead," I say, pointing at the sign as we pass.

"About time," mutters a little voice from the back. "I'm starving."

"Has there been an accident?" an even smaller voice asks.

"No," Isla replies. "It's just a police cordon on the road out of the village. Given all the celebrities attending the party, Ivy said there would be one. It must make the Duffys very unpopular with the neighbors," she adds under her breath.

"I was reading about them before we left. On the internet," I explain. "I think because they've brought so much work into the region, most people seem only to have nice things to say. I'm sure being one-half Hollywood royalty and one-half local helps."

"Actual royalty would get short shrift," she answers tartly, slowing to a stop to speak with a policeman.

"*Paparazzi!*" Isla sounds almost impressed as we're waved through the cordon, and a smattering of cameras go off. "I wonder who'll be here tonight."

"Movie moguls and models, I should imagine." Maybe I can find a dark corner to hide. I'm *no' hackit*, as Emma or Allie would say—or in other words, I know I'm not ugly—but I'm also five feet four and a little round in the places women are supposed to be. I don't much want to feel like a cuckoo in a nest full of swans.

"Oh, my."

"Wow."

Claish Castle up ahead, and it looks like it was plucked from the pages of a book of fairy tales. Blue-grey Scottish stone gleams in the afternoon sun and sparkles from mullioned windows, conical spires reaching for the heavens.

"It makes Kilblair look ramshackle by comparison, doesn't it?"

"Absolutely not. Kilblair is much bigger."

"Size isn't everything." Isla rolls her lips inward as though she hadn't meant to say that.

"True," I find myself answering, not wanting her to feel awkward and seemingly dunking myself in a bucket of the same. "But the duke sure knows how to use it—to its best advantage, I mean. The castle," I qualify. "H-He works it really well."

"I do hope we're still talking about the castle,'" she murmurs without looking at me. Which is probably just as well as my cheeks begin to sting.

The blue gravel driveway is already lined with parked cars as we approach.

Looks like we aren't the only ones staying over.

We're directed to stop outside of the decidedly plain-looking entrance, considering the glamour of the approach. A stone archway houses a domed oak door. High above it on the next floor is a Juliet balcony carved from stone. Between the two sits a weather-beaten family crest.

"Look, Mummy. A red carpet, just like on the TV!"

Archie seems tickled by the slash of red leading to the front door where stone urns at least five feet high flank the stone archway. The urns are filled with red flowers and golden ferns.

Isla's eyebrows lift to the top of her head as though to say: *Hollywood!*

Ivy Duffy trips down the velvety carpet, her dark hair pinned in braids to the top of her head and dressed in a pair of slim-fitting jeans and a painter's smock. Arm outstretched, she seems genuinely pleased to see us. "It's so lovely to see you all again. Lady Isla," she adds, beaming.

"It's just Isla," she insists in her usual way.

Greetings and admirations are exchanged before Ivy moves her attention to me, and Isla moves hers to her sons.

"Holly, I'm so pleased you could come." Her eyes sparkle with a mixture of what seems like delight and mischief as she adds, "Though I didn't know you and the duke's brother were a thing."

"What?" How does she know? "It's kind of recent."

"I thought—well, it doesn't matter what I thought. Or maybe you could come and find me later, and I'll tell you all about my observations from our stay at Kilblair."

"Sure," I answer uncertainly because whatever she's offering is about as clear as a cup of mud.

"And you'll have to forgive me for not putting you and Griffin in a room together," she says, sliding her arm through mine and turning us in the direction of the door. "I mean, I'm no prude, but when he mentioned it when he arrived a little while ago, I apologized to him, too."

"Apologized for what?" I ask warily.

"I had to tell him I couldn't put you in a room together." She adds a tinkling laugh and an inconsequential wave of her hand. "But the rooms were allotted last week in this grand housekeeping plan and obviously made up accordingly."

"Oh, well. What can I say?" Except I'm glad. And I might kill him.

"From your expression, it looks like you'll have quite a bit to say about it. At least, when you see the man himself."

"I think I might find one or two words for him." Rude ones.

At the door, Ivy directs us to follow a pair of guys in khakis and polo shirts to our rooms as she turns to greet more arriving guests. Isla and the boys are in the suite a couple of doors down from mine, though as the boys are quick to point out, they'll actually be sleeping in Alistair's playroom tonight in tepee-style tents.

"After a quick refresh, and I'll take them to find the nanny," Isla says.

"Do you want me to do it?"

She waves the offer away. "No, that's fine. They're about to explode with excitement, so I should probably do it soon." She turns in the direction of her room, where the boys are almost hopping with anticipation at the already open door.

"Hurry up, Mummy," Archie complains.

"Oh, Isla?" She half turns as I call out to her. "I forgot to say thank you for the dress. It really is beautiful." Too beautiful for a loaner, that's for sure. "I'll have it dry cleaned during the week and—"

"I'm sorry, Holly, but I don't know what you're talking about."

"There was a garment bag left on my bed yesterday. I thought—we spoke about it, didn't we?"

"I got the impression it was all taken care of," she says, taking two steps closer. "And now I feel awful because I don't know what you're talking about."

"My bad," I reply. "Sorry. Don't worry about it."

"Perhaps Griffin…"

"Yeah, that must be it." And now I feel uncomfortable. *Griffin bought me a dress?*

I guess that's a conversation we need to have.

Dress = good deed ≠ sex

Maybe that's why he thought to wrangle a room together. Kudos to Ivy for seeing that scenario for what it is. Namely bullshizzle.

If *Vogue* is a style bible, then my room is one of its verses. It's beautiful. I mean, my room in Kilblair is beautiful, but in an *old money, well-worn but built to last forever and filled with family heirlooms* kind of way. This room could be straight from the interior page of *Vogue*—the Parisienne version. Original plaster-paneled walls painted a shade of white I imagine would be called wheaten or something just as artistic sounding. The queen bed looks French, the linens pinstriped in more shades of white with accents of *toile de jouy* in a bright raspberry color dotted around the place—in cushions, on a fabric modesty screen, and on the dainty Louis-style sofa and single chair.

I unpack my case and unzip the garment bag, hanging up a dress that seems far too sophisticated for Griffin to have chosen. It doesn't flash a lot of flesh to begin with.

Maybe he got a little help from a female perspective when he went shopping for this.

Midnight blue, high-necked, and long-sleeved, this exquisite piece of tailoring is deeply cuffed at the wrists and waist and falls in a soft ruffle to mid thigh. At least, from the front. From the back, it drapes dramatically from the shoulders in a waterfall effect, forming a billowing, ruffled train that stops at my heels. *My four-inch gold heels.*

The dress is a showstopper—a thing of beauty—and something I would've never dared to try on myself. Partly because of the label. *Valentino.*

That's why I'd thought it was Isla's. The label. And the fact that the cut of it would lend itself to both our body types. Except maybe the length, which is why I'd sought to add heels. Anyway, I've died and gone to designer heaven and in truth, finding this beauty on my bed is one of the main reasons I got in the car at all.

What girl doesn't love to get gussied up like she's going to a ball?

Once my domestic tasks are taken care of, I decide to have a wander around the castle. Let's see if I can find out how the other (Hollywood) half lives.

While Claish might be nowhere near the size of Kilblair, it's still the kind of building I wish I'd brought a bag of crackers to so I could at least leave a trail back to my room. Hallway after hallway, door after door, but as I reach the first floor, I notice many people moving around confidently, so at least I can ask for directions if I get lost. *Milling around, toing and froing, fetching and carrying, at second glance.* So I decide to head on out to the gardens.

I lift my hand to shield my eyes as I step out onto a terrace furnished with teak Lutyens benches and tables shaded by huge parasols. A pair of weather-worn stone lions guard the steps down to a carpet-like lawn where a giant chessboard, complete with child-sized chess pieces, stands.

It looks more like the set of a period drama than the home of one of Hollywood's big hitters, which I think is infinitely better.

"Oh, hi!" I offer as I notice the elderly woman sitting in a wheelchair in the shade of the castle's walls. Delicate framed and silver-haired, she wears a pair of eggshell blue slacks and a matching knitted twin set. On her thin wrist is a tiny gold watch and at her neck a double string of pearls. The only incongruity in her whole outfit is her sunglasses.

Large red frames with gold studs, the designer logo emblazoned on their thick arms. *Balenciaga.*

"I wish I was," she replies, her voice papery.

"I'm sorry?"

"Hi," she repeats, as though I'd misheard. And I had not. Just misunderstood. "I wish I was. *High.*"

"Oh. Right." Weird. And unexpected in one who looks so neat and proper. *But okay.*

"Ye can get marijuana on prescription in California, you know?" *Mari-joo-wana* is how she pronounces it.

"Yeah? I mean, yeah. I heard that."

"Aye." I can feel her eyeing me through the dark frames. "I do like my holidays there. I thought you looked like an American."

"You can tell by just looking?"

"You have'nae the right skin tone to be Scots. Not blue enough," she adds with a sage nod.

"Do you mind if I sit here?" She's going to be fun, I can tell.

"No, lassie, not at all. You'd be doin' an old woman a favor by keeping her company. The name's June, by the way. I'm Dylan's concubine."

I find myself hesitating as I sit. Maybe she's going to be a little fun and a little crazy.

"Don't be a daftie. Sit yourself down," she scoffs. "I am his adopted granny. More like Ivy's, but it's himself that pays the bills."

"I'm Holly."

"A new friend of Ivy's?"

"Well, I met Ivy and Dylan just recently." When I served them haggis bonbons.

June's gaze narrows. "That'll have been over at Kilblair?"

"Yes. Do you know it?"

"Not really. Scotland has as many castles as some places have hovels. But Ivy told me she and the birthday boy had been invited."

"So, you're here for the birthday boy? The party, I mean?"

"Aye, I suppose. Truth be told, I am wherever anyone decides to wheel me." She taps the arms of her wheelchair.

"Oh. Yes. I see."

"But at my age, I'm just happy to still be here. And here's my favorite wee men!" June holds out her arms as the Duffy boys come running along the terrace with Hugh and Archie in tow.

"June-y!" Harris, the younger of the two boys, throws his arms around the woman, almost climbing onto her lap.

"Hello, my wee laddie! Oh, so strong you are. Such a squeeze! You're like Arnold Schwartzhisface! Now." She sets him back again, brushing the hair from his face. "Introduce me to your wee pals."

"This is Hugh and Archie. They're here for a sleepover."

"Goodness, you are old!" Archie blurts out, his face turning immediately red as he slaps both hands to his mouth.

"Archie!" his brother hisses, pulling on his arm. "I apologize for my brother. That was unforgivably rude. You, you, don't look old at all."

"Oh, but I am old," June replies, hunching her shoulders forward like an old crone.

"How old, exactly?" Archie asks, clearly fascinated.

"Mummy says you should never ask a woman her age," Hugh whispers, horrified.

"Wise advice, laddie. But I don't mind tellin' ye I'm seven hundred and three."

"Really?" Archie's expression twists. "I know trees can get that old, but not people."

"You are so literal," Hugh mutters, making the word sound more like *idiot* as he rolls his eyes.

"Most people die before they get to one hundred," Archie adds.

"Aye, but most people don't cook small children in the oven to eat, do they?"

I guess it's hard to scare kids who live in a place with a dungeon. But all four boys are happy when June produces a bag of candy from her purse on the back of her wheelchair, and begins to dole out the contents liberally.

"Off you go, now," she says, shooing them with one pale, papery hand. "I can't be sharing my lunch with ye." From the bag, she pulls out a pink candy in the shape of a small ear, popping it into her mouth. Giggles turn to squeals, and the boys run off.

June sighs happily, her dentures clacking on the chewy candy. "I reckon those boys are the only reason the good Lord keeps me on this side of the grass. Well, them and him," she adds with a sly twist to her mouth. I follow the path of her gaze to where a young man in blue scrubs is approaching. "That's my nurse, Raphaël." She smiles saucily. "He gives one hell of a bed bath."

"Ivy's looking for you," says the man in a rhythmical Spanish accent.

"Och, she'll be wantin' to set my hair." She pats her silver curls. "Like she doesn't have enough to do today."

"You know she likes to take care of you." Raphaël, the nurse, squats down in front of her.

"Because she's a sweetheart, just like you." June pats his cheek. "And the good Lord gave you the kind of bahoochie to keep an auld woman alive."

Bahoochie is butt, as I recall. Scandalized! Though not really. Good for June! And maybe Raphaël is new to the idiosyncrasies of the Scot language.

"You are a big flirt." Dispelling my theory, he flicks his eyes my way as he presses his hand over June's to keep it there. "All mouth and no trousers." The idiom sounds a lot more flirtatious in his accent. And I'll admit to a little tummy twist as he sends me a wink.

"I'm just too old to work what you keep in your trousers, laddie. Maybe Holly here could make good use of it?"

"Oh, no. I mean, I'm—" Did she really just offer me her nurse's—?

"Life is too short to pass up a good ride. Believe me, hen."

Raphaël laughs and waggles his finger her way. "You're making her blush."

"Like you're complaining. Go on, take her out of the way and show her what she'd be missing." She turns to me then, tapping her nose. "He has a stash of the good mari-joo-wana. For medical purposes, o' course."

"Come on, cupid." The man straightens, leaving his scrub-concealed junk in the general vicinity of June's gaze.

"Such a shame to waste good cock. It's my favorite word," she says as her gaze swings my way, her blue eyes bright over the top of her sunglasses. "Such a braw, virile word is cock."

"Come." Raphaël moves behind her and grabs the handles of her wheelchair.

"I would, but the apparatus is broke!"

He disengages the brake and wheels June around so fast she giggles like a little girl on a swing. "Maybe I'll see you around."

"Erm, maybe!"
What the hell just happened here?

42

ALEXANDER

I SEE HER LONG BEFORE SHE SEES ME. LONG BEFORE MY SISTER notices her arrival, so I alone get to watch her glide down the stairs. All lithe legs and sure steps, she holds her chin high. It's part of the version of Holland she wants us to see, that she insists upon.

It's been days. An eternity. And it turns out, sleeping under a different roof hasn't helped me sleep any better. I want her with the same fervor. Possibly even more. And I should perhaps feel bad for how I'm about to behave this evening.

But I don't.

One more evening of playacting. Only, this time it's my turn.

It had taken Van's phone call, not that he'd talked any sense. Suggesting he'd steal Holland from under me was nothing short of ridiculous. Instead, at the end of the call, I'd found myself undergoing a light-bulb moment. A eureka! Or maybe more a moment where I'd realized I hadn't been paying attention all along.

Holland wants to be seen. Or at least, she wants people

to see the version of herself she's created. By contrast, I never want to be seen for fear of the truth of my life coming out. But something has to give, and I've decided that needs to be me.

I need to give less of a fuck of being judged for who I was. For what I did.

I'm letting go of the past and letting the cards fall where they may.

I'm going to take care of the present and let the past take care of itself.

When I'd found her in the garden after that phone call, the seed of thought had sprouted and grown into a vine. A vine that wrapped itself around me. And under the roof of the dilapidated folly, with grass in her hair and that damp T-shirt sticking to her, I'd wanted to drag her out into the open, strip her naked in the rain, and claim her. To see the water cascade from her curves. But the vine gripped me tight for a reason. It held my arms to my sides as I used my mouth for something other than the worship of her.

I told her, "*I see you.*"

I see her for who she is, not the version she wants me to see or the version she wants other people to see. The woman she pretends to be. I see the woman who'd go to the pains of hiding a fucking statue so as not to bring a woman she cares for more trouble than she already has on her plate. I see the woman my nephews dote on. I see the woman who has inspired the kind of loyalty in just a few weeks that might take lesser people years. Yet none of this matters because without all the goodness in her, I know I would still want her because she's so much more. She's funny and quick-witted, and despite the trials she's suffered, she's still willing to take life by the horns and fucking ride it. The bottom line is, no matter what life throws her way, she isn't afraid to try. Except when it comes to me.

And I want her to try because I love Holland Harper. And I can't even tell her, not yet. Because I need this night to be over. I need her to feel what I feel when Griffin tells me she's his. Or when Van suggests he'll treat her better than I can. I need her to see the risk of losing me to someone else.

Frankly, I can't think of another way. I don't have a lot of time left.

So, yes, out at the folly, I'd been more than disingenuous. I'd lied. Because how could I ever admit to being able to walk away from her?

I can't admit this is over. I won't.

Not when I remember the way she'd looked up at me, rain bedraggled, her hair in disarray, her heart pouring from her eyes. She'd looked so honest and beautiful and in pain. And days later, I still suffer a frisson of sensation when I recall how she'd leaned into me as though willing me to take her in my arms.

"There she is." My sister beams, our little circle of people widening as Holland approaches. "My goodness, what a stunning dress!" Isla's gaze isn't the only one sweeping the length of her as Griffin's eyes practically fall out of his head. I tighten my grip on my glass as an alternative to slapping him across the back of the head.

I don't need to look. I drank my fill as she'd floated down the stairs, even if I wasn't the only one watching. But it's fine. I'll be the only one watching as her dress slips to the floor at the end of the night. If everything goes right.

"You look gorgeous, love." Griffin rests his hand at the small of her back. The hand I imagine snapping off at the wrist.

"Whoa!" I'm not sure that's the response any of us had

anticipated as Holland holds up her hands as though to shield her eyes. "I have no idea what you just said, Griffin. I couldn't hear over the noise of your pants."

"What?" Griffin's gaze dips to his tartan trews as Isla and my companion—the girl Van eventually brought along despite his complaints; the girl Holland has yet to make the acquaintance of—begin to titter.

"I think Holland is trying to tell you your outfit is a little loud," I murmur. The glance that passes between her and me is more than a little conspiratorial. What was he thinking? Red and green tartan trousers—not even the family tartan—a matching vest, and a forest green velvet dinner jacket.

"Are those house slippers?" Holland asks, her eyebrows raised.

Of course, we all glance down.

"No, these are Italian," he protests.

"Aw, look. Your Italian slippers even have silky little tassels to match your bow tie," she adds.

"You look like you should be on a shortbread tin." Isla chuckles as she throws back the remains of her second glass of champagne.

"He's just hamming it up for the American audience, aren't you?" Holland smiles so sweetly at him, but it's all fake.

"Unlike you," he mutters, his attention sliding to me. "Where's your sense of Scottish pride tonight? Left it with your kilt at the dry cleaners, did you?"

Holding out my glass, I glance down at my dinner jacket, inviting those around me to do the same. *Though one person in particular.* Double-breasted with a satin shawl, my jacket fits my torso like a glove. "Is there something amiss?"

As it turns out, it was a good choice for tonight, seeing as the theme of the night appears to be a nod to Hollywood's golden era. Not in an ironic sense but leaning more towards old-world glamour. Champagne saucers rather than flutes, the waitstaff dressed like usherettes. Jaunty angled pillbox hats and bolero jackets with golden-tasseled epaulettes. Ostrich feathers and swags of silk ballooning over a makeshift dance floor. It looks like Ivy Duffy has gone all out.

"You look perfect," the woman to my left purrs with perfect timing. I watch with some satisfaction as Holland's eyes track the motion of her hand as it comes to rest on my chest.

"Holland, I don't believe you've met Jessica, have you?"

"No." Such a small word for the look of challenge that meets mine. Interesting. I usually pride myself on being able to read expressions, but it's almost impossible to discern hers.

The women exchange greetings and compliments on their respective dresses, though I'll note that Holland instigates this nicety, involving my sister in the conversation. I'm not sure it would've occurred to Jessica, geniality not being part of her remit tonight.

"Holland!" Van takes that moment to join us, our circle widening to accommodate him as he presses a kiss to each of her cheeks like they're old friends. She even she seems a little surprised by this. Meanwhile, Jessica really is a better actress than I'd hoped for as she barely acknowledges him beyond a polite smile. He is her employer, after all. I wonder if they've—

Something pulls at the threads of my attention as my eyes narrow on my sister and one of my oldest friends. I might've said *best friend,* but for the way the pair seem familiar. Very familiar.

Someone has been lying.

Someone other than me.

Someone other than Holland.

What tangled webs we weave...

"Care to dance?" Van holds out his hand, and my sister responds in kind.

"I don't remember the last time a handsome man asked me to dance," Isla answers, positively beaming up at him.

"Holly, let me get you a drink," Griffin says, turning to a passing waiter and a tray.

"Sure." Her shoulders jump in a sign of agreement and perhaps discomfort. "So, Jessica, what do you do?" she asks, her tone erring on the side of brittle, somehow not quite bright.

"I'm an actress."

"I'm sure you are." Holland's gaze briefly meets mine. "I'm sure you're a great actress."

Careful, Holland. Your claws are showing.

I hide my amusement behind the rim of my glass.

HOLLY

He looks better than he has any right to in a castle full of people whose beauty is regularly portrayed on screens all over the world.

"I meant what I said. You look stunning tonight."

I lift my gaze from where Alexander is twirling his date around the dance floor like he's a puppet master and she's attached to his strings. With a stifled sigh, I force a half-smile Griffin's way.

"Thank you. I do love the dress." Not for the first time, I

spread my fingers over the fabric and glide my hand down my thigh. "It's Valentino, did you know?"

He shakes his head, uninterested in anything but my legs. I guess I can rule him out of the dress mystery, which leaves only one culprit. The man with the cool and appraising gaze. The one who'd barely bothered to lift his head as I'd walked into the room while my nerves had jangled like a bunch of keys at my first glimpse of him.

"I guess this fake dating thing worked." Griffin's gaze follows mine to where it has slid back to Alexander. *And Jessica, I guess.* "I mean, it looks like he's moved on, doesn't it? He's leaving you alone."

I refuse to bite. But, honestly, I'm not sure. Not that I could explain it to Griffin. Did I feel sick to my stomach when she slid her hand across his chest? No, I actually felt like something inside me had curled up and died. And watching them dance makes me want to throw my glass at her. Or throw myself on the floor and cry. And while Alexander has been perfectly civil to his dance partner, attentive in fact, I've sensed his eyes on me more than once. I've felt his attentions like he was peeling back the layers of my skin. I've witnessed the weight of his want when I've glanced his way. I've observed as he has seemed to breathe in my words.

Thoughts and denial and a sick kind of hope weave around my head as a cat does one's ankles. But as the song comes to an end, my contemplations turn to dust as I watch Alexander tenderly slide away a lock of her hair before he bends and traces his lips against her ear.

"I mean, just look at that."

"I am watching," I mutter. I watch as I swallow over the ache creeping up the back of my throat as he lifts her hand and presses a kiss to it.

And then I watch no more.

So much for trusting in what is meant to be.

So much for not forcing things.

Except maybe forcing me to get away from him.

"Hey, Holly." Ivy appears to my left, wreathed in a gold sheath dress and a wide smile. "And Griffin."

"Nice to see you again," he replies, holding out his hand.

"I have a bone to pick with you," she chides playfully. "When we met at Kilblair, you didn't tell me you were a QC."

"Are you in need of legal representation?" Griffin parries.

"Ha! No. But hiding your light under a bushel is so not Hollywood. But I suppose you're more at home at the Old Bailey."

"Oh, Griffin makes himself at home in all sorts of places," Isla interjects, appearing next to him. "Look at you. A rose between two thorns," she adds, linking her arm through his. "You haven't asked your big sister to dance yet."

"Do you want to dance?" he asks uncertainly.

"Only all night long," she says, tugging on his arm.

"Well, that went well," Ivy murmurs. "Do you think she's psychic?"

"Isla?" My gaze follows the pair. "Maybe she just feels a little sorry for me."

"By stealing your dancing partner?" she asks with a laugh.

"No. I—" Why am I continuing with this? "Nothing is going on between Griffin and me." I get the sudden impression she wants to squeeze my cheeks like I've been the topic of conversation. I fix on a smile and pretend I don't mind.

"I have eyes. I also have advice. And an empty glass that needs rectifying." She curls her finger comically, and I find myself following her out of the room and into another, this one with a makeshift bar.

"A wee dram for what ails ye," she says, thickening her accent as she pours two fingers of whisky into a glass and then passes it over. She pours herself sparkling water. "Up your bum," she says, touching the rim of her glass to mine. "And that's not a toast I'd recommend uttering in front of your husband on his birthday."

"I'll bear that in mind if I ever get me one of those." I bring the glass to my now smiling lips. "You know, I'm beginning to get a taste for this."

"Of course you are. What whisky will not cure, there is no cure for. Or so June would have us believe."

"Oh, I met June!"

"Yeah, she said. She's as daft as a brush, but we love her."

"I can see why." When I say I love old people, I especially love the irreverent ones.

"Did she try to fix you up with Raphaël yet?"

"Yes!" Eyes wide, I nod.

"I think she must have a camera set up in his room or something. But I didn't bring you out here to talk about our adopted granny and her wicked habits. I wanted to talk to you about the big cheese." I must pull a face. The mention of cheese always makes me think of Mookatill. "His grace, the duke." Ivy mocks a little curtsy. Oh, she's enjoying this. "I don't want to pry—actually, no, that's a lie. But I do want to say this to you. I wanted to say it to you after that awkward dinner, which you were wonderful through, by the way."

"I didn't feel wonderful."

"Well, no. No doubt you wanted to smash your plate over his head. But then you both disappeared afterwards…

and then the hubby and I went for a walk, and we heard some pretty particular noises coming out of one of the rooms." Ivy purses her lips to prevent a smile, but it spills from her eyes anyway. "Let's just say, great minds think alike."

Does that mean she was... That they were...

"It adds a wee bit of spice to the relationship," she says with a tiny shrug. "Anyway, I'm just going to say this, then move on. I just feel like a mama hen watching you. Maybe it's this pregnancy, not that you heard that news from me."

"My lips are sealed," I answer uncertainly, brushing aside the fact that this pregnancy seems to be the worst kept secret ever. I mean, if Mari knows... But what the heck is Ivy getting to?

"Men can be arseholes."

"That's it?" I mean, tell me something I don't know.

"The more powerful the man, the bigger the arseholery," she says, leaning her forearm on the bar and pinching her fingers together like some TV mafioso. "I've watched that man—I watched him over the weekend we stayed at Kilblair, and I've watched him tonight. More specifically, I've watched him watching you."

"Looks can be deceiving. We're not suited."

"Two people cannot look at each other the way you two do and it not mean anything. Yes, I've been watching you, too. And if I told you the things Dylan did to me, the pain he put me through, you'd think I was mad for being with him. But he's worth it, *we're* worth it, because I made him suffer just as much. Love makes fools of us all, Holly. It's a cliché, but—"

"Clichés are a thing for a reason." Yes, I know.

"Exactly. Now, stop trying to resist him and let him love

you. You could be a duchess or a nanny or a waitress. Me? I'm a hairdresser. It doesn't really matter what you are as long as you have love."

43

ALEXANDER

"I don't suppose you've seen Holland, have you?" I hate to open another can of worms or annoyance as I pass Van at the bar.

"Did you blink, and she disappeared?" He smirks over the top of his glass.

"What are you drinking?" I lean against the makeshift bar top and peer into his glass. "Vodka?"

"Yes." He sighs. "Sometimes, it helps me think."

"And sometimes, it helps you fall down whole flights of stairs," I reply, thinking back to our student days. "Stay away from my sister, Van." I brush a weary hand through my hair. "She's got enough trouble coming her way." Divorce. A custody battle. A mountain of debt, I shouldn't wonder. But we'll get through it together. It's what we do.

"Yes. Trouble," he repeats pensively. "But what are you going to do about your trouble, *Aleksandr?*"

"Crush it." I flick my shoulder, unconcerned. I thought that the dance might do it. A tender look. A kiss to the cheek. I thought that even my blush might've helped—completely spontaneous—as at the end of our dance Jessica had offered to take me into the garden to blow more than my mind.

I'd declined, of course. And I haven't been able to find Holland since, despite doing a couple of laps of both inside and out.

I signal to the barman and order a single malt, beginning to absently drum my fingers against the wood.

"Your sister's husband is no good."

"Tell me something I don't know."

"He's embroiled her in much trouble."

"Also, not news," I mutter, thinking back to the loss of her trust fund, and God only knows what else. God, and our lawyers as of next week.

When my drink appears in front of me, I lift it to my lips.

"If you'll excuse me," Van says, standing and placing his glass down.

"Are you all right?" He's in a weird mood. Then he often is these days.

"Yes, of course." As he passes, his hand clasps my shoulder tight. "I have some thinking to do. And you, my friend, have something a little more physical to look forward to." I stiffen at the implication in his words as he bends, bringing his mouth to my ear. "I saw Griffin lead Holland out into the gardens."

No.

Just no.

Room after room blurs, people and faces grotesque caricatures as my mind swims from scenario to scenario.

Holland behind a sofa.

Over a picnic table.

Taunting me from behind closed doors.

Because she's not in the fucking gardens, that's for sure.

I will fucking kill him, I think as sweat sticks my shirt to my back. *And probably shake the living daylights out of her.*

Which won't happen because this is all one big mistake—a figment of Van's vodka-fueled imagination. *I hope.* I round a corner, my hands balled into fists as I resist the urge to hit the wall. To pound it until my knuckles bleed. To give my mind something else to focus on.

"Hey, man. You okay?"

I blink, coming back to the hallway and the man in front of me. *And his strange company.*

"Dylan. Yes." I rouse myself, trying to focus on the next blockbuster *Batman*, the wheelchair, and the elderly woman dressed in a pink jumpsuit. "I'm sorry. I was miles away."

"You look like you wish you were miles away," the old woman says, her blue eyes penetrating.

"No, not at all," I answer, the words almost rote. Drawling and arctic. A product of my station. My breeding. My fucked head. "I don't suppose you've seen Holland, have you?" I direct my words to the taller of the pair, though possibly the less sober.

"Hey, Juney. Did we see her on our race?"

"Buggered if I know," she says, twisting her gaze to him. "I was too busy hanging on for dear life when you spun me 'round those corners."

"You were yelling for me to *go faster*," he retorts like a child. A large, multimillion-dollar earning child.

"Aye, ye have to grab excitement where ye can get it at my time of life."

"Well, I'll leave you to it." I make as though to pass when another thought occurs to me. "What about Griffin. Have you seen him?"

"Was that him in the tartan trews?" the old woman asks with a moue of distaste.

"Yes, that's him." I hadn't seen anyone else dressed in such a ridiculous way.

"That one wouldn't know his arse from a hole in the ground."

The film star snickers. "This is his grace, the Duke of Dalforth, June."

"Aye, and I'm sure he's got an arse, too."

"I've got a few of them," I mutter, "because Griffin is my brother."

He is until I strangle him.

"I know that look. Do ye believe in reincarnation?"

By this point, I think I must have steam coming out of my ears.

"Take a leaf out of my book, laddie. When you get to the pearly gates, ask Saint Peter if you can come back as a wee birdie. I know I'll be asking to because, when I come back, I have a long list of people I plan to shit on."

"June, you crack me up," Dylan says, beginning to laugh.

"I think it must be almost cake time," she orders, circling her finger in an order to about-turn.

"And Griffin?" I ask, instantly regretting it.

"The bathroom nearest the kitchen," June says. "I thought to myself when they went in together, his boaby can't be as big as all that. He can't have needed that woman to help him hold it. Don't pull that face," she warns suddenly. "Grind your teeth, and you'll end up with dentures like me."

"Thank you, June." My words sound surprisingly calm as I pivot on my heel.

"Something is rotten in the state of brotherhood." I hear her call.

"Cool," her pilot answers. "A literary pun."

"It's from *Hamlet*, aye?"

"Yep."

"Is that the one where the wife goes doolally?"

As I turn the corner, I hear no more.

I find the kitchen, and shortly afterwards, find the bathroom. Mainly due to the short queue of people waiting outside.

"Come on!" An elderly man in a white dinner jacket knocks politely on the door. "I need to shake the dew off the lily." He turns to the person next to him. "These old legs aren't what they used to be. I can't go out to the posh porta loos they have in the garden."

Portable loos. She wouldn't, would she?

I shake the ridiculousness from my head.

"Have you been waiting long?" I find myself asking.

"Long enough." The elderly man pulls a face.

I step around him, bringing myself level with the door.

"Fuck, you're such a dirty little bitch, aren't you?"

If I'm not mistaken, I've found at least one-half of my missing party.

"Yes! Yes!" comes the voice of the female contingent.

American, yes. But Holland? I can't quite tell.

"You're my dirty little bitch, aren't you? Say it!"

"I'm your dirty little bitch!"

"Someone is having a good time," the old man says.

"Yeah, a dirty little bitch." Someone snickers as I raise my fist and begin hammering on the door.

"Say it again!" Griffin demands.

"I'm your—"

"Griffin!" I bellow. "If you don't open this door, I'm going to break it down and tear off your fucking head!" With the side of my fist, I begin to hammer while imagining the block of wood is his head. "Open the door!"

And if that's Holland in there, at least blood will wash easier from tile.

I can almost see the headline—

Under my fists, the door falls open, and I fall in and almost on top of Griffin. I kick the door closed behind me to a chorus of disappointment, flicking on the lock. Before I quite understand what I'm doing, I have my feckless, treacherous, half-undressed shit of a brother by the neck and pressed up against the opposite wall.

"Al? What the fuck?" He begins to splutter, but I have no time for him, my eyes sweeping the room for—

A blue dress hangs over the top of the shower door, a pair of slender legs the only things visible through the glass. Through my rage, through the red mist that descends, my fist meets with the meat of my brother's stomach without a word.

"Oof!" Griffin bows forward, his hand reaching out for the vanity. Unsatisfied, I pull my arm back and aim for his face.

"You fucker!" he yells, but I've already whipped around, reached for the dress and pulled it down to find standing in the shower cubicle, arms crossed her chest, a near-naked not-Holland.

The dirty little bitch, I presume.

"Where is she?" I pivot back, pulling my brother straight as I see rage red again.

"Obviously not fucking here," he spits. "But not through a lack of invitation."

My hand tightens in his shirt. "You really are a fucker," I growl, beginning to shake him.

"I saw her first, you twat!" he says, his fist coming over

the top and connecting with my head. I twist and pull him against me, pressing my arm against his throat.

"You did not see her first. You don't know a fucking thing."

Fists begin to pound at the door, complains and worries filtering in.

"You're fucking choking me—"

Not yet, but I will, I think.

"She was mine from the start. Mine, do you hear? She was mine long before that cold fucking lane, and if you so much as look in her direction again, I'll more than choke you. Got it?"

"F-Fine." Spittle lands on my arm, but I don't let him go. Not yet.

"This thing between you. Real or fake."

"What the f-fuck do you think?"

I think he's going to answer the question. Especially as I tighten my grip on him.

"F-Fake."

Relief seeps out of me, my arm falling loose as my other supports Griffin under his arm. I don't see his fist, but my kidney feels it.

"I hope you piss blood for weeks," he mutters, his chest heaving as he props himself against the marble vanity.

"Fuck." I clutch my side, my other palm flat against the wall as the pain radiates up my ribs and down my flank. "I probably will."

"Good, you deserve it."

"Probably." I begin to straighten slowly, then pass the blue dress to the woman in the shower with a murmured apology.

As the hammering on the door picks up again, Griffin bellows back, "Oh, do fuck off."

"Oof." The pain worsens as I approach the vanity and slide my hand through my hair.

"You're going to find her then?" Griffin's voice sounds harsh, but if it's any consolation to him, I also feel ill.

"Yes," I answer. "I'm going to try to." Try to make her see sense.

"Well, she's not interested in me, but if she'll have your arse at all," he says, pulling himself straight and holding out his hand, "I hope she makes you fucking miserable."

And that's something we shake on.

44

ALEXANDER

"Are you going to tell me what's going on between you and Van?" I try not to wince as I lead us into a turn. I've seen snippets of Holland since I'd dragged my sore body from that bathroom, avoiding the gazes of the gawkers in the hallway. I'm sure it'll make for good gossip within the Duffys' circle. The stuffy duke and the barrister behaving like adolescents over a girl.

A girl who's still avoiding me.

"Van is a good friend," my sister answers, keeping her eyes studiously over my right shoulder. Her feet follow the rhythm of the music as a singer croons low-pitched words from a nearby stage, words that tempt lovers to run away in the night.

Van as a friend? I used to think so.

"He's not the man you think he is," I mutter repressively as my sister's gaze seeks mine.

"It's not like you to speak ill of an old friend."

"There are things I could tell you about him that—" I start as Isla increases the pressure on my shoulder in warning.

"Then don't. I have no intentions of discussing him with you, Sandy. But you don't have to worry. Not about this."

"What else do I have to worry about if not you?"

"How about the state of your own love life?"

"A state indeed."

"Well, you were the one stupid enough to bring that girl. Beautiful though she is, she's extremely vapid. Where is she, by the way?"

Fuck. It even hurts to shrug.

But I suspect Van sent Jessica to a hotel. Maybe he even went with her. Though given the way this conversation is going, that could be a case of wishful thinking.

"Holland brought Griffin," I find myself muttering defensively.

"Did she? I thought she travelled here with me."

"You know what I mean."

"Yes," she agrees. "But do you see them together?"

"That's not the point."

"No, that's exactly the point. Well, along with the fact that you were stupid enough to think bringing someone else would send her into a jealous fit, and then your arms." Isla sighs. "Honestly, Sandy. Did you really think it would help?"

"The night isn't over yet."

"Just confess. Tell her you love her."

"What was that?"

Isla sends me a withering look. "I know you better than you know yourself. I don't know if you remember, but you behaved nothing like this with Leonie."

"Leonie was different." Very different. I don't even remember why I proposed, if I'm honest. Perhaps we seemed like the perfectly sterile match. Nothing so mundane as jealousy or monogamy for us.

"You know, I remember asking if you loved Leonie. It

was before your engagement. Do you remember what you said?"

"No. Nor do I want to."

"Don't frown," she says, smoothing her hand over my brow. "You're not the man you were then."

I'm not frowning because of that. I'm frowning because my side throbs. And my head. And while I feel some relief in the knowledge that Holland isn't fucking Griffin, I still can't get her alone for five fucking minutes.

This time, my sister gives my shoulder a reassuring squeeze.

"Go on, then," I reply. "What rubbish did I spout?"

"You said, '*I'm a Dalforth.*' " Isla's tone drops in to some approximation of my voice. "'*Feelings were bred out of us before Henry chopped off his first wife's head*'."

"But he didn't chop off his first wife's head."

"Exactly."

"The folly of youth."

"And now you're old enough to know better than to play silly games. Just go and haul her over your shoulder, Sandy. Take her to your lair."

"That's not part of the problem," I answer, less than sanguine.

"Just don't let her out again until you've made sure she's yours."

"Really, Izzy?" I chastise. "And you're a supposed feminist."

"I'm a sister first, and it breaks my heart to see how ridiculous you're both being."

Oh, God, how I laugh. I laugh so hard my feet refuse to keep in time with the music.

"Look, there she is. Dancing with someone who isn't you. Let's cut in."

"Isla," I warn, but it's too late as she's already grabbed the man's arm.

"My brother keeps stepping on my toes. Mind if I cut in?"

And who would dare stop her?

∼

HOLLY

"What are you doing?" I pull on Alexander's hand as he lifts it.

"Don't look so worried," he murmurs, pulling me closer.

Did he just wince?

His hand brushes my waist as it comes to rest on my hip, my stomach swooping someplace between weightless and a jangle of knots.

"It's just a dance, Holland. Don't you want to dance with me?" His voice was made for seduction. *That devil's mouth of his.*

The bigger the man, the bigger the asshole. The worse his sins.

The greater the temptation. And the annoyance.

"You make me nervous." The words are out of my mouth without my permission, and I could curse myself.

"You know what will help with that?" He cocks an eyebrow as we begin to move across the dance floor, and before I can respond, he says, "Let me lead."

My breath hitches as I'm suddenly pressed tight to his body. He's looking down at me with the most disarming smile, and we're being swallowed by the crowd in the middle of the dance floor. Somehow, the music has changed from Nora Jones to something a little Latin. Latin for the girl who had to be dragged onto the dance floor by June's nurse. I have two left feet, and neither of them knows how to keep a rhythm.

"I don't... I can't. I don't know how the dance steps go." I'm not sure he can hear me over the sudden increase in the music's volume, but surely, he can read my expression.

"It's fine." I hear the rumble of his response and feel his smile pressed against my cheek. "I've got you." He lifts my hand, curling it around the back of his neck, his fingers making a tantalizing path down my arm. I gasp, and not just because my nerve endings dance from his touch but also because he then pushes his strong thigh between mine.

A ripple of awareness runs through us both. This position isn't our first rodeo. I've ridden this thigh once or twice before.

"I really don't think—"

"Then don't." His words are a satisfied hum, the kind that turns my grey matter to grey mush.

Just don't think about what a bad idea this is.

It's just a dance. It'll be over soon.

Just don't think about how this dance is a vertical expression of my desire to be horizontal with him.

"Just relax. If there's one place you're allowed not to think, it's while you're dancing."

Or being screwed, my mind supplies. But it's impossible not to think as his arm wraps around me, pulling my body against his until his fingers are curling around my ribs. And doubly impossible as he begins to move, all sinuous hips that encourage me to move with him. To undulate against him. Suddenly, my mind is filled with an image from the movie *Dirty Dancing*, where Johnny tries to teach Baby how to move. I remember watching the movie with Dede and

Nana, cringing and hiding behind the cushion at her ineptitude.

Oh, man. I'm Baby. Someone *please* put me in the corner!

"Don't fight," comes Alexander's honeyed coaxing. "Relax into the music. Let…"

I miss the rest of his sentence as he presses his lips to my hairline. Tiny pop rocks of pleasure explode inside me because I think I felt those words just fine.

Let me have you.

Oh, my. Stick a fork in me, for I am *done!*

His solid thigh. The way he holds me and the way his body moves against mine. The way he makes my body respond to his. It's like sex.

Like a prelude, my mind whispers.

How can I not be turned on when I'm rubbing myself against the thick thigh he's jammed between my legs? One arm around his neck, I lift the other to the broad expanse of his chest, spreading my fingers wide just because I can. I'd almost forgotten how good he smells. A woodsy-scented cologne and the inimitable musk of man.

"What is it?" he asks as I unglue my gaze from his chest. I think I was going to tell him he smells good and to ask the name of the cologne he wears. Realizing how ridiculous that sounds and how the probability of my turning beetroot when my gaze meets his, I glance left instead.

Boy, our efforts are pretty tame compared to those dancing around us.

Sexual eye contact. Sensual hips. Trailing hands. Salsa that's more simulated sex than anything else.

How are they not burning with embarrassment?

Burning with need?

These aren't questions I'm about to voice aloud. I wouldn't be able to, anyway. Not as Alexander's hands caress the side of my head, bringing my attention back to him. The look he gives me is nothing short of explosive as his fingers set a trail of fire down my arms the moment before he somehow spins my body away from his, then twirls me back just as quick. My stomach goes weightless, blood rushing through my veins with a nervous kind of excitement. There's a kind of freedom in letting him lead. An exhilarating freedom.

As he tightens his arms, bringing me even closer, my breasts are pressed flush against him. Our eyes meet, and he knows I know what he's doing to me. I can see it in that dark blue self-satisfied gleam. He can probably feel the heat pouring from me. I will actually die when this is over if I've left a damp patch on his pants.

Over his thickly muscled thigh.

Oh, Lord.

But the thoughts don't last long as he dips me backward, making the blood rush to my head. As he lifts me upright, warmth licks through my insides as our noses almost touch, and... I'm back to riding his thigh again.

And anticipating the hard brush of him.

"How are you feeling now?" Alexander's words are pressed into the soft skin of my neck, his next breath a soft grunt as I bring my hands to his hips.

Hot. I feel hot. Inside. Outside. A heated pleasure seems to pulse from my fingertips to my toes. But none of that seems like the kind of things I should be sharing. Not with him. Not now.

"I-I'm okay." If okay means primed to go off like a firework.

His low laughter seems to shock us both.

Please, Lord above, don't let me have said that.

The music begins to slow as he takes my hand in his,

sliding me a look that makes my skin hum. By silent agreement, he leads me from the dance floor. We step out of the open French doors at the far side of the room and down onto the terrace.

The cool evening air does nothing to ease my blood.

"Alexander." I hold up my hand to stop him when he brings it to his chest, where it once again becomes passive. He steps closer, his eyes glimmering like the stars in the night sky the moment before he slides his lips across mine.

Was the groan his or mine as my hands slip under his jacket, unable to find purchase against the fabric.

Another groan, this time mine as he steals my breath and feeds me his. This is the exact kind of kiss that's meant for darkened hallways in Latin clubs. For museum rooms. For castle kitchens. For bedrooms.

"We shouldn't." Even as I protest, my mouth is greedy for his as my bones liquefy and my insides turn molten.

"But we are." Alexander spins me, pressing me up against the roughness of the wall, the cool stone penetrating the thin fabric of my dress.

The soft brush of his breath against my neck feels like heaven as I reach for the hard length of him.

Patterns. We're following old patterns.

"Not here. Come to my room, Holland. Let me have you for a night. For a lifetime." Though his mouth still dances over mine, his words catch my attention.

He doesn't mean that.

I find myself pulling away.

"No. We can't do this. You came with someone else, and I'm here with—"

"Don't say it," he growls, decisive, dark, and dangerous. "Don't you dare say his name."

"But—"

"This is bullshit, and I'm putting an end to this right now."

My chest rises and falls in tight breaths as I stare up into his angry face. But evidently, I'm not looking high enough as he grips my chin, forcing it up.

"You're going to go back into the party and say your goodbyes. Then you're going to go to your room and gather what you need for the night. Then, my darling," he says, bringing his lips to my ear and causing pleasure to pulse from my toes to my skull, "in precisely half an hour, you'd better find your way to my room. Because, if you don't, I'm going to go inside and find my brother and tell him a few not quite truths."

"I don't know what you mean," I whisper unnecessarily. Maybe my mind doesn't understand well, but my body sure does, nerve endings lighting up like I'm a dang pinball machine. His threats are empty, and he doesn't even know it. *Because you're a liar,* my mind whispers. *You've lied to him, and you've lied to yourself. And you're still doing it now.*

"I'll tell him I brought you out here to fuck. And like the slut I'll make you out to be, I'll tell him you loved it. That you moaned as you sucked my cock." He straightens, his eyes hooded as he caresses my face. "Griffin already tried to get me to believe you were being chased by half of the village. Cameron. Cooper." His generous mouth pouts on the Uber driver's name. "I'll just be selling him his own lie."

Once upon a time, I might've been furious. Once upon a time, *easy* was almost a trigger word. But right now, all I can think about is what this means. This moment. This manipulation. And how I'll give in but not for the reasons he thinks.

One more time.

See what you can get away with.

Laugh tomorrow morning. Tell him his manipulations fell flat.

Be the puppet master. Pull his strings.

Call it payback.

Cry later for the mess you've made of things.

"I don't—" want to. I want him but I don't want what this means.

"Yes, my darling, you do." He pulls back, his expression as blank and as expressionless as a mask. "You've told anyone who'll listen you're with him," he utters as he jerkily straightens his cuffs. "Who's to deny it? Well, apart from me?"

Whoever said Alexander, the 13th Duke of Dalforth, was a stand-up guy and not one in the long line of the debauched, was wrong.

And I don't quite know how to feel about that.

45

ALEXANDER

I'D THOUGHT IT STRANGE HOW, AS I ENTERED THE LARGE ROOM I'd been allocated, I noticed the fire in the marble fireplace had been lit. A second glance told me the effect was achieved by a flick of a switch. Old-world charm via modern convenience allowed the heavy mahogany furniture to gleam in the lambent light. The bed linens have been turned down as though this were a hotel, the navy drapes and counterpane giving the room a masculine air. A Marc Chagall painting hangs between a long pair of windows, where I pull open one of the paneled shutters and stare out into the darkness as noise of the revelry downstairs is carried on the air.

I shrug off my jacket and top up my drink, resolutely ignoring my father's damning words as they resound through my head.

Blood will out.

I refuse to feel damned or tainted. By him. By Griffin. By Holland herself. How can this be wrong when I feel so expectant? The effervescent anticipation of what's to come twirling and twining inside me.

She'll come. I know she will.

Better still, I know blackmail isn't the reason she will.

She'll come because she wants me. Not because of my empty threats. Not because of Griffin.

If she doesn't come to my room tonight, then she's not invested in her lie. And if she's not invested, then I must examine why she went to such lengths to keep me away in the first place. She has no interest in my brother. She'd used him only as a shield. A shield to keep me away... and because she can't trust herself.

My wry smile reflects back at me in the darkened window. For two weeks, I've turned myself inside out at the thoughts of them together, despite telling myself none of it could be true. That she could prefer him, seek his touch over mine, is a thought that I'd used to torture myself.

My beautiful, beautiful liar.
I hope you're ready to pay.

I shift my gaze from my reflection to the land beyond the window, my mind drifting to Kilblair. My birthright. The chain around my neck. The land I've fought so hard to protect, and the people in it. Yet I'd risk it all for her. Risk the truth coming out, risk the disappearance of our revenue, because no one would want to be involved with a duke with the kind of reputation I risk.

The moon hangs white-gold in a black velvet sky, its reflection like a pearl dropped into a lake. I close my eyes and see the dark gardens of my ancestral home. The gardens undulate as far as the eye can see in a carpet of midnight greenery, dotted here and there with three-hundred-year-old cedar trees, each just one bad storm away from being uprooted. A fitting metaphor for how I feel when Holland is near.

Uprooted. Discombobulated. All at sea.

The floorboards creak out in the hallway, and a seismic thrill courses through me.

She's here.

And only twenty minutes late.

Does this prove how conflicted she feels?

Conflicted about wanting me.

But she does want me, or why else is she standing on the other side of the door?

Not because of a threat she knows is empty.

She might think she's using my supposed blackmail as an excuse. She might even tell herself she's safe this way. Safe from deepened feelings. From complications.

But I need to tell her the truth so we can both stop playing our parts in this farce.

The truth is that I love her. I have no intention of ever letting her go.

I turn to face the door, settling my glass and myself against the windowsill, affecting a position of studied nonchalance.

There follows... nothing. Not a sound. Not a footstep or the slightest rattle of the handle, just silence, rolling and unfolding between the door and me. A silence that grates on my every nerve because I know she's there, standing in the hallway, second-guessing herself but still wanting me.

Come on, Holland. Come to me.

Want me more than you think is good for you.

Relief washes through me as the door *clicks,* then silently opens, and she slips into the room. Closing it softly at her back, she leans back against it, almost as though she's not fully committed to being here. *Liar.* And there she stays, her eyes barely meeting mine, her hands behind her back, fingers no doubt still curled around the doorknob.

"Having second thoughts?"

My God, she is stunning. She's still wearing her evening dress, the one I'd bought. The one I'd imagined her in. The dress I'll see flutter to the floor before very long.

"I'm still processing," she replies what seems like eons later. Processing the reason she's here? It's a good attempt at a cover because looking at her now, I can see she wants me every bit as much as I want her.

Even if I can't help but push her a little bit further.

"It'll be just like old times." I cast my eyes to the bed. "Though some parts might be a little more novel."

If I don't have her soon, I'll explode.

My heart pounds as she takes a step away from the door. One step, then another, the only sound of her travels the swish of silk against her legs. And the pounding of my heart, which I'm certain must be audible to us both.

"What are you going to tell Griffin?"

My guts twist at the mere mention of his name. "I don't want to hear his name in this room," I murmur dangerously.

This wasn't what I had in mind when I thought of pushing her. Goading. I'm almost tempted to tell her she can give up the act, that I know the truth, but where would the fun be in that? "I like that you kept your dress on."

"Yeah, well, Griffin wasn't in the room to undo the zipper."

Anger flares inside me immediately, and before I register anything else, I'm across the room, falling on her like a lion does a gazelle. My fingers gripping her forearms, I press my mouth to her neck as I begin to devour the silky skin there. I want to touch her, hold her, allow myself the joy of her, but I'm afraid to let go. Then somewhere from outside of my frenzy, I realize she's evading my lips even as her chest heaves with hot, hungered sounds.

"Kiss me, Holland."

"I can't," she replies, the sound a bare rasp of want.

"You did earlier." In the garden where this madness began. Where I took. Where she gave. Where I lost my mind for a few minutes. Though, in truth, I'm not sure it has at all been regained.

"You know why." But there's no reprimand or rancor in her reply.

"What difference does it make? Now? Then? Give me your mouth for no other reason than you want to."

She gasps as I pull her to my chest, shock and desire as I cup her sweet arse, fitting her softness against where I'm hard. *So fucking hard.* "Then let me kiss you. Let me taste." My words are breath over sandpaper, my teeth sharp on the shell of her ear. She gasps, her knees weakening and allowing me to fit her body tighter against me.

"Don't be frightened, Holland." Frightened to want me. Full of pride? Pride I understand more than most. Fear I understand, too. Not fear of what comes after tonight but fear of never getting my fill of her.

"I'm not frightened. You can force me to be here, but I don't have to give all of myself to you."

The stubborn little minx. Who knew she had such acting skills?

I should be laughing. I shouldn't care, but like fuel to the fire, it doesn't seem to matter that she's fooling neither of us. I certainly shouldn't be pushing her away.

"And what is that supposed to mean?" Rage blurs at the edges of my consciousness as I almost anticipate what she'll say next.

"That I'm not yours, *your grace*," she snipes, her eyes glittering angrily. "And I never can be."

An interesting distinction—*can* over *will*.

"Is that so." My tone is low and dangerous, and she begins

to back away. Conveniently for me, it's in the direction of the bed. "Don't worry, Holland," I purr as her thighs hit the mattress. "You can tell my shit of a brother that you weren't at fault. That you gave nothing freely away. That I took."

She gasps, not in fear, nor pride, but in excitement as I press her down onto the mattress, my body following hers.

HOLLY

The noise he makes as his body meets mine is the sound I've been hearing in my dreams. Part groan, part growl as he presses himself against me, hard meeting soft as his mouth finds my neck again. I push my palms against the hardness of his chest, though not to push him away. At least, not initially, finding his rapid heartbeat a sudden comfort. I'm not the only one feeling this way.

Why wouldn't I kiss him? Why did I make such a fuss? Was it in case he discovered the truth? In case he discovered how much I want him? Or maybe it's because I'm supposed to be playing the martyr, not the blessed.

Oh, God, I'd willingly sacrifice myself on the thing he presses between my legs.

Hard. Hot. Wanting. I'm not sure if those words refer to him or to me. As he rocks against me, a clawing desperation springs to life inside me, and I curl my fingers into the soft cotton of his shirt.

"Tell me you want this." His gaze meets mine, shining with challenge and as dark as any storm. "If you don't, now is your only chance to say so."

Speak now or forever hold your peace.

Hold *his* piece.

An absurd giggle bubbles up inside me because that's something to aspire to, right?

But I don't laugh as his expression changes, the look of determination slipping from his face, replaced by something a little more bittersweet. I swallow thickly. I don't want to hurt him, but his earlier kisses were enough to unravel me. Enough to melt my resolve. Enough to make me give in. I close my eyes, opening my mouth to deny him when the tender press of his lips at the base of my throat startles me into a sob.

I expected punishment through fucking. A reprimand delivered by the rough touch of his hands. I didn't expect to feel like one press of his lips could make me feel treasured. Loved.

His mouth travels higher, heated breath and bare brushes of his lips igniting my skin. Making my heart beat a tango between us. My back arches from the bed, my dress already perfect now up around my waist as I welcome the press of him between my legs. Alexander presses up onto his arms, and for a moment, he stares down at me. Watches me. Sees the truth of me. My stupidity? His expression is barely discernible in the light, though his eyes shine quite suddenly like dark stars.

"Give yourself to me, Holland." Wrapping his arm under me, he surges between my legs, his body and voice as taut as a bowstring. "Give yourself to me because you want to. Not because of anything else."

I give him the only answer I can as I pull him down to me. Air leaves his chest, the warm scent of relief feathering across my lips. Lips that meet in a kiss. Mouth against mouth, our bodies flush, my hands grasping and a little too enthusiastic for someone who's supposed to be here under duress.

We kiss as though starved, as though this kiss is the very thing to bring us breath. My fingers are still twisted in his shirt as his hand reaches down to grasp my calf. To trail up my leg. Higher. Higher. I am pure sensation, every inch of my skin aware of each place our bodies meet. The brush of his pants against my naked thighs, his chest as it grazes mine, the press of his lips. It's all so heavenly, though not nearly enough. I begin to pull the shirt from his pants, my fingers seeking the heat of his skin, desperate for more of him. He groans a velvety sound as my fingertips reach their objective, his abdominal muscles rippling in response to my touch.

"Holland." He shapes my name against my skin as my fingers dip and begin to grapple with the buckle of his belt as my body aches for his.

Inside me. Hot. Hard. Unyielding. Punishing me.

As though reading my mind, my intentions, he takes my head in his hands, his kiss hot and urgent. Our tongues twirling and twining, our breaths shared, our half-spoken words inhaled.

"Yes—"
"Need—"
"You are—"
"Fuck—"

I arch against him as he reaches for the tiny row of gold buttons at my wrists. He begins to twist them loose.

"I didn't think this part through." His teeth gleam in the low light with his grin.

Oh, my heart. He bought me this exquisite dress.

I want to thank him. Tell him what this means to me—not because it's designer, but because it's perfect for me.

"Ah, fuck it," he growls, his accent nothing less than guttural Scots as he pulls one cuff apart, the buttons pinging across the room.

"No!" I protest, snapping my wrist away from him. "It's Valentino!" Like he doesn't already know as he grabs the other and repeats the process.

"I'll buy you another. I'll buy you a dozen."

"I like this one," I say, laughing in protest. "And I'll treasure it always."

"Darling girl." His eyes turn almost molten, his fingers brushing the hair from my face, but then he breaks contact for a moment, finding the zipper at the side. Together, we work to pull it off, the damage, the moment, no longer important.

"I want you so damned much." He cups my cheek, his rough whisper pure praise.

I screw my eyes tight against the reverence in his gaze.

"Hurry. Quickly." The two words escape in barely a breath as I fight against this. *It's just sex*, I remind myself. I can't lose myself in the way he looks at me because he bought me a dress.

He's not for me. Not for more than this moment in time we're stealing.

"No." Air fills the space between us, but still, I keep my eyes shut, my hands balled into fists at my chest as though to protect myself. "You will look at me, Holland."

His fingers grip my chin as though he could shake some sense into me. While I'm not sure that's possible, I do open my eyes. Alexander is balanced above me, his expression only half visible in the ambient light. But I can't ignore his pain.

He loosens the buttons of his shirt, one, two, three, before he pulls it over his head. His body gilded by firelight, he is Michelangelo's Adam. Though I'm not sure Adam ever wore such an expression. Nor were his eyes filled with such sin.

"Don't hide yourself from me. Not ever. Don't think I can't see the truth."

I gasp as he takes my hands in his, pressing them to the mattress above my head. His fingertips skim the sensitive underside of my arms, sliding down my face, my jaw, the pad of his thumb coming to rest on my bottom lip. Resting. Stroking.

"I know you're here because you feel the same way as I do."

His thumb presses on my lip, pulling it down to expose the moisture within. To open me to a kiss. A hard kiss. A rough kiss. A kiss that makes me moan into his mouth and my head follow his as he retracts. Makes me sigh as he trails his damp thumb down between my breasts. His hands span my ribs before slipping behind me to loosen my bra. He frames my breasts with his hands, molding the soft flesh.

"Alexander," I whimper, as his attentions turn my nipples into hard, aching peaks before he engulfs one with a masculine groan.

I arch and twist as he teases with his fingers, echoing the sucking pull of his lips, crying out as I'm overcome by a hot liquid pleasure his mouth brings. How many nights have I imagined this and played out some variation in my head? Not that my dreams came anywhere close to how this feels.

"God, you're so fucking lovely."

My hands find a home in his hair as Alexander's mouth lays claim to my breasts. Kisses and a coaxing tongue, the brush of his stubble, and the pull of his lips makes my whole body tremble, my nerve endings singing out for more.

I cry out. Not in surrender to this most delicious of torments but in a demand for more.

"Tell me you want me," he demands.

I tilt my hips in a silent reply, my mind filled with such filth.

Fuck me. Hurt me. Bruise me. Make me leave this room bearing your mark as a remembrance.

"Yes. *God, yes!*"

He swallows my cries as his mouth meets mine in a punishing kiss, a kiss that's jagged breaths, clashing teeth, and questing tongues. Until he presses my hands back to the mattress.

"So utterly frustrating but so, so lovely." His gaze burns down, his fingers linking with mine as he lowers his head and kisses me again. Gentler this time, his lips barely flirting, forcing mine to slow, my will to concede. Measured and deliberate, his lips are coaxing but not at all tentative.

My heart beats faster, my tongue meeting his, twirling and twining, inhaling—

"Lovely enough to eat." Words. They're just words he breathes into my ear, yet they detonate inside like a shower of tiny anticipatory fireworks. I recognize his fingertips, his fingernail trailing along the elastic of my tiny panties. My hips surge from the bed as Alexander's hand slips between my legs, cupping me. Teasing me as he slides a finger over the fabric of my underwear.

He makes a noise of appreciation, feeling the evidence of my arousal as his gaze flits between my face and his hand. "You're making these so, so *wet*."

Oh, God. That accent. He should record naughty audiobooks. He could get women off all over the world just by his voice alone.

"Maybe you should take them off," I whisper, arching under him.

"With my teeth?"

I begin to twist under him, to thrash, his wicked words a thrill.

"You're so sweet. I can smell how much you want me. How you want to take all of me."

"Yes," I cry, my insides throbbing emptily. *Fill me. Fuck me.*

"That's quite a mouth you've got on you." I freeze under him, not quite daring to look him in the eye as I belatedly realize I'd given voice to my desperation.

But I do look. And Alexander seems... turned on. Judging by the way his gaze travels over me in a slow, heavy-lidded glance. "Anything else you'd like to share?"

"I-I've thought of you. Every time I've touched myself since London. It's been you in my head." The words fall from my mouth, unbidden, but I don't regret them. Not as his gaze becomes pure liquid heat. "I've tried to think of others—"

"Maybe there is such a thing as being too honest," he says with a sly grin.

"—but it never worked."

"It sounds like you're trying to tell me that this belongs to me." He groans as he teases me with his fingers. "That you're so wet and so ready, and you're all for me."

"*Yes.*" This time, my agreement carries more force. It sounds more like a demand as my hands curl around his shoulders. I gasp as his hand dips under the satin, his fingers parting me.

"You're mine. Say it."

"Yes." I swallow over the admission. "I'm yours." I buck

up against him, my body offering no resistance, wet and spread, as he thrusts two fingers inside.

"You belong to me," he asserts. "And you always will."

I'm too far gone to hear the implication of his words.

My legs stiffen, and I cry out in frustration as his fingers withdraw before I realize he's slipping down my body, dragging my panties down my legs with him. The room falls quiet, but for the sound of my beating heart and my staccato breaths. I push up onto my elbows as his big hands slide my thighs wide, the look on his face more Lucifer than Adam as she shoots me a swift and wicked smile a moment before the flat of his tongue meets my inner thigh.

"So soft." A bite follows the lick. "And you smell heavenly."

Oh. My. *Lord.*

I want this so badly.

So badly that tears form in my eyes as he draws his tongue the length of my pussy.

Oh my God, yes.

I think I might...

My hands fist the sheets as though to hang on to the sensation as he repeats and repeats as though I'm the taste he craves as he absolutely savors me, drawing me closer and closer to the unseen edge as I cry and sob. As I moan for more.

"Please, Alexander," I beg. And I plead as his tongue begins to circle my clit. Circle, pet, tease until I'm pressing up into his face, my fingers twisted in his hair.

Until.

Until...

My body bleeds sensation, and I'm melting into the bed.

Spent and empty, I scarcely have time to come down before he's over me, his broad shoulders crowding out the light. His lashes flutter closed as my body accepts him, and as he fills me, my responding cry as tender as his thrust.

"I never..." Words go unfinished as he undulates above me, pressing up on his hands, his expression a mix of pleasure and pain. Of agony and ecstasy as he stretches out, throwing back his head and baring the strong column of his neck.

To watch on is almost bittersweet, yet to feel him so hard and long inside me is everything.

"I have imagined..." Alexander swallows thickly, then blesses me with a small stab of his hips. "My imagination could never conjure anything close to you. You feel like velvet, and I will *never have enough.*" He punctuates his words with his thrusts, his eyes dark and his expression so fierce. His fingers tighten as he begins to impale me again and again. And I love every second of it.

So close, I slide my legs around his waist, desperate to hang on to every perfect snap of his hips as, with each thrust, I rock up to meet him until I'm not sure where I end and where Alexander begins.

"You are mine, Holland," he grates out, burying his face in my neck. "Body and soul. I love you, and I'm never going to let you go."

Everything inside me draws tight, my orgasm springing to life almost at his words. I want to watch, watch him reach his peak. Want to see the truth of him.

But I can't.

I can do nothing but give. Give myself over to this moment. Give myself over to him as he begins to come undone.

46

ALEXANDER

IDIOT. YOU TOLD HER YOU LOVED HER WHILE YOU WERE COMING inside her.

Talk about making things hard for myself.

Difficult, I mean.

It's not quite morning, and Holland is still in my bed, lying beside me. Asleep, I think. Meanwhile, I haven't slept properly for the fear that I might wake, and she'd be gone. I have so much to say, and we're not leaving this room until we're done.

I trail my hand down her back as something swells inside me, too strong to be ignored. Love. I know now what that feeling is called.

I want to be the first person she sees when she wakes and the last person to hold her attention before sleep carries her away. When she trembles, I want it to be from my touch or from some joke I've told or even, goddammit, from the anger I've caused her. I want to be the author of her joy and the banisher of her sorrows.

I want to hold our children—if she wants them—but that's a conversation for another day. I want to hold her hand always and make her blush daily for the next forty years. And if she's the last face I see as I leave this world, I know I'll go with a smile on my face. Because there's never been another woman like her, and I know I'll love her always.

Her arms curled beneath her chest, Holland kicks her leg out from under the sheet in a wild sort of abandon. My hand lifts to her hair like a magnet to metal, my fingers beginning to sift through the silky strands.

I'm nervous. The kind of nervous I've never been before. I want to wake her and spill my guts, yet I'm afraid to. What if she still says no? What if she refuses me?

Then I guess the Duffys will be entertaining siege-style houseguests for longer than they anticipated.

My hand follows the path of her narrow back, my fingers tracing the bumps and indents in her spine. Next to me, Holland releases a breathy whisper, the noise not quite a moan as I fit my fingers to the dimples above the upside-down heart shape of her backside. I rest the meat of my palm against its rise. Rest. Settle. Press. Until she begins to move with it, grinding herself against the mattress.

An intensity washes through me as she begins to stir, the ripple of her body's pleasure making my heart trip and my throat burn. I slide my arm under her waist, gathering her to me as, with my other hand, I lift her thigh over mine and nudge my rigid cock between her legs.

Nudge? The thing behaves like a heat-seeking missile.

But I can't. Not yet

"Holland, darling. Wake up."

She purrs, pushing her arse against me, and my God, she's so wet. Wet from want. Sticky with cum. She feels heavenly as my cock glides against her. As I press my nose in her hair and inhale the scent of her.

"Holland, what are you doing to me?" I move the hair from her neck, pressing my mouth to her nape. My gut tightens, a seismic ripple of want travelling through me as she reaches down, her dainty fingers caressing the crown of my cock.

"Please," she whispers, pushing back against me, the angle of her body changing as she presses the crown of my cock to her opening.

"Wait." I can't quite believe that I do, but I lift her hand away, pressing it flat to the mattress. "Not yet." My tongue slips across the line of her shoulder as I push my fingers between hers. A scrape of teeth. A press of my lips before I bring my mouth to the shell of her ear and whisper, "You want me."

"*Yes*." Her admission is barely a breath.

"How much, my darling."

"I need you, Alexander." She tries to lift her head, but I continue my sensual assault, kissing her neck and shoulders as though it's my fetish. "Please." She pulls against my hands, tries to twist from under me.

"Do you want me enough to spend a lifetime with me?" I rest my head against hers as she inhales a gasp. "I love you, Holland. I've loved you for weeks. Forgive me. I just didn't know it was meant to feel like this."

I feel the moment she gives in. The moment she takes me at my word. The moment she stops denying.

And as I slide myself inside her, it's the beginning of everything.

HOLLY

"I love you." Alexander's knees are snug behind mine, his arms banded tight around my ribs. And I feel... happy. Like a girl on cloud nine. Like a girl who is loved.

"I know." There's a tremor of laughter in my words. "I heard you the first hundred times."

"Then you can hear it a hundred times more." His lips are soft against my shoulder, the rasp of hair on his chin not so much. *Yet it's just as delicious.* "A thousand times more." His finger reaches up, pressing to my chin as he turns my head, bringing my lips to meet his. "A lifetime of more, God willing."

Our mouths meet in a soft, teasing kiss.

"I can't believe you knew," I whisper, wondering on some level if I should be pissed while finding I don't have it in me to be.

Call it post-coital bliss. Call it being loved. *Being in love.*

He manipulated me no more than I did him. And last night, out in the garden, there was no question of me refusing to come to him. I'd told myself the joke was on him. I wasn't about to sleep with him for fear of him telling Griffin. I was going to sleep with him because I could. Because I wanted to. *Because I needed him.*

And my lofty plan was going so well until I refused to kiss him.

I'm not yours, your grace, and I never will be.

A frisson of discomfort washes over me. I'm not sure I'll ever get used to it. Accepting Alexander's love, it turns out, is easy. Accepting that a duke loves me is a little harder to get my mind around. I know it makes no sense, but there it is. The duke and Alexander are one and the same, and I'll just have to deal with my own sense of inadequacies. Get over myself.

"Where are you going?" I turn as our bodies separate, the air in the room cooling my back.

"I'm just checking the time."

"Good plan. I don't want to do the walk of shame while people are milling around."

"Shame?" he drawls.

"As in the expression, not as in the sense of disgrace."

"I should think you feel a sense of accomplishment, not disgrace," he murmurs. His hand lightly slaps the nightstand a couple of times before I hear him pick up his phone "You've drained me. I feel like a shell of a man."

"Lucky for you, I have a thing for old people."

"What a coincidence. I have a thing for you, too."

"Is that what we're calling the thing poking me? What time is it?"

"We've got hours yet," he murmurs suggestively.

"That can't be right." The room is getting lighter.

Alexander shuffles closer, pulling the pillow out from under my shoulder and throwing it God knows where. "Holland?"

"Hmm?" I smile as he presses his bristled cheek to mine, immediately going temporarily blind. "Was that your phone?" I think I might squeal, blinking away the dots of white swimming in front of my eyes.

"It was insurance."

"I saw your phone. I didn't know you were a devotee of the selfie. In fact," I say, turning to face him as I wrap myself burrito-style in the sheet, "I noticed a distinct lack of images of you on the internet."

His face lifts from his phone, his expression mildly mocking. "I'm not quite sure how to respond to that. You went *looking*?"

"Not exactly for you," I reply, feeling my cheeks turn

pink. "It pays to research a new company before an interview."

"Hmm. Sounds like I have a stalker." He presses his lips to my head. "I think I might like it."

"Why aren't there any images of you out there?" I find myself asking as I think back. "You know, falling out of nightclubs as a kid or tending to your duke-ly business, all staid and serious?"

"Because I go out of my way to avoid being in the public eye."

I make a note to come back to that point later. There was barely anything to find on the Internet about him. *Yes, I'd looked.*

"Alexander?" The tone of my voice and the way I slide my foot down his calf gets me his attention. "What did you mean when you said you didn't know love was supposed to feel like this?"

He slides a lock of hair behind my ear in an incredibly tender gesture.

"We don't know a lot of things about each other." His voice low, his words softly spoken. "And there are things we both have in our past that I'm sure we'd prefer not to share at all." I nod, because agreed. "But if we're going to be together, and we are," he adds in a surer tone, "there are some things we ought to know."

"Like?" I begin to wonder if I should've plucked this thread right now.

"Like how I know I love you because I've never felt like this before, which might sound wrong to you, considering I was once married."

I don't answer. Instead, I fix my gaze on the tattoo on the inside of his bicep. I bring my finger to it, tracing the roman numerals as I ask the question I've wondered about but have never wanted to ask.

Wanted to know, yes. Wanted to ask...

"Is this the date of your wedding?"

"No. The date I was handed the responsibility of the dukedom. The day my life changed forever."

"It must be hard to lose someone." In the way he did. I can only imagine how painful it must've been.

"How I felt about Leonie wasn't at all like this." He reaches out, drawing the backs of his fingers down my cheek. "Nothing quite so agonizing. Nothing quite so perfect." His hand retracts, and his gaze dips. "Ours was an open marriage, by design. There was passion, yes, but not just for each other. Hand on my heart," he says, doing just that, trapping my own under his. "I have never felt like this."

"You didn't love her?"

"We didn't love each other. I suppose we married because that's what was expected of us. Because we seemed suited in our pursuit of others."

"Okay." But it's far from okay, and something that's a bit of a mind phuck, if I'm honest. But maybe it doesn't have to be.

"Don't, darling." His thumb peels my lip from between my teeth. "It seems like a lifetime ago. Another world. A world I haven't lived in for some time."

I snuggle closer. "I don't think I could ever share you." Because I love you too much, I don't say. Not yet. We have time.

"Holland." My name is a low rumble through his chest before he presses a kiss to the top of my head. "I think I made it clear in the beginning, I have no intentions of sharing you with anyone else, ever."

I hide my smile as I recall him saying so.

"Before I do something monumental, is there anything you'd like to tell me?"

"Monumental how?"

"That would be telling," he answers with a sly smile.

"Well, you're getting involved with a woman who has an absent mom whose boyfriend may or may not try to hit you up for money, if he thinks you have any to spare."

"People have been trying to fleece me for years," he answers, still wearing that same expression.

"I have a sister, Kennedy. She's cool. A single parent. Her son's name is Wilder, or rug rat, depending on how I'm feeling. And the people in our hometown love our family because we're a good source of gossip."

"Your mother?"

"To begin with. Also, Kennedy has never said who Wilder's father is. But she owns her own business and pays her own bills, so it's nobody's business but hers."

"I look forward to meeting them both."

"And of course, I was jilted by the school principal. That's good for gossip, too."

"I think you'll find my family stories will trump yours when we post our wedding notice in *The Times*."

"Excuse me," I say. Splutter? Maybe laugh.

"Holland, you're where you're meant to be. By my side, now and for always. Which unfortunately for you means you also have to become a duchess."

"You are crazy." The smile I wear must be a mile wide.

"No doubt about it. I'm crazy in love."

47

HOLLY

"Hey, rugrat! How are you?"

We drive home together the same morning, though not before I'd snuck out of his room and back to mine before the sun was fully up. The walk of shame looks good on no one... except for maybe Isla, who I caught tiptoeing out of what I assume was Van's room. Our eyes met, her face turned pink, and mine burned to high heavens, then we burst into a fit of giggles before committing to a high five.

"I take it I'll see you at home?" she'd said, turning at the door to her room. I'd nodded, unable to find the words. Home is the place your heart belongs. And that's not a place but a person, as far as I can tell.

And now we're parked outside of Kilblair after a very different drive to the one out to Claish Castle. A drive filled with much less introspection and much more laughter, grabby hands, and fun. I'm pretty sure the smile I'm wearing will eventually result in cracked cheeks or something.

"Nephew?" Alexander whispers, pointing at the phone in my hand. I nod.

"Please stop calling me that." I smile as Wilder's deep sigh sounds down the line. "You know that's not my name."

"Isn't it? You mean you've changed it? Did you get a lawyer? Make an affidavit?"

"No." Another sigh. "You already know my name is Wilder. You even write it on my birthday cards. Only you call me rug rat."

And that's precisely why I don't ever want to stop.

"Are you sure? I'm kind of old, you know. Maybe I've gotten confused."

Or maybe my jokes are getting old, judging by the look Alexander slides me. Leaning across the console, he presses his lips to my cheek and gestures he'll get the bags.

"Yeah, I'm sure."

"Okay, nephew Wilder. How've you been? Did you do anything interesting today?"

"Well, I had to go and see the principal, but that was just a misunderstanding."

"Oh. How so?" The kid is usually so well behaved it's frightening. He definitely takes after his mother in that sense.

"I asked my new teacher if she had any kids."

"And the punchline is..."

"She said no. I told her that was probably for the best."

"Oh, dear." I try not to chuckle but not too hard.

"She's not a good teacher." I can almost see him shrug. "She doesn't understand kids."

"Who does?"

"I guess you might have a point," he answers with more wisdom than a child of his age should possess. Kennedy has always said he was born an old man.

"Well, that's maybe something you want to keep to yourself in the future, bud."

"I've already been to the principal. What else are they going to do?"

"Give you extra homework? Teachers are despicable creatures, you know that."

"You're not despicable. Well, not too much."

"Not when I'm booking vacations to Florida, I'm not."

"I want to come to Scotland. Mom told me you're working for a duke." *A dook.*

"Yeah, I am."

"Does he have a crown?"

"I... don't know." I glance in the rear-view mirror at said *dook,* now wondering the same thing. "I'll ask him next time I see him." Maybe I'll ask when I'm seeing quite a lot of him. Like, maybe tonight, when we're curled up in bed together. If he does have a crown, maybe he'll let me borrow it. Because who doesn't want to wear a crown, especially when you're naked in bed? "Where's your mom?"

It's not unusual for Wilder to call before handing the phone over to his mom.

"She's busy making coffee. And arguing with a man. That's why I called."

"Is he a customer?" And why are my spidey senses tingling?

"I guess so," he answers doubtfully. "I mean, he's here plenty. It's the Australian I told you about."

"Huh."

"Jenner says he's dreamy." Wilder fake barfs. "And he said he's seen the man's face on a billboard."

It was probably a wanted poster, knowing Jenner, Kennedy's part-time barista.

"Why do you think he's hanging around so much?"

"I don't know. He seems to like it when Mom is mean to

him. Do you think you could come home? Things are getting really weird around here."

"Well—" Shit. Maybe men are like buses. We've both been waiting for one while going in different directions when it seems they—the men, not buses—have turned up at the same time.

"Uh-oh. She's just thrown a glass of ice water over his head," the kid whisper-hisses. "That's the second time this week," he mutters to himself. "I gotta go, Aunt Holly. Can you at least give her a call and tell her she's acting weird?"

I agree I will and take Alexander's hand as he opens the car door.

"Everything all right?" He wraps his arm around my waist as we walk to the door.

"It's hard to tell with my family."

"Families are complicated," he agrees as we step into the echoing hall. He puts down our bags and turns me to face him as my heart begins to cartwheel in my chest. "Are you ready to start a new adventure?" he asks, smoothing back my wild hair.

"With you? Absolutely." He lowers his head, though I stop him, pressing my hand to his chest. His hard, unyielding, could-rent-the-space-for-advertising chest. His chest that houses his heart. A heart that is my home. "Do you have a crown?"

"I'm sorry?" He frowns down playfully at me.

"Never mind." I shake my head. "Silly question."

"I do have a crown," he growls against my ear, making me shiver. "Though technically, it's called a coronet."

My head snaps back as I stare into his teasing expression. "You do?" My tone might be a little too excited for the moment, but the man has a crown! I reach around to slap his ass, but he winces as I end up catching him a little higher. "What is it?" I try to slide around him when he catches my arms. "I saw a bruise there—"

"It's nothing. Just a bump. Now, what about this crown."

"Well, if only you'd told me about it weeks ago—maybe that night in London? It might have saved us a lot of fuss."

"I've enjoyed the fuss myself but go on."

"Fuss, yes." I get a little lost in his indigo gaze and the lick of warmth between my legs that look creates. I clear my throat. "Because I have this motto in life—"

"You have a motto? What a coincidence. I have one, too. It's a family motto." Pulling me under his arm. "Does yours have a heraldic shield?"

"If you stop interrupting, I might tell you."

Alexander turns to face me, throwing back his head as he laughs.

"I'm sorry," he says, assuming the appearance of seriousness. "Please tell me about your motto, Holland." His hands are warm against my hips, and as he begins to rub his thumbs over my hip bones, I go all melty and liquid between. Not that he can tell. Not the way I sniff, glance away, and then give a little shrug. *Whatevs.*

"It's called... I just want to see what I can get away with. That's it. That's my motto." His hands tighten as he slides me a sly glance. "And do you know what I've always wanted to get away with?" He shakes his head slowly like he thinks he knows exactly what I want to get away with. Or what he'd like me to. I tip up on my toes and bring my lips to his ear. "Falling in love with a man who owns a crown."

His hands slide lower, cupping my butt and pulling me against him.

"You know," his low tone rumbles, "I think you might be in luck."

"No, Alexander." I press a kiss to the little v against his collarbone. "I think I might be in love."

"Oh, Holland." His hands band at my back in a hug that's nothing short of fortifying.

"I've been trying very hard not to fall in love with you, telling myself I wasn't, that I couldn't—"

"This is just perfect," says a woman's voice from somewhere behind his broad shoulders. Alexander's hug turns to a hold, that kind that squeezes the air from my lungs.

"What is it?" I look up, realizing his complexion is now the color of milk, and the expression he'd been wearing, that sly amusement and joy, has gone. "Alexander?" I repeat. He doesn't move when I slide my head around him. A caramel blonde stands on the stone steps. She looks at home there. Tall and attractive, she also looks expensive from the roots of her shiny hair to the pointed tips of her even shinier designer high heels. She also looks familiar.

"Sandy," she purrs, "haven't you a better greeting for your long-lost wife?"

48

HOLLY

"Aren't we going to the family apartments?" the woman asks as Alexander marches her into the nearest room, almost throwing her into it.

No, not the woman. His wife. His long-lost wife.

I think I must be in shock. Or maybe I've hit my head, and this is all some kind of nightmare. One minute, I'm professing my love for him, and the next, he's... married. As in, no longer available.

"You're not family," he mutters. "Not anymore."

"I like what you've done with the place up there, by the way."

"Start talking," Alexander growls, glancing back at me as he prepares to close the door. He hasn't looked at me once since he'd turned the color of soured milk and stumbled away from me. Shock, I guess. But he's looking at me now. Glaring. Because he expected me to follow them into the room.

"Did you know?" I ask, not moving from the spot he'd left me. Two steps and he's back in front of me. And I don't need his answer, not after taking a good look at his expression.

"Do you think I would be on the brink of proposing to you, that I—" He grabs my elbow. "If she was going to come back from the dead, of course it would be right at this moment." This he almost mutters to himself before his grip tightens and his attention turns outward again. "You want to know how I know I love you? Because love is the absolute opposite to hate. And that's what I feel for that woman in there."

"But she's your wife." *Now*, I almost add. *Still?*

"No, she is not." A shudder vibrates down his arm, transferring to mine. Anger. Frustration. Panic, maybe? But then he seems to gather himself before me. Straightening, he takes back command. "Holland, please. Just don't go anywhere. Promise you won't leave."

I nod my head in agreement, unable to find the words. I wasn't about to go running for the hills, probably because my leaden feet wouldn't carry me there.

Clasping my hand, he kisses me again, his mouth hard and unforgiving as though he'd punish me for my words. "Call Isla," he whispers quickly as he pulls away again. "Tell her not to bring the boys back here. We don't know what we're dealing with." His phrasing brings a strange kind of relief. What *we're* dealing with.

"Is she dangerous?" I ask haltingly.

"Leonie is..." He shakes, like he still doesn't believe she's here. "Ruthless."

Back out in the hall, I almost bump into Griffin immediately. Him and his dark and swollen eye. A bruise to match the one I'd noticed on Alexander's lower back this morning. The one making him wince. *At least that makes sense.*

"What—" His gaze flicks to the door behind me. "Fuck." His hand to his mouth, he looks like he's seen a ghost. And I guess he's not the only one.

"Oh, good," drawls the feminine cut-glass accent from the other room. "The whole gang is here now. Just like old times."

The whole gang? As in, the three of them? Is this the cause of the animosity between Alexander and Griffin? And the bruises?

No, at least, not these ones.

"Hey." Back to the matter in hand, I whisper into the phone as the call connects. "It's Holly."

"Hello, Holly," Archie chirps.

"Hey, Arch, could you put your mom on."

"You're on speakerphone. Mummy's driving," he explains happily.

"Oh." *Damn.*

"I called shotgun, and Hugh is in a huff."

"Am not," mutters his brother, his tone quieter.

"Isla, Alexander has asked me to ask you not to come home. Not right now, at least. Not until he calls."

"Why?" There's surprise in her tone. Suspicion? A hint of amusement. "I'm quite sure the place is big enough to—"

"Could you pull over?" I say hurriedly. "I need to speak with you."

"Hang on."

The boys murmur questions, and Isla shushes them. Meanwhile, I begin to bite the skin around my thumb, my ears straining to hear what's going on in the other room. I do what I can do and lower my hand. This is an old habit I'm not about to pick up again.

"Okay." The car door slams shut, the change in the

background noise immediate. Cars. The whistle of the wind. The no-nonsense clip to Isla's tone.

What do I say to her? How can I explain?

The bitch is back? But maybe she isn't a bitch. She's *definitely* a bitch, and not just for coming back from the dead with bad timing. But it happened—what's done is done. There's no use pretending things are otherwise. How do you tell someone that. without them seeing it with their own eyes? Will Isla have the same response as Alexander? Disbelief. Anger. Abhorrence. There was no relief there. Not even a little.

"Holland," Isla utters tersely, bringing me back to the phone in my hand.

"Leonie. Leonie's here." My heart drops as the words hit the air.

"What? No, that's not possible."

"Alexander said to tell you." Who could make this shit up? "And for you not to come home."

"How? I mean. Jesus Christ."

"Alexander doesn't want you and the boys here."

"Who else is with you, Holly?" she asks impatiently. "Who is with Alexander right now?"

"Griffin. And her."

"Right. Okay. Do you think you could make your way to the gun room?"

"What?" From my stomach, my heart drops to my boots. "Why? I don't even know where that is?" It wasn't on the itinerary when Chrissy showed me around, strangely enough.

"Okay. Right. Well, that's not going to work. Never mind. I'll call Van. Just... stay with him, please. Holly, let me know he's okay."

"I will," I promise, even though I don't quite know what I'm promising.

I hang up as Alexander bellows, "You knew! And you didn't think to mention it to me?"

"I didn't know," Griffin shouts back. "I told you, I thought it was a hoax. I thought she was dead, the same as you did!"

"Did you really?" *Raaally*, comes the word. "Even after I sent you those little reminders of our time together?"

"You didn't think any of this warranted mention?" Alexander bites out. "That my dead wife had sought you out by some other medium than a fucking séance?"

Wife. I swallow over the pain in that, crossing my arms over my stomach as though it would somehow protect me. Ward off the words.

Alexander still has a wife.

How can he have a place for me in his life?

Yet I'm still drawn into the room.

"It was a man on the phone. I thought it was some chancer, some fuck, trying to blackmail me."

As I enter the room, only Leonie looks my way. Like a cat eyeing a canary over a bowl of cream. Maybe even two bowls of that decadence.

"It's true," she says, her voice a cut-glass drawl. "The chancer was me, though it's not like I made the calls myself. I didn't even watch the recordings." She gives a tiny shrug. "Actually, that's a lie. I enjoyed a wander down memory lane, as I'm sure you did too, Griffin."

"You're a mental case," he retorts. "Off your fucking rocker."

"What recordings?" Alexander whips around, his tone nothing short of frightening.

"I told you, he was trying to extort money from me, but I didn't for one minute think—"

"Of course, the bad man didn't tell you. Silly Griffin." She glances indulgently his way. "That was the point. You were supposed to run to your brother for help," she says, making a running motion with two fingers of her right hand.

"No one sorts out my problems but me," he retorts, his words hard.

"What recordings?" Alexander demands again, louder this time.

"Of you and me," she says, turning back to him. "Of me and him," she says, glancing his brother's way. Things are suddenly beginning to make sense. *Apart from her not being dead.* Her attention moves to me as I stand at the far side of the room. "Of the three of us together," she adds meaningfully.

I inhale a sharp gasp as the whisper of his words come back to me.

There are things in our past that I'm sure we'd prefer not to share.

What a fool I am, worrying about my own petty secrets, conscious of them impacting *his* life, conscious of *his* abhorrence of media attention. When all along the real story was that there would be no marriage because he already had a wife. My mind flips through scenarios and situations, my stomach, head, and heart at war.

They slept together? They fucked? All three of them?

That is wrong—so wrong.

Is she the reason he said those weeks ago that he'd never settle down? The reason Isla said Hugh would be his heir? Maybe he's known all along she wasn't dead, and he's been waiting for this.

No. That's not true. I saw his face. But that he didn't know doesn't make it any easier to bear.

What do you call a widower who isn't a widower anymore?

A man who's in need of a divorce and the kind of scandal that could stick to us both for years. These thoughts swirl and grow and pound in my head, the ache in my chest becoming so tight I suddenly find I'm struggling to breathe.

"Holland." I blink up into Alexander's worried expression, his eyes. "Sit down." He leads me to a window seat the long way around the room, as though he fears her reaction or some form of contamination. *Or maybe he just doesn't want either of us to be near her.* "Put your head down," he encourages, the bite gone from his words. The five points of his fingers feel like sweet relief against my back. "Yes, just like that. Deep breaths. That's it. Slow and steady. I can explain, I promise you. Everything is going to be okay."

But it isn't. It'll never be the same again.

I would never share you. Not with anyone.

Oh, my God.

How have we gone from declarations of love to this? Is he really that man? The kind of man who would allow his brother to screw his wife? Take part in it? And—I release a sudden, hiccupping sob—what about me? Didn't I use his brother as ammunition, too.

Maybe I do deserve to be in this clusterfuck.

"How sweet, Sandy. Here I was beginning to think you'd never get over me."

"You must know finding you missing from the yacht was almost a relief." Alexander's growling response makes my chest ache, but when I try to sit up, he applies a little more pressure, so I stay there.

Breathe. In. Out. In. Out. I try to relax into his touch as his hand moves over my back in reassuring circles.

"Yes, I suppose you're right. Things weren't right between us."

So why not divorce like a normal couple?

"But then you never remarried and," she continues, "as far as I could tell, you've never been interested in anyone since. Well, perhaps until now."

"I'm touched you've been keeping tabs on me." I'll credit his words as sounding less pleased than they might.

"Just lately. Needs must, you see. My circumstances have changed, and I am in need of money."

"So that's why you're here?"

Relief floods my chest. She's not staying. Should it matter? Shouldn't we call the police? My breathing becomes a little more even, my shock a little less immense

"Actually, I was on my way to see Griffin in London. To tighten the thumbscrews, as it were. But now I don't need to as another opportunity has presented itself."

I sit up as he steps toward her quite threateningly. And then I notice why. The way she's looking at me.

"And let me guess," Alexander begins, "you thought, what the hell, I'm passing, I'll pop in and say hello to Alexander. Why not?" He throws up his hands. "I'm in the area, and I'm *not fucking dead!*"

His voice reverberates off the walls so hard, I'm surprised they don't shake. They might've been built to withstand siege warfare, but I doubt they've ever witnessed this man's temper.

"I was in the country certainly," she replies serenely, crossing one tanned leg over the other. "Though I had little expectation of seeing you again. Sorry, darling. I hope that doesn't hurt too much."

"Not at all. I'd hoped the next time I'd see you, you'd be in a coffin."

"So you didn't pine for me?" Her mouth becomes a small moue.

"Not unless we're talking about pine boxes. And you?" Alexander's attention swings to his brother.

"If I'd thought she was alive, do you think I'd be here?"

"It never stopped you before," the woman murmurs, examining the buff-colored polish on her nails. "Sometimes your car was barely down the drive when Griffin's was on the way up. Not here, of course. We conducted our little affair out of the London house."

"Is it an affair when your marriage is a sham of an open relationship?" Alexander folds his arms across his chest. "Or when you don't care who your wife fucks?"

"You are a first-class bitch," mutters Griffin. "I know I was in the wrong," he says, his attention swinging to Alexander. "I shouldn't have gone anywhere near her, and I'm not sure it makes any difference, but I've hated myself for it since."

"Sandy, it wasn't his fault, she murmurs, all sulky-lipped. "He was just young and impressionable." She makes as though to stand.

"Sit back down," Alexander growls. "Don't come near me."

"He couldn't say no," she says, lowering herself again. "At least, not to me."

"I really don't care who you fucked or when. Any kind of emotion around you is wasted, Leonie. Besides, it's not like either of us felt the need to share who we were screwing. No doubt she pursued you relentlessly to get back at me for some perceived slight," he says, his attention touching Griffin. "If only I'd known guilt was the reason for your bitterness, we could've laid the past to rest long ago."

He glances meaningfully Leonie's way. *Some things just won't stay dead,* his look seems to say.

"Oh dear, it looks like he's been tying himself up in knots for nothing. Actually, that might be my fault," Leonie adds with an evil-sounding titter. "I told him you'd kill him if you ever found out. And, of course, that you were better in bed. Did you find that out, too?" Her malicious question is directed my way.

"Leave her out of it." Alexander's voice is soft. Frighteningly so.

"She's not quite who I imagined you'd be with," she says, ignoring him. "She's very young. I would've thought more like an entrée not a main course."

"I guess that makes you the remains of a buffet that nobody wants to touch," I retort.

Griffin barks out a laugh as Alexander's gaze finds mine. I see pride there, I think. Maybe warning, too.

"Well, this is all very nice," she says, disregarding me, "but what about that money?"

"What are you talking about?" Alexander growls.

"Obviously, the jig is up. Blackmailing you through Griffin is a lost cause." Her head turns like a shark sensing blood in the water. "But it looks like you're ready to move on."

"It looks like I'm in need of a divorce."

"No, not technically," Griffin interjects. "Scottish jurisprudence might not be my specialty, but—"

"Oh." She presses a hand to her head. "It seems my amnesia is lifting! I remember who I'm married to. And I remember who he used to make me screw."

"Make you? I couldn't stop you," Alexander spits.

"The press would still have a field day anyway. By the way, that's a splendid black eye, Griffin." Leonie slides a compact and a lipstick from her jacket pocket. "Was it Alexander's gift?"

"It's not what you think."

From my position, I see Griffin's fists ball.

"No?" Her eyes slide my way. "Who decided this time? Or is our meek maiden over there pulling the strings. I know they say the quiet ones are always the worst, but I've never really been convinced about that." She casts a sly glance my way as she begins to apply her lipstick.

A creeping sensation slides up the back of my neck, its tendrils slithering into my head, turning to realization with crystal kind of clarity. She's going to use me against him. Use the knowledge of our relationship, our love, as leverage against this all coming out, just when we're at our most vulnerable. Just when we were about to start a life together. The one thing he fears she'll use against him.

The truth coming out.

"How much do you want?" Alexander turns, clearly surprised to find me by his side.

"You know nothing about me or us." My voice rings clear, my convictions carrying me. "And you know nothing about our love."

Leonie scoffs, but I push on because she really has no idea what I'm feeling right now. This wave of emotion, this overwhelming desire to protect the man next to me.

"We all make mistakes." My eyes find Alexander's, and I see hesitancy but also concern. "And we judge. We *all* judge. And maybe we judge ourselves most of all. But the thing about love is you can't turn it off, no matter how much it might hurt in the process. So we do the only thing we can do." I press my hand to one cheek and my lips to his other. "We keep on loving anyway."

I pull away, sliding my hand down his shoulder and arm, our fingers linked until the very end of our fingertips.

"How much do you want?" His voice is brusque as I move away. All business.

"Quite a bit, I'm afraid," she answers, her tone like a kid in anticipation of candy as my quiet steps carry me out of the room.

49

ALEXANDER

"What are you doing?"

The moment I realize Holland has left the room, I take the stairs two at a time after her.

She can't leave.

Not after what she'd said.

Not after what's passed between us.

Yet as I swing open the door, there the evidence lies: a suitcase open on her bed, clothes dropped into it, onto the bed, between the wardrobe and the bed, and pretty much everywhere in the room.

Though my heart beats against my ribcage, I force myself to smile. "This reminds me of your hotel room." The first night when I'd switched on the lamp to find the room festooned with clothes. Used cups. Hair products. I'm sure that night was a peek into our future. *Our future bedroom.*

"You were supposed to be leaving then."

"No supposing about it. I am leaving," she retorts, dry-eyed and stony-faced.

"Looks more like you're running away."

Her denial is a vigorous shake of her head. "Wilder, my

nephew, asked me to come home. He's worried about Kennedy."

"When was the last time you went home?" I stroll over to the window and lean against the windowsill.

"He's worried about a man who's hanging around the coffee shop," she says as though she hasn't heard me. "That's Kennedy's business. The coffee shop." She drops a pile of underwear into the case. "She runs our grandmother's old place."

Oh, look. Another penny the information miser parts with.

"I mean, it sounds kind of worrying," she says, hurrying on. *Withe her words and her packing.* "But I'm sure it's not as bad as all that. I think it might have something to do with Wilder."

Back at the armoire, she flings open the doors and begins tugging at the hangers.

"Okay. I'll get on and book a couple of flights." I pull out my phone. "Into Portland?"

"What?" She swings around.

"You have family trouble, yes?" Holland nods. "Your family will be my family soon. Besides, I really should introduce myself to your sister, don't you think?"

Holland blinks. A hanger clinks to the floor. Then she shakes her head as though this is the most ridiculous thing she's ever heard.

"Nana also left Kennedy her shotgun." She begins to move again, dropping her pile of clothes to the case before swinging back to the armoire again. My eyes remain on the case where shirt arms dangle like wraiths trying to escape.

How to play this? Explain this?

I lift my head when I sense her eyes on me.

Holland Harper is beautiful when she's frustrated.

Sublime when she's laughing.

When she's hiding her thoughts, she looks like someone else.

"You're not coming with me," she says decisively. "You have enough to take care of here. You don't need to involve yourself in my little life."

"That's where you're wrong." I push up from the windowsill. "There is nowhere I'd rather be in this world than by your side."

"You already have a wife."

She looks so pale. Barely hanging on to her hurt. To see her hurt will hurt me—crush me—but it has to be better than this façade of feigned indifference.

"No, actually, I don't." I pause at the foot of her bed and hook my arm around one of the bottom posts.

She shimmers with agitation, her hands jerky as she pulls at the hem of her shirt. "Have I had a stroke? Or is this some kind of lucid dream? Because I swear, I just met the duchess downstairs."

"Hardly what I'd call an introduction," I say, running my finger along my cheek as though to satisfy an itch. "And she's certainly not a duchess. The sometime girlfriend of a Russian mobster, perhaps. She just said so herself."

"Girlfriend or not, she's still your wife first."

"I beg to differ. Pseudocide."

"What?" Holland's hands find her hips, anger causing some cracks in her mask.

"I'd never heard the word before myself. Griffin just taught it to me. He'd taken a leave of absence from work and had a private investigator examine the blackmail attempt. They asked him to consider the possibility of Leonie committing pseudocide. Apparently, it's increasingly common, but he told them that couldn't be the case."

"That she couldn't fake her death," she deadpans. "You mean like she has."

"Whether she faked her death or not, she's no longer my problem."

"Oh, I'd say otherwise. And I guess she would, too." Changing her stance, Holland wraps her arms around herself.

"According to Scottish law, our marriage was legally dissolved the year she committed pseudocide. As far as I was concerned, and as far as the courts are concerned, she was lost at sea, dead as far as the Presumption of Death Act is concerned. To say otherwise would mean she faces a long spell in prison. Meanwhile, I face remaining as I am. In love with you."

"Alexander, what are you doing?"

"Well." I glance down at my now dark phone. "I was about to book us flights. To Portland. Do you want to get married there, in Mookatill?"

With a noise that isn't quite a cry and isn't quite a yell, she takes a step to her left and whips up some of the clothing from her case. Then she yells. Swears, actually. Really quite profusely, though it's mostly muffled by her clothes.

As she lifts her head, I discover that Holland Harper is magnificent when she's steaming angry. Her eyes take on a coppery edge, her chin, which she holds high anyway, holds the hauteur of queen.

"Stop torturing me. Just fucking stop!"

"Then unpack your clothes," I say, my own temper rising as I lean over and begin plucking sweaters and jeans from the case. "Hang them up. Put them away."

"Stop that! You fucking stop that!"

"I will not!" I bellow. It doesn't have the desired effect.

Because the desired effect was not a sneaker to my head. "Ow!"

"Get fucked!" I catch the next one. Feint and avoid the third. The fourth, a heel, glances off my shoulder.

"You nearly had my eye out with that one!"

"Boo-hoo!" She eyes the lamp on the nightstand to her right but seems to think better of it. It's interesting how she's only weaponizing the things she owns.

A bottle of perfume. *That one I catch.*

A book. I look down at the title. "*One Dirty Scot*?" I can't help but smirk.

"I thought you might pick up a couple of pointers!"

"Oh, you think you're being clever, now?" I consider throwing the book onto the bed, but I don't want to increase her ammunition, so I drop it to the floor.

"No, I think this is my life falling apart!"

She swings around, looking for something heavier than her Prada purse, so I lunge for her before she can grab something else. I tighten my arms over her shoulders and chest when she swings the purse upwards, catching me on the jaw as I swing away just in time.

"Were you just looking for a couple of bricks to put inside?"

"No one puts bricks in a Prada handbag, philistine!"

I can't help but chuckle as I hug her tighter. This woman. There isn't another in the world like her. And she's all mine.

"Your life is not falling apart," I murmur, bringing my mouth to her ear. But dear God. Where do I go on from here? Do I tell her how I want her there, by my side? How I need her? How I can't imagine a life without her? How I was already half in love with her before either of us had set foot in the castle?

I might not have my riding boots and jodhpurs on, but I can still be the arsehole duke.

"When I thought I couldn't offer you long-term devotion, I was fooling myself. I might be selfish in my motivations, and perhaps even a little morally corrupt, but I find I no longer care whether you deserve to be embroiled in the clusterfuck that is my life. I can only think of how I must keep you in it. Keep you here. With me. And if that makes me a terrible person, I really don't give a fuck. That woman downstairs means nothing to me. She has no hold over me."

"You're fooling yourself," she whispers with a sad shake of her head.

"And I'm here with you because Griffin assures me he can handle this." By legal means or Russian-led otherwise, is something else I don't care about.

"Is that the same Griffin you tag teamed your wife with?" With this, she pulls against me and tries to stamp on my foot.

"Yes," I answer simply, sidestepping her efforts. "We were both different people then. I didn't know he was my brother. He was just a pretty face in a club we used to play at." Should I tell her the whole truth? "A club I once owned a very long time ago."

"Oh, you just keep setting them up for me, don't you?"

"Reasons to leave?" I find myself asking. "Except you forget," I whisper a touch threateningly, "I'm not letting you go."

"You can't keep me here."

"I beg to differ."

"You have to let me go." This time, her words are a little plaintive.

"You are better than this, Holland. We both are. I know

we both want, on some level, to be seen as someone else. Someone better. Someone stronger. Someone without a past. I'm no innocent, and I've been guilty of bad judgement and bad taste. Of living in fear of becoming just another in that long line of men who came before me, instead of recognizing myself for who I truly am. I'm done with that. There's no hiding from our experiences and there's no denying who we are. But we can be better, stronger, more. Because together, you and I, we're a whole new entity."

"But if I leave," she says in a small voice, "she has no hold over you, and you won't be seen as that man."

"But I am that man. I was that man. If you leave, my heart will break. There's no contest, my love. And this is monumental." I press a kiss to her cheek as I reach into my pocket and pull out my phone. "You remember I said I was going to do something monumental this morning?"

"Yes," she whispers, taking the phone from my hand and staring down at it.

There on the screen is the photograph I'd taken this morning. We're in bed together, white sheets and wide smiles, her dark hair in disarray and my jaw covered in sandy bristles. There will be no disputing the facts; it's perfectly obvious what we've been up to. *Our smiles. The sheets. Her hair.* And though there's little flesh on show, it's obvious we're both naked.

"Now, this," I say, sliding the image closed and opening the newly installed app, I navigate to Kilbair Castle's Instagram page.

"What are you doing?"

"Isla gave me the login details. I have more followers than you. Are you jealous?"

"Alexander, please, what are you doing?"

"See, I've already loaded the photograph. Isla tried to

talk to me about hashtags, but we'll ignore that for now, and I'll just finish up with my post. Post?" Over her shoulder, I tilt my head in question.

"Yes, it's post," she murmurs.

"Good. I've got the vernacular down. It's a good photograph, isn't it?"

"It's wonderful, but if you post it—"

"Oh, I'm not going to post it."

Holland stills in my arms, her fingers infinitesimally tightening around my phone.

"I think sometimes our lives have to be shaken and thrown about like a leaf blown from a tree if we're to get to be where we're meant to be. Where are we meant to be, Holland?"

"I don't know," she whispers.

"I think you do. We're meant to be in each other's arms. That we're meant to grow old together. The rest, darling, is up to you."

With that, I leave her in her messy room with my phone still in her hand.

EPILOGUE

HOLLY

"So, do you consider yourself a Scot or an American?"

I pretend to consider the question like it hasn't been asked already a hundred times.

"I guess I'd have to call myself an Americot, mainly because the alternative sounds like a spinal complaint." *Scomerican?* Sometimes I say, "sounds like a hemorrhoid cream", but I'd judged this crowd a little more sophisticated than that gag.

Queue a round of husky chuckles and rasping giggles from the participants of Grey Nomad Tours. Well, it is Wednesday, and Wednesday at Kilblair Castle is our senior specials day. As well as hump day, but that usually comes after the castle has closed for the day to visitors. Because the Duke and Duchess of Dalforth are nothing if not conventional.

My ass.

Anyway, I like Wednesdays because I get to hang with this crowd.

"And do we address you as your grace or your ladyship?" asks another of the crowd.

"Just Holly will do." Anything else sounds a little ridiculous, quite honestly. Technically, I'm Her Grace, the Duchess of Dalforth. Because almost a year ago, as I'd stood in my bedroom with Alexander's phone in my hand, I truly debated how I'd felt like that leaf. Tossed about in the wind, shaken in more ways than I thought I could deal with. I'd imagined myself as that tiny piece of foliage being swept from problem to problem, from catastrophe to catastrophe. And then I thought of where I'd landed. Of where I belonged. And Alexander was right. I belong in his arms.

Leonie left. Without money and without a reason to come back. Before Alexander's foot had reached the bottom step of the grand staircase, I'd pressed the little button to send the Instagram post live. I'd outed our relationship to the world in a monumental fashion, just as he'd planned.

Meet the future Duchess of Dalforth

was all the post read. Just that and our smiling faces. It wasn't quite a wedding announcement in *The Times*, as is the usual way. And it caused an internet sensation, making the front page of most of the European newspapers. *A couple of US ones, too.*

It turned out that Leonie had become involved with a high-powered criminal, and the attention a divorce would draw was not to his liking. So, she'd faked her death to slink off with him. But when the relationship soured, she needed money to escape.

If you ask me, I think she has a few screws loose in her head.

But she left knowing full well her sordid tales would

never provide her with money from the Dalforth estate because Alexander had reached the point when he no longer cared if the truth of his past came out. He'd laid it to rest that morning as he'd held me in his arms, trusting me to do the right thing for us both. If she wanted to throw stones that resulted in her incarceration, well, all the better. Pseudocide is a very serious offence. I understand Griffin stepped into his own at that moment, and the brothers have begun to take steps to mend what's between them. Which can only be a good thing, I think. Because he was right about us being stronger together. The concept doesn't just relate to us.

But we are stronger together, Alexander and me. And we're stronger as individuals because of the support and love we show each other.

"And here we have the castle's pride and joy," I say as my little band of grandparent types gather around the painting in a small semi-circle. "A landscape scene by the 17th-century painter Paul Peter Rubens. I mean, Peter Paul Rubens." Ack! I always get his name the wrong way around.

"I read on the website that there has been some contention regarding the provenance of this piece," says an elderly man in a green turtleneck and houndstooth jacket.

In my head, I do this whole shocked, grabbing my pearls thing. *Are you contradicting the Duchess of Dalforth! Off with your... turtleneck. It's July, for gosh sakes!* But Her Grace is gracious. So I don't.

"Scholars have been debating this for more years than I've been around, and I'm sure they'll be debating it for many years more. But whether Ruben or an Antwerp contemporary of the man himself painted this piece, I think we can agree, it's beautiful." Eh. It's not my favorite.

Let me put it this way—I wouldn't give it wall space in

my bedroom. In fact, none of the paintings along this hallway are my favorite. My favorite piece is only for private viewing.

"And here we have something a little more contemporary…"

We move along the hallway to another painting, and I do a little two-handed flourish like a flight attendant doing the pre-flight safety demonstration. Actually, I sometimes like to pretend I am a flight attendant.

In the event our airliner becomes a cruise liner, you may use your seat cushion as a floatation device. Lights on the floor will illuminate to guide you to the exit. Or you could just follow me because you're not getting off this thing first.

I think I could get away with actually saying something along those lines one day, though not on Wednesdays. The oldies crowd are nothing if not attentive.

And that's why I love them.

Anyone who tells you they became a teacher because they love kids is a liar. Teachers become teachers because they want a captive audience. And the teacher in me loves the oldies and their rapt attentions.

"Are those knickers?"

"I believe the correct term is breeches," I reply, trying not to sound too smug.

"No, not in the painting. Those." The rake-thin granny wearing sensible tweed points over my shoulder. "Hanging from the corner of the frame."

I whip around and spot what she means.

Dammit.

No taking photographs of the Duchess of Dalforth jumping up and down, trying to retrieve a pair of silver La Perla panties please!

"These—"

"Are—"

"Just—"

"Need a hand, darling?" My husband's honey-dripped drawl sounds from behind me, followed by the usual murmurs of pleasure, plus one exclamation.

"Ooh, look! The duke is here!"

"Ah, yes. Hello, sweetie." I turn and shoot him a smile as a chorus of "ahhs" sounds around us.

"Oh, look, the duke is joining us."

"Such a handsome man. So well... *put together*."

That one usually comes up when he has those damn polo jodhpurs on. They don't leave a lot to the imagination.

The duke joins our little tour groups occasionally, and I hear it's become a bit of a treat that the tourists look forward to. Will he be joining us? Won't he?

Just typical. I lead the tours, and he gets the accolades.

No one seems to have gathered that he prefers to tag along on Wednesdays. He likes the Wednesday tour groups best because the oldies tend to be a little deaf and a little slow. It means they miss his filthy whispers, and when he grabs my hand, pulling me ahead of them, they generally can't keep his pace. He likes to whip me around some corner or other and kiss the living daylights out of me.

My husband does seem to have a thing for hallways and walls, come to think of it.

But if you're wondering if that's how my panties come to be dangling from a picture frame, it's not the result of a wall-based assignation. He'd peeled them off with his teeth last night after catching me halfway up the staircase.

I was running away from him.
We both love the thrill of the chase.

But back to the matter in hand.

"I think one of the cleaners must've left behind a cleaning cloth."

With a languid ease, Alexander plucks down my underwear. That sounds worse than it should have, considering we're standing in front of a party of twelve senior citizens.

"I think we must be paying the cleaning company too much," he murmurs, sliding the silver-colored lace into the pocket of his pants.

"Maybe. I mean, yes, if they're not doing their job properly."

"He means because they were La Perla knickers," another woman offers up. All heads turn to her. Puffed up with the sudden attention, she carries on. "I used to work in the lingerie department in Selfridges, the department store."

"Oh, how interesting!" I say, using some approximation of Isla. I'm thinking of having a little bracelet made with the acronym WWID to remind me, when in doubt in the role of the duchess, I just need to think:

What. Would. Isla. Do.

"Now, if I can just direct your attention to—"

"Three hundred pounds, some of their knickers cost. Scandalous, prices for a tiny scrap of fabric!"

How much?!

A round of scandalized "oohs" and "aahs" break out, along with one or two discussions about how you can get a three-pack of knickers from Marks and Spencer's for under ten pounds.

I pull a meaningful face at my husband. A sort of, see what your shenanigans have done.

But he just chuckles. Then he rouses the crowd.

"Ladies and gentlemen, the chef has just asked me to let

you know there are scones and clotted cream in the kitchen if you'd like to pop down there and sample them."

"Will there be tea?" asks a little old lady with a walking stick and vivid red hair. "Can't have elevenses without a proper cuppa."

"I'm sure you'll manage to charm him into popping the kettle on."

"Dougal is going to kill you," I say as they trudge off towards the kitchen. "And so will Isla when she finds out." We're supposed to direct them to the coffee shop after the tour, which you can only get to through the gift shop.

Cha-ching!

"Who's in charge here? Me or Isla."

I fold my arms. "Come on. You know better than to ask that."

"My name is above the door," he protests.

"If you want to keep buying expensive panties to use as slingshots, you let her do her thing."

Isla isn't in charge of the day-to-day running of the castle anymore, being too busy with her own life and businesses, but I still defer all Kilblair matters to her. This place runs through her blood.

"You've got that look in your eye," I tell him as he takes my hand and leads me along the hallway.

"Where are we going?"

"To your favorite room."

"Our bedroom isn't along here," I tease. But I know what is. My office. My study space, not that I do a lot of studying, but I do store a lot of books there.

Without letting go of my hand, Alexander opens the door, allowing me to precede him.

"You just want to look at my ass." I direct my words over my shoulder and flutter my lashes just a touch.

"Always," he replies as I turn back and smile at my favorite piece of artwork in the building. Hanging on the wall next to my mint green couch is a montage of posts printed from Kilblair's Instagram page, the page I now curate. But it's not all fun and games being the duchess. Sure, I get to take pretty pictures, and I get to hang out with the older folks once a week. But there's a seriousness to the job, too. Like coming up with events to raise funds for a new roof and helping out at the local primary school, as well as hosting a vast array of fancy parties. McCain does most of that, but I've had to learn the ropes. I bet I could get a job as a butler now. You know, if I ever get sick of being a duchess.

As if!

"You know why I let you go ahead of me?"

"In case Archie has balanced a bucket of water above the door?"

"That happened once, darling. And you got him back quite spectacularly."

A hose is much more efficient than a bucket, even if the bucket was meant for his brother and not me. Payback is payback.

"You let me go first because you're a gentleman." I wrap my hands around his waist and snuggle in close. He's no ordinary gentleman, that's for sure.

"Well, yes. Ladies first in all things."

"Because that didn't sound smutty at all. Not even a little bit."

"No? I must be losing my touch." He chuckles as he turns me in his arms so we're both looking at my Kilblair montage. "When you come into this room, your eyes immediately fall to that picture," he says, folding his hands over my waist. "And your eyes light up. That's why I let you go first. It reminds me I must be doing something right."

"Or lots of things," I murmur, my eyes running over the moments. Our Christmas Eve wedding held at the tiny ancient chapel in the village with just a dozen people watching on. Our family, both blood and chosen. We'd come back to the castle afterwards and celebrated until the wee hours before collapsing into bed. Our first Christmas morning together. Our honeymoon. The memories go on and on. "But I think we're going to need a bigger picture frame," I murmur, sliding my hands over his as anticipation bubbles inside me.

"I'm sure we'll need lots of them as the years go by. I look forward to many years of making memories with you."

I press his hands on my stomach as a shiver of something sweet rolls down my spine. "It's a good thing the castle has so many rooms." I take a deep breath and try not to giggle as I say, "Remind me again. Do twins skip one generation or two?"

ABOUT THE AUTHOR

USA Today bestseller Donna is a writer of love stories with heart, humor, and heat. When not bashing away at her keyboard, she can often be found hiding from her responsibilities with a book in her hand and a mop of a dog at her feet.

Get to hear all the news by joining her newsletter or come say hello in her private reader group, Donna's Lambs.

Donna's VIP Newsletter
mail@donnaalam.com
www.DonnaAlam.com

Printed in Great Britain
by Amazon